Days of
BLOOD
and
FIRE

Days of
BLOOD
and
FIRE

A Novel of the Westlands

Katharine Kerr

Bantam Books
New York Toronto London Sydney Auckland

DAYS OF BLOOD AND FIRE

A Bantam Spectra Book / September 1993

Spectra and the portrayal of a boxed "s" are trademarks of Bantam Books,
a division of Bantam Doubleday Dell Publishing Group, Inc.

Library of Congress Cataloging-in-Publication Data

Kerr, Katharine.
    Days of blood and fire : a novel of the Westlands / Katharine
Kerr.
        p.   cm.
    ISBN 0-553-37204-1
    I. Title.
PS3561.E642D38   1993
813'.54—dc20   93-20229
                                                         CIP

Published simultaneously in the United States and Canada

PRINTED IN THE UNITED STATES OF AMERICA
FFG 0 9 8 7 6 5 4 3 2 1

For Richard Wilfred Ashton
My grandfather

ACKNOWLEDGMENTS

I owe special thanks to

    Barbara Denz, who taught me ferret lore and took the time to correct my mistakes,

    Ken St. Andre, whose comments on an earlier book made me think about dragons in a new way, and

    Karen Lofstrom, who climbed a real volcano and told me about it.

CONTENTS

APPENDICES

The
Roof of the
World

N

To the
High Plains
(Horse Kin)

The Fire
Mountain

Haen
Marn?

Haen
Marn?

To
Dwarveholt

Lin Serr ✦

Cerr Cawnen

Penli ✦

THE
RHIDDAER

Cengarn ◉

ARCODD
PROVINCE

To the Seven Cities
(Gel da'Thae)

To
Deverry
(Humans)

To the
Grasslands
(Elves)

0 ▭▭▭▭▭ 300
Miles

✦ Cities
◉ Capital
Hills
Mountains

©1993 A·Karl/J·Kemp

The Westlands
Summer, 1116

RUBEUS

Of all the figures that give us omens in the element of Earth, this be the most dangerous and dissolute, unless it pertain, thanks to the overall reading of the map, to days of blood and fire. And should it fall into the House of Iron, then the loremaster must destroy the map immediately, proceeding no farther, for naught good will come of peering into such a future.

The Omenbook of Gwarn, Loremaster

1

PUER

*Unless this figure fall into the House of
Bronze, that is to say, the seventh country on
our map, or into the House of Gold, the fifth
country where dwell art and song, then it be
ill-omened, bringing dissension, injury, and
the lust for revenge.*

The Omenbook of Gwarn, Loremaster

ROUND CERR CAWNEN THE MEADOWS lay marshy, crossed by a thousand streams, most no more than rivulets, and dotted with pools and bogs. With his face and hands lard-smeared to keep the blackflies from biting, Jahdo picked his way through the high grass to hunt for brooklime and colt's foot. To the north the mountains that the dwarven folk call the Roof of the World towered out of blue mist, their peaks shining white in the summer sun. To the south the rolling meadows spread out into farmland, dotted with trees, and here and there a plume of smoke from a farm wife's kitchen rose like a feather on the sky. In his pure boy's tenor Jahdo sang aloud, swinging his wicker basket in time to the song. He was so entranced with this wide view, in fact, that he stumbled, stepping out into empty air and falling with a yelp some four feet down into a gully carved by a stream.

He landed on soft grass and marshy ground, but the basket went flying, hitting the water with a plop and floating away. He scrambled up, decided that the sandy streambed offered the best footing, and splashed after the basket as it rounded a turn and sailed out of sight. Jahdo broke into a shuffling sort of trot, keeping his feet under the knee-high water, traveling, quite inadvertently, in near silence, hidden by the banks of the deepening stream. At another twist in the watercourse, he caught his runaway basket, which had beached itself onto a strip of shore at an eddy. When he picked it up, something shiny caught his eye, a little disk of metal, pierced and hanging from a leather thong. He grabbed it, hoping for a dropped coin, but the thing was only pewter, engraved with a strange squiggle. He slipped it into his pocket anyway, stood for a moment panting for breath, and realized that he heard voices.

Just ahead the leafy shadows of trees danced on the water. Up on the banks stood a copse, where a man and a woman talked on the edge of anger, though they kept their voices down so low that Jahdo could guess they met in secret. He began backing away, slipped, and fell with a splash and a curse.

"Here!" the woman shrilled. "A spy!"

"I be no such thing, good lady." In a wail of protest Jahdo clambered up. "Don't hurt me."

Tall, blond, with ice-blue eyes as cold as the northern peaks, a young man jumped down onto the sandy strip of shore bordering the stream, grabbed his arm, and hauled him out of the water. When he recognized Verrarc, a member of the Council of Five that ruled the city, Jahdo began to stammer apologies. Verrarc grabbed him by both shoulders and shook him hard.

"What are you doing here?"

"Gathering herbs, sir. My sister she be ill. Gwira the herbwoman said she'd treat her, but it was needful for me to go and do some gathering. To give her due fee, I mean."

Verrarc threw him to his knees. As he looked up at the tall, hard-muscled man towering over him, Jahdo felt the world turn all swimmy. Verrarc's blue stare cut into his soul like the thrust of a knife.

"He does tell the truth." Verrarc's voice seemed to come from far away.

"That's of no moment. Kill him." The woman's voice hissed and cracked. "We mayn't risk—kill him, Verro!"

Jahdo whimpered and flung up his hands, half warding a blow, half begging for his life. When he tried to speak, his tongue stuck to the roof of his mouth, and he gasped for breath. Verrarc laid one hand on the jeweled hilt of the sword slung at his hip, then considered him for an achingly long moment. His stare seemed normal again, merely the look of an angry man, not some strange ensorcelment.

"I know you. You be the rat boy."

"I am, sir." He found his voice at last, but in his terror he could only whisper. "Jahdo Ratter."

"Kill him now." Wrapped in a black cloak with the hood well up, the woman crouched on the edge of the gully.

"Hold your tongue, Rae!" Verrarc snapped. "I'll not be hurting the boy. He's but ten summers old, and no threat."

"Verro!" Her voice, this time, whined, as petulant as a toddler. "Kill him. I want to watch."

"Hold your tongue! He be valuable, this lad, and besides, the herb-woman does know he's out here."

With a snarl she sat back on her heels. All Jahdo could see of her was gray eyes and pale cheeks, streaked with sweat. No doubt she found the black cloak a burden on such a sunny day. Verrarc ignored her, slipped one arm around Jahdo's shoulders, and turned him round.

"Look, lad, as one man to another, I ask you: are you really going to be telling anyone about what you did see here today?"

All of a sudden Jahdo understood: a love affair.

"Of course not, sir. It be none of my business, bain't?"

Verrarc winked and grinned.

"Not in the least, lad, not in the least. And don't you go worrying. No harm will come to you, as long as you hold your tongue."

"Thank you, sir, oh, a thousand thanks. I'll never say naught, I swear it. And I'll gather my herbs somewhere far away, too."

Verrarc looked deep into his eyes and smiled. It seemed that his blue eyes turned to water, that his gaze flowed over the boy like warm water.

"Good. Good lad. Now, just trot back down along the stream, like, and go on your way."

Jahdo followed orders, running as fast as he dared, never looking back until he was a good mile away. He climbed out of the gully and stood for a moment, shaking his head. Something odd had happened, down there by the water. Or had he fallen asleep and dreamt it? He'd seen something, someone—Councilman Verrarc and a lady, and they were sneaking out behind her husband's back, and he'd sworn to speak not a word of it. Fair enough, and he'd certainly keep his promise, especially since he wasn't even sure if it was true or just a dream, or even a rumor. The city was full of rumors, after all. Maybe he hadn't seen a thing. He was sure, as he thought about it, that he'd seen no one but Verrarc, sitting by a stream.

By the time he'd filled the damp basket with herbs, he'd forgotten the councilman's name, and by the time he was heading home, all he retained was a sense of fear, linked to the grassy bank of some stream or other. A snake, perhaps, had startled him; dimly he could remember a sound much like the hiss of a snake.

Although there were a scattering of villages farther west, Cerr Cawnen was the only town worthy of the name in that part of the world, the Rhiddaer (the Freeland), as it was known. In the midst of water meadows lay Loc Vaed, stretching in long green shallows out to blue deeper water and a rocky central island, the Citadel, where stood the fine homes of the best families and, at the very peak, the armory of the citizen militia. The rest of the town crammed into the shallows: a jumble and welter of houses and shops all perched on pilings or crannogs, joined by little bridges to one another in the rough equivalent of city blocks, which in turn bristled with jetties and rickety stairs leading down to the stretches of open water between them, where leather coracles bobbed on ropes. Toward the edge of town, where the lake rippled over sandy reefs, big logs, sawn in half and sunk on end, studded the surface of the water and served as stepping-stones between the huts and islets. On the lakeshore proper, where the ground was reasonably solid, stood a high timber-laced stone wall, ringing the entire lake round. Guards stood on constant duty at the gate and prowled the catwalk above, turning the entire town and lake both into an armed camp. The forty thousand folk of Cerr Cawnen had more than one enemy to fear.

It was late in the day by the time Jahdo trotted through the gates to the stretch of grass that ringed the shore, and he knew he'd best hurry. Not only did the memory of his fear still trouble him, but he was worried about his elder sister, who'd woken that morning doubled over with pain. Clutching his basket tight, he jumped his way across the shallows from log to log, then climbed some stairs up to a block of buildings, all roofed with living sod or vegetable gardens. Most of the stilt houses had wide wooden decks round them, and he leapt or clambered from one to another, dodging dogs and goats and small children, ducking under wet laundry hung to dry, calling out a pleasant word here or there to a woman grinding grain in a quern or a man fishing from a window of his house. At the edge of the deeper water he climbed down and helped himself to a coracle tied to a piling. These little round boats were common property, used as needed, left for the next person wherever one landed them. With his basket settled between his knees, Jahdo rowed out to Citadel.

Normally, poor folk like him and his family never lived on the central island, but his clan had occupied two big rooms attached to the town granaries for over a hundred years, ever since the town council had chartered the lodgings to them—on condition, of course, that they "did work most diligently and with all care and patience both of man and weasel" to keep down the swarms of rats in the granary. Everyone knew that rodents were dangerous enemies, spreading filth and fleas, befouling much more food than they outright ate. To earn their food, clothing, and other necessities, the Ratters, as their family came to be known, also took their ferrets round from house to house all over town. Wearing little muzzles to keep them from making kills, the ferrets chased the vermin out through holes in the walls, where the family caught the rats in wicker cages and drowned them and their fleas both in the lake—not the most pleasant of jobs, but growing up with it made it tolerable.

The squat stone buildings of the public granaries clung to a cliff low down on the citadel island. Getting to the Ratters' quarters required some of a ferret's agility: first you climbed up a wooden ladder, then squeezed yourself between two walls and inched along until you made a very sharp turn right into the doorway. When Jahdo came into the big square chamber that served as kitchen, common room, and bedchamber for his parents, he found white-haired Gwira, the herbwoman, brewing herb water in an iron kettle at the hearth. The spicy scent, tinged with resin, hung in the room and mingled with the musky stink of ferrets.

"Where's Mam, Gwira?" Jahdo said.

"Out with your da and the weasels. They'll be back well before dark, she told me. Don't know where Kiel's gone to."

Dead-pale but smiling, his elder sister, lanky, dark-haired Niffa, was sitting at the rickety plank table nearby and drinking from a wooden bowl. Although she glanced his way, her enormous dark eyes seemed focused on some wider, distant view. A dreamy child, people called her, and at root very strange. Jahdo merely thought of her as irritating.

"You be well?"

"I am, at that." Niffa blushed as red as the coals. "I never were truly ill."

When Jahdo stared in puzzlement, Gwira laughed.

"Your sister be a woman now, young Jahdo, and that's all you need to know about it. It's needful for us to set about finding her a husband soon."

Vague boyish rumors of blood and the phases of the moon made Jahdo blush as hard as his sister. He slung the basket onto the table and ran into the bedchamber. At one end of the narrow room lay the jumble of blankets and straw mattresses that he, his elder brother, and his sister slept upon, while at the other stood the maze of wooden pens, strewn with more of the same straw, where the ferrets lived. Since his parents were out hunting, only one ferret, a pregnant female, was at home and surprisingly enough awake in the daytime, scooting on her bottom across the straw as if she'd just relieved herself. Jahdo leaned over her slab-sided pen, built high enough to keep the other ferrets out and away from her tangled ball of a nest, all heaped-up straw and scraps of cloth. Tek-tek deigned to allow him to stroke her soft fur, then reached out her front paws in a long stretch, casually swiping her bottom across his fingers to mark him as hers.

"Oh, ych, Tek!" Jahdo wiped his hand on his trousers, then remembered the pewter trinket in his pocket. "Here's somewhat for your hoard."

When he dropped the disk in, she sniffed it, then hooked the thong with her fangs and, head held high to drag her prize, waddled back to her nest and tucked it safely away. Some ferrets were worse than magpies, stealing shiny things to wad up with rags and bits of old leather into a treasure ball. They liked socks, too, and stole belt buckles if you didn't watch them, dragging them belt and all into their nests.

As promised, his parents came home not long after, bent under their burdens of caged ferrets and damp traps. Dark-haired Lael, going gray in his beard and mustaches, was a tall man, built like a blacksmith, or so everyone said, while blond Dera was a mere wisp of a woman even now, after she'd born three healthy children and two that had died in infancy. Yet somehow, when she got in one of her rages, no one thought of her as slight or frail, and her blue eyes always snapped with some new passion or other.

"Back, are you?" Lael said with a nod at Jahdo. "Help me with the weasels."

They carried the cages into the bedroom and opened them one at a time, grabbing each ferret and slipping off its tiny leather hood. As much as they hated the hoods, the ferrets always seemed to hate having them off even more, twisting round and grunting in your lap. For creatures that weighed no more than five pounds at the absolute most, they could be surprisingly strong. Jahdo got the first pair unhooded easily enough, but their biggest hob, Ambo, was always a battle, a frantic wiggle of pushing paws.

"Now hold still!" Jahdo snapped. "I do know you do hate it, but there's naught I can do about it! Here, just let me get the knot undone. It's needful for you to wear them, you know. What if you ate a big meal and then fell asleep in the walls? We'd never get you back, and you'd get eaten yourself by one of the dog packs or suchlike. Now hold still! There! Ye gods!"

Free at last Ambo shook his sable length and chittered, pausing to rub himself on Jahdo's arm, all affection now that his workday was over. He backed up for a running start, then leapt and pranced, jigging round Jahdo's ankles. When the boy could finally catch him, he dumped Ambo into the common pen, where the ferret began rummaging round in the straw on some weaselly concern. Dera came in with clean water in a big pottery dish and a wooden bowl of scraps of jerky. She set them down inside the common pen, then laid down some fine-chopped meat for Tek-tek.

"Food for you later," she announced to Jahdo.

"Is Gwira still here, Mam?"

"She is. Why? Don't you feel well?"

"Naught like that. I just did wonder."

"Well, then, don't stand in the straw like a lump! Come out and see for yourself."

Jahdo followed her out to find his elder brother home, sitting at the far end of the big table and sharing a tankard of beer with Lael. The eldest of the three and almost a man, really, Kiel was a handsome boy, with yellow hair like their mother's, and almost as tall as their father, but slender, with unusually long and delicate fingers as well. At the nearer end of the table, the herbwoman stood, picking over the herbs Jahdo had brought back.

"Be those herbs good?" he asked.

"Perfectly fine, indeed," Gwira said.

The herbwoman stayed to dinner that night, sitting down at the end of the table next to Dera and across from Niffa, where they could all gossip over their sauced pork and bread about possible husbands, while Lael mostly listened, voicing only the occasional concerned opinion about one suitor or another. Kiel and Jahdo pretended indifference, but at the same time, they said not one word to each other, either, lest they miss something. As the second oldest person in Cerr Cawnen, Gwira knew a good bit about most everyone.

"Well now, with your pretty face," the old woman said at last. "You might nock an arrow for high-flying game, young Niffa. Councilman Verrarc's been known to stop by here for a word or two on occasion."

"He does come to see Mam, and I'd not be marrying him if he were the last man left alive under the moon."

Although Niffa spoke quietly, cold steel rang in her voice.

"I doubt me if he'd marry a ratter, love," Dera broke in. "So don't you worry."

"Beauty's bettered a lass's fortune before this." Gwira paused to hack a bit of gristle with her table dagger. "Why do you hold him in disdain, lass?"

"He's like reaching into a pond and touching a big old slimy newt. I hate him."

Dera and Lael both raised an eyebrow at this outburst. Niffa buried her nose in her cup of watered ale.

"Well, there *was* that scandal," Gwira said. "Him and that Raena woman, the chief speaker's wife from over in Penli."

"That near cost us the alliance, it did," Lael said. "A lot of us might not vote for the young cub again, I tell you, after that botch."

"Worse for her, it were," Gwira broke in. "Her husband did put her aside, didn't he? Who knows what happened to the poor woman after that?"

"If the young cub did want her as much as all that," Lael growled, "he might have married her decently when he had the chance."

"I hear Raena did go back to her people in the north in shame." Dera turned thoughtful. "But I don't know. It takes two to twist a rope, I always say, and there was somewhat about that woman I never did like. I doubt me if she were but an innocent little chick to Verro's fox, like."

"Um, well, mayhap." Gwira pursed her lips. "Our Niffa might not be able to do better when it come to coin and calling, but there's no doubt about it, she can do much better when it come to character. I'll be putting some thought into this, over the next few days, like."

"Think of Demet," Niffa mumbled. "The weaver's second son."

Everyone laughed, relaxing. Gwira nodded slowly.

"Not a bad choice he'd be. Good steady man, his father, and prosperous, too."

Jahdo laid his spoon down in his bowl. All this talk of Councilman Verrarc had made him feel sick to his stomach, and cold all over, as well. He should tell Gwira how he felt, he knew, should tell her about—about what? There was some incident he wanted to tell her, just because she was old and wiser than anyone else in town. Something about some event out in the meadow. Hadn't something scary happened? Yet he couldn't quite remember what it was, and the moment passed beyond returning.

Yet, not two days later, the boy recovered a brief glimmering of the memory, though not enough to save him. Early on that particular morning, Dera sent Jahdo over to town to claim some eggs and meat that one of the townsfolk owed them.

"Your da be across, too, love," she said. "See if you can find him when you're done."

Jahdo had rowed about halfway across the lake, his back turned to his destination, of course, when he saw the ceremonial barge pushing off from Citadel and heading his way. With a few quick strokes he moved off its course and rested at his oars while the squat barge slipped past, painted all silver and red, riding low in the water. In the middle stood a false mast to display the yellow and green banners of Cerr Cawnen, which hung lazily in the warm summer air. At the bow clustered a group of men in rich clothing, embroidered linen shirts belted over knee-length trousers, the common style in this part of the world, with short cloaks thrown back from their shoulders. Jewels and gold winked in the rising sun.

As the barge slid past, Jahdo saw Councilman Verrarc standing at the rail. His heart thudded once as the councilman looked his way. Since only some fifteen feet separated them, Jahdo could clearly see that Verrarc had noticed him, that the councilman frowned, too, and turned to keep him in view for a minute or two after the barge went past. Again Jahdo felt his mouth turn parched, and the sensation made him remember his meadow fear and the image of a woman, wrapped in black and hissing as she spoke. Yet all the boy knew was that in some obscure way Verrarc's image had sparked the memory. With a cold shudder he forced the recollection away and rowed on to town.

The family who owed them for the ratting, the Widow Suka and her son, had slaughtered a goat just the day before. Some hundred feet from the lake's edge, her house perched on a crannog piled up so many hundreds of years before that the construction had turned into a real island, with trees and topsoil of its own, a little garden, and a pen for goats, which, every day in summer, the widow's son rowed over to the mainland for the grazing. While she nestled eggs safely in the straw in Jahdo's basket and wrapped chunks of goat up in cabbage leaves, Jahdo strolled to the edge of the crannog and looked over to shore.

Down by the gates in the wall a crowd of people stood round, all staring toward the gate itself. Jahdo could just pick out the tall form of Councilman Verrarc toward the front of the mob.

"Now what's that?" Suka said. "Looks like a merchant caravan's coming in."

"It does, truly. Ooh, I wonder where they've been?"

"If you want to go see, lad, I'll keep the food here and cool for you."

Leaving the boat behind, Jahdo made his way to shore on foot, hopping from log to log. He arrived at the edge of the crowd just as the gates swung wide and a line of men and mules began to file through. Since he was the shortest person in the crowd, Jahdo couldn't see a thing. For a few minutes he trotted this way and that, hoping to find a way to squeeze through to the front, decided that he might as well give it up, then heard muttering and oaths from the front of the crowd. The press began to surge backward, men swearing and stepping back fast though without turning to look where they were going. Jahdo tried to run, nearly fell, nearly panicked, and cried out.

"Here, lad!" Lael grabbed him. "This be a bit dangerous for someone your size. Hang on, and I'll lift you up."

"Da! I didn't even see you."

"Ah, but I did see you, and I was heading your way."

Riding secure on his father's shoulders Jahdo at last discovered the cause of the commotion. A pair of merchants on horseback, a pack of ordinary guards, and a string of heavily laden mules had all marched by when, at the very end of the line, a manlike figure strode in, leading an enormous white horse laden with sacks and bundles. It was one of the Gel da'Thae, swinging a stout staff back and forth and side to side in front of him as he walked, as if he were clearing something out of his path.

He stood perhaps seven feet tall, roughly man-shaped with two short-ish but sturdy legs, a long torso, two long arms, and a face with recog-nizable manlike features—but he was no man nor dwarf, either. His skin was as pale as milk in the places where it appeared between the lacings of his tight leather shirt and trousers, but his black hair was as coarse and bristling straight as a boar's. At the bridge of his enormous nose his eyebrows grew together in a sharp V and merged into his hairline. His hair itself plumed up, then swept back and down over his long skull to cascade to his waist. Here and there in this mane hung tiny braids, tied off with thongs and little charms and amulets. The backs of his enormous hands were furred with stubby black hair, too. His cheeks, however, were hairless, merely tattooed all over in a complex blue and purple pattern of lines and circles.

As he walked, he turned his head this way and that, to listen rather than look, because where eyes should have gleamed under his furred brows were only empty sockets, pale and knotted with scars.

"Oh!" Jahdo spoke without thinking, in his piping boy's voice that cut through the noise of the crowd. "He be blind."

With a toss of his maned head the Gel da'Thae stopped walking in front of Lael and swung toward the sound of Jahdo's voice. He bared strong white teeth, with more than a hint of fang about the incisors.

"Do you mock me, lad?" Although he spoke in the language of the Rhiddaer, his voice growled out and rumbled, echoing back and forth like the waves of a storm slapping off a pier.

"Never, never," Jahdo stammered. "I be truly sorry. I were just so surprised."

"No doubt. But you're an ill-mannered little cub nonetheless."

"I am, sir, truly, and I'll try to learn better."

"Ill-mannered and cowardly to boot." The Gel da'Thae paused, sniffing the air. "Huh. I sense a man carrying you. Are you the lad's father?"

"I am," Lael said, and his voice was steady and cold. "And I'll speak for him. He be no coward, sir. He be shamed that he might have wounded your feelings."

The Gel da'Thae grunted, tucked his staff under one arm, and reached out an enormous hand to pat the side of Lael's face. He reached higher, found Jahdo's arm and patted that, then took his hand away and smelt his own palm.

"Huh, sure enough, I sense no fear on the lad, but by all the gods and demons, as well, the pair of you stink of ferrets!"

"So we do, no doubt. You've got a keen nose."

"Hah! I may be blind, but a man would have to be dead to miss that scent." He seemed to be smiling, pulling thin lips back from his fangs. "Well, a good day to you both and your weasel friends as well."

With a whistle to the huge horse, the Gel da'Thae walked off, tapping his way with the staff as he followed the jingling of the caravan along the curve of the lake, where a grassy stretch of shore was set aside for traveling merchants. Lael swung Jahdo down with a grunt.

"You'd best mind your mouth after this, lad. You always did have a cursed big one."

"I know, Da, and I truly, truly be sorry."

"No doubt. But the last thing we do want is to give insult to one of the Horsekin. That's all they need, one word for a thin excuse, and they cry war. I hate to see one of them here for just that reason. If that bard goes taking offense, we'll have his clan riding at the head of an army to siege us."

"How do you know he's a bard?"

"Because his eyes are gone. That's what they do, when they decide one of their boy children has the voice to make a bard. They do scoop his eyes right out with the point of a knife, because they do think it make his singing sweeter."

Jahdo nearly gagged. He turned sharply away, found himself staring up at Councilman Verrarc, and felt the blood drain from his face in a wave of cold fear.

"Somewhat wrong, lad?" Verrarc's voice was mild, but his stare was sharp and cold. "You look frightened."

"Oh, he had a bit of a run-in with that Gel da'Thae bard," Lael said, smiling. "He's never seen one of their tribe before."

"Enough to scare anyone, that."

"What's he doing here, anyway?" Lael went on.

"Cursed if I know." Verrarc shrugged, visibly worried. "That's why the guards did fetch me and the rest of the council before they did let that lot in. We're going to pay him a visit, just to ask, like, down at the campground."

"Think it be trouble?"

"I wish I knew, Lael, I wish I knew. As he walked by, he did tell me that he'd come to claim a tribute we owe his kind. We've got a web of treaties and obligations with these people, much as I wish we didn't, and so who knows what he means by it? I'd best be finding out."

Verrarc turned away with a pleasant nod, but Jahdo felt his fear deepen to a clot like goat's hair in his mouth. With a dreamlike clarity he knew that showing his fear of the councilman was dangerous, that if Verrarc thought he remembered—remembered what? The terror in the meadow. The hiss of a snake.

"Well, lad," Lael said. "You do look as white as I've ever seen you. What be so wrong?"

Jahdo was about to tell, then realized that the councilman lingered within earshot.

"The bard's eyes, Da, that's all. I keep imagining how that knife would feel when they did it."

"A nasty thing, sure enough." Lael shuddered a bit himself. "But they're a strange lot all round, and cruel enough as well. Come along now, let's get home. We need to stop to claim a fee, too."

"I did it already, Da. Mam told me to. I got a lot of roast goat from the Widow Suka."

"Splendid. Let's go fetch it home, then."

The news had preceded them to Citadel. As they were tying up the coracle, a handful of militiamen surrounded them. With the swing of one broad hand and a toss of his blond head, Demet pushed his way to the front. The family had known him all their lives, just as most everyone knew everyone else in Cerr Cawnen.

"Be it true, Lael?" Demet burst out. "Is one of the Horsekin in the city?"

"He is, and we did see him. A bard, and blind as a mole. Councilman Verrarc says he's come to claim some ancient due or service."

All the men swore, laying automatic hands on sword hilt or knife.

Demet looked away to the distant shore and shaded his eyes with one hand, as if he were hoping to see the stranger.

"I don't see why we had to go and make treaties with them, anyway," Jahdo said.

"Better than being their slaves, lad," Lael said. "Or the slaves of the wild tribes up to the north. Better to bargain with the Horsekin we know than fight the ones we don't, bain't?"

"True spoken." Demet turned back to them. "But I'll wager we call council fire tonight over this."

No one bothered to argue with him, and rightly so. Just at sunset the big bronze gong that hung at the top of Citadel began to clang and boom across the water. More ominous than thunder, each huge stroke hung in the darkening air. When Jahdo and his family left their quarters, he could see boats and coracles, skittering on their oars like so many waterbugs, as all round the shore the townsfolk swarmed across the lake. Every person who dwelt within earshot of the gong had the right to attend these councils and make their wishes known, man and woman alike, just as everyone had the right to vote for the town council, too. Out in the Rhiddaer there were no lords and kings. As the citizenry hurried up the steep streets of Citadel in a tide of rumor and fear, the family made its own way to the assembly ground.

In front of the stone council hall, which sported a colonnade and a flight of shallow steps, stretched a plaza, paved with bricks. Off to one side, the militia was heaping up wood for a bonfire to light the proceedings. Jahdo and Niffa scrambled to the top of the thick wall on the uphill side and watched the murmuring crowd grow larger and larger. Every now and then Jahdo would turn round and look back at the lake. Already in the cooler evening mists were rising over deep water. Since it was fed by hot springs, the lake ran warm. Just as the night grew thick, and the flames began to leap high from the fire, casting enormous shadows across the arches and pillars of the hall, the council barge tied up down at the jetty. From his perch Jahdo could see the torches bobbing along the twisted streets of Citadel and pick out the council members, too, as the procession panted its way up the steep hillside. Striding among them was the Gel da'Thae bard.

"I be scared," Niffa said abruptly. "I don't know why. I just feel so cold and strange, like."

"Oh, he's not so bad, really. The bard, I mean. And this won't have anything to do with us."

"Don't go being so sure, little brother. I never feel like this for no reason at all." Her voice stuck in her throat, and she paused, gulping for air. "Let's get off this wall. Let's go find Mam and Da."

"I don't want to. I can't see anything down in the crowd."

"Jahdo, come on! You can't stay here."

He hesitated, considering, but taking orders from his sister rankled.

"Won't. You go down if you want to."

"You dolt! Come with me!"

He shook his head in a stubborn no and refused to say a thing more. After a moment she slid down and plunged into the crowd like a swimmer into waves. He could just make her out, heading from clot to murmuring clot of townsfolk, until at last she fetched up next to Demet, standing guard near the fire itself. So that's it! Jahdo thought. She just wanted to find him, not Mam and Da at all.

Brass horns blared at the gates to the plaza. The crowd shrank back into itself, opening a narrow passage through for the councilmen, with Verrarc in the lead and Admi, the chief speaker, bringing up the rear. In the middle strode the Gel da'Thae, surrounded by councilmen, all murmuring to him at once, whether or not he could hear over the crowd and the horns. As they reached the steps, a squad of militiamen escorted them to the big stone rostrum near the fire. After some confused milling round, the clot opened again to let Admi climb the rostrum. A tall man with narrow shoulders but a big belly, he was going bald rather badly, so that he seemed made from perched spheres. In the firelight his head gleamed with sweat, and his tiny eyes peered out at the crowd through slits in heavy flesh. Yet when he spoke, his dark voice rang like gold.

"Fellow citizens! We do have among us a guest, the honored bard Meer of the Gel da'Thae."

Dutifully everyone clapped their hands, a patter of sound, dying fast.

"He does come on grave purpose and with serious intent. Trouble brews in the far west. The wild tribes of the northern Horsekin are on the move."

It seemed that everyone in the plaza caught their breath hard. Even over the crackle of the bonfire their dismay hammered on the surrounding walls. Admi wiped his forehead with both hands, unconsciously pushing back hair he no longer had.

"May the gods allow that this trouble stay among them!" Admi went on. "Yet who knows what the gods intend? The western Horsekin, our allies for all these long years, are fortifying their cities. From what Meer does tell me, it behooves us to look to our own. We go on full guard and military alert."

Murmurs, nods—the crowd moved within itself, then fell silent. Jahdo inched closer along the wall. He could just see Meer, turning his head slowly back and forth, as if listening to the temper of the gathering.

"Since Meer did travel long and hard to reach us, he will claim a reward," Admi continued. "He would journey farther on, where none of our merchants do go, and he does need a servant and guide. Sightless as he is, he requires a lad to wait upon him in his roamings, now that he can no longer travel with a caravan."

Too late Jahdo remembered his sister's premonitions. He clung to the wall, paralyzed like a rat cornered by a ferret, as Councilman Verrarc walked to the edge of the steps and looked his way. The traitor fire flared up and sent long lines of light to bind him to Verrarc's cold blue stare. In the crowd several men called out a question.

"He's heading east." In the stress of the moment Admi dropped his rhetoric. "He says he does have business at the border. The one we share with the Slavers."

Jahdo turned so weak and cold that he nearly fell. He grabbed the rough stones to steady himself and swung down to hide in the muttering swarm of townsfolk. Too late—Verrarc was speaking to the militiamen, summoning a pair, plunging into the crowd and heading straight for him. Jahdo tried to run, but caught in the forest of grown-ups he found no path. Verrarc laid a heavy hand on his shoulder and swung him round. The councilman was smiling.

"Meer did remember you, lad. Bring me the boy who smells of ferrets, he said. That one owns a brave heart."

Jahdo stared into his eyes and felt again that he was spinning in a mind eddy, down and down, drowning in the lake of Verrarc's eyes. From what seemed like far away he heard a woman screaming in rage. The screams grew louder, rushed close, turned into his mother's voice. The spell broke. His mother's face hovered above him.

"You mayn't, you mayn't! How can you even think of it?"

"It be the treaty bond, Dera!" Verrarc shoved himself back, raising one hand ready to ward blows. "It's needful that someone go. Do you want a whole pack of Horsekin sieging us for breaking the treaty?"

"He be but ten summers! Send some other lad. Send one of the militia."

"Meer didn't ask for some other lad."

With an animal snarl Dera turned away and began shoving her way toward the steps. In his mother's strong grip Jahdo found himself dragged after as the guards and Verrarc followed, with Verrarc arguing with Dera the entire way. Jahdo could just sense the crowd thinning, swaying, as most of the citizens headed for the gate. He was willing to bet that the family of every other boy there was running for safety. In the flaring torchlight by the colonnade Meer stood waiting, his arms crossed over his chest.

"Listen, you!" Dera growled. "I do care not if you be one of the gods themselves. You're not taking my son away."

"Dera, please, hold your tongue!" Verrarc looked terrified. "You'll insult our guest."

With Niffa, Demet, and Kiel right behind him, Lael pushed through the crowd. Dera ignored him and the councilman both and waggled one finger under Meer's flat nose.

"Just who do you think you are, anyway," she went on. "Marching in here and—"

"My good woman, please!" Meer held one huge hand up flat for silence. "I come to you as a suppliant, as one in need. Please, I beg you, allow your son to come with me. I promise you I'll treat him not as a slave, but every bit as well and tenderly as I would treat my very own first-born nephew."

Dera hesitated. Verrarc muttered astonishments.

"A mother's words are law, Councilman," Meer snapped. "My good woman, as I traveled this day through your city, everywhere I smelt fear, except on your son. He's like one of your weasels, very small, but with the heart of a wolf. I cannot travel alone." He reached up to touch the rim of an empty eye socket. "My own mother wept when they blinded me, but in the end my calling pleased her well. For all I know, some great destiny lies in wait for your lad. Would you stand in his way?"

"Well now." Dera let out her breath in a puff. "Well now. If you were going anywhere but east—"

"Truly, the name of the Slavers is not one to speak in jest. Among my own people we call them Lijik Ganda, the Red Reivers. An aeon ago they swept down upon us, and the slaughter drove us from our homeland and into sin and degradation. Woe, woe to the people of the horse that our desperation drove us to such sins! Do you think we've forgotten such terrible things? I will not lie to you. I take your son into danger, but I would take my own nephew, had I a nephew, into the same."

"This thing be as important as that?" Lael broke in.

Meer turned slightly in the direction of Councilman Verrarc, just a brief involuntary gesture. Fortunately Verrarc was whispering to one of the militiamen and, at least, seemed to notice nothing.

"It is to me. To no one else, mayhap. My mother laid a geas upon me concerning my brother, and I have reason to believe he's gone east."

To Jahdo the bard's voice sounded entirely too smooth, too glib, making him wonder if Meer was lying, but he supposed that he might have felt that way because he too had something to hide from the councilman. As he thought of Verrarc, he felt words bursting from his mouth.

"Mam, I want to go."

The moment he spoke he was horrified, but there was no taking the words back. Dera threw her hands into the air and keened aloud, just one brief sob of sound, quickly stifled. Lael turned to him, his mouth working.

"If we do owe this thing under treaty," Lael said at last. "And if you want to go, well, then, there be naught much your mother and I can say about it. But be you sure, lad? At your age and all, how can you know your own mind?"

Jahdo felt his entire body trembling, trying to squeeze out the words his traitor mouth refused to speak: no, no, I didn't mean it, I don't want to go, I don't. His heart pounded the words like a drum, but he could not speak.

"He smells great things on the move, my good man," Meer said. "Even a child may sense destiny."

"Destiny?" Dera spat out the word. "Hogwash and turnip wine!"

"My good woman, please. With luck we'll never even cross the Slavers' border."

"Hah! That sort of luck does have a way of running short. I'm not letting my lad—"

All at once Dera stopped speaking. Meer caught himself as he was about to speak, as well, and turned, moving his huge head from side to side as if he were straining to hear some small sound. Jahdo realized that he himself was—that they all were—turning to Niffa, staring at Niffa, even though she'd said not a word. Her face had gone dead-pale, and in the broken torchlight her eyes seemed huge pools of shadow, as empty as those of the bard himself. Demet grabbed her arm to steady her.

"Let him go, Mam." Her voice was a hollow whisper. "He'll be safer there than here."

Involuntarily Jahdo glanced at Verrarc, standing just behind her, and saw the strangest smile on the councilman's face. It reminded him of a playmate caught cheating in a game. Dera considered for a long moment, taking her daughter's strange pronouncement seriously, as indeed she always did whenever Niffa came out with one. For a moment she seemed about to speak; then she burst into tears and rushed off, dodging her way through the remnant of crowd. Swearing under his breath, Kiel followed her.

"Well, then, that's settled." Rubbing his hands together, Verrarc stepped forward. "Lael, since your son's fulfilling an obligation for the entire town, the council will of course provide him with a pony and such supplies as he'll be needing for this journey. Meer, the chief speaker and I did think that we could spare you some armed guards as well, a squad of militia, say, and some packhorses."

"You can't spare them, Councilman," Meer said. "That's the point of my journey here, wasn't it now? Besides, the child and I will be safer on our own. I know a trick or two about smelling my way to safety when I have to. If need be, the lad and I can always hide in wild places, but hiding a whole pack of armed men in the forest is beyond me."

"Hiding?" Lael stepped forward. "From what? Now wait just a moment, good bard. I had no idea—"

"Da!" Niffa snapped. "It's needful that you let him go."

"Come now, my good sir," Meer said. "The lore teaches that one of the fifty-two fixed things is this: when women lay down the law, men must do as we're told."

Lael turned to him, utterly baffled by this statement, a gesture, of course, lost on the bard.

"He does agree," Niffa broke in. "Jahdo, come home now. We've got to get your gear ready."

Lael started to protest, then merely threw his hands in the air to reproach the gods and followed the two children as they hurried across the by-then empty plaza. When Jahdo looked back, he saw Demet running after as well. Standing where they'd left them, Verrarc and the Gel da'Thae conferred, heads together, while the rest of the town council hovered anxiously nearby.

The family spent a miserable evening round the central hearth, where two candle-lanterns stood, sending long shadows flickering on the walls. No one wanted a fire on such a muggy night. For a long time Dera and Lael paced back and forth, squabbling and cursing each other and the town council both while the family merely listened. Niffa and Demet sat on a wooden bench; Kiel leaned in the doorway and glowered; Jahdo scrunched into a corner with a ferret cradled in the crook of his arm for comfort. All at once he realized that his father was speaking to him.

"Why? Why did you say you wanted to go?"

Jahdo opened his mouth to answer only to find that he had no words. Although he tried his best to remember what had made him speak, the entire episode by the council fire had blurred in his mind into something much like a half-remembered dream.

"The adventure of the thing, maybe?" Lael said, softening his voice. "Lad, lad, you can tell me." He crouched down to Jahdo's level. "What be wrong? Second thoughts?"

Jahdo nodded. Lael let out his breath in a puff.

"Too late now, lad, to get out of it. You should have thought of this then. Ye gods, it's not like we can spare you here. There be a passel of work, this time of year."

"Lael?" Demet broke in. "If my sergeant does release me, I'll come take Jahdo's place."

Niffa gave him a brilliant smile that made him blush. Lael pretended not to notice.

"Now that be decent of you, lad," he said. "I'll speak to him myself. It's been many a long year since I served my turn in the militia, and I wouldn't mind having someone good with a sword round the place."

"Why, Da?" Jahdo found his tongue at last.

"Don't know." Lael hesitated, suddenly uneasy. "It's just that somewhat be wrong. I can feel it, like."

"Everything be wrong." Dera began to weep. "Jahdo, Jahdo! Naught will ever be right again."

Jahdo clutched Ambo so tight that the ferret whipped his head round and nipped his wrist, then slithered free and dashed for the other room. Jahdo stood up.

"Mam, don't be crying! Please! It's needful that I do this." He felt as if he were struggling to open a locked door, shoving and pushing and banging against some huge expanse of solid oak, but he simply could not voice the truth, that he'd never wanted to agree.

"You could at least tell your mother why," Lael snapped.

The entire family was staring at him, waiting for him to speak.

"I can't. I don't know why. I can't say it."

Lael sighed and threw his hands into the air.

"To think that a son of mine!" he snapped. "Ye gods!"

"Da!" Niffa came to Jahdo's rescue. "Leave it be. There's no help for it now, anyway, no matter what the reason."

Dera wiped her eyes on a bit of rag and nodded agreement.

"And I'll say one thing for that Gel da'Thae bard," she snarled. "He's got some respect for a mother's heart, not like our Verro. Here I've known him since he was a tiny lad, a pitiful little thing with that rotten father of his, and me the only woman in this town who'd stand up to old Renno, at that, and tell him to keep his belt off his lad's back. To think he'd treat one of mine this way now that he's made his way in the world!"

Jahdo tried to speak so hard that he began to tremble, but words would not come. Dimly he remembered that Verrarc had somehow or other spared his life, but he could not tell his mother, could not find one word.

"Now here, the lad be exhausted," Demet said. "Lael, a dropped plate's past mending, isn't it? Might as well let Jahdo get his sleep. He'll need it."

Jahdo decided that as prospective brothers-in-law went, Demet had a lot to recommend him. Before his parents could start in on him again, he retreated to the bedchamber.

Although Jahdo was sure that he'd never fall asleep, suddenly it was dawn. Wrapped in their blankets, Kiel and Niffa were sleeping nearby; the ferrets lay tumbled in pairs and threes in their straw. Jahdo got up, considered waking everyone, then decided that he could never bear to say good-bye. The night before, he'd gathered into a sack his few pieces of extra clothing, along with his winter cloak and the bone-handled knife his grandfather had given him, and put the lot by the front door. He dressed, pulled on his heaviest pair of boots, and slipped out of the chamber, tiptoeing past his parents' bed. At the door he stopped, looking out into the gray light brightening on the passageway outside. If he turned round for a last look at home, he would cry. He grabbed his sack and hurried out.

He slithered down the passageway, climbed down the ladder, bolted into the wider street, and nearly collided with Councilman Verrarc. In the rising light Verrarc looked ill—that was the only word Jahdo had for it, anyway. His skin was dead-pale, and his eyes seemed huge, sunk in the puffy shadow of dark circles. Behind him stood two guards, armed, wearing chain-mail shirts under the loose red tabards that marked them as servants of the Council of Five. Even though his family knew their families, Jahdo saw them as jailers.

"There he is," Verrarc sang out, and he was making some attempt at a smile. "Jahdo, the council does send its official thanks. Do you realize what that means? By taking up this burden of the treaty bond, you do work for everybody—the town, the council, your family—everybody. Why, lad, you be a hero!"

The two guards nodded their solemn agreement. Jahdo merely shrugged. He knew that if he tried to say one word, tears would pour and shame him. And yet, when they reached the main jetty and discovered the entire council assembled to hail the rat boy, Jahdo found himself caught by the moment. Admi himself stepped forward to take his hand and lead him onto the barge, where the town banners snapped and rustled as the mists blew away. The councilmen bowed, the oarsmen saluted, the militia all watched him with awe. Jahdo's heart began to pound from the honor of it. Maybe he was a hero, after all. Maybe he really did believe them. Maybe he really did want to go.

At the main gates out Meer stood waiting beside his huge white horse. With his staff in one hand he turned his sightless eyes their way and boomed out a greeting as the procession made its way up. The honors evaporated like summer mist from the lake.

"Well, Jahdo lad, are you ready for our journey?"

"Not truly." The words leapt from his mouth. "Meer, I be scared."

The councilmen winced and looked this way and that, but the Gel da'Thae laughed.

"Good. So am I. We've every right to be. Neither of us are warriors, are we?"

"So we're not," Jahdo said. "I wish we were."

Meer laughed again and swung his head round.

"Councilman Verrarc? Where are you?"

"Here, good sir." Verrarc stepped forward. "My men tell me you don't want the lad to have a pony."

"Just so. The pack mule and supplies will do us, and very generous you townsmen are, I must say. Jahdo and I will walk, because warriors we are not, only a blind man and a lad, and much more fitting it will be for us to stay on our two feet. And safer, as well. All during my long journey from the trading stations of the east, I've been studying to be humble, and, Jahdo my friend, I recommend the same to you. When a man runs the risk of meeting his ancestral enemies, humility becomes him."

No one seemed to be able to think of fine words to answer those.

"Let us address the gods," Meer went on, "and beg them for a safe journey as we go about our business. All our doings lie in the hands of the gods, after all." He flung himself to his knees, bowed his head, and stretched out his arms like a suppliant. "O you gods who dwell beyond the sky, all-powerful and all-seeing, and especially the gods of roads, O you, Tanbala of the North, O you, Rinbala of the South, Thunderers and Shakers, hear our prayer!"

Meer prayed for a long while, both in his language and that of the Rhiddaer, while the men looked this way and that and Jahdo watched fascinated. The folk of the Rhiddaer prayed, when they prayed at all, standing on their feet and facing the home of whatever god they were invoking, whether it was a tree or a hot spring or a fire mountain. He'd never seen anyone grovel in front of the gods before, and the sight embarrassed him. At last, however, Meer finished and rose, dusting off the knees of his leather trousers as if he'd done something perfectly ordinary. The men standing round all sighed in relief.

Verrarc handed Jahdo the lead rope of a fine brown mule, laden with canvas panniers.

"Farewell, lad, and may we meet again soon."

Jahdo had never heard anything less sincere in his life.

As the gates swung open, he took the lead, urging the mule along with little clucking noises such as he'd make to encourage a ferret. One of the guards handed him a switch.

"Beat the mule as much as it needs," he remarked. "Stubborn ugly things."

"Here!" Meer bellowed. "What did he give you? A stick or suchlike? Throw it away, lad. I'll teach you how to handle a mule, and beatings have no part in it."

Secure in Meer's blindness the guard grinned and rolled his eyes, but Jahdo tossed the switch away.

All that morning they followed a hard-packed dirt road east through reasonably familiar country. Although Jahdo had never been more than a mile or two away from Cerr Cawnen, the farmers round about were still his people. Their wooden longhouses, all painted white and roofed with split planks, stood in the midst of fields of volcanic earth so rich some thought it magical. Often, as they walked past a fenced field or a pasture, a well-dressed man or a couple of plump children would leave their plowing or cattle to run to the side of the road and stare at them. For the first few miles, Meer strode along in silence, swinging his stick back and forth on the road with one massive hand as he led his horse with the other. Wrapped in his instant homesickness, Jahdo was glad to be left alone at first, but the farther they went, the harder it became to keep back his tears.

Since he'd never eaten that morning, as the sun rose high in the sky his stomach began to growl. He could imagine his family coming back home for their noon meal, gathering at the long table, and watching while Mam dipped soup from the kettle and cut bread into chunks. He caught his breath with a sob.

"What's this?" Meer bellowed. "What do I hear?"

"Naught, good bard."

"Hah! You can't fool my ears, lad. Don't even try. Huh. The sun feels hot on my back. Is it near midday?"

"It is, truly."

"Time for us to stop and see what kind of provisions your councilmen gave us, then. Look round. Do you see a stream nearby? We should be watering our animals, anyway."

About a quarter mile down the road Jahdo found them a shallow stream with a grassy bank. Working under Meer's direction, he unbuckled the pack saddles, but Meer himself had to heft them down. Despite his affliction the Gel da'Thae moved remarkably surely when it came to tending his horses. Watching him rub down the white horse, Baki, with a twist of grass, with the bard talking under his breath all the while, or seeing him patting the horse and leading him to the stream, it was hard, in fact, to remember that Meer was blind. The mule received the same attention.

"We'll name you Gidro," Meer announced. "That means strong in my people's talk, and a fine strong mule you are."

Gidro leaned its forehead against the bard's chest and snorted.

"Mules are one of the thirteen clever beasts, young Jahdo. Your people abuse them and call them stubborn, but by every demon among us, who can blame the mule? Here, he thinks to himself, why should I be sweating and straining my back all for the benefit of some bald, two-legged thing that smells of meat and piss? All I get out of it is sour hay and a drafty shed. A pox on them all, thinks the mule."

Jahdo found himself laughing.

"That's better, lad," Meer said. "I know it's a hard thing I've asked you to do. Now go through those packs, there, and find us a bite to eat."

Much to his delight, Jahdo found a lot of food wrapped and cached in various cloth bags, including some chewy honey cakes. Meer had him bring out some dark bread and cheese, which Jahdo sliced up with his grandfather's knife. Before they ate, however, Meer recited yet another prayer, though mercifully it was a good bit shorter than his effort back at Cerr Cawnen, to thank the god Elmandrel for the food.

"The gods do matter a fair bit to you, don't they, Meer?" Jahdo said.

"They do, and so they should to all the Gel da'Thae, for we are sinners in their sight, more loathsome than worms." Meer held out his hand for lunch. "Thanks, lad. That cheese smells good, I must say. At any rate, we all sinned mightily against the three hundred sixty-five gods and the thousands upon thousands of the Children of the Gods, back in the old days, when the Red Reivers fell upon us. Your people, now, they suffered much at the hands of the Lijik Ganda, but as victims they did not sin."

"Er, well, that be splendid, then."

Meer merely grunted and bit into his bread and cheese. Jahdo followed suit, and for a long time neither of them spoke. Jahdo had heard stories of the old days from priests and singers among his own people, who recited them at public feast days, such as the celebrations of spring and the harvesttime, but he had never considered that those ancient events would someday reach out dead hands to touch his own life. The Slavers lived only in stories, didn't they, to frighten children into behaving? Stop pinching your sister right now, or the Slavers will come get you—that sort of thing. But he'd just found out that they were real, and he was heading their way.

Far, far to the east, or so the stories ran, lay a beautiful kingdom that once had belonged to the ancestors of the Rhiddaer folk, where they lived in peace and prosperity near the trees and springs of the ancient gods. One dark day a new people appeared, warriors who thundered down on horseback and killed or enslaved the peaceful farmers. On their stolen land and with their slave labor, these invaders built stone towers and towns made of round houses, where they lived at ease while the ancestors were forced to work the fields. A few at a time, though, the ancestors had slipped away, seeking freedom. Some died in the attempt; others escaped to found a new country, the Rhiddaer, where kings and lords such as commanded the Slavers were forbidden forever by law. Finally, the Slavers' bloodthirsty ways brought ruin upon their own heads, when a huge civil war, lasting five and a hundred years, tore their kingdom apart. Most of the ancestors escaped during those days of retribution and made their way to freedom in the Rhiddaer. For a long time everyone hoped that the Slavers were all dead, but unfortunately, the warring madness had left them in the end, and their kingdom was prospering again.

"Meer?" Jahdo said. "The old stories do say that the Slavers used to cut off people's heads and then tie them to their saddles and stuff. The heads, I mean, not the rest of the people. That be not true, bain't?"

"I fear me it is, lad. The lore passed down from bard to bard confirms it."

Jahdo dropped his face into his hands and sobbed. After this whole long horrible day, the lore was just one thing too many to endure. He heard Meer sigh and move; then a broad hand fumbled for his shoulder and patted it.

"Now, now, we've got to put our trust in the gods. They'll guide us and protect us, and the Slavers will never even know we were walking their border."

Jahdo sniveled back his tears and wiped his face on his sleeve.

"Well, I be sorry I did cry."

"Don't you think my heart aches within me, too? I tell you again, lad, warriors we are not, and thus the gods will hold us not to the warrior's harsh honor."

"All right, then, but if ever I do get home again I'll have to be a warrior when I grow up. I'll have to join the militia, I mean. Everybody does. I guess it's not like that in your country."

"It's not, indeed. Only the chosen few become warriors, the best among us, and a grim lot they are, soaked in blood and death from the time they're but colts."

"They be just like the Slavers were, then."

Meer laughed, a rumble under his breath.

"So they are, but I wouldn't say that to them, if ever you meet some. And truly, you just might in the days ahead. You just might indeed."

After they'd eaten, they loaded up the horse and mule again and headed east on the familiar road for the rest of that day. At times as they walked Meer would sing, or at least, Jahdo supposed that you could call it singing, a far different thing from the songs and simple tunes for dancing that his people knew. Meer's voice rumbled deep and huge to match the rest of him, but it seemed he sang with his throat squeezed tight and forced the air out his nose, too—Jahdo wasn't exactly sure—so that his notes hissed and wailed as much as they boomed, and the melody flowed up and down and round about in a long cadence of quarter tones and sprung rhythms. Every now and then, Jahdo could have sworn he heard the bard sing chords, all by himself with no instrument to help him. At first the music threatened headaches, but by the third song Jahdo heard the patterns in it, and while he never grew to like it, he found it tolerable.

That night they made camp beside a duck pond in a farmer's pasture, within sight of the wooden longhouse and big stone barn. After they'd eaten, Jahdo collected wood and tinder for a little fire, but he saved it for the actual dark. As the sunset faded to twilight, Jahdo found himself staring at the farm, watching the gleam from a lantern dancing in the windows, wondering how big a family lived there and if they were happy. When he wondered if he'd ever see his own family again, he started to cry, and this time Meer let him sob until he'd got it all out and felt better for it.

"Well, lad, are you sorry you said you wanted to come?"

Jahdo tried to speak and found his throat frozen. All he could do was make a small choking sound.

"Here, what's that mean?" Meer said.

"Naught." Jahdo grabbed a handful of grass and blew his nose.

The Gel da'Thae swung his massive head round as if he were looking Jahdo's way, but he said nothing. All round in the velvet evening insects buzzed and chirred. Jahdo tossed the ill-used grass away.

"Meer? Why are you going east?"

"That's a fitting question, considering how I've dragged you away from hearth and home, but I'm not going to answer it."

"Here! Not fair!"

"Fair has naught to do with it."

Jahdo felt all his homesickness boil and turn to rage. He scrambled to his feet.

"Then you may just find your way without me. I'm going home."

He grabbed a bag of food from the ground and marched off, sighting on the last glow of the setting sun. Behind him Meer howled, a huge sound as if ten wolves sang.

"Come back, come back!"

Jahdo heard stumblings and cursings, but he kept walking.

"Stop!" Meer's anguish floated after him. "Wait! I'll tell you, then."

Jahdo stopped and turned round, but he hesitated. In the last of the light he could just see the bard's silhouette, flailing round with his stick as he tried to follow over the rocks and hummocks. He moved remarkably well, considering, but he was angling away fast from the path that Jahdo had actually taken. He'll die out here without me, Jahdo thought.

"Meer, stop! I'm coming back."

The bard sobbed once in relief and held still. Jahdo led him back to their camp, sat Meer down on a log, then busied himself with striking sparks from his flint and steel until the readied tinder at last caught. Jahdo blew the spark into a flame, fed in a little dried grass, then some twigs, and at last pieces of broken branch. As the light leapt and spread he moved back from the unwelcome heat. Meer was sitting with his head between his hands, his face turned as if he were staring into the fire. Seeing him look so defeated brought Jahdo a strange insight: never before had he argued with, much less bested, a grown man, and rather than exulting, he was frightened. Yet he refused to back down.

"Well, tell me now. Why are you going east?"

"It's a long and bitter story, but you're right enough that you should hear it. Pay attention, though, because I can only bear to repeat it this once." Meer cleared his throat several times before he went on. "I have an elder brother who became a powerful razkan, what you'd call a captain in your tongue, I suppose, the man who leads a group of warriors. And what with his raiding and then the legitimate battles between our various cities, he became famous, gathering many a free-born warrior round him, as well as the usual slave soldiers he bought with all his booty."

"Hold a moment. Slave soldiers? How can you give a slave weapons and make them fight?"

"They've been bred and born among the Gel da'Thae, and they know that if they fight well, they'll be set free."

"But still, I don't understand. You think they'd just kill this razkan fellow and run away."

"Run to what? The wilderness? They know the civic authorities would hunt them down, and the gods wouldn't help them the way they helped your people escape, because they'd be rebels and traitors."

"The gods helped us?"

"Of course they did. They sent their own children to save and succor you, out on the grasslands to the south."

"I never did hear that before. I heard that it was some people who raised horses or suchlike. Why did the gods help us?"

"Now here!" Meer spoke with some asperity. "Do you want me to finish this tale or not? Fewer questions, if you please."

"I be sorry."

"Very well, then. Now, as I say, my brother, Thavrae his name is, his warrior's name, I mean, though Svar was the name our mother gave him. Ah alas, woe betide the day she birthed him, and woe betide that his kin and clan have lived to see his infamy!"

"What's he been doing?"

"Whoring after strange gods. Gods? Did I say gods? One of the three hundred sixty-four kinds of demon, more like! False gods, anyway. They're supposed to be new gods. Now I ask you. If a god wasn't around to help make the world, what kind of a god can she be? Gods don't just pop up all of a sudden like, out of nowhere, appearing at your table like some unmarried uncle in search of a dinner!"

Jahdo giggled.

"Just so." Meer nodded firmly. "But for some years now these false prophets have been coming round, preaching these new gods to anyone stupid enough to listen. These so-called seers come from the wild tribes of the far north, where the demons have been appearing and working marvels, or so *they* say. Alshandra's the name they mention most, a powerful goddess of war, or so they call her."

"Your people, they'd be liking her, then."

"Just so. But most of these prophets are gone now. Some got themselves caught and strangled in the public square by the authorities, and the rest haven't been seen for some while. They've turned sensible, if you take my meaning, but a few fools have listened to them. And my brother, my own blood kin, little Svar as I'll always think of him, he's one of them, claiming allegiance to this Alshandra creature. It broke my mother's heart."

"I'll wager it did. That be too bad, Meer, really 'tis so." Jahdo was trying to imagine what the mother of a man such as Meer would be like—even more formidable than his own mother, he supposed. "I guess she could talk no sense into him, huh?"

"No one could make him listen to reason, no one, not our mother, not our aunts, not our uncles. But anyway, some weeks ago Thavrae led his men out east."

"Why?"

"Well, partly to spare our city outright war between his warband and that of his rivals. He did listen to our mother about that, when she begged him to take his men away before citizen slaughtered citizen in the streets. The authorities wanted to strangle him for blasphemy, you see, but you don't just arrest a razkan when he's got his warband round him."

"Then he does have some honor left."

"Some, truly, though a poor comfort to our mother it is."

"Wait a moment. You said these demons live in the north, right? Why did Thavrae head east?"

"I'm coming to that part. Hush. Apparently he'd received an omen from the gods, sending him to fetch a particular thing from the lands of the Slavers."

"What was it?"

"How would I know? But I was sent to find him and beg him to come home."

"Sent by your mother?"

"Just so."

"Do you think you—I mean we—can find him?"

"I don't know." Meer sighed, running both hands through his tangled mane of hair. "By now he and his men should have found whatever this mysterious object is and be returning. I hope we'll meet them on the road back."

"What road? We don't even know where we're going."

"True."

"Then how do you think we'll ever find him?"

"If I can get within a reasonable distance, the brother bond will guide us."

"The what?"

"The brother bond." Meer hesitated for a long time. "Now, that's one thing I can never explain to you, Jahdo, even if you were to walk away again and leave me here to starve. It's a magick, and some magicks are Gel da'Thae. They cannot be shared. In the temple we swear holy vows."

"Well, all right, then. My mam does always say that if you swear a thing, it's needful for you to do it. But I still don't see how we're going to find him. What if he goes north and we go south or somewhat like that?"

"It might happen, truly. But a mother's charge is a sacred charge, and I must travel and try."

Jahdo hesitated, considering.

"Be you sure this is all you're doing? I did hear you talking to Verrarc back home, Councilman Verrarc I mean, and you were talking about your mother and stuff, but I did get this strange feeling. You weren't telling him everything, were you?"

Meer laughed.

"I figured I was choosing the cleverest lad in town, and I was right. But actually, I wasn't lying. I was merely editing. I didn't want to go into detail. There is somewhat about Councilman Verrarc that creeps my flesh. I hear things in his voice, somehow."

"Things?"

"Overtones, odd hesitations, a peculiar timbre. He sounds enraged, but at the same time, he reeks of fear." Meer paused, considering. "I can barely put it into words, it's such a subtle thing. But he's an ominous man, in his way, an ominous man."

Jahdo shuddered. Yet once again the buried memory tried to rise, bringing with it a cold shudder. He caught his breath with a little gasp. Meer turned an inquiring ear his way.

"Geese walking on my grave," Jahdo said. "Oh, ych, I wish I hadn't said that."

"More likely the evening breeze, lad. I wouldn't take it as an omen."

Later, as Jahdo was falling asleep, he remembered that Meer had found him clever. In spite of the trouble this opinion had got him into, he was pleased.

It took three more days of their slow journeying before they left settled country behind. The road climbed steadily, and the last few farms they passed nestled in hills where sheep, not cows, grazed the sparse pasturage between huge gray boulders. What trees there were, scrubby pine and second-growth alders and suchlike, hugged the narrow valleys, leaving the hilltops to grass and the wind. As the road diminished to a rocky path, Meer began to worry about the horse and mule, stopping often to run a huge hand down their legs to check for swellings and strains. He told Jahdo how to pick up their hooves and look for tiny stones or thorns that might have got stuck in the soft frogs. Although Jahdo was afraid of getting a kick for his trouble, as long as Meer was holding their halters or even simply touching them, the horse and mule stood still and docile.

"If either of these creatures comes up lame, lad, we're in for a miserable time of it."

"I do see that, truly. Well, I'll be real careful and take good care of them."

The next day early they left the Rhiddaer behind, not that there was a formal boundary or cairn to mark the border. It was just that Jahdo happened to glance back from the top of a hill and realized that he could see nothing familiar—not a farmhouse, not a shepherd, not a cultivated field nor a coppiced wood—nothing to mark the presence of human being or Gel da'Thae, either. For a long moment he stood looking back west and down across the low hills to catch a glimpse of the valley, all misty in the blue distance, where he'd spent his entire life. He felt torn in half between missing his family and a completely new sensation, a wondering what lay ahead, not behind, a sudden eagerness to see the new view that would lie east of these hills.

"Jahdo?" Meer called. "Somewhat wrong?"

"Naught, truly. Just looking behind us. Meer, you'd better let me lead the way now. This be a road no longer, just sort of a trail. I don't think your staff will be enough of a guide."

"Well and good, then. Lead on. And please remember, lad, that you're my eyes. You've got to tell me everything you see."

"I will then."

Remembering to keep up a running commentary for the blind bard turned out to be difficult. At first Jahdo had no idea what information would be useful to him, and he tended to describe distant vistas rather than the footing just ahead. Thanks to Meer's constant and sarcastic comments, he did learn fast that a lovely view of trees in a valley wasn't half so valuable as news of a rock blocking the path.

The path, such as it was, wound along the sides of hills and ran, basically, from one grassy spot to the next, which confirmed Jahdo's guess that it was a deer trail. It was a good thing they were heading directly east; without the sun's direction to guide them, they could easily have circled round and round the broken hillsides and steep valleys. Water, at least, ran clean and abundant in a multitude of little streams and springs. Here and there they came to a deeper stream, roaring with white water at the bottom of shallow but steep ravines. It was one of those, in fact, that nearly proved fatal.

Late in the afternoon, as they skirted the edge of a fast-moving stream, Jahdo was so intent on telling Meer where to walk that he lost track of his own feet and stepped too close to the ravine edge. The moment his foot hit he felt the damp soil crumble under his weight. He tossed the mule's lead rope back toward the animal just in time to avoid pulling Gidro after him.

"Meer!" he shrieked. "I'm falling!"

The sky spun blue and bright, and the roar of the water far below seemed to fill the world as he went over, twisting, flailing, grabbing out at empty air. With a smack he hit a wall of pain and lay gasping for breath on a little ledge. Above, what seemed like miles and miles above, he heard the frightened mule braying and Meer yelling his name, but though he fought sobbing for air he could not speak or call out. My ribs be broken, he thought. I'll never be able to walk. I'll have to die here.

All at once he realized that the sounds from above had stopped. His first panicked thought was that Meer had left him behind, but he realized almost immediately that the Gel da'Thae needed him too badly for that. His second panicked thought was that Meer was going to fall over the edge himself.

"Meer!" he managed to force sound from his burning lungs at last. "Careful! The edge be soft!"

"Jahdo! You're alive! Thank every god! Lie still, lad, lie still and get your breath."

Jahdo did as he was told, letting the pain subside as he listened to odd scrapings of sound above him. Suddenly Meer's face appeared at the cliff edge. Jahdo realized that the bard was lying on his stomach and feeling for the edge with one hand. In the other he held a rope.

"Make noise," Meer called out.

"You be right above me."

"Hah! Thought I heard you panting down there."

If Meer had heard him breathing, no matter how noisily, over the sound of the white water below, then, Jahdo decided, his hearing must have been amazingly keen. When Meer tossed the rope, the end spiraled down and fell across his chest. Jahdo grabbed it with one hand and carefully felt round him with the other. He had just the room to sit up, and as he did so, he realized that while he ached from bruising, nothing was broken.

"I be whole enough, Meer!" he called out. "And I do have the rope."

"Splendid, splendid. Tie that end round your waist, lad, not too tight, now. You'll need to ride her up like a sling. I've got the other end on Gidro's packsaddle."

With the mule pulling and Jahdo walking up the steep side of the ravine, he got to the top easily enough, but scrambling over with the rim so soggy and soft was something of an ordeal, because his back and shoulders ached like fire. At last he was crawling on solid ground. By grabbing Gidro's packsaddle he could haul himself up to his feet. Meer inched back from the edge and sat up into a crouch.

"My thanks," Jahdo said. "You did save my life."

"And my own as well, eh?" Meer felt the front of his shirt and began brushing off mud and grass clots.

"I do thank you anyway. You could have fallen and broken your neck, trying to save me."

"I feared your mother's curse worse than I did dying. A mother's curse follows a man into the Deathworld, it does. And I thought we'd lost you for sure, lad. What happened?"

"I did step too close to the edge, that's all. This soft dirt, it be a jeopard, Meer. It's needful that you do test every step with that staff you carry."

"And so I shall from now on. Here, do you see a good place to camp? How late is it? I feel a powerful need to rest, I do."

"Well, the trail runs downhill from here, and I see some trees and grass down over to our left."

"Downhill, does it? Huh, I wonder if there's mountains ahead. Can you see any, off on the horizon?"

"I haven't yet, not even from the top of a hill. I did never hear any stories about mountains between us and the Slavers. I think that's why the ancestors could escape. They never would have survived in mountains."

"True. Huh. Another thing I wonder. This city, where Thavrae was heading, I mean, is it northeast or southeast?"

"You don't know?" Jahdo heard his voice rise to a wail.

"I'm afraid I don't. The lore's a bit sketchy when it comes to details like that. Well, we're in the hands of the gods. In them lie our true hope and our true safety. Let us pray for guidance."

Although he never would have dared to voice such a thought, Jahdo decided that he'd rather put his trust in a man who'd traveled there and back again. Yet, much to his surprise, not long after they did indeed receive a sign from the gods—or so Meer interpreted it.

For the next few days they traveled slowly, stopping often to let Jahdo rest his sore back. Although he soon realized that out of sheer luck he'd broken nothing, he hurt worse than he'd ever hurt in his young life. Sleeping on the ground did nothing to ease his bruises, either. At times, thinking of his warm mattress at home would make him weep. At others, he would simply wish that he had died, there in the fall, and put himself out of his misery. Yet, of course, he had no choice but to keep traveling. Going back would have hurt as much as going forward, after all, and he learned that much to his surprise, he could endure a great deal and still cope with the work of tending animals and making camps, to say nothing of a hard walk through broken country.

On the fourth day it rained, a heavy summer storm that boiled up from the south. Although they were soaked within a few moments, they took shelter from the wind in one of the wooded valleys. Meer insisted that they unload the stock for a rest while they waited out the rain in this imperfect shelter.

"They might as well be comfortable, anyway," Jahdo said. "Even if we can't. I hate being wet. I do feel all cold and slimy, and my bruises from that fall, they do ache in this damp. My boots be wet inside, even. This be miserable, bain't?"

"I take it, lad, that you've not spent much time in wild country."

"Why would I?"

"No reason, truly. You're not Gel da'Thae. Our souls belong to the wild places of the world, you see, and deep in our souls, all of us yearn for the northern plains, the homeland, the heartland of our tribes."

"But I thought you did live in towns, like we do."

"Of course, so that we may better serve the gods here in the latter days of the world. But in our souls, ah, we yearn for the days when we rode free in the heartland. Our warriors make their kills to glorify its memory, and singers like me make our music in its honor."

"Well, if you do miss it so much, why don't you go back?"

"We can't. Jahdo, listen. This is very important. When the Slavers attacked the homeland, we fled. We deserted our north country and fled south, stinking in our shame, cowards and slave-hearted, every one of us. For what is one of the thirteen worst things but to desert one's homeland in its hour of need? And in our rage and shame we fought and burned and pillaged our way through the cities of the south. Oh, woe to the Gel da'Thae! That we should desert the homeland and then destroy the cities that the gods themselves had built for their children! Woe and twice woe, that we raised our hands against those children themselves and did slay and smite them! And for that shame and that sin, we can never return. The long meadows of the north, the fire mountains of the ancestors, and the warm rivers that forbid winter their banks—all, all are lost forever. Do you understand?"

"I don't, truly. Meer, you must be awfully old, to remember all that."

"I don't remember it, you irritating little cub. This is lore."

"Well, I do be sorry if I were rude again, but it does seem to mean so much to you. It's like it just happened last winter."

When Meer growled like an enormous dog, Jahdo decided to let the subject drop.

Once the horses were tended and tethered, Meer hunkered down beside the leather packs, which they'd piled up in the driest spot. Although Jahdo was expecting him to pass the time in prayer, instead he merely sat, as still and in the same way as one of the tree trunks around them, alive but utterly silent. At times he turned his head or cocked it, as if he were hearing important messages from every drop of rain, every scuttling squirrel. Even when the rain slacked and died, Meer sat unmoving, until Jahdo finally could stand it no longer.

"Meer? I feel so awful."

"No doubt you do, lad. My apologies. Here, take off those wet boots. Wet boots rub wet feet raw. What does the sky look like?"

"Clearing up pretty good. It must be 'twixt noon and sunset by now."

"Huh." Meer considered for a moment. "And what does the land ahead look like?"

"More hills. Bigger ones, and all broken up, like."

"We'll camp here, then. I hear a stream nearby."

"I can just see it, truly. I thought I'd take the waterskins down. Do you want a drink?"

"I do, if you don't mind fetching me one. The lore says that one of the fifty-two contrary things is this: sitting in the rain makes a man thirsty. And as usual, the lore is right."

Jahdo slung the pair of waterskins, joined by a thong, across his shoulders and picked his way through the trees and tangled bracken. The little stream flowed between shallow banks, all slippery with mossy rocks and tiny ferns; predictably enough, he lost his footing and slid into the water. Stones stung his bare feet, and he yelped, righting himself.

"Careful." The voice sounded directly behind him. "It's not deep, but it's treacherous."

When Jahdo spun round he saw a strange man sitting on the bank and smiling at him. He was a tall fellow, slender, dressed in a long green tunic and buckskin trousers. His hair was the bright yellow of daffodils, his lips were the red of sour cherries, and his eyes were an unnatural turquoise-blue, bright as gemstones. Yet the strangest thing of all were his ears, long and delicately pointed, furled tight like a fern in spring.

"That Gel da'Thae has no eyes," he said.

"He be a bard. They get them taken out."

"Disgusting custom, truly, but no affair of mine. You're his slave?"

"I am not!"

"Then what are you?"

Jahdo considered.

"Well, I didn't even know him a fortnight ago, but he's my friend now."

"Very well. Give him a message. What the legends say is right enough, and east lie the Slavers, sure enough, but south, south is the way to turn. Follow this stream, and it will swell to a river. Cross at the ford marked with the stone, and head into the rising sun. Beware, beware that you go too far, or you'll reach the Slavers' towered dun. Can you remember that rhyme?"

"I can indeed, sir, but please, who are you?"

"Tell the bard that my name's Evandar."

"I will, then. But, sir, will you come back if we get lost?"

"Now that I can't promise. I have other affairs on hand."

With that he disappeared, so suddenly and completely gone that Jahdo was sure he'd dreamt the entire thing—until he realized that he could never fall asleep standing knee-deep in cold water. He filled the skins and rushed back to the bard, who was currying the white horse.

"Meer, Meer, the strangest thing just happened! I did see this man, and then he were gone, all at once like."

"Indeed? Suppose you start at the beginning of this peculiar tale, lad, and tell it to me slowly."

Jahdo did, paying particular attention to the fellow's directions. For a long time Meer said nothing, merely laid his huge hands on the horse's back as if for the comfort of the touch and stared sightlessly up at the sky.

"Well, now," he rumbled at last. "I told your mother, didn't I, that you were marked for a great destiny?"

"Well, you said maybe I was."

"And I was right." Meer ignored the qualification. "To have seen one of the gods is the greatest honor a man can have."

"That were one of your gods?"

"It was. Did I not pray for guidance in our traveling? Did he not come to provide it?"

Jahdo shuddered. He felt as if snow had slipped from a roof down his back, and it took him a long time to be able to speak.

"You be sure that were a god? He didn't look like much."

"You ill-got little cub! It's not for us to question how the gods choose to appear to us."

"My apologies, then, but you be sure it weren't one of those demons you do talk about?"

"Not if he gave his name as Evandar the Avenger, the archer of Rinbala, goddess of the sea, he whose silver arrows could pierce the moon itself and fetch it from the sky."

"Well, he only said Evandar, not all the rest of that stuff."

"The rest of that stuff, as you so inelegantly put it, happens to be two of his major attributes and one of his minor ones, as attested by the holy hymns themselves. Humph. I can see that I'd best attend to your education. Besides, if he'd been a demon, he'd have tried to snatch you away, to make me fail in my quest."

Jahdo went cold again, a bone-touching chill worse than any god-induced awe.

"I smell fear," Meer said.

"Well, do you blame me?"

"Of course not. Lead me over to our gear, lad, and open the big gray saddlebags. I've got some very powerful amulets in there, and a feather talisman wound and blessed by the high priestess herself, and I think me you'd best wear them from now on."

They met on horseback and alone at the boundary of their two domains, which lay far beyond the physical world in the peculiar reaches of the etheric plane. In this empire of images, a dead-brown moor stretched all round them to a horizon where a perennially setting sun fought through smoke, or so it seemed, to flood them with copper-colored light. Evandar rode unarmored, wearing only his tunic and leather trousers as he lounged on his golden stallion. Since he sat with one leg crooked round the saddle peak, a single shove of a fist or weapon would have knocked him to the ground, but he smiled as he considered his brother. Riding on a black, and glittering with black enameled armor as well, the brother was more than a little vulpine. Since he carried his black-plumed helmet under one arm, you could see his pointed ears tufted with red fur and the roach of red hair that ran from his forehead over his skull and down to the back of his neck. His beady black eyes glittered above a long, sharp nose.

"You're a fool, Evandar," the fox warrior snarled. "Coming here alone like this."

"Am I now? Your message said you needed my help. Was it all a trap and ambuscade?"

He grunted, slung his helmet from a strap on the saddle, and began to pull off his gauntlets. Russet fur plumed on the backs of his hands, and each finger ended in a sharp black claw rather than a nail.

"First you lose your wife, your dear darling Alshandra," he said at last. "And now I hear you've lost your daughter as well."

"Alshandra's gone, true enough, and good riddance to the howling harridan, say I! My daughter? Not lost in the least." Evandar paused for a grin. "I know exactly where my Elessario is, though indeed she's gone from this place. Elessario lies safe in a human womb, and soon she'll be born into the world of men and elves."

The fox warrior shrugged, indifferent to the fact now that the barb had missed its mark. He turned in his saddle and spent a long moment staring at the horizon, where the bloody-colored light fumed and roiled. It seemed that the smoke was stretching higher, sending long red fingers toward the horizon.

"What have you done to the Lands? Hah?" His voice at times barked like a fox's as well. "You've done somewhat, you bastard swine, you scum of all the stars. We can feel it. We can see it. The Lands are shrinking and fading. My court sickens."

"What makes you think that's my doing?"

"It's always your doing, what happens to the Lands." He stared at the ground, grudging each word. "You made them, you shaped them. Doesn't Time feed in your pasture as well?"

"And what does the flow of days have to do with one wretched thing?"

"Don't you see? The turning of the wheel brings decay, and Time runs like a galloping horse these days. You're the only one who can grab its reins. Make it slow, brother, for the sake of all of us, my court as well as yours."

For an answer Evandar merely laughed. A weapon flashed in his brother's hand, a silver sword held high and ready. Evandar unhooked his leg, leaned forward in the saddle, stared into the black, glittering eyes, and stared him down. The fox warrior snarled, but the weapon swung into its sheath.

"You won't kill me, younger brother," Evandar said, but quietly, lest a grin or a laugh be taken as mockery. "Because you don't know what will happen to you if I die. Neither do I, for that matter, but I'll wager it would be naught good."

The fox warrior shrugged the statement away.

"What have you done to the Lands?" he repeated. "Tell me."

"Tell me your name, and I'll tell you."

"No! Never! Not that!"

"Then I'll say naught in return."

For a long moment the fox warrior hesitated, his lips half-parted as if he would speak; then he snarled with a jerk of his reins, swung his horse's head round, and kicked him hard. As he galloped away in a rise of dust, Evandar watched, smiling faintly.

"You stupid fool," he said aloud. "It should be obvious what's happening to the Lands. They're dying."

He turned his horse and jogged off, heading for the green refuge along the last river, where his magic, the enchantments that had carved kingdoms out of the shifting stuff of the etheric plane, still held.

Although he most certainly wasn't the god Meer thought him, Evandar held enormous power, drawn straight from the currents of the upper astral, which shapes the etheric the way that the etheric shapes the physical. He knew how to weave—with enormous effort—the shifting astral light and twine it into forms that seemed, at least, as solid as matter, though he'd also had to master the art of constantly channeling energy into those forms to keep them alive. In the thousands of years of his existence, which he'd spent trapped in a backwash, a killing eddy of the river of Time, he'd had plenty of leisure to learn.

Unthinkably long ago, in the morning light of the universe when Evandar and his people were struck, sparks from immortal fire as all souls are, they'd been meant to take up the burden of incarnation, to ride with all other souls the turning wheels of Life and Death, but somehow, in some way that not even they could remember, they had, as they put it, "stayed behind" and never been born into physical bodies. Without the discipline of the worlds of form, they were doomed. One by one, they would wink out and die, sparks flown too far from the fire—or so he'd been told, and so he believed, simply because he loved the woman who'd told him the tale and for no other reason of intellect or logic.

After Evandar left the dead moor behind, he came to a forest, half green trees and burgeoning ferns, half dead wood and twisted thorns. At its edge stood an enormous tree, half of which thrived in green leaf while half blazed with a fire that never consumed the branches nor did it go out—the beacon that marked the boundary proper between the lands he'd made for his brother's Dark Court and those he kept for his own, the Bright Court. Once the beacon lay behind him, he could relax his guard. As he rode, he thought of his daughter, who had chosen to leave this less than real, more than imagined place and take on flesh in a solid world, one that endured without dweomer to feed it, but one that promised pain. She would be born to a human mother soon, would Elessario, and take up the destiny that should have claimed all his folk. If she were to be safe, there was much he had to do in that other world, the only one that most sapient souls know. What happened to his glamoured lands, or the images of lands, that he had spent an aeon building up no longer much concerned him. Without his concern, they dimmed.

All the green plains, dotted with glades and streams, had turned misty, billowing as he crossed them, as if they were embroidered pictures on a coverlet that someone was shaking to lay out flat upon a bed. The distant towers and urban prospects fluttered and wavered as if they were but banners hung on a near horizon. Only one particular river and the meadows round it remained real, the gathering place for his court, and it seemed to him that they too had shrunk into themselves, turned smaller, fainter, flames playing over a dying fire.

Yet still they were a beautiful people. Since they had no proper bodies or forms of their own, they'd taken the form of the elves that their leader loved so much, with hair pale as moonlight or bright as the sun to set off violet eyes, gray eyes, and the long delicate curled ears of that earthly race. For the most part their skin was as pale as milk, just touched with roses in the cheek, but some had seen the human beings of the far southern isles, and those who had wore a rich, dark skin like fresh-plowed earth under a rain. They clustered in the golden pavilion, listened to sad songs played by indifferent bards, or sat in the pale sunlight, merely sat and talked in low voices, their dancing, it seemed, all done forever.

Whether their numbers had shrunk as well, he couldn't say. Counting the court lay beyond him or any being, truly, because most of them were like shapes half-seen in clouds or flames, at times separate, at others merging into one another, rising into brief individuality only to fall back to a shared mind. Only a few had achieved, as he had, a true consciousness. One of these, wearing the form of a young page, ran to take his horse as he dismounted. Although the boy stared at him, hoping for a few words, Evandar merely shrugged and walked away. As he hurried through the scattered crowd, faces turned toward him, eyes came to life, hope bloomed in smiles that he would save them as he had before. He doubted that he cared enough to try.

Down by the river, flowing broad and slow between rushy banks, sat a woman with steel-gray eyes and silvery-blond hair that tumbled down her back. When she rose to greet him, he abruptly saw her slender body as a shaft of granite, hard and cold and real among the shifting forms of the Lands. Round her neck she wore a tiny figurine, seemingly carved from amethyst, that echoed her body in every detail. It actually was her body, in fact, once physical meat and blood and bone but transformed by his magic so that she could live in his country. Dallandra was one of the truly-born, a member of that race called elves or Westfolk by men and the "Children of the Gods" by the Gel da'Thae, though they called themselves simply "the People." She was also a dweomermaster of great power, though no human or elven sorcerer could ever match Evandar's skill.

"What did your brother want?" she said.

"To blame me for letting his territories fall into disrepair. Let him build his own, if he wants them as badly as all that. I've no time to waste upon his snouted, hairy pack." He walked to the riverbank and looked into the astral water, thick and silver, oozing rather than flowing between the clumps of water reeds and the rushes. "No matter what I do, this river remains. I wonder if it will still exist—after I'm dead and scattered into nothingness, I mean."

"It might well, at that. Of course, there's no reason for you to die with your domain. You could choose birth like your daughter has."

She spoke casually, barely looking his way.

"I've made my choice," he snapped. "Never shall I go live in the world of blood and muck and pain and mire."

"Well, then there's naught I can do about it, is there?"

His hurt that she would sound so indifferent to his death stabbed like a winter wind. For a moment he was tempted to change his mind, just to spite her.

"But I do have to visit it now and again," he said instead. "I've started a few more hares upon this field, and I have to go see how they run."

"I hope you know what you're doing."

He laughed, tossing back his head.

"I hope I do, too, my beloved. I sincerely hope I do. Don't you trust me?"

"It's not a question of trust. It's just that everything's getting so dreadfully complicated. You seem to have so many schemes afoot."

"Only the one, to keep Elessario safe once she's born."

"But you've a fair number of meats simmering in this particular stew. And I worry about Time, my love. It runs so differently here in your world than it does in mine."

"Why must you always refer to that world as yours? I want you to stay here forever with me."

She hesitated, but in the end, although he could see longing in her eyes, she shook her head no.

"My place is there, in the world of men, the world of Time."

"And the world of Death."

"It is, at that. Some things are beyond changing. But after death comes new birth."

He tried to speak, but no words came. Whether it was beyond his changing or not, he knew that Time and her daughter Death were beyond his understanding. The knowing gave him doubts. Maybe he didn't understand the universe as completely as he thought he did, maybe his power was far more limited than he thought it was. With those doubts, a distant city vanished from his lands forever, wiped away like a smear of charcoal from a hearthstone.

Although it seemed to Evandar that a mere hour or two had gone by since he'd seen the Gel da'Thae bard and spoken with Jahdo, ten whole days of Time as we measure it in our world had passed for them. They'd been following the stream south, stopping often to rest the horse and mule, since by then they were long out of oats. Although they skirted hills, rising off to the north and east, the river itself seemed headed for lower country. As the river deepened, the banks turned flat and grassy, so that the walking became much easier, even though the forest grew thick and wild to either hand. As Jahdo described the terrain to the bard, Meer remarked that someone must be inhabiting this country, whether they'd seen them or not.

"Trees hug water, lad. Following this river should be a battle, not an easy stroll. Someone cleared this bank, and not so long ago, either, or second growth would have taken it over."

"Well, maybe so. I hope they don't mind us using the road."

"So do I."

Thinking about what might happen to them if they ran into hostile natives made Jahdo nervous enough to sharpen his eyes. As the river began turning east, he found himself studying the bank as they walked.

Here and there he found brown traces of crumbling horse dung, and the rare hoofprint, too, cut so deeply that the rains hadn't washed it away.

"Do you think that's dung from Thavrae's horses?"

"It sounds too old from the way you describe it," Meer said. "So it more likely came from horses belonging to the natives. Hum. If they drive stock through here, clearing the bank would make sense."

"I wonder if they be the same people from the old tales? The ones who helped the ancestors escape."

"Those were the Children of the Gods," Meer snapped. "The lore says so."

"But what would gods want with real horses?"

Meer had to chew over this piece of heresy for a long time before he answered.

"Perhaps your helpers were indeed horseherders, as your lore says, but acting under the direction of the gods or their children, as our lore says. That would make sense, all nice and tidy, like."

"Very well, then. If they are the same people, then we don't have to worry. The tales talk about how decent they were, feeding the ancestors and giving them knives and mules and stuff so they could farm up in the Rhiddaer."

"Hum. Goes to show, then, that they were guided by the gods for purposes of the divine wills."

"Why?"

"Well, any ordinary folk would have enslaved the ancestors all over again."

"The tales do say that these people were against keeping slaves, on principle, like, just like we are. They thought it was dishonorable and just plain rotten."

Meer snorted in profound skepticism.

"Not likely that anyone would believe such a thing, is it?" he said. "Well, not to insult your tribe or suchlike."

"Oh, never mind." Jahdo had always heard the grown men say that trying to change a Gel da'Thae's mind about anything was like trying to stop a fire mountain from spewing. "Everyone be different."

Round noon they came to an enormous meadow, ringed with rotting tree stumps, which gave credence to their theory that the mysterious horseherders had cleared some of this land. After they'd unloaded the stock and let them roll, and Meer had prayed, they unpacked a scant dinner and settled down to eat. Although they still had a good amount of cheese, hard tack, and jerky left, they'd used up half of their supplies, and Jahdo was beginning to worry about what they'd eat on the way home. Meer, of course, was convinced that the gods would provide for them when the time came.

Jahdo had just finished his meal when he heard a strange sound, a rasping birdcall, up in the sky.

"What's that?" Meer said. "Sounds like a hawk."

Jahdo looked up.

"It is, truly."

Far above them, silhouetted against wispy clouds, the bird was circling the meadow. From the backward sweep of its wings and its color, dark gray on its back, a very pale gray on its belly, Jahdo could tell that it was a falcon of some variety or other. Even though it soared high, he could see its slender gray legs and the mottling on its breast so clearly that, he realized suddenly, it had to be enormous. As he stared up, the bird suddenly flapped and flew, just as if it knew he watched. Yet he thought little of it at first. Toward evening the falcon, if indeed it was the same bird, reappeared to hover above them as they made their camp. Again, when Jahdo stood for a better look, it flew abruptly away.

On the next day Jahdo kept watch for it, and sure enough, in the middle of the morning it reappeared, flying in lazy circles and holding its place even when he stopped walking to scrutinize it. With a call to Meer to hold for a moment, he shaded his eyes and studied the bird, which seemed to be flying lower than it had the day before.

"Meer, here's an odd thing! Way above us there's a falcon, circling round, like, but it's the biggest falcon I've ever seen. It's way too big for a peregrine, which is sort of what it does look like."

"How big, lad? This could be important."

"Well, huge, actually." He paused, trying to gauge distances and size. "You know, I'd swear it were as big as a pony, but that can't be right. It's all the clouds and stuff, I guess, making it hard to see. I mean, not even eagles do grow so big."

Meer howled, a cry of sheer terror, and flung both hands in front of his sightless eyes. With a flap and a screech, the falcon flew away.

"It be gone now," Jahdo said. "What be so wrong?"

"Bad geas, lad, bad, bad geas! Don't you understand? There's only one thing a bird that large could be!"

"But there can't be a bird that large. That's what I did try to say."

"Hah! You don't understand, then. I should have known you didn't, when you didn't sound afraid. A mazrak, lad, that's what it must be. The most unclean magician of all, a shape-changer, a foul thing, using a coward's magic."

"Huh? You mean someone who can turn himself into a bird?"

"Just that. If a mazrak's spying upon us, then things are dark indeed."

Jahdo quite simply didn't know what to say. While they'd been traveling, Meer had been teaching him lore, just as he'd promised. The bard's tales had introduced him to an entirely new world, one where the gods moved among men and demons fought them, where spirits roamed the earth and caused mischief, where magic was a necessary part of life, as well, to fend all these presences off or to bend the weaker ones to your will. Automatically Jahdo's hand went to his throat to touch the thongful of talismans that hung there. He would have laughed all the tales away if he hadn't seen with his own eyes the being called Evandar disappear. As it was, he was prepared to believe almost anything.

"Well, it *were* an awful huge hawk," he said.

"Of course it was. Mazrakir can't shrink themselves or suchlike. They can only change the flesh they have into another form. It's only logical that their totem animal, the one they change into, I mean, would be about the same size they are."

"There be other ones than birds?"

"Some are bears, some wolves, some horses. All kinds of animals, depending on the nature of the mazrak." Meer turned his head and spat on the ground for luck. "But it's bad geas to even talk about such things. Let's move on, lad. And we'd best travel ready to duck into the forest, where spying hawks can't follow or see."

"All right. And can we sleep in the woods, too?"

"We'd best do just that, indeed."

The very next morning Jahdo became a believer in the power of mazrakir to bring bad luck. Just at dawn he woke, sitting bolt upright and straining to hear again the sound that had wakened him. From far above it came again, the shriek of a raven, and a huge one, judging from how loud it squawked. In his blankets nearby, Meer rolled over and sat up.

"Jahdo, what?"

Jahdo rose to a kneel, peering through the tree leaves overhead. He could just see a black shape flapping off, a bird as large as a wolfhound at the least, thwacking the air with huge wings.

"It be another one," he burst out. "Meer, another mazrak."

Meer whimpered under his breath.

"It be gone now," Jahdo went on. "I hope it doesn't come back."

"Never have I echoed a hope so fervently!" Meer considered for a moment, then pushed his blankets back with a huge yawn. "I'm tempted to try traveling through the forest edge, out of sight, like, but the footing will be too hard on the horses. Besides, if we lose the river, we're doomed."

"Well, I was kind of thinking the same thing, about the river, I mean."

"We will pray to the thirteen gods who protect travelers before we set out today. But first, let's lead the horses to their drink, and break our own night's fast."

After the horses were watered and tethered out on the grassy bank to graze, Jahdo knelt by the gear, took out a few small pieces of flatbread and some chewy dried apples, a scant handful each for him and Meer, and laid them on a clean rock while he repacked the saddlebags to balance. Behind him Meer was strolling back and forth, singing under his breath and rehearsing phrasing, as he always did with a particularly important prayer. All at once the bard fell silent. Jahdo slewed round to find him standing frozen, his mouth slack, his head tilted as if he listened for some tiny sound.

"What is it?" Jahdo got to his feet. "What be wrong?"

Meer tossed back his head and howled. Never had Jahdo heard such a sound, a vast vibrating ululation of grief, all the world's mourning, or so it seemed, gathered and rolled into this long wail, wavering and shrieking up and down the bard's entire register.

"Meer!" Jahdo ran to him and grabbed his arm. "Meer! Tell me. What be so wrong?"

Another howl answered him, then another, long cascading waves of grief and agony, while Jahdo shook his arm and begged and shouted and, in the end, wept aloud in sheer frustration. The sound of his tears cut through the bard's wrapped anguish.

"Forgive me, lad," Meer gasped. "But my brother, my brother! I think he's dead."

"What?" Shock wiped the tears away. "Dead? When? I mean, how can you know?"

"Just now, and the brother bond told me."

Meer shook the boy's hand away and stalked into the forest. Jahdo hesitated, then decided that Meer would need to be alone, at least for a while. He wiped his face on a dirty sleeve, then picked up the food again, packing Meer's share away, eating his own while he squinted up at the sun. Not even half of the day's first watch had passed since the mazrak's cry had wakened them.

"I'll bet it was the mazrak, too," Jahdo said aloud. "I'll bet that ugly old raven does have much to do with this."

Thinking of the mazrak made him shudder in cold terror. He ran across the open space, hesitated on the edge of the forest safety, groaned aloud, then dashed back again to grab the tether ropes of the horse and mule.

"I don't even want to think about that raven getting you," he told them. "Come on. Let's go find Meer."

He'd led them to the forest edge when he remembered their gear, spread out near the riverbank. Without Meer to lift the packsaddles, he couldn't load the stock. Sniveling and crying in sheer frustration, he led the horse and mule onward. Fortunately, Meer was quite close, standing at the edge of a small clearing. Jahdo urged the horses into this sliver of open ground and dropped their halter ropes to make them stand.

"Meer?" He hesitated, wanting to ask the bard how he fared, realizing that the question was stupid. "Meer, it be Jahdo."

Meer nodded, turning his sightless eyes the boy's way.

"Meer, we can't just stay here. Forgive me, but we've got to do something. If that mazrak—"

"True." The bard's voice sounded thick, all swollen with grief. "No need to beg forgiveness. You're right enough."

"Are we going to go back west now?"

"Can't. I've got to make sure he's dead. In my heart, I know, but how can I tell my mother that I learned of his death without bothering to find out how or why or where he lies buried?"

"Well, truly, that would be kind of cowardly. She'll want to know."

Meer nodded his agreement. Jahdo chewed his lower lip, trying to find the right words. There were none, he supposed.

"Meer, I be so sorry."

Meer nodded again.

"Uh, I'm going to go get the food and what I can carry."

The bard said nothing, sinking to his knees, his face turned to the earth.

Jahdo went back and forth, carrying armloads of sacks and bags, dragging the heavy packsaddles, staggering under their bedrolls, back and forth until at last he was exhausted but their gear safe in the tiny clearing with the horses. During all of this the bard never moved nor spoke. Jahdo went back to the river one last time for a long drink. He splashed water over his head and arms, as well, then knelt for a moment, looking up at the sky. A few stripes of mare's tail clouds arched out from the west, but nothing moved below them, not even a normal bird. Shuddering, he hurried back to the forest.

This time the bard looked up at the sound of his footsteps.

"Do you want to stay here for a while?" Jahdo said.

"I need to collect myself." Meer's voice was thin and dry, the sound of reeds scraping together. "My apologies, Jahdo. My apologies."

"It be well. I do be real tired, myself. I just wish there was somewhat I could do."

Meer shrugged and sighed.

"I guess you wouldn't know where your brother is? I mean, well, you know."

"I don't, I'm afraid, no more than I knew where he was when he was alive." His voice choked on the last word. "But we don't need scrying crystals to guess what's happened. His false goddess has deserted him, and in the end no doubt she'll do the same to all who believe in her! A curse upon her and her evil prophets both!"

"I guess all we can do is keep going east and hope and pray and stuff. I be so scared."

But wrapped in his grief the bard never heard him. Meer clenched one enormous fist and laid rather than pounded it against a tree trunk. Under his breath he keened, a low rumble rather than a wail, yet it rose and fell with agony. All at once Jahdo realized a small horror—without eyes Meer couldn't even weep. At last the Gel da'Thae fell quiet. For a moment he stood silently, then turned and spoke in an unnaturally flat voice.

"Best be on our way. Whatever that may be."

All that day they headed more south than east, following the river and luck as well, to make a grim camp at sunset. Meer spoke only to the horse and mule, and in his own language at that, leaving Jahdo to bad dreams of seeing some member of his own family killed beyond his reach to stop it. For Meer's sake he kept hoping that the bard was wrong and his brother still lived, but some days later they found that Meer's inborn magic had revealed the truth.

It was getting on late in the afternoon when the river, which had turned due east, grew suddenly wider, suddenly shallow. They might be drawing near to the ford Evandar had told them about, Jahdo supposed. He was beginning to think of finding them a campsite, when the boy saw black specks wheeling against the sky at some distance and, as far as he could tell, anyway, on the other side of the river. Meer stopped walking.

"What's that?" he snapped. "Do you see birds? I hear them calling a long way off."

"I can see them, sure enough. There be a lot of them. I don't know what kind they are. They fly too far off, but they look really little, not like mazrakir."

"Good. Well, let's see what they're up to. Lead on."

Some yards on they came indeed to the ford, and on their side tall white stones marked its spread, just as Evandar had told them. Although the water ran shallow enough for Meer and the horses, Jahdo had to pick his way across the rocky bottom in water up to his waist, but he didn't dare ride one of the pack animals and leave Meer to guide them. Since the river fed off the mountain snowpack, he was chilled deep by the time they scrambled onto the grassy bank at the far side. Meer felt his damp tunic, then laid the back of one furry palm against the boy's cheek.

"We'd best keep walking. Warm you up a little."

"Well and good, then. Do you still want to see what those birds are?"

"I do. I have dread round my heart, but I must know the truth."

Meer's fear turned out to be more than justified. As they traveled on, heading more south than east, the distant bird cries resolved themselves into the harsh cawing of ravens, wheeling and dipping over some unknown thing.

"It might just be a dead deer," Jahdo said.

Meer only grunted for an answer and strode onward, swinging his stick back and forth before him like an angry scythe. After some hundred yards the horse and mule suddenly tossed up their heads and snorted. Their ears went back and they danced, pulling on their lead ropes.

"Oh, by the blessed name of every god," Meer whispered. "Do you smell that?"

"I can't. What?"

"Count your human weakness a blessing, then. It's the smell of death, much death, death under a hot sun."

Jahdo felt his stomach clench.

"Let's go back a ways and leave the horse and mule behind. Jahdo, forgive me. If I could go on alone and spare you what's sure to lie ahead, I would, because you're not a Gel da'Thae colt, raised to this sort of thing, but without you, how can I tell if my brother lies there or not?"

"Well, true spoken. I'll try to help."

They retraced their steps a ways and found a good campsite near the river, then unloaded and tethered the animals. Meer had Jahdo find pieces of old rag, soak them in water, and tie them round their noses and mouths before they set out again. As they walked, Meer prayed, a low rise and fall of despair.

First the sound of the birds, and all too soon the stupefyingly foul smell of rotting flesh, led them down the grassy bank, then east of the river for some hundred feet. The land there rolled back rising from the river to a high wooded knoll that climbed like a grave mound behind the carnage. For a long time Jahdo could only stare at what he saw; every time he tried to speak he gagged from the smell. The air bludgeoned him, even through his pitiful mask; it shoved a dirty fist down his throat; it wrenched at his stomach with filthy fingers. Yet he was too horrified to vomit, which was perhaps the worst thing of all. I have to go through with this, he told himself over and over. What if it were Kiel lying dead there? How would I feel then? I've got to be Meer's eyes. At last he convinced himself into courage, and he could speak.

"Meer, there's a flat space, like, and it's all covered with dead men. They're not buried or anything. They do just lie there, and they be all puffy. And the birds do crawl all over them like ants. The birds keep fighting with each other, and that's why they keep squalling and flying."

"Indeed." Meer's voice was very thin but steady. "How many men?"

"Oh, lots and lots. They're all human beings. Off to the north there's an overturned wagon. It be all broken, and there's someone really tall lying by it."

"I hate to ask you this, lad, but can you bear to lead me there?"

"I'll try."

Fortunately they could skirt the edge of the battlefield rather than walk across it, but even so, Jahdo was caught by the horror and found himself staring at the corpses. He would never forget that sight, not as long as he lived, of bodies heaped and tumbled like firewood, broken, slashed, tangled, left there for wild things in a last gesture of contempt. Whenever the singers back in Cerr Cawnen had told lurid tales of battlefields, they'd always spoken of red blood and deathly silence. Here all the bodies lay gray and swollen, streaked with the black of dried blood or the dull maroon color of torn flesh where the birds were feeding. The field itself pulsed with life and noise as ants swarmed, ravens screamed and chattered, broke to fly only to circle and settle again, while under it all sounded the vast drone of thousands of flies.

"I think they were killed with swords. There lie hoofprints all round, too, and a couple of dead horses, but only a couple. Oh, wait, here's an arrow, just lying here."

Although the shaft was broken, the point was mercifully clean. When Jahdo stooped down, he saw the tiny paw prints of foxes on the horribly moist ground—no doubt they crept up at night to share this banquet. He concentrated on the arrow, picked it up, and ran his fingers down the wood.

"I've never seen an arrow so long. When it were whole it must have been longer than my arm, and the feathers are from some kind of blue bird."

"None of my people would loft a thing like that." Meer was whispering. "Ah, evil, evil, evil come upon us!"

Jahdo wanted to agree, but he didn't dare risk speaking for fear he'd sob aloud. Between them and the wagon lay a scatter of corpses, as if they were a few sticks of wood tossed in the eddy of this river of death. A young man lay on his back, his head tilted in an unnatural angle, his eyes pools of slime in a bloated gray face. The body of a comrade lay slung over his legs. Nearby lay an arm, torn clear off and as gray as stone, with the bone exposed and picked clean all down the wrist. Flies crawled between the fingers.

"Meer, watch out!" Jahdo's voice came out all strangled. "Step round to your right."

"Very well." Meer was tapping with his stick, but gingerly, afraid no doubt of what he might touch. "Lad, what are these dead men wearing?"

"Some of them aren't really dressed at all. The others have shirts with big sleeves and these leather vest things, and trousers that come all the way to their ankles, and there's these thong things that tie them in."

Meer whimpered in a way that said he recognized this garb.

They came at last to the overturned wagon and the enormous warrior stretched out beside it. At their approach a scatter of ravens shrieked and flew, but someone had dropped a cracked shield over the man's face and folded his arms over his chest, too, with a cloak upon his hands, so that the birds had barely got a start on him. When Jahdo described these scant signs of respect, Meer made a long keening sound under his breath.

"What does that shield look like?"

"Well, it be wooden, and sort of egg-shaped, and whitewashed. In the middle there does lie this circle of metal with funny designs on it, and down at the bottom someone's scratched this little picture that I guess is supposed to be a dragon."

"A little more detail, if you please, about that metal plate."

"Well, the design runs in circles, and one's like when you braid a horse's tail, three strands, and then there's one that's like a lot of knots, like someone did tie all these sheep-shank knots in a long rope but then never did pull them tight."

Meer shrieked.

"Slaver work, may the gods all help us! Can you bear to lift the shield, lad?"

Gagging profoundly, Jahdo used the broken arrow to hook the shield rim and shove it to one side. At the motion it broke in half, the pieces sliding apart. All puffed with heat rot a huge distorted face looked up with eyes glazed and milky. His mane of coarse black hair lay tangled and clotted with dried blood, which also streaked one tattooed cheek.

"Meer, I be sorry. He be Gel da'Thae."

Meer tossed back his head and howled, a cry of such pulsating agony that all round the ravens flew, flapping indignantly in circles overhead as the bard shrieked again and again, clutching his staff in both hands and raising it high as if to lay his plaint before the very gods themselves. Thanks to Meer's teaching of the lore, Jahdo knew that the charms and amulets braided into Thavrae's hair were for his protection in the Death-world and had to remain with him. The cluster of talismans on the thong round his neck, however, needed to go back to his kin. On the edge of vomiting Jahdo drew the knife his grandfather had given him, knelt down, and cut the thong while Meer's rage and grief swirled round him like a storm. When Jahdo yanked the talismans free, the head flopped to one side. Retching and gagging, he stood up fast, shoving the charms into his pocket.

"Meer, Meer!" He grabbed the bard's arm. "It's needful for us to get out of here. We don't know where the enemies are. What if they're still close by?"

Meer wailed once more, then let the sound die away with a rattle in his throat.

"True spoken, lad. It behooves us to head west as fast as we can travel."

Leaning on his stick, Meer let Jahdo lead him away, but doubled with grief the bard moved slowly. Once they were back at their camp, Jahdo sat Meer down by the packsaddles, handed him one of the water-skins for a drink, then tore off the mask and threw it onto the ground. He rushed to the river, knelt, and plunged his head and shoulders into the water. Gasping and crying, he flailed round with his arms until his entire upper body was soaked and free of the smell. He sat back on his heels and wondered if he should vomit, but by then the gut horror had faded, leaving him with memories that nothing would ever purge.

Meer began keening again, more softly, this time, but he was rocking back and forth, hands clasped round his drawn-up knees, rocking and moaning in a ghastly kind of music that had a certain beauty to it. Jahdo walked back and laid a hand on his shoulder.

"Meer, can you travel? We've got to get moving, Meer. I be so scared."

The Gel da'Thae never heard him, merely keened and rocked, all knotted with grief. Jahdo grabbed his shoulders and shook him.

"Meer, Meer! Listen to me, Meer!"

"Go on without me, lad. Let my house die here. Thavrae was the last hope of our house, a warrior who might win the right to claim a daughter as his own and hand over our name to her like a treasure chest. No daughters has my mother birthed, and woe, woe unto our clan and kin, that the gods would wipe our name from the face of the earth. Leave me, Jahdo, and let me die with the name of our house."

"I'm not going to do anything of the sort. If you stay I'll stay with you, and then I'll die, too, and here you did promise my mother that you'd look after me."

Meer whimpered and trembled.

"Well, you did," Jahdo snapped. "You promised."

Meer fell silent for a long while, then all at once laughed, a hysterical sort of rumble.

"Jahdo, lad, one day you'll no doubt be a great man among your people, the chief speaker, I'd say, wielding power with words as your people do. Very well. Bring Baki over. I'll saddle him up first. All day we shall travel, and in the night I'll mourn."

Yet they made only a few pitiful miles that afternoon. Meer was exhausted with his mourning, Jahdo with the horror he'd seen and smelt, and in the hot sun it seemed they could barely put one foot in front of the other. At times Meer would burst into a mourning song, half music, half keening, only to break off in midphrase and fall silent again. As if they picked up his mood, the horse and mule walked head down and weary, ambling to a stop unless Jahdo yanked their lead ropes to keep them moving.

"It be useless," Jahdo said at last. "Just ahead does lie that little stream where we camped last night, and there's grass for the horses here, and so why don't we just stop?"

And there the Slavers caught them. It was still afternoon, and Jahdo was scrounging dead wood for an evening's fire, when Gidro and Baki became restless, throwing up their heads, sniffing and snorting into the rising wind, finally whickering out a greeting. Distantly a horse answered, then another. Jahdo leapt to his feet and grabbed his grandfather's knife, but Meer sat unmoving, hunkered down by their gear, his head on his knees. Hoofbeats sounded, riding fast, riding hard, and straight for them out of the east. Jahdo could see a plume of dust skittering along like a live thing.

"Meer, Meer! We've got to run."

Slowly the bard raised his head and turned toward the sound.

"You run, Jahdo. Head west and hope you find those horsemen who aided your people once before. I might as well die a slave, so long as I die soon. A man is nothing without a clan, and my future holds no kin to serve the gods in my old age."

"Stop that! It's needful you come, too."

The hoofbeats came louder, tack jingled and rang, men yelled, a wordless high shriek of triumph. The dust resolved itself to a mounted squad. Meer rose to his feet, grabbing his staff, but he only leaned upon it as he waited, turned toward the noise.

"Run, Jahdo! Grab that bag of food and run to the forest."

Jahdo hesitated, and in that moment it was too late. With a whoop and a yell, like men driving cattle, the horsemen swept round the camp and surrounded them, about twelve of them, mailed and armed, and wearing loose long trousers tucked into high boots. When they edged their horses into the firelight, Jahdo stared in fascinated terror at their gear, but he could discern not one severed head—all the comfort he was going to get. He sobbed once, then drew himself up to full height with the knife clutched in his fist, as two of the men dismounted, tossing their reins to others in the squad. Both of them were over six feet tall, hard-muscled under their mail, but one was blond and young, with a heavy mustache drooping over his mouth, and the other had dark hair, streaked with gray, and his road-filthy stubble of beard sported gray saltings as well. Each of them carried at their belts a peculiar dagger, narrow and sheathed, with three silver knobs on the pommel, and a heavy long sword.

"A blind man and a lad?" the blond said. "This is our ever so important prize?"

Jahdo goggled. He could understand their speech, a thing he'd never expected. Although they rolled every R and RH they spoke, and pronounced half their words deep in their throats, too, or so it sounded, by paying strict attention he could at least make out the main sense.

"Any Gel da'Thae's a rare enough thing." The dark-haired man was smiling. "I'd trust that Jill knows what she's doing."

Jill? That was a Rhiddaer name! Automatically he turned toward Meer, hoping for answers to these puzzlements, but the bard stepped forward at that instant and knelt at the dark-haired man's feet.

"If I'm the prize," he rumbled, "then let the lad go. Let him take what food we've got left and try to make his way home."

The dark-haired fellow hesitated, visibly touched, but the blond strode forward, gesturing at the squad.

"All right, saddle up those pack animals! Let's get on our way back to the main camp." He turned to the dark-haired fellow. "Rhodry, the child can ride behind someone's saddle, and we can load this hairy dog onto a packhorse, I suppose."

"Maybe so." Rhodry strode over to Jahdo. "Hand me that knife, lad."

In sheer instinct Jahdo stabbed at him, but Rhodry caught his wrist in a huge grasp and half lifted him from his feet. The knife dropped.

"Here, now, you've got guts." Rhodry was smiling at him. "But this is no occasion for heroics, like. Are you going to behave yourself, or are we going to have to tie you up?"

Jahdo tried to think of a really good insult, but at that moment the blond man grabbed Meer's arm.

"On your feet," he snapped.

"You leave him alone!" Jahdo snarled. "You treat him with respect, too. He be a bard."

Although the blond man started to laugh, Rhodry hit him on the shoulder and made him stop. He walked over to Meer and knelt down in front of him on one knee.

"Does the lad speak true?" he said, and politely.

"He does. A bard I am, and a loremaster as well, to the twelfth level of the thirteen levels of the deepening well of knowledge, not that I'll ever see my homeland and my master again, most like, to complete my studies."

"And the lad's your slave?"

"He is not that, but free born, traveling with me at my request."

"Well and good, then." Rhodry got up, turning to the blond man. "Yraen, put your saddle on that white horse, because the bard and his lad will be riding in comfort. You'll have to make do with bareback, unless you want to clamber into that packsaddle yourself and shell your own nuts."

"What?" The man called Yraen was practically spitting. "Have you gone daft?"

"A bard's a bard, lad, and due all respect."

Laughing and calling out jeers, the other men in the squad gathered round to see what Yraen would say to that—nothing, as it turned out, because Rhodry caught his gaze and stared him down.

"Have it your way, then." Yraen heaved a melodramatic sigh. "You stinking bastard."

Although Jahdo expected swords to flash, everyone merely laughed. Rhodry's laugh taught Jahdo the meaning of that old saw, that a sound could make your blood run cold. It was daft and furious, merry and murderous all at the same time, a high-pitched chortle that reminded him of ferrets in a rage. The rest of the men, however, seemed to take it for granted, as if they heard him laugh that way often. With a shake of his head, Yraen strode off to get the squad ready to ride. As Jahdo watched them, he wondered why the view had turned so hazy, wondered why he felt so trembly, all of a sudden. Then he realized that he was crying, the tears running down his face of their own accord. Still kneeling, Meer held out one enormous arm. Jahdo rushed to him and flung himself against the Horsekin's chest to sob aloud while Meer moaned and whimpered under his breath.

"Forgive me, Jahdo lad, forgive me, and may your mother forgive me, too!"

In a river twist the etheric water puddled like a mirror, slick silver, edged with green. Evandar knelt on the bank nearby and stared down at the surface, but his eyes moved, following a vision rather than contemplating himself. All at once he laughed and sat back on his heels.

"They have them," he announced. "The bard and the boy, I mean.

Rhodry and his squad have seized them upon the road. They're all heading off to Cengarn."

"I feel sorry for that poor child," Dallandra said. "He must be terrified."

Evandar merely shrugged.

"Don't you feel anything for these people?" Dallandra burst out. "You're moving them round like pegs in a game of Wooden Wisdom, knocking them off the board and ruining their lives. Don't you care?"

"I love you, and I love my daughter, and I love the memory of Rinbaladelan, the seacoast city I was telling you about. Beyond that, my darling, no, I don't care. Not one whit."

2

AMISSIO

A good omen for the taking of prisoners, but otherwise, evil in all things, though with great hope of mitigation. If it should fall under the presidency of Tin, the ninth land upon our map, it signifies evil without any such hope, for in all matters pertaining to the gods and their worship, this figure works naught but ill and harm.

The Omenbook of Gwarn, Loremaster

Approached from the west, Cengarn loomed. The day when Jahdo saw it for the first time was beautifully sunny and fresh, too, as if the gods were mocking his fate and making sure he could see every detail of the Slavers' evil city. As usual, he and Meer, doubled up on Baki, were being led along at the rear of the squad. When it crested one last hill, the men spread out to rest their horses, and Jahdo could look ahead. Down below the view stretched out, the sparse woodlands dropping to a valley of rolling meadows and green crops. Toward their side of the valley stood a solitary farmstead. Some ways beyond that ran a stream, bordered with trees.

"The house be round, Meer, and there does stand this dirt wall, a mound like, all round it. I can see some cows, too, and it looks like they be white. It's kind of hard to tell from here." Jahdo shaded his hand with his eyes. "Oh! I do think that's the city."

In the strong morning light he could pick out, far across the valley, three gray hills surrounded by what seemed to be stone walls, being as they were too smooth and circular to be cliffs. Spread across the hills were the tiny shapes of whitewashed houses, all of them round, and some larger stone buildings. Over it all hung a faint haze—the smoke of cooking fires, most likely—out of which, at the top of the highest hill, rose a cluster of round stone towers with flat roofs, just like the ones mentioned in the old tales, as dark and grim and ugly as chunks of iron. When Jahdo described this view, Meer sighed, but he said nothing.

"It be not far." Jahdo swallowed heavily. "We should get there before noon."

"To find out our fate at last. I can only pray that some kind and decent master buys you, lad. What happens to me is of no moment, for I am a broken man with no house or clan, but you have a life ahead of you."

"Not much of one."

Meer stayed silent. Over the past three days, as the squad rode for Cengarn, Jahdo had run out of tears for his lost family, his lost freedom. He felt numb, as if he'd been so ill with a fever for so long that life had receded to some far distance.

"Come on, lads!" Rhodry called out. "Almost home."

In a clatter and jingle of tack and hooves the squad jogged off downhill. When they came onto the flat, Jahdo got his first omen of what their welcome might be like. Just by the road they saw a young girl, her blond hair hanging in one long pigtail down her back. She was wearing a dirty brown dress, cinched in at her waist with a length of old rope, and carrying a wooden crook, apparently to help her herd the cows. At the sound of the horses' hooves and the jingle of tack, she turned toward the road and watched as the men rode by. When Rhodry made her a gallant bow from his saddle, she laughed and waved, until she got a look at Meer. At that she turned and ran screaming for the farmstead.

"Stop!" Rhodry called out. "We won't let him hurt you."

When the other men laughed, Jahdo remembered how he hated them. Although the girl stopped screaming, she kept running, darting inside the earthwork wall. They could hear a gate slam, and dogs began barking hysterically—an entire pack, from the sound of it.

"Better trot, men," Rhodry said, grinning. "Let's get out of here before they set the dogs on us."

Since they passed the farmstead with no more trouble than the din of angry hounds, Rhodry called the squad to a walk. Apparently he was in no hurry to reach the city, for all that he'd called it home earlier, not on such a lovely day, perhaps, with songbirds warbling and the sun glinting on the stream. As they rode closer, Jahdo found himself thinking of the city as a storm cloud, floating nearer and nearer, rising high and dark on the horizon at first, then looming to fill the view. He couldn't decide whether he wished that they'd reach the city and get it over with or that Time would slow and they'd never quite arrive.

At length, though, they came to the West Gate, where a sheer rise of cliff, hacked smooth with tools and reinforced at the base with stone blocks, guarded a winding path up to the town. By tipping his head back Jahdo could just see the tops of the towers, rising over a dark gray wall at the brow of the highest hill. The gate itself stood partly open, a massive thing of oak beams bound with iron strips and chains. In the shadows inside he could just make out a huge winch. Armed guards stepped forward and hailed the squad.

"So, silver dagger," one of them said to Rhodry. "You had a good hunt, I see."

"Well, we've netted what Jill wanted, sure enough. Tell me somewhat. Are there a lot of people out and about in the streets today?"

"More than a few, it being so warm and all. Why?"

"I don't want the prisoners stoned and injured."

Jahdo felt briefly sick.

"True enough," the guard said. "You'd best dismount, I'd say, and put them in the middle of you." He jerked a thumb at Meer. "The rumors have spread about that fellow you killed, and his kind's not exactly well loved round here."

Meer grunted, just once, but it was close to a sob.

"Don't worry, good bard," Rhodry said. "We'll get you through in one piece. Yraen, we'll wait here. You go fetch Otho the dwarf. I'll wager he and his kin have ways through this city that are out of the common sight."

Although he grumbled, Yraen dismounted and puffed off uphill to follow orders. A few at a time the entire squad dismounted as well, leading their horses through the gates. Opposite the huge winch was a small wooden guardhouse, and everyone drifted over in front of it to stand round gossiping with the guards about things that had happened during their absence. Meer stood stiff and straight, his hands clasped tight round his staff, his lips trembling. When Jahdo laid a hand on his arm to comfort him, Meer shook it off. Rhodry noticed the gesture.

"I won't let anything happen to the pair of you," Rhodry said. "That's why we're waiting here."

"It's not that what does ache his heart. The Gel da'Thae you did kill was his brother."

The moment he spoke Jahdo rued it. Even though he was visibly trying to choke back the noise, Meer keened, just briefly before he forced silence. Rhodry winced and swore.

"Well, my apologies." And oddly enough, he sounded perfectly sin-cere. "But, Meer, your brother was doing his cursed best to kill me."

"No doubt." Meer let out his breath in a long sigh. "You are a warrior as he was a warrior. Your kind lives and dies by a different code than we ordinary men."

Jahdo noticed the squad looking at Meer with a trace of new respect. Rhodry seemed to be trying to find something further to say, but Yraen came bustling back with three men in tow, two of them armed and mailed, the third elderly with a long white beard, but all of them the shortest, stockiest people that Jahdo had ever seen. The shortest of all, though obviously a grown man, was just his height, though twice his breadth. Jahdo frankly stared until one of the axmen glanced his way with a scowl, frightening him into looking elsewhere.

"My thanks for coming," Rhodry said. "What do you think, Otho? Can we pass by one of your roads?"

"Up to Jorn, here." Otho waved in the direction of the taller axman. "By the by, silver dagger, young Yraen had the cursed gall to remind me about that little matter of the coin. I'm waiting for somewhat to sell at a good price, and then I'll bring it to you, so stop your badgering." He turned, looking Meer up and down. "Ah, he's blind! I couldn't imagine what you were thinking of, asking us to take a spy up this way, but if he can't see, then the secret's safe enough."

Meer bared his fangs but said nothing.

"Can't bring the horses through." Jorn stepped forward. "What about having Yraen and the squad take 'em up to the dun?" His voice turned contemptuous. "You don't need twelve men to guard a blind man and a boy."

"Ah, but they're wily, wily." Rhodry was grinning. "Yraen, the rest of you—I'll see you back in the great hall."

Collecting the horses, including Baki and Gidro, the squad moved off, leading the stock up the steep hill. As he watched, Jahdo realized that he was sorry to see them go. Even though he hated each one for helping capture him, they were at least familiar, men he'd grown used to in the horror of the past few days.

"Come round here." Otho gestured at a twisting lane that led behind the guardhouse.

With Jorn in the lead they walked to the base of the hill just beyond the gates, where the slope had been cut to the vertical, then faced with stone blocks to produce an artificial cliff. When Jorn pounded on one block with his ax, a good quarter of this structure creaked back three inches to reveal a sliver of face and a suspicious eye.

"Ah, it's you already," said a voice from inside. "Stand back, and I'll open up."

With much groaning and the crunching of dirt and the bouncing of pebbles the massive door opened just far enough for everyone to slip in sideways, one at a time. The two younger men ushered them down a long, cool tunnel of worked stone, a good ten feet wide but a bare six tall, so that both Meer and Rhodry were forced to walk stooped. Once everyone was safely in, the doorkeeper seized an enormous lever and pulled. The door inched shut to groan into place so tightly that Jahdo could see not the slightest crack of sunlight round it. The only light, a sickly blue glow, oozed from phosphorescent mosses and fungi, gathered into baskets and hung from iron pegs in the wall. Jahdo shuddered, wondering if a rat felt this way, caught in one of his family's traps. Remembering how the creatures squealed and clawed when the trap splashed down and water rose to cover them made him want to weep.

"Come along, come along," Otho snapped. "Stop goggling, lad. Haven't got all day."

The tunnel ran straight for some ten feet, then turned into a flight of stairs, climbing steep and narrow for an ordeal of hundreds of yards. Before they'd gone halfway up Jahdo's heart was pounding, and he fought for breath in the stuffy air. Once he stumbled, and his sore and sweaty hands slipped from the narrow stone ridge that did for a railing. For a brief moment he thought of letting himself fall backward and plunge down to die, but Rhodry caught his arm and yanked him up.

"No hurry, lad," the warrior said. "Get your feet under you."

Jahdo had no choice but to keep climbing. By the time they reached the top, everyone was panting for breath, but Meer was downright sobbing. Rhodry allowed them a few moments of rest.

"Tell me somewhat, lad," Otho said. "You seem to have great respect for this creature you serve. Were you raised among his kind?"

Jahdo started to tell him the truth; then it occurred to him to wonder if he truly wanted these people to know about his homeland.

"I was," he said instead. "But he be a bard, and it's needful that you respect him, too."

Otho shrugged in insulting dismissal.

Another corridor, another stairs, another massive door—at last they came blinking out into the sunlight before another pair of guarded gates, as massive and iron-bound as the first. Behind these rose the towers, as grim as a giant's clubs, stuck into the earth.

"There you are," Otho said. "We'll be heading back now."

As the three dwarves started back into the tunnel, Rhodry called after them.

"Remember that coin you owe me, Otho."

It struck Jahdo as viciously unjust that these people would be haggling over the ordinary details of their lives, something as petty as a gambling debt, probably, while they were dragging him off to slavery.

As they walked through the gates, Rhodry laid a heavy hand on Meer's shoulder, and Jahdo took the bard's arm, because his blind man's staff made a poor guide for leading him through the confusion in the vast ward. Clustering round the towers and the inside of the walls stood wooden sheds, mostly round and thatched. Incorporated into the outer walls were long rectangles of buildings, stables on the lower level, though Jahdo couldn't see into the upper. Scurrying round through the midst of this jumble were servants—tending horses, carrying firewood or sacks of what seemed to be vegetables, or even pulling a squalling goat along or driving a couple of pigs before them. Somewhere close by a blacksmith's forge rang with hammering; dogs barked; people yelled back and forth. Every now and then an armed man strolled by, knocking any servant in his way out of it.

"Straight ahead," Rhodry barked. "Quick like, before I find myself defending you. See that long straight building there past the pigsty, lad? That's where we're heading."

Fear made Jahdo cooperative. He hurried Meer along while Rhodry kept a nervous watch behind them, and the various servants all shrieked at the very sight of them and rushed to goggle. When the armed men started jeering, Jahdo was more than glad to duck into the long stone structure, even if it did reek of the nearby hogs and something worse, too, an undertone of human filth. Inside he found a narrow passageway, lined with doors, each with a small opening near the top and a heavy oak bar across to lock them.

"The dungeon keep," Rhodry remarked, confirming Jahdo's worst guess. "With luck you won't be here long."

An elderly man, dressed in brown tatters that had once been clothes, came hobbling out of a room at the far end of the corridor.

"Prisoners of war," Rhodry said to him.

"Put them here, silver dagger." With arthritic hands he lifted a bar and swung a door back. "Shove them right along."

Jahdo helped Meer cross the high threshold, then stepped in after, his heart pounding as badly as it had on the underground stairs. He was profoundly relieved to find a small window, barred, on the opposite wall, and thick straw, reasonably clean, on the floor. In one corner stood a leather bucket, crawling with flies—otherwise, nothing, not so much as a blanket.

"I want them decently treated," Rhodry was saying to the old man. "Plenty of food, mind you, and clean water, and none of that moldy bread, either. I'll be stopping by now and again to see that you've made it so."

"It'll be done, it'll be done."

The door eased shut, and the bar fell down with a thump. Jahdo could hear Rhodry and the old man squabbling down the corridor for a moment; then the old man returned.

"Lad, lad! I'm handing you water in through the window."

A clay pitcher appeared in the slit in the door. Jahdo could just pull it through. A clay cup with a broken handle followed, and after that a loaf of brown bread, reasonably fresh.

"There," the old man snapped. "Cursed arrogant bastard of a silver dagger, giving an honest man orders like that."

"Bain't Rhodry a lord, then?"

"What did you say, lad?"

"Bain't Rhodry a lord?"

After a moment the old man laughed, and hard.

"Not half, lad, not half. A stinking mercenary and naught more, fighting for coin, not honor like a decent man. Little better than thieves, all of that lot. Got into trouble young, they did, or they wouldn't be riding the long road at all, would they now?" There was the sound of him spitting onto the floor. "The gall, a silver dagger giving me orders."

Muttering under his breath, the fellow stumped away, and this time he never returned. Jahdo poured Meer a cup of water—it was indeed clean, even cool—and helped him drink.

"I can break this bread up with my fingers," he said. "You know what I really hate, Meer? They did take my grandfather's knife, and it were the only thing of his I ever did have that were just mine."

Meer moaned as he passed the cup back.

"If only I'd never brought you on this fool's errand!"

"It's what the gods did decide for us. I guess." Jahdo heard his voice break as he wished from the bottom of his heart that he'd never come, either. "You couldn't know Thavrae was going to be killed." He swallowed hard, concentrating on pouring himself water. "Oh. You know what? I do have somewhat to give you, and I never did remember it till this moment." He gulped the water, set the cup down, and began fishing in his pocket. "Here they are. It's the stuff Thavrae wore, the amulets and things. I did cut them off for you."

When Jahdo laid them in Meer's palm, the bard tightened his fingers over them for a moment, then muttered a curse and flung them hard against the wall.

"I have done what our mother asked. I will do no more. If it weren't for him and his foul demons, his false gods, his blasphemy, and his heresy, then our clan would still have the hope of life, and neither you nor I would be caged here in this loathsome dungeon. Is it not one of the seven worst things in all of life, to fall into the hands of one's enemies?"

Jahdo tried to find some comforting thing to say and failed. He broke the bread up into chunks and gave Meer a big one, but the bard handed it back.

"Eat it all, lad, the whole loaf. You are young, and you have hope. Many a faithful slave's been rewarded with freedom."

"But bain't you hungry?"

Meer shook his head no.

"Meer, you must be—oh, Meer, don't. Don't starve yourself to death. You mayn't, you mayn't! You're all I've got, Meer. Please eat some of this bread. Please."

Meer folded his arms over his chest and turned his head away. No matter how Jahdo begged and wept, he spoke not one word. In the end Jahdo gave up. His own stomach was growling from the scent of food. He wiped his face as best he could on his filthy sleeve and began to eat. Meer must have heard, because he allowed himself a brief smile.

Jahdo finished one chunk and started on another. He was wondering if they'd be fed more later in the day, or if he should be saving half the loaf, when he heard a slight sound without the door, or so he thought until he looked up to find someone inside the cell with them.

In the dim light she seemed to glow, a beautiful woman, tall and slender with long ash-blond hair that cascaded down her back, deep-set eyes the color of storm clouds but slit vertically like a cat's, and the strangely long and curled ears he'd seen on the god by the stream. She was dressed in clothes of silvery gray, a full shirt, belted at the waist, a pair of doeskin trousers, and boots of the same.

"Evandar wouldn't come himself, but I can't bear to leave you this way, child. Fear not: things aren't as dark as they must seem. I promise you that."

She seemed to swirl like a trail of smoke above a campfire; then she was gone.

"What was that voice?" Meer snapped. "Who was that?"

"It were a goddess." Jahdo had never been so sure of anything in his life. "A goddess did come to us, Meer. It's needful for you to eat now, bain't it? She came and did say that all be well."

When Jahdo handed him the bread, Meer began to eat, slowly, savoring each bite in something like awe, while Jahdo poured himself more water and drank it the same way.

After he made his final threats to the jailor, the man who preferred to be known only as Rhodry from Aberwyn stood in the ward for a moment, considering how badly he wanted a bath and some clean clothes after a fortnight in the saddle. He knew, however, that he'd best make his report to those who'd sent him on this hunt. He headed across the ward to the broch complex, aiming for one of the smaller towers that were joined to the flanks of the main broch. Although he was planning on slipping in quietly, he found waiting for him a man he couldn't ignore. A tall, hard-muscled fellow with moonlight-pale blond hair and gray eyes, Lord Matyc of Dun Mawrvelin was leaning against the door with his arms crossed over his chest. Since he had no choice, Rhodry made him a bow.

"Good morrow, my lord. Somewhat I can do for you?"

"Just a word, silver dagger. Those two prisoners you just brought in? By whose order did you take them?"

"The gwerbret's himself, my lord. He sent me and Yraen out with a few of his own men."

"I see."

His lordship peeled himself off the door and walked away without so much as a fare thee well. And since it was the gwerbret, Rhodry thought, there's not one wretched thing you can do about it, is there? He would have disliked so arrogant a man as Matyc on principle alone, but recently an incident or two had left Rhodry wondering just how loyal the lord was to his overlord, Gwerbret Cadmar of Cengarn. What interested him about this latest brush with his lordship was not that Matyc had asked him a question—simple curiosity would have explained that—but the lack of further questions, such as a wondering about who Meer might be or how he'd been found, the normal sort of things you'd expect a man to ask. Rhodry watched Matyc until the lord had gone into the main broch, then went on his own way.

Right inside the door of the side tower a wrought-iron staircase led up every bit as steeply as the dwarven stairs, spiraling round and past all four floors of the small and wedge-shaped chambers belonging to various of the gwerbret's honored servitors. On the fifth and final floor was an open area for storing sacks of charcoal to one side and one last chamber to the other. Rhodry stood for a moment catching his breath, then knocked. A woman's voice called for him to enter. He hesitated ever so slightly before he opened the door and strode in.

Dressed in pale gray brigga and a heavily embroidered white shirt, Jill was sitting on a curved, three-legged chair with a large leather-bound book on the table in front of her. Her hair, cropped off like a lad's, was perfectly white, and her face was thin, too thin, really, so that her blue eyes seemed enormous, dominating her face the way a child's do. Overall, in fact, she was shockingly thin, and quite pale, yet she hardly seemed weak, her eyes snapping with life when she smiled, her voice strong and vibrant as well.

"Well?" she said. "Success?"

"Just that. We followed your directions and found them just about where you said they'd be, one human lad, one Gel da'Thae. I've stowed them in the dungeon keep."

Jill made a face.

"Oddly enough, they're safer there than anywhere," Rhodry went on. "Feeling in the town's running high. A lot of townsfolk lost kin to those raiders, and the word's gone round that their leader was a hairy creature straight out of the third hell. How are they going to feel about having another of the same lot right within reach? Here, an odd thing. That Gel da'Thae I killed was this bard's brother."

"Odd, indeed. How do you know the prisoner's a bard?"

"His servant told me. And here's the oddest thing of all. They speak the same tongue as Deverry men do. I've never been so surprised in my life, Jill. The lad just spoke right up, and I could understand him. Not easily at first, mind. His way of speaking's a fair bit different, all flat and watery, like, and he uses a lot of words that I'd say were very old. The kind of thing you find in my esteemed ancestor's books—words that haven't been spoken round here in two hundred years."

"No doubt they haven't, and no doubt he was as surprised as you were. If I'm guessing a-right, his forefathers were escaped bondmen. The bondfolk came from many different tribes, you see, before our ancestors conquered the lot. And each of those, or so the lore runs, had its own language, a hundred of them all told, or so the priests say." She tapped the book before her with reed-slender fingers. "The only tongue that they all had in common was the language of their old masters, and they were forced to use it to survive."

"I'll wager it griped their souls. It would have mine."

"No doubt." She smiled briefly, then glanced at the book. "It must be a strange place, the Rhiddaer. I haven't been able to learn much about it, which is why this pair of prisoners is so important. But there's no High King, and no lords nor gwerbrets, either, to keep order or form alliances—not that I can truly blame the people for wanting to leave all that behind forever. The High King's justice never did apply to them, did it? But as for the lad and the bard, I hate to do this, but I'd say leave them where they are for a while, at least, until they're scared enough to consider talking to me and the townsfolk find somewhat else to gossip about."

"Done, then."

"Tell me, was your ride quiet enough?"

"It was. No signs of trouble, no sign of more of those raiders, but we might have ridden right past them, and they past us, with no one being the wiser. It's wild country out that way."

"It's wild country all round here. That's the problem with Cengarn, isn't it? Ye gods, we're isolated! Tell me somewhat, Rhoddo. How many men do you think Cadmar could field, if things came to some sort of war?"

"Not all that many. Let me think. Matyc's his only vassal to the north, and then Gwinardd is his richest vassal, which should tell you somewhat about this place when you look at the kind of gear his men have. There's a lot of small lords round here, with, say, five, ten men sworn to them. But anyway, our gwerbret has alliances farther east, of course, but Arcodd province isn't exactly a rich and settled place itself. Say five hundred men easily, another five hundred if all his nearby allies sent their treaty-bond due. And of course, the common-born are all free farmers, out this way. They'll fight for their own, and they could field what? Say another thousand men, half armed and half trained, but brave and determined."

"And if the entire province were threatened, the High King would march, wouldn't he?"

"Of course, but it would take months to mobilize and get an army out here." All at once the implications of all these questions sank in. "Jill! What are you saying? Do you really think we're in that kind of danger?"

"I don't know. I hope not. But all my life I've expected the worst and planned for it, and you know what? I've never been disappointed yet."

Rhodry tried to laugh, then gave it up as a bad job.

"I honestly don't think we've seen the last of this trouble," Jill went on. "But how big the danger is? Well, I have no idea. As soon as I find out anything, I'll tell you and the gwerbret both."

"Fair enough, and speaking of his grace, I'd best find him and tell him I've brought his men back."

"Just so. And give him my thanks, will you?" She turned another page in the book. "I'll come down the great hall in a bit."

The great hall of Gwerbret Cadmar occupied the entire ground floor of the main broch. On one side, by a back door, stood enough trestle tables and backless benches for a warband of well over a hundred men; at the hearth, near the table of honor itself, furnished with actual chairs were five tables more for guests and servitors. On the floor lay a carpet of fresh braided rushes. The walls and the enormous hearth were made of a pale tan stone, all beautifully worked and carved, while huge panels of interlacement edged the windows and were set into the walls alternately with roundels of spirals and fantastic animals. An entire stone dragon embraced the honor hearth, its head resting on its paws, which were planted on the floor, its winged back forming the mantel, and its long tail curling down the other side. Even the riders' hearth on the far side of the hall was heavily decorated with interlacing and dragons' heads. When Rhodry walked in, he found the hall mostly empty, except for a couple of servant lasses over by the warband's hearth, and a page, polishing tankards up at the table of honor. When Rhodry hailed the page, the boy ignored him.

"You, Allonry! I know your father's a great lord, but you're here to run errands for anyone who asks."

Scowling, the lad slouched over, a willowy lad of about ten summers, red-haired and freckled.

"Where's his grace?" Rhodry said.

"Out in the stables with the equerry."

"Will he be there long?"

"I wouldn't know. Go ask him yourself, silver dagger."

Rhodry restrained himself with difficulty from slapping the boy across the face. Although he himself had served as a page in a gwerbret's dun, he couldn't remember having been this arrogant. He'd been terrified, mostly, of making a wrong step and disgracing himself, but young Allonry seemed to have no such worries.

"I will, then," Rhodry said. "But I wouldn't strut like this around Lord Matyc and his ilk, if I were you."

The boy ducked his head and looked away. Rhodry turned to go, but the gwerbret himself made the point moot by coming in, trailed by the equerry and the chamberlain. Even though he limped badly on a twisted right leg, Gwerbret Cadmar was an imposing man, standing well over six feet tall, broad in the shoulders, broad in the hands. His slate-gray hair and mustaches bristled; his face was weather-beaten and dark; his eyes gleamed a startling blue under heavy brows. As he made his way over to the table of honor, the page bowed, and Rhodry knelt.

"Get up, silver dagger, no need to stand on ceremony." The gwerbret favored him with a brief smile. "You're back, are you? I've heard that you brought prisoners. I take it Jill was right, then, and there were spies prowling round my borders."

"Well, Your Grace, we found a couple of prowlers, sure enough, but I doubt me if they're truly spies. One's but a lad, you see, and the other's blind."

The equerry and chamberlain exchanged startled looks, and Cadmar himself grunted in surprise.

"Cursed strange, then. Why were they riding in my lands?"

"I have no idea, Your Grace. I do know that Jill has great hopes of getting information out of them."

"No doubt she'd like me to leave the matter in her hands?"

"If his grace agrees, of course."

"Well, most likely I will." The gwerbret turned to the page. "Alli, run up to Jill's chambers and ask her, and politely, mind, but ask her to come down for a word with me."

Although the boy bowed and ran off fast, he was obviously smarting at the vertical hike ahead of him. Cadmar glanced at the chamberlain.

"Think he'll learn courtesy one of these fine days?"

"I can only hope so, Your Grace," the old man sighed. "I'm doing my best to teach the wretched little snot."

Cadmar laughed, then remembered Rhodry and turned to him with a quick wave of one hand.

"You may go, silver dagger. No need for you to be standing round here."

"My thanks, Your Grace."

Rhodry went out to the barracks, those structures built into the walls that had so puzzled Jahdo, and drew himself water at the stable well for a cold bath. Once he was shaved and reasonably clean, he went back to the great hall to keep an eye on things. He got himself some ale, dipping his own tankard to avoid giving a servant lass the chance to snub him, then found himself a seat at a table on the far side of the hall, where he could watch the noble-born from a proper distance. A few at a time, the honor-bound men in the various warbands quartered at the dun came drifting in, chivvying the lasses and settling down at one table or another to wait for the evening meal. Unlike the servants and the noble-born, most of the men had a friendly greeting for Rhodry or a jest to share. They'd seen him fight, after all, and judged his worth on that.

The hall filled up fast. For the war against the raiding party captained by Meer's brother, Cadmar had called in two of his closest vassals, Lord Matyc and Lord Gwinardd, and as their oaths of fealty demanded, they'd brought twenty-five men apiece with them to add to Cadmar's oath-sworn riders. One of the latter, a young, brown-haired lad named Draudd, sat himself down beside Rhodry.

"Where's Yraen?"

"Don't know, but he'd better be cleaning himself up," Rhodry said. "I thought he'd be in by now. Why?"

"Just asking, wondering if he's up for a game of carnoic or suchlike." Draudd yawned profoundly. "He plays cursed well. Here, Rhodry, some of the men have a wager on, like, that Yraen's noble-born."

"Do they now? I hope they don't go asking him outright and hope to live to collect it. Prying into a silver dagger's past is bad for a man's health."

Draudd snorted into his ale.

"I'm not having a jest on you," Rhodry spoke quietly, levelly. "Tell them to lay off."

Draudd looked up sharply, his good cheer gone.

"And another thing," Rhodry went on. "Am I included in this little game?"

Draudd turned beet-red in silent confession. Rhodry grabbed him by a twist of shirt that nearly choked him and hauled him face-to-face.

"Lay it off, lad. Do you understand me?" He let Draudd go with a thrust of his wrist that sent the lad reeling. "Do you?"

"I do, and I will, then." He hesitated, rubbing his throat with one hand, then swung himself free of the bench. "I'll just go have a word with the captain, like."

Rhodry realized that a clot of men were hovering in the door and watching. He ignored them and picked up his tankard again. When he checked a few moments later, he found them gone.

Soon after Jill appeared at the far side of the great hall and hurried up to the gwerbret's table, where Cadmar himself rose to greet her, insisting she take the place of honor at his right hand. Although he was too far away to hear their talk, Rhodry could guess that the gwerbret was trying to winkle information out of her—never the easiest task in the world. Rhodry suspected that she knew a great deal more than she was saying about this mysterious bard from so far away. In a few minutes the gwerbret's other vassal in residence, Lord Gwinardd, joined the honor table, a young man, brown-haired and bland, his title newly inherited, sitting diffidently at the far end from his overlord and not saying a word.

As the afternoon drowsed on, Rhodry started keeping a watch for Lord Matyc, who would be expected to join the other noble-born men for the evening meal if not before, but he had a long wait before Matyc finally strode in. Right behind him came Yraen. Rhodry allowed himself a small smile as the two parted company, Matyc to greet his overload, Yraen to stroll down and join Rhodry.

"And where have you been?" Rhodry said.

"Keeping an eye on his lordship. What do you think? I caught him showing a bit too much interest in those prisoners for my taste, so I stood on guard for a while. When he kept hovering round, I distracted him, like, with talk of horses, and maneuvered him into taking a look at the gwerbret's new mare and suchlike."

"And how did our lordship take that?"

"Badly." Yraen shrugged. "Let him. I don't like the look of the man. Somewhat about him turns my gut."

"Mine, too. I'll try to get a word with Jill, and as soon as I can. I wouldn't mind having our prisoners moved to some fresh place, and that without our lordship knowing."

Round sunset the jailor brought Jahdo and Meer a fresh loaf of bread, more water, chunks of cheese, stiff with rind but not bad tasting and plenty of it, and a couple of fresh peaches, which, he said, came by Rhodry's direct order. Although he was glad of the food, thinking that they were dependent on the goodwill of the man who'd killed Meer's brother and then captured them made Jahdo profoundly uneasy.

"I do feel that we shouldn't eat it," he said to Meer.

"Slaves take what they can get, lad."

"I know that, but then it really creeps my flesh, thinking what will happen to us if Rhodry's killed or suchlike. How will someone else treat us?"

"Slaves live one day at a time, as well."

While they ate, sitting in the straw, Jahdo looked up and out the barred window on the opposite wall. Outside the sky, streaked here and there with gold clouds, was darkening to a velvet blue. He could hear voices passing, harried servants, laughing men, the occasional bark of a dog or whinny of a horse. When he was done, he walked over to the window and found below it on the wall a couple of uneven stone blocks. By stepping on them and grabbing the window bars to hoist himself up, he could look out to a view of two storage sheds, the pigsty, and in the distance the massive outer walls of the dun, all of which he described to Meer, mostly to pass the time.

"And then round the top of the dun there's these wooden catwalks, like we have back home, for the militia to walk round on and guard things. These are kind of broken in places, though, like they haven't been kept up right. Maybe they don't have a lot of wars here or suchlike."

"This dun seems to be the strong point of the entire area and not very likely to be attacked. I wonder what a gwerbret is? The lord of this place, obviously, but I've never heard the word before."

"Neither have I."

Meer considered the problem for a moment, then felt for his staff, lying near him in the straw.

"Do you need the bucket?" Jahdo said.

"I don't. Help me to stand, lad."

When Jahdo did so, Meer tapped his way to the door and felt for the little window. Once it was found, he put his face close to the bars.

"Jailor!" he roared. "Jailor! Come here!"

He kept it up until the old man appeared, cursing and complaining as he stumped down the hallway. A whiff of sour ale came with him.

"And what's wrong with you, you hairy cow? Disturbing an honest man at his hard-earned meal, not that I'll be making much of a profit feeding the likes of you, and that worm-riddled silver dagger giving me orders."

"I require the meaning of a word."

The jailor stared, his mouth flopping open and silent.

"I am Meer, bard and loremaster," Meer bellowed. "Tell me what this word *gwerbret* means. Such lore is my due."

With a shake the jailor recovered himself.

"Oh, is it now? Since when do hairy dogs have bards?"

"You better watch your tongue!" Jahdo snapped.

"Hush!" Meer waved him away. "Old man, first you called me a cow, now a dog. In my homeland you would have been publicly strangled for those insults. Here, as a slave, I have no choice but to forgive you. Yet even a slave-bard is a bard still. You will answer me my question, or I'll call down the wrath of the gods."

"Call away. I'll not be telling you one wretched thing."

As the jailor turned to go, Meer sang a high, piercing note whose harsh texture made Jahdo squirm. Louder and louder he sang, and longer and longer, until the jailor shrieked.

"Very well! Hold your ugly tongue, bard! I'll tell you. I should have known that hairy savages like you would be as ignorant as you are ugly. A gwerbret's a kind of lord, see, the most powerful lord there is, except for the princes and suchlike of the blood royal. He's got vassals what owe him service and pay him dues. And he judges criminals and suchlike, and I hope to every god that when it comes to the judging of you, he hangs you good and proper."

This time when the old man hurried off, Meer let him go.

"May his heart burst within him," Meer remarked. "Or better yet, may the gods plug his kidneys so that he dies in a stink of piss. Ah well. At least I've got my bit of new lore."

Jahdo felt a profound relief. Obviously Meer had truly decided to live if he'd go worrying about some funny name. He got the bard settled, then climbed back to his window perch to watch the twilight fading. After a few minutes he saw a familiar figure come striding out of the main broch.

"Someone's coming. It be Rhodry, and he's got Yraen and a couple of men from the squad with him."

When he heard Rhodry's voice in the corridor, and the jailor's sniveling answers, Jahdo climbed down from his perch and handed the Gel da'Thae his staff. Meer rose to his feet just as they lifted the bar and opened the door. Rhodry made them a formal bow, but he was grinning all the while.

"Feel like a stroll in the evening air?" Rhodry said. "The ward's nice and quiet at the moment, because most everyone's still eating. I think we can get you across to the broch safely, *if* you hurry and *if* you cause me no trouble. Agreed?"

"We don't have any choice, do we?" Jahdo said.

Rhodry laughed as hard as if the world were one daft jest.

"None," Rhodry said. "So march."

Jahdo caught Meer's arm, and they hurried out, striding fast across the ward with the men disposed around them—not that they could hide Meer, tall as he was, of course. Jahdo, however, had trouble seeing through them, although he could just make out the many-towered broch complex, looming against the darkening sky and drawing closer and closer. They ducked suddenly into a door, which Rhodry slammed behind them, turning wherever they were as dark as pitch.

"Curse you, Rhodry!" Yraen snarled. "I'm not climbing all those stairs in the dark."

"Then get yourself into the great hall and grab us a candle-lantern. The servants should be lighting them about now. Draudd, Maen—when Yraen returns, you're dismissed, but say one word about this, and you'll have me to deal with."

"I've forgotten already," Draudd said. "Even though I'm still here."

Once Yraen came back with a punched tin lantern, they climbed the staircase by its mottled and flickering light, up and up, round and round, until Meer and Jahdo both were panting for breath. At the landing up top, Rhodry let them pause among the heaped sacks.

"Now mind your manners in here," he whispered. "We're going to see Jill, and she holds your fate in her hands."

Jahdo immediately pictured some great queen out of the ancient tales. He was not, therefore, prepared for the reality when Jill flung open the door. The chamber behind her glowed with a peculiar silver light that clung to the ceiling and sheeted down the walls as if it were water, and backlit as she was, he honestly thought her a skeleton or corpse. He screamed, making Meer grab his shoulder hard.

"What is it?" the bard snapped. "What is it?"

Jahdo tried to speak but could only stammer. When Rhodry howled with his usual crazed laughter, the boy burst into tears.

"What are you doing to him?" Meer bellowed with full bardic voice. "He's done no harm to aught of you."

"It's all right," Yraen broke in. "Jahdo, stop sniveling."

"Ye gods," Jill snarled. "Will you all hold your wretched tongues? Do you want half the dun running up here to see what the commotion is?"

That sensible question silenced everyone.

"Much better," Jill said. "Come in, come in, and my apologies for frightening you, lad."

With new courage Jahdo led Meer straight into the chamber. Now that he could see that she was a perfectly normal woman, though certainly not an ordinary one, he was expecting to find the peculiar glow just some trick of moonlight or torches. Unfortunately, it was nothing of the sort.

"Meer, there be magic at work here," he whispered. "The light does shine all over everything, like dust or suchlike, I mean, if moonlight were dust it would look like this, and she's got books, great big books. There must be twenty of them."

Jill grinned at that. The Gel da'Thae was turning his huge head this way and that, listening to every sound he could register, and his nostrils flared, too, as if he were sniffing the air like a horse. Since his hand lay on Meer's arm, Jahdo could feel him trembling. All at once Jahdo remembered hearing Rhodry and Yraen speak of this woman during the long ride back to Cengarn.

"You be the mazrak!" he burst out. "The falcon I did see following us."

Meer clutched his staff hard between both hands and growled under his breath.

"I have no idea what a mazrak may be," Jill said mildly. "So how could I be one?"

"But the falcon. We did see it, and then Rhodry and Yraen did come with the squad, and they knew right where we'd be, didn't they? They did speak of you and said your name, and I could tell they were following your orders."

Jill glanced at Rhodry.

"I agree with you," she said. "This child's much too bright to be locked in a stinking dungeon."

She was admitting he'd guessed right, that indeed, he was facing a real sorcerer. Jahdo clutched the talismans at his neck.

"I understand that you're a bard," Jill said to Meer. "So you shall have the only chair I've got. Rhodry, Yraen, if you'll just stand by the door? In fact, Yraen, if you wouldn't mind standing on the other side of it to keep the curious away, I'd be grateful. Jahdo, get your master settled, and then, I think, it's time for some plain talk."

Jahdo helped Meer sit, then knelt beside him on the floor, which was covered with braided rush mats and reasonably comfortable. The room itself seemed ordinary, except for the presence of books, containing only a small table, a chair, a charcoal brazier, an alcove with a narrow bed, a pair of carved storage chests. Jahdo realized that he'd been expecting sorcerers to live somewhere grand and cluttered, with demons standing round in attendance, not in an everyday sort of room like this. There was, however, no explaining away the silver light. When Jill leaned against the wall facing him and Meer, the drape of light parted, as if dodging her.

"Well, good bard," she said. "My apologies for the rough treatment you've received, but your people are not so well liked round here, thanks to the raiders."

"So I've noticed." Meer's voice was stiff and cold. "Wait. What do you mean, raiders?"

"A band of men, led by one of the Horsekin, have been raiding hereabouts, burning farms, killing the men and any pregnant women, enslaving the rest."

"What?" Meer tried to speak, sputtered, caught his breath at last. "Lies! Disgusting, demon-spawned lies! No man of the Horsekin would ever harm a pregnant female, no matter whether she were kin or utter stranger, horse or Horsekin, human or hound, and he'd kill any man under his command in an instant for doing the same. Never! The gods would send down vengeance on him and strike him dead."

"Well, in a way they did," Rhodry said, rubbing his chin with one hand. "But, Meer, I'll swear to you it's true. I saw one victim myself, a woman not far from giving birth, lying dead in the road from a sword slash, and her babe butchered inside her."

Meer turned toward the sound of the silver dagger's voice, then hesitated, his mouth working. Jill stood utterly still, watching all of this with her blue eyes as cold and sharp as thorns, as if she could bore through the faces of the men into their very souls.

"Do you believe me?" Rhodry said. "I can bring you other witnesses, Yraen for one."

Meer shook his head in a baffled gesture that might have meant either yes or no.

"One thing," the Gel da'Thae said at last. "Are you sure that the raiders you fought were indeed the same band that committed these heinous sins?"

"We are. The men they'd taken for slaves? After we rescued them, they gave evidence against the raiders, and they all swore that the man of the Gel da'Thae was the leader, ordering the murders."

Meer grunted, his hands clasping and twining round his staff, then loosening again, over and over.

"I'll bring you witnesses," Jill said.

"No need." Meer's voice rasped in a whisper. "Are we prisoners of war, then, or slaves?"

"Never slaves," Rhodry broke in. "Never would I lend my hand and sword to the enslaving of anyone, good sir, and I'll swear that on anything you like."

Jahdo goggled, desperate and afraid both to believe him.

"Did Rhodry and the men treat you decently?" Jill asked.

"Better than prisoners of war can usually expect," Meer said. "I have no complaint to lay before you."

"Good."

Jill leaned back against the wall, waiting, letting the silence grow.

"Answer me one thing, Meer," Rhodry said at length, "if you can without dishonoring yourself, anyway. Are there going to be more of these raiding swine coming our way?"

"How would I know?" Meer snarled. "This first lot should never have been here in the first place. To send more would be infamy compounded, outrage and abomination writ large, if they've come to break every law of god and Gel da'Thae by killing females in foal! Who am I to say what men like that will do or not do next?"

Jill nodded, considering his outburst carefully.

"It sounds to me, then," Rhodry said, "like this was no ordinary raid."

Meer glowered with his lips tight-clenched.

"It were the false gods," Jahdo burst out. "The false goddess must be making them do that."

"False goddess?" Jill swung her head round fast. "What false goddess?"

"Her name be Alshandra, and she's only a demon or suchlike, but some people do worship her, just as if she were a true god from the Deathworld."

Never before had a mere bard's servant got such a profound reaction with a tale as Jahdo did with that blurt. Rhodry went dead-white, then swore a long string of foul curses while Jill laughed, a nervous giggle and much too high.

"Alshandra a goddess!" she said at last. "Oh, by all the ice in all the hells!"

Rhodry made a sputtering sort of noise under his breath.

"I agree," Jill said, grinning. "Well now, this may bode ill, or it may bode worse, but I'll wager it proves interesting. My thanks, lad. That makes a great deal clear."

"Answer me somewhat in return," Meer said. "I take it that you know about this Alshandra creature?"

"I do, and a goddess she's not and never will be. You're right a thousand times about that."

"What is she then? A demon?"

"A meddling bitch," Rhodry snarled. "That's what she is."

"Whist! Let me finish." Jill waved a hand in his direction. "She's not a demon, and neither human nor Horsekin, but a very strange sort of being indeed. Let's see, how can I explain this clearly?" She thought for a long moment. "I'm not sure I can. She doesn't live in this world, so in that respect she's like a spirit of the sort people call demons, but she's vastly more intelligent. She can move about much more freely than a demon, as well, and when she's here in our world she can make herself a body of sorts. She can work magic, some truly spectacular magic, in fact, from what I've heard, enough so I can see how some people think her a god."

"She sounds even more dangerous than I thought her, then."

"Unfortunately, that's very true. What's even worse is she's quite mad."

"Mad? May the gods preserve us!"

"I wouldn't mind their help, truly." Jill smiled in a wry sort of way. "Now here, did your brother worship this creature?"

Meer nodded, his mouth slack, then bent his head as if he were staring at the floor. His hands rubbed up and down his staff for the comfort of it.

"The infamy!" he snarled. "That my own brother's dishonor and sin would lead me to trust strangers who are no doubt no better than he and perhaps a good bit worse! Are you truly a mazrak?"

"I have no idea." Jill turned irritable. "If you'd deign to tell me what one is, I might be able to answer."

"A shape-changer, one who takes animal form."

"Oh. As a matter of fact, I am that."

She spoke in such an ordinary way that Jahdo shuddered, a long convulsion of terror. Meer growled under his breath and showed fang.

"But which one are you? The falcon or the raven? My servant here told me of two."

"What?" Jill hesitated. "The falcon's the form I take. Are you sure you saw another dweomer shape, Jahdo, or were you just scared or suchlike? I wouldn't blame you, mind. There's no shame attached, none at all, to being frightened of such things."

"I do know I did see it. It were a raven, and it were huge, and I did see it the morning Meer knew his brother was dying. It was flying close over the trees, so I could see how big it were."

"Well, well, well, could you, then?" Jill glanced Rhodry's way. "You didn't happen to see any birds that looked unnaturally large, did you? When you were riding to fetch Meer and Jahdo, I mean."

Rhodry shook his head no. He'd gone white about the mouth.

"But all those weeks ago, when you and Yraen were riding to Cengarn, you saw a raven, didn't you?"

"So we did," Rhodry said. "It was just when we stumbled across that farm the raiders destroyed, the one where that poor woman was lying dead and her unborn babe with her. Ye gods! I made a jest about the wretched bird, teasing Carra, like, and saying it was a sorcerer, most like."

"Were you really only jesting?"

Rhodry grinned, briefly.

"Not truly. Are you telling me I was right, and a dweomermaster it was?"

"I'm not telling you anything. But I begin to think it likely."

"Ah, infamy and abomination!" Meer whispered at first, but slowly and steadily his voice grew louder, till it rumbled in bardic imprecation. "O Thavrae, how could you, brother who is no longer no brother of mine! May your spirit walk restless through all the long ages of ages! May the gods turn you away from their doors! May their gardens be forbidden you! May you never drink of their drink, may you never taste of their food! That you could commit such sin, such perfidy! That you could break every law of every god! A brother's curse fall upon you! And in the end, if ever our mother should learn your evil, may her curse pierce your spirit as you writhe in the thirteen pairs of jaws of many-headed Ranadar, the Hound of Hell!"

"So be it," Jill said, and her own voice boomed like a priest's. "May the gods be his witness."

The room seemed to ring for a long, long moment. As he crouched beside Meer and watched the dweomer light swirling over the walls, Jahdo felt a peculiar intuition, that this moment marked a great change for more than the few individuals in this chamber, that some mighty thing, a destiny indeed, had begun to rouse itself from some age-long sleep, or that some vast night had begun to turn toward day—he could not find words, not even for himself, but he knew, he knew.

"You look solemn, lad," Jill said. "What ails you?"

He stared up at her, then rose, laying one hand on the back of Meer's chair.

"I just felt—I don't know—" The moment was passing, the insight fading, even as he struggled to grab it and pin it down. "That some great thing will happen, and I be glad I'm here to see it."

Meer swung his head round and grunted.

"Have you gone daft?" he snapped.

"I have not. You were right, that's all, when you did tell me that great things were on the move. This be all real important, bain't it, Jill?"

"It is, truly, or so the omens tell me. Great things or evil things, or, most like, a fair bit of both."

• • •

Although by then the evening was growing late, by the light of candle-lanterns Gwerbret Cadmar lingered at the head of the table of honor with Lord Gwinardd sitting at his right hand. Nearby a bard waited, drowsing over his harp, in case his lord should ask him to sing. Across the great hall the riders' tables were mostly deserted, and a few servants sat yawning by the empty hearth. Jill hesitated in the doorway for some moments. She'd been hoping that she'd find his grace alone. Matyc at least was gone. Although she herself had nothing against Matyc, she trusted Rhodry's judgment in such matters. If he said he smelt festering meat, then doubtless something had died under the stairs. On the other hand, no one had ever said a word against young Gwinardd, and she refused to keep silent and send Meer and his boy back to the dungeon for the night.

When she approached the table, Cadmar greeted her with a smile and a wave, calling for a servant to bring up another chair so that she could sit nearby without displacing Gwinardd from his honored position. The lord rose, bowing her way, then sitting down again rather than leaving. As usual, Gwinardd looked puzzled at the honor in which his grace held this common-born old woman, even though he knew that her herbcraft had saved the gwerbret's life the winter past. She wondered if he suspected her other skills as well.

"Well, Jill," Cadmar said. "Have you spoken with those prisoners yet?"

"I have, Your Grace, and it's about them, in fact, that I've come. Spies they're not, as you might expect with one of them blind. That Gel da'Thae is a bard and here on a tragic errand indeed. I'd like to treat them as guests—well, guarded guests, if you take my meaning—and put them in a chamber here in the broch. Is that possible?"

"And have I ever turned away a man who deserved my hospitality? But—"

"I'll explain, Your Grace," Jill went on. "When these raiders first showed up in your lands, I thought they were after the usual sort of booty. Do you remember the talk we had about that, what they wanted, I mean, after you tracked down and destroyed the raiding party?"

"I do, not that you told me much in the way of hard fact." Cadmar allowed himself a smile. "You were starting to get a different idea, you said, but you didn't tell me what you meant."

"Well, my apologies, but my idea sounds farfetched, you see, so much so that I'm still not sure of it. I do think, though, that Meer can tell me what I need to know, that he's got the missing piece of this puzzle somewhere in his stock of bard lore. But if we don't treat him well and show him some trust, he's not going to trust me enough in return to tell me one word of what he might know."

"That's quite true." Cadmar snapped his fingers at a serving girl. "Run fetch the chamberlain. Tell him that we have a guest to accommodate and him a traveling bard at that."

The lass curtsied and hurried away. Gwinardd was staring, as shocked by this ready acquiescence as young Jahdo had been by her dweomer light.

"My thanks." Jill rose, nodding his way in lieu of a bow, since she was wearing brigga and thus had no skirt to curtsy with. "May I have your leave, Your Grace?"

"Of course. But where is this sudden guest, then?"

"With Rhodry and Yraen. Look. Here he comes now, across the hall. The lad will have to stay with him, of course, not be quartered with the other servants."

"Of course. I'll have the chamberlain tend to it."

"My thanks, Your Grace. I thought that if you received him here in the open hall, everyone would know he's your guest now, and the threats against him and his kind would stop."

"No doubt, Jill. They had better."

When the gwerbret and his vassal turned to look at Meer, Jill slipped away. Although no dweomerworker can make herself truly invisible, despite what the old tales may say, Jill could gather her aura so tightly about her and move so silently and smoothly that she could pass unnoticed unless someone happened to be looking straight at her. Wrapped in these shadows she hurried up the staircase to her chamber. Judging from what she'd heard about this mysterious raven, she had to keep a close watch on Cengarn and the countryside round about, and for that she needed to fly.

For all that Meer hated and feared mazrakir, the process by which a dweomerworker takes on animal form is really only an extension of the perfectly ordinary procedure of constructing a body of light, in which the magician makes a thought-form in human or elven shape as a vehicle for his or her consciousness out on the etheric plane. Although at first he has to imagine this form minutely every time he wishes to use it, eventually a fully realized body, identical to the last one, will appear whenever the dweomermaster summons it, out of no greater dweomer than "practice makes perfect." This happens in exactly the same way as a normal memory image, such as the memory house a merchant uses to store information about his customers, becomes standardized after a long working with it. A shape-changer starts with the same process, substituting an animal form for the human, although, of course, the mazrak does take things a fair bit further.

That evening Jill followed her usual practice. First she took off all her clothes, because not even the mightiest dweomermaster can transform dead matter like cloth, and opened the wooden shutters at the window. She laid her hands far apart on the windowsill and stared up at the starry sky, letting her breathing slow and her mind clear as the cool night air swept over her. She felt power gather, invoked more, until it flowed through her mind like water. In her mind, as well, she formulated the image of a gray falcon, but many times life-size, and by a mental trick sent this picture out through her eyes until she saw it perching on the windowsill. Now, at this point the falcon image existed only in Jill's imagination, though an imagination that had been highly trained and disciplined by years of mental work, and it was only in imagination that she transferred her consciousness over to the bird until she seemed to perch on the sill herself and look down at the ward below through the bird's eyes.

Now came the first tricky step. Keeping her concentration firmly centered in the falcon, she transferred her consciousness up a level to the etheric plane. A rushy sound washed over her; she felt as if she were falling; then she heard a sharp click, like a sword striking the metal edge of a shield. When she looked round, she saw the chamber and the sky bathed in silvery blue light. Behind her on the floor her physical body lay slumped in trance, joined to the hawk form by the silver cord. At this point she could have used the falcon as an ordinary body of light to scry on the etheric or lower reaches of the astral. Instead she took that last step. The etheric double of a person is a matrix that forms and holds flesh. If the double and the trained will are strong enough, flesh will follow its lead. Jill began to chant and intone strange words of power that only a few masters know, until with one last convulsion of will, the etheric falcon drew the physical into its mold.

Jill the woman was gone from the chamber. Only the falcon stood on the windowsill, stretching its wings and ruffling its feathers in a last shudder against the cold.

With a soft cry she leapt and flew, flapping steadily till she cleared the dun, then gliding on the currents up, ever up, circling round the hills of Cengarn. Although the falcon form existed on the physical, Jill's consciousness remained on the etheric plane, so that she saw the trees and fields glowing a dull brownish-red from their vegetable auras, spotted here and there with the yellow ovoid auras of cows or horses huddled together. The dun, the walls, the town itself—all wore the dull black of stone and dead wood. Here and there a brightly colored aura of a human being moved down a street or strolled across the dun ward and once, down in town, she saw the metallic aura, copper streaked with steel-gray, of a dwarf trotting purposefully along. Out in the valley to the west of the town the fast-running stream sent up its exhalation of elemental force, like a towering silver veil shifting and hovering above the physical water.

Everything seemed peaceful, everything seemed safe, even when she circled out some miles. She saw no enemy soldiers, no ravens, no dweomerworkers, nothing or no one out of place. She decided that this other shape-changer, if indeed there were one, had to be flying for home and safety as fast as his or her wings could beat, wherever that home might be. Without the band of raiders for support, to carry its food and human clothing, the raven would be helpless in a wilderness. And where was that home? That, she hoped, Meer could tell her, or, at the least, give her the information she needed to discover it on her own. With a flip of a wing she turned, riding the night wind, heading back for the dun.

And yet, just as she had the town in sight, she saw something—someone—circling high above the walls, a bird form, all right, but far too large for an ordinary creature. As the other bird turned and began flying in her direction, Jill sprang higher, soaring in an easy circle to gain height and thus advantage. Yet, as the other mazrak flew close, she could see that it was no raven, but rather a strangely indeterminate gray bird, something like a linnet, but its feathers bore no markings at all. Dallandra—come through to the physical plane in the bird form! Without thinking Jill stooped and plunged, plummeting straight down like the falcon her body indeed was. With a shriek of terror the gray linnet broke course and flapped wildly away, heading for a copse. Cursing her bad manners, Jill broke from her plunge and followed more slowly, though she could still outfly the clumsier linnet.

"Dalla, it's just me!" Jill sent the words on a wave of etheric thought rather than sound. "My apologies! I didn't mean to frighten you. The wretched falcon took me over for a moment."

A wave of wordless relief floated back in answer.

Since the trees were far too small to shelter a pair of birds of their size, they circled down and lighted on the ground underneath, hopping a little to find footing on the uncongenial earth. The linnet shook herself and preened a few feathers on her breast to calm herself down.

"I *am* sorry," Jill thought to her. "I somehow thought you'd recognize me."

"You're not the only master who flies in hawk form, you see. Alshandra's been known to take the nighthawk at times."

"Indeed? Is one of her other forms a raven?"

"It's not, but a swan."

"That's a strange thing, then, because I've just heard of a shapechanger in raven form. A lad from the far west claims he saw it but an eightnight ago."

"No one I know flies as a raven. Ye gods! Talk about ill-omened! That would be too grisly even for Alshandra."

"Judging from some of the things I've heard I wouldn't have put it past her. But here's an even stranger thing, and thrice ill-omened at that. It seems that our Alshandra's been pretending to be a god, and she's collected herself a band of worshipers, too, among the Horsekin."

The linnet opened and shut her beak a few times, just as if she were trying to speak with a physical voice.

"She would." Dallandra's thought flowed on a wave of sheer bitterness. "She's just the sort who would. Jill, let's fly. I can't bear it, perching here and listening to sour news all at the same time."

With a few hops and a jump they launched themselves into the air, flying till they were high enough to be invisible from the ground. Up this far from the anchoring earth, the etheric sight turned the night sky into a swirl of black, studded with enormous silver stars, flaring and gleaming so close that it seemed they might have felt heat. Down below the countryside receded to a dull red glow. Slowly they rode the air currents in long aimless loops centered round Cengarn, a black lump rising from the red.

"What's Alshandra been doing?" Dallandra thought to her. "Working magic in front of the Gel da'Thae?"

"I suppose, but I don't know for sure. My one witness doesn't trust me in the least, and I can't blame him, either, but he's not going to bare his heart and soul to me. From what he *has* said, though, I've gathered that her worship is considered heresy, fit only for outlaws and suchlike."

"That's somewhat to the good, then. Are you still convinced that the Horsekin are those demonic Hordes the old elven lore speaks of? The ones who destroyed our cities?"

"More convinced the more I learn, though they're most certainly not demons."

"Well, I never really thought they were. My teacher, Nannanna, always said that they were most likely flesh and blood the same as us, whether they had the manners of demons or not, and she'd heard the tales a good bit closer to the destruction than we have."

"Just so. Here, Dalla, you'd know this. Wasn't there an elven king named Ranadar?"

"He was the last of the Council of Seven Kings, as a matter of fact. After the cities were destroyed by the Hordes, and all the other six kings killed, Ranadar gathered a warband from the survivors and lived in the mountains like a bandit, raiding and harrying the Hordes, taking what revenge he could. He's the one who witnessed the horrible plagues that very nearly destroyed the Hordes. In fact, until you started talking about Gel da'Thae, I'd always assumed that the invaders had been completely wiped out."

"Most people did, and I gather, from what I've been able to piece together, that the tribes who'd conquered the southern part of the elven homeland did die, down to the last child. But in the north some remain, and now they seem to be coming east."

The linnet dipped and shuddered.

"But this Ranadar," Jill went on. "He was a real historical figure, then?"

"Very much so. Eventually he joined the other refugees out in the grasslands, when he realized that he and his men weren't going to be able to reclaim the dead cities and suchlike all on their own. Why?"

"Meer—that's the Gel da'Thae bard I've got in custody—Meer used his name, but he called him the Hound of Hell with thirteen pairs of jaws. Rhodry told me that he's heard the bard pray, and that all of his gods have elven names, but odd and distorted ones, mostly fragments of the names of the old cities and palaces."

Jill felt the linnet's mind shy briefly away, then return.

"Rhodry's here?" Dallandra thought to her.

"Very much a part of this, truly. Why so surprised? You mentioned once that you'd met him."

"Only very briefly and some years ago. But that's a strange thing, truly, about the elven names. This whole situation's getting too complex, and I'm beginning to worry that everything's slipping out of control. I doubt very much, I truly do, if Evandar knows what he's doing with all his meddling. Foresight and understanding consequences are most definitely not talents of his."

"But other talents he has in good measure. Dalla, how much can I count on his aid?"

"I don't know. I honestly don't know. He cares about his daughter and her coming birth more than anything else in the three worlds, but there's trouble in his own lands. I've been planning, you know, to come back to the physical plane and stay in the dun with you and Elessario's mother, but now I'm afraid to."

In human form Jill would have sighed aloud, but as it was the falcon made a chirruping little sound.

"What kind of trouble?"

"I can't say for sure. Bad blood between Evandar and his brother, bad blood between the Bright and the Dark Courts. Evil things are brewing, Jill. I can feel them—or no, not evil exactly, but malice and spite and old hatreds."

"That, my dear friend, sounds evil enough for me. And please, be careful! You're in constant danger these days."

"I suppose so. I can't even blame Alshandra for hating me so bitterly. After all, I did steal her husband away, didn't I? And I'd best return to Evandar now. I'll be back, as soon as I can. Trouble or no, my place is here."

Jill felt the wave of fear from Dallandra's mind like a cold wind.

"My thanks. And if I need you badly before then, I'll send the Wildfolk as messengers."

"Do, please."

The linnet began to fly lower, dropping down toward the countryside and heading straight for the water veil rising up from the stream in the valley. Jill was just ready to shout a warning, because the currents of elemental force above moving water would tear an etheric form apart, when she remembered that not only was Dallandra very much in the physical, but that she was also a master of the strange dweomer of hidden roads. The linnet swooped, skittered, fluttering along the water veil, then suddenly spiraled up to disappear through one of the mysterious gates that led into the country where she lived with her beloved.

Ye gods, Jill thought to herself, how she puts up with Evandar for two days together is beyond me! There's all his riddling and wild talk, and besides, he's neither human nor elven, not truly incarnate at all—it's too perverse for the likes of me! Then she had to laugh at herself, that in the midst of all these strange events and mighty dweomers, she could still worry over a friend's choice of men. She soared back to Cengarn, reaching the dun just as the first dawn touched the eastern sky.

When Jahdo woke and found himself in their new chamber, high up in the main tower of the broch, he lay still for a long time and wished that he were dreaming, that he'd wake to find himself home, but the big wedge shape of a chamber stayed stubbornly real in the gray light of early dawn. Home or not, their new lodging was certainly better than the dungeon keep. Across the room, Meer lay snoring in a proper bed, surrounded by embroidered hangings, while Jahdo had a trundle bed with good blankets all to himself. In one corner of the room stood a bronze charcoal brazier in case some night turned chilly. Under the window lay a wooden chest, covered at the moment with bags and sacks. The night before, Rhodry had hunted round the dun and found most of their captured gear, although much to Jahdo's sorrow, his grandfather's knife had never turned up. Most likely it lay on the riverbank by the forest where Rhodry had made him drop it, back in what seemed like another life.

Since he was hungry, he got up, pulling on his trousers, and padded across the floor barefooted to find the chamber pot at the far end of the chamber. When he was done, he went to the window and began rummaging as quietly as he could in the sacks to see if there was any food left in them. All at once the entire pile shifted and slid, thumping onto the floor. Meer woke with a snort and a curse.

"My apologies," Jahdo said. "I was trying to be quiet. I just did drop some sacks and stuff."

Meer snorted again and yawned, rubbing the sides of his face with both hands.

"It be dawn out and light in here," Jahdo said. "Down in the ward there's servants walking round and stuff. I was just wondering if we had any food in these sacks."

"A good wondering, that. Hand me my clothes, and I'll get out of bed."

Down in the corner of one sack Jahdo did find a few slices of dried apple, and there was a flagon of fresh water and a wooden cup in the chamber, as well, so they had a bit of a meal to tide them over. When the sun was brightening on the dun wall, a servant unbarred the door to their chamber and came in with a loaf of bread, some fried bacon, and a pitcher of milk, brought specifically because Meer had asked for it the night before. The lass looked at Meer in such terror that she probably would have thrown the food onto the floor and run if Jill hadn't been standing right behind her.

"Jahdo, come take these things, will you?" the mazrak said. "I thought I'd come in for a bit of a chat."

Jahdo could think of nothing more likely to spoil one's breakfast than a conversation with a sorcerer, but he smiled politely and did as he was told. Jill perched on the recently cleared chest at the window while Jahdo served Meer his food and got his own. The boy and the bard sat on the edge of the bed to eat.

"Now," Jill said. "Meer, I know that you're a prisoner of war. For me to question you about your homeland goes contrary to all the laws of honor, but I'm desperate enough to try."

Meer merely grunted and fanged a rasher.

"Consider the evil that your own people will suffer," Jill went on. "This false goddess will lead them into great harm."

"My own people realize that very thing, mazrak," Meer said with his mouth full. "With the exception of my ill-begotten foal of a brother, she has no followers there."

Jill hesitated, cocking her head to one side, honestly puzzled.

"It's the wild tribes," Jahdo said. "The ones in the north, not Meer's people in the west. That's where all the prophets do come from."

"The what?" Jill turned to him with her icicle stare, stabbing into his very soul. "Where is this?"

Jahdo felt suddenly sick. Deep in his mind a memory tried to rise, another pair of ice-blue eyes, another stare that had pinned him down. He whimpered and broke away, flinging up a hand as if to ward a blow. Meer turned toward him with a questioning sort of growl.

"Here, lad!" Jill's voice softened, and her eyes were normal again. "I won't hurt you. I'm sorry if I frightened you. I never knew there was such a thing as wild tribes, you see, till this very moment, and it took me by surprise, like."

"All right." He was surprised to find his voice steady. "Meer, may I tell her about the tribes? Or would that be dishonorable? I be worried about what's going to happen to my own people if they get attacked and stuff. My father says we should always be scared of them, you know."

The bard considered, wiping his mouth on the back of one hairy hand, while Jill merely sat and waited for his decision. In the strong sunlight she seemed more frail than ever, as if her skin and flesh were translucent. Jahdo found himself thinking of bayberry candle wax.

"I will speak for us both," Meer said at last. "The tribes may be Horsekin, but they're no allies of the Gel da'Thae. If they've gone over to the false goddess, then they be enemies indeed."

"My thanks, good bard." Jill sounded profoundly relieved. "Is there a difference between Horsekin and Gel da'Thae?"

"Of a sort. We were all the same people, though a people made up of warring tribes, in a past very long gone indeed. But now my people live in the ruined cities of the Children of the Gods, while the wild tribes still roam the untamed plains of the north with their horse herds. Ah, the plains! The treasure that we Gel da'Thae have lost! And cursed poor custodians the wild tribes have proved for it, too. Huh, they dare to wage war without any of the proper rituals and procedures. In war it behooves a man to be ruthless, but they've stooped to using any and every weapon at their disposal, including the four evil magicks and the seven cowards' tricks. You wouldn't be alone there, mazrak."

Jahdo flinched, hoping that Jill wasn't about to blast Meer with lightning or suchlike, but she merely smiled.

"I see," she said. "And it's those tribes who worship Alshandra?"

"They do, indeed."

"Ah, things are beginning to fall into place. Now, when you say the wild tribes are to the north, do you mean due north or north and west?"

"North and west. Not so far west for my folk, though far, far west from here."

"One last thing, Meer. What do you mean when you say ruined cities of the Children of the Gods?"

"That I will not tell you."

"Very well. Let me guess. Long, long ago the Horsekin conquered seven rich cities, filled with marvels, and in their rage and ignorance destroyed them utterly. To this day the people known as Gel da'Thae eke out their lives near the remains of the beauty they destroyed."

Meer tossed back his head and howled, a thin keen of rage and mourning mingled. She be dweomer indeed! Jahdo thought, to ken such things and them as old as old. Jill smiled, sitting calm and easy, until Meer at last fell silent. For a moment he turned his head this way and that, focused at last on the sound of her breathing, and swung his head toward her.

"It's true," he whispered. "You've seen our ancient shame, mazrak. How? In a scrying crystal? Did the spirits come to you and bring you visions? How?"

"Not magic at all, but memory, the story passed down and down the long years by bards, or even written in books. I have a book, Meer, that tells the story whole and speaks of your people as well, but as they were that thousand years or more ago. Not all the folk who lived in those cities died. Some escaped to find a refuge and remember the harsh Wyrd that had fallen upon their people. Some live west of here. Others sailed in boats far, far to the south across the sea, and there they live to this day."

For a long time Meer sat with his head turned as it would have been if he'd had eyes to stare at her. At last he turned away with a long sigh.

"I will speak no more to you, mazrak. I am, however, going to think about what you say."

"My thanks, and that's all I'd ask of you." She turned to Jahdo. "So, lad. You come from the Rhiddaer, do you?"

"I do. I mean, uh, I didn't know you'd know about that. Or be that writ down in one of them books, too?"

"It is, indeed. But I'm probably the only person in all of Deverry who's both heard of the Rhiddaer and cares one whit about it, so don't let it trouble your heart. I can understand why you don't want the Slavers to come meddling with your country."

"Good, 'cause we don't." Jahdo summoned every shred of courage he had. "We be free now, and free we'll stay."

"And I promise you somewhat, lad. I'd die myself before I'd let anyone enslave your folk again. I mean that from the very bottom of my heart. It was a wrong thing that Deverry men did when they stole your people's land and freedom, and those of us who serve the dweomer have condemned it from the very beginning."

The quiet way she spoke convinced Jahdo that she meant every word of it. His eyes filled with tears again, and he found he couldn't speak.

"Tell me somewhat, mazrak," Meer broke in. Apparently he could no longer stand his self-imposed silence, not when there was lore to be had. "May I ask you a question in turn for those you've been asking me?"

"Of course, though I may not answer, since at times you won't answer me."

"Fair enough. You know about Jahdo's people, and your name sounds as if it came from his country. Have you lived there, then?"

"I haven't, but I've heard tales from the Westfolk, the horseherders who live out on the grasslands between our two peoples."

"Horseherders!" Jahdo blurted. "See, Meer, I were right."

"Just so. Now hush."

"There are some of them in the dun right now, Jahdo." Jill smiled, attempting to be kind. "You'll see them sooner or later. I've made it my affair to gather as much information as I can, you see, about both the Rhiddaer and the Gel da'Thae—not that it's been much of a harvest."

"Indeed? But what about your name?"

"Just a nickname my father gave me, but I wouldn't be at all surprised to find it goes back to some ancestor of mine who was a bondwoman.

Jahdo, from what I've been able to learn, while your people may have adopted the Deverry language, your names spring from the old tongues of your ancestors, not from ours, because people cling to their names and pass them down. And not all your ancestors escaped Deverry entirely. Many years ago, when we were having some horrible wars, a lot of bondfolk found themselves without masters. Some claimed their land as freedmen and stayed where they were; others went to other provinces to settle down and farm there."

"No one made them go back?" Jahdo asked.

"They were too valuable where they were. The noble-born learned an interesting lesson, back in those days of civil war. If there weren't any farmers to give them food in taxes, they'd have to farm themselves if they were going to eat, and well, now, they wouldn't have been very noble, then, would they?"

Jahdo laughed.

"Now we come to my case," Jill went on. "I was as aminheddic as a lass can be. Do you know that word? You look puzzled."

"I don't, my apologies."

"Well, a binheddic man is a man with a pedigree, a man who knows who his ancestors were, a noble-born man. When you don't know and care a fair bit less, then you're aminheddic, lacking a family tree, common-born."

"Oh. And that matters?"

"It matters a great deal, here in Deverry. Never forget that. Your life might depend on it, remembering that the noble-born see themselves as a good bit more valuable, like, then the aminheddic. But anyway, I've got a bondwoman's name, sure enough, and so I'm guessing that somewhere back in my family there were freedmen."

"And that doesn't ache your heart?" Meer said with some surprise.

"Not at all, good bard, not at all. All souls are the same to me, noble or common, human or otherwise. I was given the dweomer to serve them all."

Meer sucked his fangs as he thought this over.

"I have never heard of a sorcerer who used her tricks to serve anyone or anything but herself."

"Then I'll wager you never heard of a sorcerer who had anything more than tricks at her disposal."

Meer seemed to be about to speak, then sat back. Out of sheer nerves Jahdo giggled, which earned him a cuff on the shoulder.

"My apologies, Meer. I wasn't mocking you or anything."

"Good. Don't."

"Meer, bard, loremaster," Jill said. "I truly believe that we must be allies, not enemies, in this time of danger. Pooling what I know with what you know will be of great profit to both our peoples."

"You believe so, do you?" Meer paused for a sip of milk. "Strange stuff, this cow's milk you people drink. It's so thick and oily."

Jill smiled at the evasion, then merely waited, letting Meer drink his cup of milk as the silence grew thicker in the room. All of a sudden Jahdo wasn't hungry anymore, though he couldn't say why. He laid his half-eaten piece of bread down on the wooden trencher. From outside and down below came noises, horses' hooves clopping on stone, people laughing and talking, the rumbling bump of a barrel being rolled, but they all seemed to be sounding from a great distance away. In the chamber the silence seemed so thick that he felt he'd touch it if he reached out a hand. Meer handed Jahdo the cup, then wiped all round his mouth with the back of his hand in case he'd spilled a drop or two. Jill merely waited, her hands folded in her lap.

"Ah well," Meer said at last. "I do happen to know why Thavrae led his men east to your country."

Jill smiled again.

"Thavrae?" she said. "That's your brother, isn't it?"

Meer growled.

"My apologies," Jill said and quickly. "The man who used to be your brother."

Meer grunted, satisfied.

"I'd very much like to know that," Jill went on. "If you could bring yourself to tell me."

"I might, mazrak, but in return, I'll want a promise out of you, that you'll do everything you can to make sure young Jahdo here returns to his homeland before he's much older. What happens to me now is of little moment, but I made his mother a promise."

Jahdo felt his eyes fill with tears, which he wiped away as unobtrusively as he could.

"Done, then." Jill reached out a hand and touched Meer's arm. "You have my sworn word."

They clasped hands for a brief moment.

"And you have mine that this is the truth, as much as I know of it," Meer said. "When the man who once was my brother fled our city with his band of soldiers, because by our laws he'd be strangled for heresy should he stay within the city bounds, the high priestess came to my mother, and my mother in turn sent for me. The priestess swore that the god Evandar the Far Archer, he who serves the goddess Rinbala, had appeared to her while she did vigil in the temple and had delivered unto her tidings of great import. The man my mother had birthed before me was fleeing east on his false goddess's bidding, to fetch some valuable thing for the demoness. The Alshandra creature had charged him with the returning of this precious object to her. As to what it is or was, none of us knew, except that she claimed it was hers and that it had been stolen from her."

"Evandar?" Jahdo broke in. "He's the one who did tell us which road to take!"

"So he did," Meer said. "Now don't interrupt."

Jill sat watching them with an expression of stunned surprise.

"I see," she said at last. "And we know that Thavrae failed."

"Just so, mazrak, just so. I think it likely that this pus-and-pride-swollen false goddess will send others after the thing, don't you? I was present when some of these heretic prophets were put to the torture in our public square. All claimed their demoness was implacable and un-yielding. She is a goddess of war, they cried, not of mercy, and she will revenge us upon you for this torment. Those were their exact words. You may trust that, being as I'm a bard and trained to remember such things."

"So you are, though it's an ill-omened thing you've remembered this time, I must say." Jill paused, thinking for a long moment. "I think I'd best have a word with the gwerbret."

"He's likely to see more raiders on his lands, truly."

Jill nodded, distracted. Jahdo suddenly wondered if she knew what Thavrae had been sent to fetch, simply because she looked so troubled.

"Meer, you have my profound thanks for this information. I can only hope you'll tell me more if I should need to ask more. I promise you, I swear to you on my honor, that if you do so, you'll be helping your own people, not betraying them in any way at all."

"Listen, mazrak. Fair words mean little between those who have just met."

"True enough, bard." Jill seemed more amused than insulted. "As time goes on, I hope we come to know each other better." She rose, nodding at Jahdo. "I'll speak to Rhodry and the gwerbret on your behalf. I see no reason for you two to stay penned up like hogs."

"Well, neither do I. It's not like we could escape without any food and stuff."

"Just so."

Jill walked across the room, opened the door, then turned back for one last look Jahdo's way. He felt that she was appraising him the way a man might judge a horse at a market fair, and for a good long time that morning, he was afraid, just from remembering her cold stare.

"Someone's meddled with that lad's mind," Jill said.

"What?" Rhodry looked up sharply from the bridle he was cleaning. "What do you mean?"

"Jahdo. Somewhat's wrong with him. I wonder if he's been ensorcelled? I don't find all the usual evidence, but maybe it was done very cleverly."

"Do you think it happened here in the dun?"

"Couldn't have. I'd know if someone were working evil dweomer nearby."

Out in the warm sun they were sitting in front of the stables, Jill on a bound shook of hay, Rhodry on the cobbles while he cleaned his tack. Although the ward was its usual busy chaos, the various servants and riders walking by all gave the pair of them a wide berth.

"Besides," Jill went on. "Every time I look him in the eye he cringes, while I've never noticed him do that to anyone else. I think me he's felt the touch of magic on his soul."

"The lad's got guts, true enough. I remember the night we captured them. He stood his ground, bold as brass, looking me right in the eye, and when I went to lay a hand on him, he tried to stab me with this miserable little knife, practically a pen-trimming knife, it was. I thought then that he'd make a grand warrior someday, but he's clumsy. Ye gods, is he!"

"Oh." She paused for a smile. "Think he'll outgrow it?"

"Some lads do, truly, but somehow I doubt it in this case."

"Well, maybe the gods have other plans for our Jahdo."

"What?" He looked up again to find her solemn. "Thinking of making him your apprentice?"

"Oh, not truly, not now that I say it aloud. He seems a stolid sort of lad, all common sense and suchlike. But you know, it's getting on to be time I thought of finding someone."

Rhodry winced and concentrated on drawing a rag through a bronze bridle ring to wipe away the green.

"Well," Jill said in a moment. "I know you don't like to think of my dying, but I've not got over that fever I picked up in Bardek, and it's not likely that I ever will. Rhoddo, we're both well on in years, even if you do look but half your age."

The tarnish lay thick on the inside of the ring. He scrubbed hard.

"Oh, very well, I'll hold my tongue."

"Curse it, Jill!" He let the bridle fall into his lap. "How do you expect me to feel when you turn all morbid like that?"

"Is it truly morbid?"

"Well, I suppose not, because you're right enough that we're a good bit older than the people we know would think, but—" He hesitated. "It's not my own death I mind. You know that. It would be losing you."

"My thanks. Huh—so I'm morbid, am I? I'm not the one who's half in love with my own death, like some as I could mention."

He shrugged and ignored her. In a moment she laughed, just softly and in defeat.

"Tell me somewhat," she said. "When did you meet Dallandra?"

Worse and worse. He rose, sweeping up the bridle.

"A long time ago, the year I took Yraen on as an apprentice. It was over that silly matter of the bone whistle."

"The what?"

"Oh, come now, surely you've heard that tale."

"I haven't. Will you sit down and tell it to me? What you and Dalla may have done together is no business of mine."

He felt his face burning, but he sat.

"How did you know? Did she tell you?"

"Not at all, but I felt her mind skip the same way yours just did. What bone whistle?"

Rhodry picked up the rag again and started in on the buckles on the cheek piece.

"Come to think of it, you should hear this," he said. "Uh, you're sure you're not jealous?"

"It's been how many years since we rode together? A long, long time, for certain. Of course I'm not jealous. Why? Is your vanity hurt because I'm not?"

He growled under his breath.

"Ah, it is." She sounded amused. "But what about—"

"The whistle, truly. It was a thing Evandar left with me by accident one Samaen day, you see, and sent Dalla to fetch back. It was made of bone, and it looked like a human or elven finger, but it was far too long for that. It had a cursed sour sound to it, I tell you. And all these peculiar creatures came prowling round to steal it. A thing that looked like a man but with a badger's head tried to murder me for it, so I killed our snouted friend and gave Evandar the wretched whistle back when he came for it himself." He paused, frowning at the buckle. "Well, there's a bit more twists to the tale than that, but I don't truly remember them well."

"Ye gods!" Jill's voice hissed in surprise. "And you never told me?"

"And when have I had the chance? I don't see you for years and years, and all at once, you pop up. Not much more than a fortnight ago, was it? And what do you do then? You send me haring off round the countryside, battling raiders and capturing mysterious bards and suchlike."

"Well, true spoken, but, Rhoddo, please, after this, tell me straight-away if anything happens that smells of dweomer. I don't care how small or strange it is. Tell me."

"I will then, and gladly. I'll pass the message along to Yraen, too."

"Do that, and my thanks." Jill thought for a moment. "How big was this whistle?"

"Oh, let me think." He laid the bridle down and held up his hands about a foot apart. "About so long. Or maybe a little shorter. Much too long to be the finger bone it looked, at any rate. And someone had cut a couple of holes in it, to make a few sour notes."

"Indeed? Huh, I wonder. It looked like a finger bone, did it? It could be. It just could be."

"Could be what?"

"I'll tell you when I know. I've got to be sure first."

"You're as full of riddles these days as Evandar."

"I begin to have more sympathy for him, truly." She smiled, but only briefly. "Do you remember when you first rode into Cengarn, and we had a talk out in the barracks here? I told you that Alshandra had sworn to kill Carra's child?"

"I do remember it, indeed. I've been wondering if that's why the raiders—"

"You're right, I think, but shush a moment."

Rhodry glanced round, then made a show of reaching behind him for another rag. Sure enough, Lord Matyc was standing some yards away, perhaps out of earshot, perhaps not. Rhodry scrambled to his feet and made the lordship a bow.

"Good morrow, my lord. Do you need me for somewhat?"

"I don't, silver dagger. Just passing by."

Matyc was forced to turn and stroll away. Rhodry sat down again, but at a different angle, so that he could keep an eye on the various approaches to their position.

"Anyway," Jill said. "I'm as sure as I'll probably ever be that Alshandra sent Meer's brother and his warband here to kill Carra and the child."

"Whatever for?"

Jill hesitated.

"Well," she said at last. "You actually do know already. I've told you, here and there, all sorts of things that I never should have let slip, bits of secrets about the dweomer, I mean. I've been tired, Rhoddo, worried sick and truly sick with this wretched shaking fever, and for all that I haven't seen you in so many years, I trust you more than any man on this earth, you know."

Rhodry was surprised at how pleased he was to hear her say so. Rather than admit it, he grinned.

"I don't recall hearing any secret knowledge of ancient dweomer. No arcane spells nor exotic wizardry seem to have lodged in my soul."

"As long as you think of it like that, then you won't remember. Good."

Rhodry had the distinct feeling he'd been outmaneuvered. Jill rose, plucking odd bits of straw from her clothes.

"I've got work in hand, scrying and suchlike," she said. "Ask me more later—if you dare."

Jill hurried off, leaving him irritable behind her. Just what did she mean, if you dare? And all this cursed talk of secrets! And yet he knew deep in his memory what she meant, or rather he knew he would know if only he let himself know, if only he pieced together the odd scattered hints that indeed he did remember, whether he wanted to do so or not.

Once Jill had mentioned that Alshandra had a daughter who'd been somehow lost to her. And he was sure that Carra's unborn child was a daughter. Why, he'd been sure enough to tell the child's father that a daughter it was, weeks ago now when they'd been hunting the raiders together. There could be no logical connection between those two daughters. Of course not. It's not like the soul of one could be born again as the other. Could it? Why was he wondering if souls could put on new bodies, the way he put on a shirt? And why, he wondered most of all, did that wondering frighten him?

With a toss of his head like a spooked horse, he rose, gathering up his tack. He refused to let himself answer those questions, and all because they brought him to the edge of an insight he refused to face. He strode into the stables, hoping for some company, but no one was there but the horses and the stable cat, sunning herself in the straw in front of the tack-room window. He hung his gear on the pegs allotted to it, then strode out again, heading for the great hall and a tankard of ale. About halfway across the ward, though, he heard boys' voices, yelling, taunting, and giggling behind one of the storage sheds. When Rhodry hurried over, he found Jahdo, red-faced with fury, in the center of a circle of pages and scullery lads. Young Allonry seemed to be the chief tormentor. He was waggling a dangerous-looking stick in Jahdo's direction and so wildly Rhodry angled round to come up behind the page.

"Slave born, slave born," the lordling was chanting. "Jahdo is a bondman, Jahdo is a bondman."

"I was born freer than you are," Jahdo snarled. "We don't have any stinking old lords where I come from."

Alli swung the stick right for Jahdo's head. Rhodry caught his wrist just in time and so hard that the page squealed.

"Drop it," Rhodry said.

Alli dropped it because he had no choice, sniveling with pain as he was. When Rhodry let him go, the page danced back out of his reach.

"I'm going to tell the chamberlain on you!"

"No doubt you are. Honor doesn't seem to be one of your strong points, lad. Go on—run to your wet nurse, then."

All the other boys howled with laughter. Flushing scarlet, Alli stood his ground for a moment, looking back and forth at his erstwhile allies. When all they did was look right back at him, he turned and ran for the broch complex. With a last round of giggles the other boys straggled away, some to their work in the kitchen hut, some to the great hall. Jahdo watched them go.

"My thanks, Rhodry," he said at last. "Are you going to get in trouble for this?"

"I doubt it, lad. Our Allonry may be noble-born, but he's a cowardly little get, all in all. I'd watch your back around him, though, if I were you. You're smaller than him."

Jahdo grinned. Rhodry was frankly disappointed that the boy had proved himself so clumsy; he had mettle, did young Jahdo, in his solid little way.

"How badly has the pack been hounding you?"

"Not very, truly. No one did cause me grief at all till Alli started in on me just now. Cae and Bran were even kind of nice to me, this morning, like."

"Well, I suspect that if you just keep on taking Alli's insults like a man, then Cae and Bran will be nice to you again."

"Probably so. This be a strange place, Cengarn. I guess the old tales about the Slavers be true. You do all really be cruel and fierce, bain't?"

Rhodry was honestly shocked.

"Well, here, I suppose we'd seem such to you, but—"

"At least you don't take heads anymore. Or do you? I haven't seen any hanging on walls and stuff like the tales talk about."

"Of course we don't!" Rhodry stopped, nagged by a memory of a time he'd seen a lord run the head of a particular enemy onto a pike. "Well, only if we're truly provoked."

"You've never cut off anyone's head and tied it to your saddle, have you?"

"Never. I can give you my word on that, lad. Ych! And I never will, either."

Jahdo sighed in a relief so profound that it was comic. Rhodry was about to make a jest when he glanced round to see Matyc, standing between two sheds and watching them. And just how long have you been there, you bastard? Rhodry thought. Lord Matyc was beginning to gripe his soul, and badly.

"Rhodry," Jahdo was saying. "Cae did tell me that there's a princess in the dun. Be that true?"

"It is. Would you like to be presented to her?"

"I would. I never did see one, you know. I mean, my father would think I'm being silly, wanting to see her just 'cause she be a princess, but I do."

"Well, she's a pretty young woman, but ordinary enough, not like a two-headed calf or suchlike. Here, let's go into the broch and see if we can find her, and then you'd best get back to Meer. He shouldn't be left alone."

"He was going to nap for a bit, you see, and so he did say I might go outside if I wanted."

If Carra had been up in the women's hall, forbidden to all men except for the very eldest, Jahdo would have had to go without meeting his real princess, but as it was, they found her sitting down in the great hall with the gwerbret's wife, Labanna, and her two serving women. With their sewing in their laps, all four of the ladies had made themselves comfortable in curved three-legged chairs near the table of honor. At Carra's feet lay a big gray dog with a roach of black hair down his back, or perhaps, judging by his yellow eyes and the feral look in them, he was as much wolf as dog. Although Labanna and her women were the matronly sort, stout and gray-haired, Carra was more beautiful than merely pretty. Her wavy blond hair, cut abnormally short for a woman, due to some odd circumstances, framed a delicate face and set off large blue eyes. That particular day she was wearing a dress of fine blue linen, heavily embroidered with alternating bands of interlace and flowers around the neck and down the sleeves, and kirtled rather high to allow for her early pregnancy. Round her neck hung a pendant of reddish-gold, ornamented with roses in bas relief. Jahdo frankly goggled at her.

"Oh, she be lovely," he whispered. "And never have I seen such a fancy dress."

The Rhiddaer, Rhodry supposed, had to be a fairly rough place, then. As he led the boy over, he wondered what Jahdo would make of the finery round the High King's court in Dun Deverry. At their approach the dog rose to a crouch and growled.

"Lightning, whist!" Carra snapped her fingers. "Come round here. That's a good lad."

Reluctantly the dog slunk to the side of her chair and lay down with a small whine. Rhodry knelt in front of Carra and Lady Labanna and motioned to Jahdo to do the same.

"My ladies," Rhodry said. "May I present Jahdo to you? He's never seen a princess before, he says, and would like to meet one."

Carra laughed softly, and Labanna smiled.

"Well, by all means," Carra said. "But you'll have to tell me what to do. I'm rather new at princessing, you know."

"Very well, then," Rhodry said. "I say: Your Highness, may I present to you Jahdo of the Rhiddaer? If you accept, you incline your head in a slight and regal manner. Don't smile, now. Haughty's the look you want."

Carra tried to follow his instructions but ended up giggling. The older women smiled and shook their heads.

"It'll do," Rhodry went on. "Now, I say: Jahdo of the Rhiddaer, you have the honor of being in the presence of Princess Carramaena of the Westlands and her grace, the Lady Labanna, wife to Gwerbret Cadmar of Dun Cengarn. Then you bow from the waist—one hand behind your back, lad, and stay as straight as kneeling will allow—that's right. Bow to the princess first, and then the lady."

Carefully, solemnly, Jahdo followed his instructions.

"Very good," Lady Labanna pronounced. "And very well taught, silver dagger, I must say."

Rhodry noticed the serving women assessing him with shrewd eyes.

"My thanks, my lady," he said hurriedly. "We'd best leave your presence and not impose ourselves upon you any longer."

"Oh, Rhodry, don't be so stiff!" Carra laughed. "It's not like I've

got much to do this afternoon. Dar—er, the prince my husband, I mean—
is out hunting with his men again."

"Your Highness?" Labanna leaned over and laid a firm hand on her
arm. "The silver dagger is quite correct. There is a limit to the time he
may tarry in your presence."

Rhodry got up, motioning to Jahdo to join him, and bowed all round.

"I bid you ladies a good day," he said, smiling. "Come along, lad.
Time for you to get back to your master."

As they hurried out of the great hall, Jahdo was babbling about how
beautiful the princess was, but Rhodry barely listened. He was reminding
himself that if he wanted his past to stay hidden, he'd best roughen his
manners. All at once he heard the boy shriek in terror. Rhodry spun
round, found he'd drawn his sword without even thinking, and saw nothing at all, except for a pair of men riding in the main gate.

"What is it?" Rhodry snapped.

"Gods." Jahdo was shaking from head to foot as he held out a
trembling hand, pointing to the gate. "Gods. Riding in there."

"What?" Rhodry sheathed his sword again. "That's only a pair of
Prince Dar's men."

The two men of the Westfolk were dismounting, tossing their reins
to a waiting stableboy. Tall and slender, with moonbeam-pale hair, they
were both handsome fellows, except for their eyes, slit vertically like
those of a cat, and their long ears, as delicately curled as seashells. Jahdo
tried to speak but only made a choking noise deep in his throat. All at
once Rhodry realized that the boy had most likely never seen an elf
before.

"Here now," he said. "They're real flesh and blood, just like you
and me. They look different, truly, but they're much the same as us under
the skin. Why, doesn't a wolfhound look different than a gwertrae? But
both breeds are still dogs, and you could even get healthy pups out of
mating a pair, couldn't you? Prince Daralanteriel is a man of the Westfolk,
and Princess Carra's a woman of Deverry, and here she is, growing bigger
with his child every day. So you know that they must be much like us."

Jahdo's terror turned to puzzlement. The two elves waved at Rhodry
and strolled on by, heading toward one of the side brochs, where they
were quartered.

"But they do look like gods," Jahdo said at last. "Two times now I did see a god, and they both looked just like that."

"Uh, are you sure you didn't just see two elves?"

"As sure as sure, because the gods did appear out of nowhere and then disappeared again. One of them did come to the cell, when we were locked up, I mean. She just walked right through the wall and said we were going to be safe, and then she were gone. And not long after that you did come and take us to Jill, and Jill did make things well for us, and we were safe, just like the goddess prophesied."

It was Rhodry's turn for the surprise.

"Oh, indeed?" he said. "You run along and tend to your master, lad. I'm going to find Jill and tell her about this. I think me she'll find it interesting."

To Dallandra, the long night and morning that Jill had spent returning to Cengarn and questioning Meer and Jahdo passed as a bare couple of heartbeats, the brief interval of Time in which she flew over the water veil from the dark of a Deverry night to the gold of day in Evandar's country. Simply making that transition stripped away her bird form, and in the semblance of her real body, and in illusions of elven clothing, she found herself standing on a hilltop overlooking the silver river. All round her the grass stretched green, but stunted, browning in the shade of sickly trees. When she turned and looked in the other direction, she saw a mound of tangled weeds and muddy bricks, all that was left of a once-lovely garden.

On impulse she walked down for a closer look. When she'd first come to Evandar's country, well over two hundred fifty years past as men and elves reckon Time, he'd created this garden to please her. She remembered it as precisely geometric, a huge square marked off by brick walls and hedges and divided corner to corner by graveled walks that led to a central fountain. In each division red roses bloomed, surrounded by various other flowers she couldn't name, purple and blue and gold. Now the walls had fallen, the hedges gone wild or died back altogether, the walks lay hidden by burdock and dandelions, the roses fought with the weeds for sun. The few blooms she saw were no longer the doubled flowers of the cultivated rose but the simple five-petaled wild variety. In the middle, the marble basin of the fountain had shattered. Mossy chunks lay round the cracked shaft.

Out of sheer grief for something once lovely Dallandra started to walk in through the remains of a gate. In the snarl of weeds near the fountain, something moved with a scurrying little sound. She went frozen, one foot over the threshold, the other not, and waited till the sound came again. This time she saw someone peering at her for a brief moment before it drew back into the foliage—elven eyes in a pale gray face, snouted like a hog, though with a human mouth. One of the Wildfolk? But for all their pranks and malice those elemental spirits, sprite and gnome, undine and salamander, were harmless at root, especially to a dweomermaster like her. Here she felt danger, a sharp hard stab of dweomer warning stinging her heart. Carefully, slowly, she stepped back out of the precinct; carefully, slowly, she moved back a few steps, never turning round, keeping a close watch on the ruined garden.

"Dalla!" It was Evandar's voice from the hilltop. "What are you doing down there?"

"Come join me."

Although she could hear him hurrying down to join her, she never turned nor looked away from the garden.

"What's all this?" he was saying. "Oh, your garden's fallen into rack and ruin. Shall I build it up for you, my love?"

"Whist! Just be silent for a moment and watch. I thought I saw a member of your brother's court lurking round in there."

Out in the weeds something moved, stirred, then rose, standing up with a scatter of torn foliage—the owner of the snouted face, roughly human in form though stooped and twisted, wearing a tattered pair of brigga and naught else. At the sight of Evandar it whimpered, holding out clawed and clubby paws.

"Help us! Without you we have nowhere to live."

"You have everywhere to live," Evandar said. "All the world between the stars belongs to you."

The creature whimpered, shaking its head in a stubborn no.

"We want a real home, the home we know, the grass and the rivers of the Lands."

"Build your own, then. Or better yet, get that lord you serve to build them for you."

With one last cry, like a despairing baby falling into tear-stained sleep, the creature scuttled off. His arms crossed over his chest, Evandar watched it skittering over the billowing meadows till it disappeared.

"I suppose you think I should help them," he said at last.

"I honestly don't know what to think. The best thing for them would be to choose life and birth, just as your people should, but would it cost you so much to save their lands for them?"

"But I don't understand. Why should I do a thing for them that I don't want to do?"

The question was perfectly calm, perfectly civil, not petulant nor angry in the least. Its very placidity made her remember how alien he was, no matter how much an elf he looked.

"It would be a compassionate thing, a right thing, a—well, a loving thing to do."

Evandar laughed.

"But they're ugly."

"That's true." Dallandra was choosing each word carefully. "But they suffer, they have feelings even as you do."

"Them? My brother's little monsters? His ugly wretched brutes?"

Something came clear in Dallandra's mind.

"You made a country for your brother, but he had to fashion the bodies for his folk."

"Just so, and a botched job he did of it. Looking here, looking there, at the beasts as much as at the elves and men, taking a piece here, a piece there. Ych! Well, it's his concern now and none of my own."

"But you made him his country. Why?"

"I don't want to talk about him anymore, nor about the Lands, either."

"But I need to know more."

"I shan't tell you."

Evandar turned and began striding back uphill. Cursing his stubbornness under her breath, Dallandra followed, catching up with him at the top.

"Will you listen to me, please?" she snapped. "We've got to talk. I've learned some rather ghastly things."

"Elessario!" A flicker of real alarm crossed his face. "Is she safe?"

"She is, but for how long I can't say. You know that Alshandra's sworn to bring her back to this world, by murdering the child's new mother if all else fails. Well, she's raising an army to help her."

"Indeed? Then we'll deal with her once the army's raised." He hesitated, but only briefly. "Don't trouble me with all this now, not when there's been a spy skulking round my lands."

"He didn't look like a spy to me. He looked terrified."

Evandar turned away without bothering to answer. He snapped his fingers, and out of nowhere a silver horn appeared. When he blew three deep notes, like flames leaping out of the ground soldiers of the Host came charging up the hill. They gathered round him—how many, she couldn't tell—in a glitter of copper-colored mail and helmets, each man armed with a long bronze-tipped spear. His page hurried forward, leading two golden horses with silvery manes and tails.

"Evandar!" Dallandra snapped. "This news I've got—"

"Will have to wait. Ride with me, my love. It's not safe for you to linger here alone."

As Dallandra mounted, she saw that the foot soldiers had turned into cavalry, as suddenly as changes always came about in this country. In the clatter and jingle of silver-studded tack they followed Evandar as he led the way out with a whoop and a wave of his arm. Dallandra urged her horse up next to his as the road beneath flattened out along the river.

"We ride to the battle plain," Evandar called out.

Behind him the Host roared their approval, and silver horns blew.

As they trotted across the billowing plains, the ground steadied beneath them, and the grass turned green, swishing high around their horses' legs until they were forced to slow to a walk. On the horizon the distant cities settled down and turned solid, too, and gleamed here and there with lights in their windows or glints atop their walls as the day faded into a greenish twilight. A moon hung pink and bloated just above the horizon, never rising, never setting.

In that ghastly light they entered the forest, half dead, half living, and picked a slow way down a trail so narrow that they were forced to ride single file. Deep among ancient trees things moved and scurried, just at the limits of Dalla's vision, until she felt like screaming. Intellectually she knew that they were merely Wildfolk, but the intellect had little place in Evandar's country. Every twig that caught her hair or brushed her shoulder made her heart race. When she saw the beacon lighting the sky ahead she sighed in such relief that she sobbed aloud.

Evandar turned in his saddle to look back at her.

"How do you fare, my love?"

"Well enough." Since she hated to show him weakness, she forced out a smile. "It's a long ride for a dark night."

"True. But we'll be there soon."

He turned back again to guide his horse round the beacon, half the tree blazing, half as green as spring. In an uncertain dawn the army rode out of the forest. By then the river had sunk and dwindled to a white-water stream, cutting a canyon some twenty feet below and to the left of the road. Ahead lay plains, stretching on and on to a horizon where clouds—or was it smoke—billowed like a frozen wave, all bloody red from the bloated sun. Far out in the grasslands this hideous light winked and gleamed on spears and armor. Evandar laughed and held up his hand for the halt. When Dallandra rode up next to him, he grinned at her.

"I sensed him here, waiting. My brother, that is."

"I assumed that's who it was."

Out in the plain, the fox warrior broke ranks and trotted to meet them, but he tucked his helm under one arm and held his spear loosely couched and pointed at the ground. When Evandar called out orders, the Bright Court clattered to a stop behind him and reined their horses up into a rough semicircle by the river. Clad in glittering black helms and mail, their opponents wheeled round to face them, but they kept their distance. The fox warrior pulled off his helm and smiled with the glint of strong white teeth.

"Riding your border, are you?"

"I am," Evandar said, "and with good cause, it seems, being as I've found you here."

"If you'll not heal my lands, then someday I just might have to come take yours."

Evandar tossed his head back and howled with laughter.

"You mean you'd *try* to take mine. Do you truly think you'd win, young brother of mine?"

The fox warrior snarled with a draw of black lips that showed fang.

"You'd have attacked me long ago," Evandar went on, "if you'd thought you had a hope of winning."

"The matter's not been put to any kind of test, elder brother." In his mouth the word *brother* was an insult. "Did I not weave bodies for my folk when you mocked me and said I never could?"

Evandar merely looked him over with a small smile.

"So don't go puffing yourself up with pride," the warrior went on, rather too hurriedly for dignity's sake. "Besides, I came here on another errand, not on a matter of war at all, so you were twice wrong."

"Indeed?"

"You have a whistle that was stolen from me."

"I have it, truly, but stolen it was not. I found it upon my lands, and long ago you told me that it belonged to a rebel from your court."

"I told you that?" For a long moment he sat silently. "Well, he stole it from me."

"I don't believe you."

The warrior growled with a long flash of fangs.

"Why do you want it?" Evandar said.

"Because it's mine."

"That's no answer at all, and how can I gift you with it if it were already yours?"

"You'd give it to me?"

"Tell me why you want it, and I might."

The fox warrior considered, turning in his saddle to look back at his court, then swinging round again to face Evandar. His horse stamped and tossed its head. Dallandra felt a cold dread. She didn't want that evil whistle in enemy hands, and especially not after Rhodry had carried it for so long in the lands of men. Just as she was about to speak the fox warrior got in before her.

"I need it as a ransom," he said. "The rebels have taken one of my women, and they'll not give her back till I fetch them the whistle."

"They've grown so bold?"

"They have. They camp on my borders, and I've seen some of your folk among them, too, rebels all and gone off to follow Alshandra."

Evandar turned his head and spat on the ground.

"Then I'd recommend, younger brother, that you ride your borders as carefully as I ride mine."

"How can I when the Lands sicken and pale?"

Evandar ignored the question. When he snapped his fingers, the bone whistle appeared, clasped in his hand. The fox warrior started to lunge forward, then pulled himself and his horse under control.

"The loss of a woman is a painful thing," Evandar said. "Here."

When he tossed the whistle over, his brother snatched it from the air, then jerked his horse's head round and spurred it hard. As he galloped off toward the sunrise, the Dark Court howled and screeched, then spurred their own mounts to ride after him, until out of the retreating army it seemed that a vast storm rose up and raged, charging toward the horizon like a living thing. Just as suddenly it collapsed in a swirl and scatter of brown dust. The plain stretched empty and silent.

"I worry, my love," Dallandra said. "Why do those rebels want that whistle so badly?"

"Probably for the same reason they made the wretched thing in the first place rather than some new mischief."

Evandar turned his horse and jogged back to the waiting Host, leaving her no choice but to follow and to hope that he was right about the whistle. There were dweomerworkers who could pick up visions and the astral equivalent of scents from objects that a person had handled for a long time. She didn't want such on Rhodry's trail to work him harm.

"The border lies secure!" Evandar called out. "Let us return, and as a reward I'll raise the golden pavilion. Feasting and dancing, my friends! There'll be feasting and dancing."

Although the Bright Court roared its approval, Dallandra was troubled. She'd never seen him reward them before, and she suddenly wondered if he were trying to buy their wavering loyalty. As they returned home, she noticed again that the lands along their route seemed solid and renewed, as if he were pouring energy into them as they rode through. When they reached the meadow by the riverbank, they found the trees growing green and tall, with wild roses and daffodils sprinkled in the grass. The Host cheered, howling out Evandar's name over and over. He raised a hand in acknowledgment, but said nothing. They fell silent and dismounted, leading their horses away and disappearing as they reached the river, only to reappear without their mounts. Evandar sat on horseback and watched them unsmiling.

"What's wrong?" Dallandra said. "Somewhat is."

"Oh, I was merely wondering"—Evandar spoke so softly that only she could hear him—"if I've done a weak thing and thus a wrong thing. By giving my brother the whistle, I mean."

"It seems to me that you did a noble thing, helping him rescue his woman."

"True, in your mind and the minds of men and elves, and even in my own mind, that was a noble thing. But in his mind? It's likely that in his mind it was a sign of weakness and naught more. Well, what's done is done, even here in my country."

Much later, when it was far too late to turn ill into good, she was to remember this conversation and to realize that indeed, Evandar's profound mistrust of his brother had been justified.

While Dallandra was riding with the Bright Court, Jill had shut herself up in her chamber and devoted herself to scrying and meditation in a kind of border ride of her own. Occasionally a frightened page had knocked on the door to deliver food and water and take away leavings, but no one else had dared come near. Since despite its great power the dweomer has strict limits, Jill was working under considerable disadvantages. If she had ever seen these magical enemies in the flesh, she could have scried them out, or if they'd been nearby she could have scouted them on the etheric plane in her body of light. As it was, of course, she didn't even know their names, and they were apparently staying away from Cengarn, judging from the utter lack of any evidence of their presence.

When Jill traveled on the etheric, she used not the elaborate hawk form, but a simple, stylized version of her own body modeled out of the bluish etheric substance and joined to her physical body by a silver cord, navel to navel, along which energy passed back and forth to sustain both her flesh and her consciousness. Although this creation wasn't alive in any sense, it did serve as a vehicle for her consciousness and for her true etheric double, such as every person possesses. Unfortunately, this process has its own limits, particularly in the distance away from the body that a dweomermaster can safely travel. Without a constant influx of new energy, the body of light, as this thought-form's called, tends to start breaking up, leaving the etheric double naked and vulnerable, at the mercy of the winds and currents of pure force that flow constantly through the higher planes. Damage to the etheric double can kill a person, even a great master of dweomer. Any damage to the silver cord will kill the person instantly, by snapping the major link between the flesh and the upper levels of consciousness.

So Jill was forced to stay fairly close to Cengarn on her night hunts. She could travel farther in this form than she could as the hawk, but not truly far enough for her tastes—some hundred miles in any one direction, a good five days' ride for a raiding party, and a fair warning, certainly, compared to none at all, provided of course that she'd chosen the right direction in the first place. But always she was mindful that any new lot of raiders would have dweomer with them, powerful dweomer, no doubt, from a system alien to her. She simply didn't know what this other mazrak might or might not be able to do, though she doubted that the ability to hide an entire army would be among his or her powers.

At about the same time that Dallandra and Evandar were returning to the riverbank—though in their world only a few hours had passed— Jill decided that four days of futile effort were enough. First she had the pages bring up hot water for a bath, so she could change her clothes and make herself presentable; then she went down into the great hall to confer with Gwerbret Cadmar. As she was leaving the side broch, she saw Jahdo watching the kitchen boys kick a leather ball back and forth over the cobbles. When she hailed him, Jahdo came over, but she could see how frightened of her he was.

"How come you're not joining in the game?" she said.

"They won't let me. Alli won't let them let me."

"Oh. He *is* a little snot, isn't he?"

Jahdo merely shrugged, misery graved on his face.

"I'll have a word with the lad, if you'd like."

"Well, my thanks, my lady, but that'll only make it worse. Rhodry says I should call you my lady, by the way. Be that right?"

"It is, though I doubt if our arrogant Allonry considers me one."

"I don't suppose you could turn Alli into a frog, could you? Just for a little while, like?"

Jill laughed.

"I'm afraid I can't, Jahdo lad, though I'll admit that the sight of him hopping round would bring us all a good laugh. But here, other than our puffed-up lordling, have you and Meer been well treated? It's important to me, you know, and I left orders to that effect."

"We have, truly."

"Good. Run an errand for me, will you? Go find Rhodry for me, and tell him I've come down from the tower."

"I will." Jahdo brightened up considerably. "You know, I did hate him when he captured us, but now I kind of like Rhodry. He can't have done anything that dishonorable. Just because he be a silver dagger, I mean."

"Well, actually he didn't, but I don't dare tell you more. He'd be in a temper over it, if I did."

"Oh, well, now, I wouldn't want that."

Jahdo trotted off on his errand, and Jill went inside the great hall. At the dragon hearth of honor the gwerbret was sitting with his lords, while nearby the bard and Meer sat together, a harp between them, and discussed how it was played in low voices, so as not to disturb the noble-born. Jill was honestly surprised at how easily the Gel da'Thae and his boy had fitted into the life of the dun—until she remembered that they'd had days to do so, while she'd been shut up working. She still didn't want Meer going into the town, though, where the citizens would have no way of knowing that he was under the gwerbret's direct protection, and she made a mental note to tell him to stay away from it. At her approach the gwerbret rose, calling for a chair, and Matyc and Gwinardd inclined their heads in her direction. Jill made an impersonal bow all round.

"Your Grace, I've come to tell you that as far as I can tell, Cengarn's in no immediate danger. But I can't swear to you that the raiders won't return and soon. I believe that they have good reason to make another strike upon us."

"Indeed?" Cadmar said. "I see. Well, that's grim news."

"Your Grace?" Gwinardd broke in. "You know that my men and me are at your disposal for as long as you need us."

"And mine, too, of course," Matyc said, much more slowly.

"But you've got a few affairs of your own that could use a little tending, eh?" Cadmar smiled. "And the same goes for you, too, Gwin-

ardd, I'm sure. You both have my leave to return to your own lands if
it's needful, just so long as you return if our enemies do."

"I don't know if it is or not, to be honest, Your Grace," Matyc said.
"I'll send a messenger to my lady straightaway, by your leave."

"Of course. We all need to discuss this matter at some length, once
you've heard from your wives and stewards."

Matyc and Gwinardd rose, bowed all round, and strode off. Cadmar
watched them go, then turned Jill's way with a questioning eyebrow raised.
It was time, she realized, for honesty, but although she was perfectly
willing to tell the gwerbret everything she knew, she wondered how much
he would understand. A version of the truth would be, no doubt, truer
than the truth itself, and she had one ready.

"Your Grace," she said. "Let me put the matter simply. Someone is
trying to kill Carra in order to kill Dar's unborn child and heir. They
had faulty information about her whereabouts and sent that raiding party
into your territory too soon. I doubt me if they know what she looks like,
either."

"And so they killed every pregnant woman they found." Cadmar
looked physically sick for a moment. "Our prince has some ruthless enemies, I'd say. More like demons than men."

"Well, they're not truly human nor elven, either." Jill considered
for a moment, then decided to let him continue to think of the prince
as the enemy's target. "If they can kill him, you see, his clan will be
dead. He's the last heir to any of the seven thrones of the far west, so
that makes him the only heir to all of them, well, such as they are."

Cadmar smiled in a brief and painful way.

"The prince has told me the situation. Weeds and nettles, broken
stones and wild animals—that's my kingdom and courtiers, Your Grace,
or so the lad always says. But I take it that someone else wouldn't mind
having the title to the wrack and ruin, eh?"

"As far as I can tell, that's the case. The ancestors of the Gel da'Thae
destroyed the kingdom somewhere back in the misty past, and judging
from what Meer tells me, they still rule what's left of it. I wouldn't be
surprised to learn that some ruler or other wants to legitimize his claim.
It's a story that's happened many times before."

"They're human enough for that, eh? Wanting their title to rest
secure, without the true king running round siring heirs to it. An old

tale, indeed. Hum. I wonder if there's a faction seeking to overthrow this ruler? They could easily be threatening to bring back the old line."

"That's also happened, many times over. Meer's cursed close-mouthed, Your Grace, not that I blame the man, but there we are. I'm only going on partial information, but I think we can say that the situation's dangerous."

"You do have a gift for understatement, Jill. Very well. The prince and his people have done me many a favor in the past, and we have a treaty of sorts between us, too. Let's be honest. Without the Westfolk trading us horses, we'd all be walking to war, not riding, up here in these rocky hills. And now these raiders have caused me and mine great harm. I think me we can say it's war." The gwerbret rose, and of course, she stood with him. "I'll have a little talk, like, with my captain and the chamberlain, just to see how we stand in the way of provisions, men, spare horses, such things as that."

Jill bowed and left him, reaching the back door of the great hall just as Rhodry stepped in. Seeing him silhouetted against the sunlight made a dweomer warning clench round her heart. She turned so cold that she swore, shuddering. All his life Rhodry had been marked for some strange Wyrd, though none had ever been able to read all its omens, not even her master and teacher, who'd been the greatest sorcerer in all of Deverry's history. But at that moment in Cadmar's hall, Jill saw Rhodry's Wyrd hovering over him, as if on wings, and while she knew not what would bring it to him, she did know that it meant the death of everything he had ever been or ever hoped to be. Before she could stop herself, she cried out, clasping both hands over her mouth. Rhodry laughed, striding over.

"What's so wrong?" he said. "It's just me."

Jill let her hands fall.

"I've too much dweomer spinning round and round in my mind these days, Rhoddo. Forgive me—you just startled me, that's all."

He smiled, rocking a little on the balls of his feet, glancing round, as wary as a wild animal even in his temporary lord's hall. For a moment she could remember what it had been like to love him, all those many years ago.

"Forgive me," she said again. "My heart aches, just from sheer weariness. I'll need to talk with you, but there's no hurry."

"You're not ill again, are you?" His smile turned to alarm, and he reached out an automatic hand.

"Not in the least."

She dodged round him and made her escape, hurrying out to the fresher air of the ward, before she made a horrible mistake and told him what she'd seen. Some omens were best left unread. Yet all afternoon she found herself thinking of Rhodry, just in odd moments as she went about her magical work in the tower. All men die, she reminded herself. He's courted death for years, whether he was a silver dagger or a warlord in Aberwyn, and now he's pressing his suit night and day, him with his strange talk of his lady Death and the love he bears her. He's growing old. We both are. That's no doubt all the omen meant.

As twilight began to deepen over the dun, she found it impossible to stay in her chamber alone, as she usually did. She went down, slipped into the great hall, and got a seat back in the curve of the wall where none would notice her. That evening Meer performed, the first time anyone in Deverry had ever heard a Gel da'Thae bard. In the dancing light and shadow from torch and candle-lantern, Meer stood by the dragon hearth to sing. For the occasion he had put on a leather tunic that was painted in strange designs—characters from the elven syllabary, but oddly distorted and forming no words, set round with bands of flowers and looping vines that had obviously been copied from some elven source. He'd washed and redone his huge mane of hair, too, and all the little charms and amulets braided into it caught the light and glinted when he moved. As he sang he kept time on a small drum, slapping it with one huge hand, while his new friend the bard struck chords on the harp behind him.

Strange though the music was, every person in the hall sat rapt, aware that this was a momentous event they were witnessing. As Jill listened to the music rise and fall, wail and tremble, she came close to weeping, just from feeling the eternal sadness of the life that all sentient beings, whether Horsekin or elf or human, must share upon this earth.

3

PUELLA

A fortunate figure, especially when it disposes itself into the House of Gold and the House of Steel, and yet, such are all things female that at times it does undermine the figures round it and turn them into twisted ways. If it fall into the House of Lead a great heaviness shall wear it down, and sickness prevail over the strong.

The Omenbook of Gwarn, Loremaster

THE WOMEN'S HALL OCCUPIED the entire second floor of the main broch, except for the small, closed-off landing round the spiral staircase. In the company of the gwerbret's wife, Labanna, and her two serving women, Princess Carramaena spent much of her time in this ample chamber during the day, while her husband was off with the men, hunting and tending to other important affairs. Since before her marriage Carra had been only the third daughter of a very poor lord, down south Pyrdon way, she had never had the luxury of an entire hall at her disposal before, with cushioned furniture, tapestries on the walls, fresh braided rushes for carpeting, and silver oddments scattered round on little tables. Since it was up above the ward, the air there smelled clean and sweet, unlike the smoky den of the great hall, filled with men who smelled of horse sweat as much as their own.

She'd never had so much company or entertainment, either. If either the gwerbret or the prince were in attendance in the hall—and they could only enter with their wives' permission—a bard was allowed to join them as well, either to sing or to perform tales in the form known as "Conversations." When the women were alone, Labanna would devote herself to her work. She had the entire dun to administer, with all its problems of managing servants and supplies. The other women, and Labanna herself when she had time, occupied themselves with their perpetual sewing, since every piece of clothing that anyone wore in the dun was made there as well. Being as she'd always loved to sew, Carra was perfectly happy to do her share. She'd never had such a choice of fine cloths in her life before, either, nor so many colors of thread.

Carra had come to Cengarn only a few weeks before, fleeing a mar-

riage to a rich but ugly old lord that her brother had arranged, all unknowing that she was already pregnant by her elven prince. Since the
journey had been anything but easy, she'd arrived utterly exhausted. At
first, sitting in a sunny chair and basking in the attention of other women
had been the greatest luxury of all. Yet soon enough she'd recovered her
strength, and with the recovery she began to realize how greatly her
marriage had changed her life.

Back when she'd been living in her brother's dun, a useless third
sister dumped onto his care by the death of his father, Carra had had a
great deal more freedom to go about alone and on her whims. Now,
whenever she announced she wanted to go for a walk in the ward, Labanna
summoned pages to attend her. Whenever she wanted to leave the dun,
vast consultations occurred, and the equerry or chamberlain, if not both,
along with several men from her husband's warband, escorted her. If
Labanna had orders to give, such as to the cook in the kitchen hut, then
Carra was allowed to go with her, but again, the two women were never
alone, always moving in a crowd of pages, servants, and the noble-born
servitors themselves.

"I used to love to go riding," she remarked one day. "Just me, you
know. Or maybe I'd take a couple of dogs, and we'd just go trotting round
my brother's lands. Naught evil ever happened to me, really it didn't."

The three older women merely smiled, leaving her wondering if
she'd actually spoken aloud or not.

"Well," Carra went on. "Soon I'm going to be really pregnant, and
I won't be able to ride then. So that's why I want to go now."

"My dear child," Labanna said at last. "You're not some scruffy
younger daughter anymore, but a married woman and a princess. Soon
you'll be traveling to your husband's country, and that will simply have
to be enough adventure for you."

"Which reminds me," Ocradda broke in. As the elder of the two
serving women, she was Labanna's main confidante in the dun. "Is it
really wise to allow the princess to ride so far in her condition?"

"I feel fine," Carra said. "And I rode all the way here, didn't I?"

"A good point, Occa." Again, Labanna spoke as if Carra had said
not a word. "But I'm afraid her place lies with her husband's people.
When he rides out, she'll have to ride with him."

Carra decided that she hated hearing about her "place." She felt that she'd become a treasured plate or goblet, put safely on a shelf where none could harm it.

Her mood wasn't helped any by her husband's attitude. Every evening Dar appeared at the door of the hall to escort her down to dinner, and he spent of course his nights in the chamber they shared, but by and large he seemed to be leaving her alone as much as he could. She did realize that often he and his men went out hunting to repay the gwerbret's hospitality, because in this rough part of the country, venison provided much of the meat. At other times, though, it seemed to her that he was merely lounging round with his men instead of sitting with her. When she complained to him, he seemed mostly puzzled, remarking that he knew she had her woman's life to live and that he didn't wish to be in her way. She knew better than to complain to Labanna, who saw her own husband as rarely. But theirs was an ordinary sort of marriage, she would think, all fixed up by their clans, and Dar said he married me out of love. At times it seemed to her that all the best parts of her life were long over, and she was, after all, but sixteen summers old.

The long days they spent worrying about the foreign raiders began to get on everyone's nerves as well. The women had heard all the reports of farms burned, families killed, pregnant women butchered by men little better than beasts. The threat hung large that these raiders might only be the advance scouts for an army. One particularly hot afternoon they found themselves squabbling over very little until Labanna took charge.

"I think it would do everyone good if we set about planning some sort of feast or entertainment," Labanna said. "I'd best go down and consult with my husband, but this waiting must be hard on his riders, too." She glanced Carra's way, imparting a small lesson. "Morale, my dear, is very important out here in the border country."

"I'll remember that, my lady. If you're going down to the great hall, may I come, too?"

"Of course, dear. Just call the others, and we'll all go down together."

In a crowd of women Carra made her way into the great hall to find it filled with the various warbands, all drinking hard and looking, indeed, grim-faced and tired. At the table of honor Prince Daralanteriel was sitting with the other lords, but when Carra started to run to him, Labanna caught her arm with a motherly hand.

"The men are discussing matters of supply and suchlike, dear. We'll just take the second table over here. It gets a bit of a breeze, anyway."

Carra was forced to sit at the lady's right hand and watch her husband from some ten feet away. He was a handsome man, Dar, exceptionally so even for one of the Westfolk, with jet-black hair and pale gray eyes, cat-slit to reveal a lavender pupil. Yet it wasn't his good looks that had snared her heart, but the way that he'd always been so kind to her, when she'd been unhappy in her brother's dun. Now it seemed that he barely noticed she was there. She told herself that she was only being foolish, to say nothing of vain and selfish, but she'd left behind everything she'd ever known for Dar, her family and clan, a group of friends built up over her entire life, the familiar sights of her ancestral lands and those of her neighbors. Soon she'd be leaving the very country of her birth and her own people. When she wondered if perhaps she'd made a mistake, her heart thudded in sheer panic.

Eventually Labanna caught her lord's attention and was summoned to join the gwerbret. In the great hall men came and went; servants rushed round trying to keep everyone's tankard full; dogs barked and squabbled among themselves. When Labanna returned, the noble-born servitors came with her to discuss plans for a feast and a series of mock combats. As the great hall grew hot as well as thunderously noisy, Carra began to feel sick to her stomach.

"My dear?" Ocradda leaned over and touched her hand. "You look pale. Let me summon a page to escort you upstairs. I think a little nap would do you a world of good."

"I think my lady's exactly right," Carra said. "And my thanks."

Once she was back in her chamber, however, and lying down in the cool, she felt quite recovered. For a few moments she dutifully tried to sleep, then got up and wandered over to the window. When she looked down she could see all sorts of people scurrying round the ward. Probably Labanna had already set things in motion for this feast, a vast event that would take days to plan and prepare. It occurred to her that she might be able to go down for a walk and not even be noticed. Better yet! All at once she remembered the boy's clothes she'd worn when she rode away from her family to join Daralanteriel. If she put those on, perhaps she could sneak out to the stables and get her horse. She'd usually saddled her own horse, back in the days before her marriage. I'm not *that* pregnant yet, she thought. No reason I can't do it again!

Her plan worked. Dressed like a dirty page, with her hair hidden by an elven leather hat, she seemed to have turned invisible. Her own gelding, Gwerlas, a buckskin Western Hunter, turned out to be stabled right at the end of a line of stalls. She had him out and saddled without a soul noticing. Getting out of the dun through the guarded gates was, of course, a different matter altogether. She led Gwer up by a roundabout way, then waited in the partial shelter of a stack of firewood until the two guards started talking with a gaggle of servant girls. Carra mounted and trotted out, looking straight ahead as if she had every right to do so. Neither guard hailed her, and she turned down into the streets of Cengarn.

After a few hundred yards she dismounted again, because in that twisting maze, cluttered with townsfolk hurrying about their business, leading a horse was much easier than riding one. By traveling as straight downhill as the streets would let her she eventually found the South Gate, and there luck tossed her a fine roll of dice. Some twenty feet inside the gate a wagon had overturned with a spew of turnips. Teamster, townsfolk, and guards alike were clustering round, yelling at one another about the best way to get it righted. Carra mounted, urged Gwer to a trot, and was out and gone before anyone noticed the lad on the buckskin horse.

As soon as she was well clear, she kicked Gwer to a canter, turning off the road and heading to the west, riding randomly, and singing as she rode in the warm summer sun. Because of the sun, and because Gwer hadn't been getting the exercise he needed, she soon slowed him to a walk. They ambled through the meadows round Cengarn, ending up due west of the town, resting there to let Gwer cool down and Carra look up at the cliffs and the impressive dun above, then rode on to the trees that lined the little stream. She dismounted to let Gwer drink, stood beside him while he did, and simply watched the water flow in the dappled shade. For a few moments she was no longer a married woman and a princess, and that was all, truly, that she'd wanted—a few moments respite.

"I don't want to go back just yet," she remarked to Gwerlas. "This really is silly of me, but oh, it feels so wonderful to not be anything for a while, just me again. And besides, it's a good jest, slipping out on everyone like that."

He snorted, tossing drops from his muzzle.

"We should have brought Lightning, too. He'd have liked this, getting free of the dun. Oh!"

All at once her heart sank. As soon as they noticed she was gone, they'd be right on her trail to fetch her back, because Lightning would lead them straight to her. She'd forgotten about that when she'd carelessly left him behind. Unless—she could remember what the heroes always did in the bard songs, when their beloved's husband or some other enemy was hunting them down. She knelt, tested the water, and found it cold but not dangerously so to a horse's legs.

"It might work. Look, Gwer, the stream's really shallow, and it's nice and sandy on the bottom, so you won't slip or suchlike."

She mounted, urged him into the ford, and after a brief moment's argument got him to start picking his way upstream, heading roughly north. They were hidden, too, by the corridor of trees hugging the banks, so that none of the cowherds from the nearby farm even saw her as she rode past without leaving a scent that a dog could follow.

Rhodry was sitting in the great hall, drinking with Yraen over on the riders' side, when Prince Daralanteriel came racing in from the ward. In a towering panic he rushed right by the gwerbret and the table of honor, ran cursing through the crowd, and finally fetched up at Rhodry's side.

"Carra's gone!" he burst out in Elvish. "I've looked all over for her. Her dog's here, but her horse is gone from the stables."

All the men near slewed round to stare at this foreign outburst. Swearing in two languages Rhodry swung himself clear of the bench and stood.

"Tell the gwerbret! We'll get every man in this dun out scouring the countryside for her. By the Dark Sun herself, Your Highness, who knows what's out there, waiting for a chance at her?"

Dar made a keening sound deep in his throat, then turned and ran back to the puzzled lords, who had all risen from their chairs to stare at his untidy progress through the hall. Every other person in it was whispering in a buzzing tide of speculation. Rhodry quickly translated Dar's tale for the other riders, started to give Yraen an order, then stopped in sheer surprise. His friend had gone dead-pale.

"Do you know somewhat about this?" Rhodry snapped.

"What? Not in the least. What do you mean?" Yraen hauled himself to his feet. "I'm just—well—worried, that's all."

Terrified was more like it. For a moment Rhodry flirted with the implausible idea that Yraen might be a traitor; then the obvious occurred.

"Ye gods!" he hissed. "And a fine choice of a woman to fall in love with! She couldn't get much more above you."

Yraen swore and hit him in the ribs so hard that it hurt. Rhodry laughed, but under his breath to keep the others from hearing.

"No time to discuss the proprieties now," Rhodry said. "Go saddle our horses, will you? I'm going to stick right close to Lord Matyc in this hunt. You do the same."

Yet, in any event Rhodry and Yraen ended up separated, simply because not even one of the gods could organize a search party of over two hundred men without some confusion. Rhodry suspected, in fact, that Yraen had slipped away from him to avoid awkward questions. He reminded himself that tormenting a man like Yraen about a hopeless love affair was as much dangerous as cruel and put the matter firmly out of his mind.

When the search parties left the town, Rhodry simply joined Lord Matyc's men without waiting to be asked. Just in case Matyc took this chance to arrange some kind of accident for the princess, he was determined to be near enough to stop it.

While Carra may have been headstrong at times, she was never stupid. Even as she plotted a careful route from stream to thicket to rocks to stream again, she made sure that she kept the towers of the town always in view and close in case she needed to make a strong gallop back to safety. With his bloodlines Gwerlas could no doubt have outrun most of the horses in the entire province if he'd had to; to make sure, she rested him often.

When she first heard the hunting horns blowing, she was riding well to the east of Cengarn down a little lane between two plowed fields. She rose in the stirrups, cocking her head to listen just as they came again— a lot of horns, spreading out from the direction of the dun. At first she wondered why the men would start a hunt so late in the day; then she realized that Dar must have called out the warbands to look for her. Her pleasure at her joke turned sour.

"They're all going to be furious."

Gwer snorted with a toss of his head.

It occurred to her that if she could stay undiscovered long enough, she might be able to cut round behind them and slip back inside unseen, where she could, perhaps, pretend she'd never left. She might have fallen asleep in one of the gardens, perhaps, where Dar might not have thought to look for her. It was worth a try. She turned back the way she'd come and began retracing her circuitous route, from cow shed to stream to thicket to duck pond, spiraling in toward the city gates. Although she heard horns and even saw, at a great distance, horsemen galloping by, no one ever came her way.

When she was in sight of the south gates, she paused, rising in the stirrups to peer at the walled town, marching up its hills and looming over her. She could just pick out the tiny figures of guards, pacing back and forth. The east gate, she decided, would offer her the best chance of getting in unseen, simply because it was narrow and old, opening onto a little-used track that existed for the convenience of cowherds and farmers come to market with produce. Sure enough, when she approached the town from the east, she saw no one at the gates, neither standing watch nor loitering.

"Good," she remarked to Gwerlas. "The hard part, though, is going to be getting back through the dun gates. Well, one thing at a time."

She dismounted and led the horse in. The wall here stood a good ten feet thick, and the "gate" was more a tunnel with a stout oak and iron-bound door standing half-open at the far end. As they hurried through, heading for the sunlight and the town, she passed big piles of rocks, stockpiled to clog the opening in case of an attack. Just as she led Gwerlas out into the dusty street, a man stepped in front of her. She screamed aloud when he grabbed her arm, but it was only Yraen, snarling as he barred her way.

"I thought so," he snapped. "If you were clever enough to get out, I figured you were clever enough to try to get back in and pretend naught had ever happened."

"You let me go! I'm a princess now, and you're supposed to be humble round me."

"Don't you realize what a scare you've given us all? Ye gods!" He gave her arm a shake. "You could have been killed, riding out on your own."

"I was safe enough. I made sure of that."

"Hah! You without even a table dagger in your belt! And with all this talk of shape-changers riding the winds and evil spirits under every bush and stile! Are you daft?"

"All I wanted was to be alone for just a little while. You don't know what it's like, being shut up like a prized mare, never getting to do anything without half the court following you round."

At that he let her go.

"Well, I do know, as a matter of fact. But ye gods, Carra! I mean, Princess, Your Highness—you're right. My apologies. I forget myself."

"Well, it's hard to remember to be formal and all that when we nearly got ourselves killed together."

Yraen nodded, looking absently away.

"So we did, so we did. Here, mount up, will you? And I'll lead your horse back for you."

"I can walk, thank you very much."

"Ye gods, don't come over all haughty on me, will you? Get on your wretched horse before I put you on him."

"Just try." Carra set her hands on her hips.

For a moment they glared at each other.

"Well, I don't suppose your husband would take it kindly if I did lay hands on you. Walk if you want to."

Yraen turned on his heel and strode off toward the dun. Grabbing Gwer's reins, Carra followed, keeping his broad back in sight as he found them a path through the round houses and looping alleyways that led this way and that but always uphill. Finally she could stand it no longer.

"Yraen, don't be a rotten beast, will you? I'm sorry."

He stopped and let her catch up with him.

"I'll escort you back," he said. "Then I'd best ride out after the others and tell them you're safe."

"Well, truly, that's a good idea. Or I can find my own way back." She grinned at him. "I found my way out, didn't I?"

For a moment he kept his face expressionless, then slowly, as if he begrudged the effort, he smiled in return.

"I've got to get a fresh horse anyway. Here, I really should be leading Gwer for you."

When he held out his hand, she gave him the reins, and they walked side by side when they went on. Carra never knew what to think of Yraen. Although he was technically a handsome man, he was as cold and hard as a steel blade in winter, occasionally smiling, rarely laughing, always, it seemed, on the edge of some great rage. Even Rhodry, with his wild berserker fits, seemed more human, more warm that Yraen ever did. As they plodded along, his silence began to get on her nerves.

"I'm still surprised you knew where to look for me," she said.

"I know what a sneak you can be, that's all. So I thought, well, if I wanted to slip back into a dun, what would I do? And so I waited at the east gate, because that's the one I would have chosen, and lo! in you walked."

"A sneak! I do like that."

"Well, look at the clever way you plotted your escape from your brother. And I still don't know how you worked on Rhodry, after you met us on the road, I mean, to get him to guard you for the journey here."

"I still don't know, either. He was so odd, that night in that miserable little tavern where I met you both. He kept talking about his lady Death, and how I was carrying his death with me. It made me feel awful, actually."

"Don't take it to heart. He's talked that way for all the years I've known him." Yraen sounded deeply aggrieved. "I don't know why I keep riding with Rhodry, I truly don't, but I always stay even when I get a chance to ride some other road."

"Well, I suppose that two silver daggers are safer than one. On the roads and suchlike, I mean."

"That's true, of course."

They had reached the top of the market hill, the second highest in Cengarn, and a vast open space, partly grass, partly cobbled, where on each full moon of spring and summer the town held a fair, although its real purpose was providing pasture for cattle during a siege. From its crest they could look across to the dun, rising dark and grim, towering over everything round it.

"Oh, I hate to go back!" Carra said with a dramatic sigh. "Couldn't I run away with you, Yraen, and be a silver dagger?"

She started to laugh at her own jest, but the look on his face stopped her. For one brief moment his heart lay open like a night sky, so that she could pick out every constellation of desire and grief and frustration. Then he turned away with a snort.

"As if a skinny lass like you could ever learn to handle a sword!" he snapped. "Besides, there's this small matter of your baby to consider."

"Oh, I know." She could barely speak, desperately searched for some jest to cover her unconscious cruelty of the moment before. There was none. "And I have my place and all that. Yraen, I'm sorry."

He merely shrugged, staring across the little valley at the dun. For a few moments they stood together, wrapped in the misery of a revealed truth. Although Carra knew she was pretty, in her world beauty meant so much less than position and a good dowry that she had never thought of herself as desirable to men of her own kind. That Yraen would love her was completely unexpected, and more frightening than pleasing.

"I'm tired," she said at last. "Could you please lead Gwer and let me ride? You were right, back at the gate."

He smiled, briefly, and held the bridle while she mounted. During the rest of the trip back to the dun, neither of them said a word.

Although Carra had been hoping that she would somehow manage to slip past the women waiting for her in the great hall, her luck had left her for the day. As they walked through the gates, the guards shouted, calling out her name and cheering. Labanna, with the serving women and Jill right behind them, came racing out into the ward. Carra dismounted, bracing herself for the scolding of her life.

"My dear child! What could you have been thinking of?" Labanna started right in. "Of all the stupid, heartless—"

"Hush." Jill stepped in between them. "Your Grace, my lady, please. Will you leave her to me?"

Labanna scowled, but she made the dweomermaster a small curtsy and retreated to the company of her ladies. When Jill laid a firm hand on her arm, Carra wished that she could faint or perhaps even die. She was never going to be able to work Jill round by being contrite and winsome the way she'd planned to do with Labanna.

"Come up to your chamber with me, Carra," Jill said. "It's time we had a little chat." She glanced at Yraen, still standing nearby. "Are you going to fetch the others?"

"I am. Just going to get a fresh horse and find a hunting horn."

"Good. Tell Dar to come talk with me when you find him. Now. Carra, come along."

Feeling like a dog about to be whipped, Carra trailed along behind as Jill led the way up the spiral staircase. Once they were safely shut up in the chamber, Jill perched on the windowsill and motioned for Carra to sit down. She sat on the edge of the bed and wondered if she could pretend to faint—not and fool Jill, she supposed. For a moment the dweomermaster considered her with cold blue eyes that seemed to bore deep into her soul. All at once she laughed, a pleasant chuckle under her breath.

"Good for you," she said, still smiling. "I always knew you had spirit."

Carra felt herself goggling openmouthed like some village half-wit.

"Carra, listen," Jill went on. "Things will be different once you and Dar get out on the grasslands with his people, very, very different. Your life will have a much wider horizon there than any Deverry woman ever has here at home. Your life's likely to become more than passing strange, mind, but restricted it will not be. Now, until then, you need to behave like a Deverry woman. Can you understand that? I have naught but sympathy for you, lass, but there's no help for it. While you remain here in Deverry, you've got to be the lady and the dutiful wife. Can you do that?"

"Of course. Haven't I been trained for it, all my life?"

"Good." Jill smiled again. "But remember my promise. I don't know when you and Dar can return safely to his people. It might not even be till after the child is born. That depends on things that—well, on things, and some of them are matters of war. These are not the best of times, Carra." She stood up. "Don't worry about Labanna and the other women. I'll tell them that you've been properly scolded."

Jill left the chamber without another word, leaving Carra utterly confused. Yet, despite Jill's talk of war, she felt strangely cheered, thinking that some new and exciting life lay ahead of her. She rested for a while, then had a wash and changed her clothes. Although she had to summon all her courage to go to the women's hall, the other women made a great fuss over her, as if compensating for the terrible things Jill had said. Carra managed a few proper snivels for the look of the thing, but all in all, the matter was closed.

There remained her husband, of course. She was dreading his home-coming, but much to her surprise his reaction was similar to Jill's—a laugh and a certain sympathy. Once they were alone, he kissed her repeatedly, then sat her down in the single chair in their chamber while he paced back and forth. By then it was night, and in the glow of the candle-lanterns his chiseled face seemed leaner than ever, picked out as it was by deep shadows.

"Forgive me, my love," he said. "I thought that you'd want me to leave you be, here with the other women. Isn't that what Deverry women expect from their lords?"

"Well, most of them do, I suppose. Dar, your people must be very different from mine."

"Worlds and worlds different, my love, and I wish to every god of both our tribes that I could take you there straightaway. Life is cleaner out on the grasslands, clean and free and honest, not like here, all shut up in stone tents like animals in pens with the smell of filth hanging round everything. And everyone's always scheming and plotting and trying to get the gwerbret to like them best of all the lords and suchlike. Sometimes I want to heave, just sitting at that table with Matyc and Gwinardd and watching the fencing for favor going on between them. Truly I do."

His vehemence shocked her so much that she found nothing to say. He knelt beside her and caught her hand in both of his.

"Forgive me, I don't mean to insult your people."

"I'm not insulted, just surprised. I didn't realize how much you hated it."

"That's why I hunt so much. To get away, out to the wild country."

"I wish you'd told me! I thought you didn't love me anymore."

He laughed, then kissed her hand, first the back, then the palm.

"The gwerbret's a decent man," he said. "But he thinks of me as some kind of savage. He's been telling me how to treat you, you see, since you're a civilized woman with civilized expectations and all that. And of course I've been following his advice. Like a dolt. I thought you'd want me to."

Carra laughed and threw her arms round his neck to kiss him.

"Well, then," she said. "I must be a howling savage myself, because I fell in love with you long before you took the gwerbret's lessons."

"Good." He sat back on his heels and looked away, his eyes pools of shadow. "By the Dark Sun herself I wish we could just get out of here."

"Why can't we? What's so wrong?"

"A very great deal, my love. The Wise One talked with me when we returned."

"The who?"

"Jill. My apologies. Wise One is what we call dweomermasters, out on the grass. She didn't tell me very much, or I should say, she wouldn't tell me any details, wouldn't answer any whys and hows and wherefores, but she said over and over that some great danger's brewing, whether raiders were riding for Cengarn or not."

"She said somewhat about a war to me, too, but naught that was clear."

"They deal in omens and strange speaking, the Wise Ones." Dar sighed profoundly. "I wanted to take you along the next time we hunt, you see, but she absolutely forbade it."

"Oh, I wish she hadn't! I used to love to ride to the hunt. Why did she say I couldn't go?"

"Because of the danger. Carra, I don't understand all of this, but someone's trying to kill our baby."

She clasped both hands hard over her mouth to stifle a scream.

"Jill said I shouldn't tell you, as if you were a child yourself, but you have to know."

Carra shuddered, turning in her chair to see if the drape over the window had blown back in some cold wind, turning back again, feeling sick and frozen and furious all at once.

"I do have to, truly." Her voice sounded so thin and high that she was shocked. "Why? Who?"

"I don't know. An enemy with the dweomer, Jill said, and that's all she'd tell me. But that's why we've got to stay near a dweomermaster. Right now she can't travel with us to the Westlands, because of the danger here to everyone else, and so here we are, stuck where she can watch over us. Eventually, she said, she'll help us get home again and find another Wise One to protect us. But for now, well."

She nodded her understanding, feeling her heart pounding hard in her chest. All she could think of was weapons and killing. She wanted to find that enemy and rend it, stab it, send it screaming to the Otherlands to freeze in the third hell for ever and ever. What happened to her seemed unimportant, but her child—that they would threaten her child!

"What's wrong?" Dar snapped. "You're dead-pale. Do you need to lie down?"

"I don't. Dar, I'm so glad you told me this. I understand a lot of things now, like why I have to be so careful." Unconsciously she laid her hands on her stomach. "For both of us."

"Good." He kissed her, then a second time. "Shall we go down to the great hall together? The Gel da'Thae bard is singing again."

"Let's. I do hate sitting up here in the same old room, and it's going to be worse now, wondering what this enemy's plotting and all of that."

"Well, as long as we're under Jill's protection, we'll be safe enough, I suspect. She seemed to think so, anyway, and after all, there are soldiers all round you, the gwerbret's men as well as mine."

"Oh, I know. I wish I knew how to use a sword, though, just in case."

He laughed, kissing her on the forehead.

"I don't think that's truly necessary, my love. You have me to do the fighting for you."

For a moment Carra felt like kicking him. There were some ways in which the men of the Westfolk and the men of Deverry were much alike.

Apparently rumors of her escapade spread into the town, for the very next morning Otho the dwarf came up to the dun to visit, just to see for himself, or so he said, that the princess was safe and sound. He brought along with him a young, dark-haired fellow, as short and stocky as he was but beardless except for some bushy sideburns, whom he introduced as Mic, his nephew.

"Do you remember the letters I sent off weeks ago?" Otho said. "To my kin, like, telling them I was here in Cengarn? Well, turns out that some of 'em are glad enough to see me again. My cousin Jorn was already lodging in Cengarn on business, and now young Mic here shows up with another cousin, Garin. Looks good, looks good—not that everything's settled yet."

"That's wonderful," Carra said, smiling. "Come upstairs with me. I have a special chamber, you see, for receiving visitors."

During the visit Mic said little, mostly ate his way through the tray of sweet cakes that Carra's maid brought up, but Otho was full of gossip from town and dun both.

"When are you going to pay Rhodry?" Carra asked him finally. "He keeps grumbling about it."

"Oh, I've had the coin for him for a good long time now. It's a jest, like, that's all, me putting him off. Him and Yraen both, they get so indignant over their wretched hire!"

"Well, maybe so, but you can't blame them. It's all they've got in life."

"Hah! They could have chosen better. Well, that's unfair to Rhodry, but young Yraen decided that he had to have the dagger, and not one word of sensible advice would stop him from leaving his kin and clan and riding the long road."

"Really? Here I thought he'd done some awful thing, like all the rest of them. All the rest of the silver daggers, I mean, not his kin."

"Not Yraen, neither. That's not his real name, of course. No mother names her cub for an ingot of iron, not even among my people. But he was glamoured of the idea of riding the long road, you see, and badgered Rhodry into taking him on. He's from a noble house, Yraen." Otho drooped one eyelid and held up a sly finger. "A very, very noble house, or so I think. Close to the throne, like."

"By the goddess herself! How very odd!"

"It is, truly. Why anyone would leave the High King's court to ride the long road is beyond me. He's a strange one, Yraen, though he has his reasons, I suppose, whether he knows them himself or not." All at once Otho looked away, as if something had pained him.

"Is there a draft from that window?" Carra said, glad to have a change of subject. "I can get my maid to—"

"No need, no need. I was just remembering somewhat, like, from a long time ago." Otho seemed profoundly sad. "I should pay those coins over, my lady. You're right, you're right. The jest's gone on too long."

"Well, I—" Carra hesitated, profoundly uncomfortable, blaming herself for the odd turn in the talk. "Mic, would you like that last cake? Don't be shy. Help yourself."

The young dwarf blushed scarlet, but with a sidelong glance at his glowering uncle, take it he did. For the rest of the visit Carra kept the conversation firmly on the subject of Otho himself and his kinsfolk in

Cengarn. But later that day, as she walked in the ward with the other women and their usual escort, she saw Yraen standing by the stables as they passed. He turned to watch her, his face carefully arranged into indifference, all the while that they were walking by. As they turned to go into the walled herb garden and out of sight, she glanced back to see him watching still.

From her tower room Jill happened to see the women passing by below, as well, but she never noticed Yraen, not that she would have thought much about him if she had. All that morning she'd been studying the books she'd brought back with her from a recent trip to the Southern Isles, looking for one last clue to a puzzle that had haunted her for years. Rhodry wore a ring given to him by his father a long time past, a simple silver band, graved with roses on the outside and a word written in Elvish characters on the inside, although when sounded out the word made no sense whatsoever in any language. She'd determined that it was a name, and a very peculiar kind of name indeed, and that Evandar had graved it there before passing it along to Rhodry's father. Apparently Evandar believed that the owner of the name had some crucial role to play in the dark days ahead. Most likely it would act as a guardian to the unborn child.

So far, so good, but why give Rhodry the name and naught more? The name must have had some special significance beyond identifying its owner, but Evandar refused to unravel his own riddle, simply because he was Evandar and for no better reason at all. At times Jill wondered if she hated him, meddling with all their lives this way, but there was no doubt that she needed his help if she were going to keep Carra and the child safe. As she read, turning page after page of obscure lore, Wildfolk gathered to watch her, a gaggle of gnomes upon her table, poking things best left alone, sylphs hovering above her like bubbles in the glass of air, sprites wandering back and forth at her feet. One particular gray gnome, all long limbs and warty nose, materialized right on top of her book, in fact. With a laugh she moved him to one side.

"This must seem tedious to you," she remarked. "It's beginning to be so for me, I'll tell you. I wish I knew someone who's got more lore than I—ye gods! Meer."

When she banged the book shut, dust puffed, and the Wildfolk disappeared.

After a lot of asking and searching through the dun, she found Meer round back of the stable, sitting on a wagon bed and taking the sun while nearby young Jahdo curried their white horse. The pair spent a lot of time with their horse and mule, or so she'd noticed, and when she found them Meer was holding one of the stable cats in his lap as well, stroking the animal absentmindedly while he chatted with the boy.

"Good morrow, Jill," Jahdo sang out as she approached. "Meer, it be Jill, come to see us."

"And a good morrow to you, mazrak," Meer rumbled. "I assume your coming bodes good, at the least."

"Probably not," Jill said, smiling. "It never does these days. I've come with a lore question for you, good bard."

"Indeed? Well, answer me one and I'll consider answering yours."

"Fair enough."

"Jahdo here tells me that Princess Carra is married to a man of a tribe called the Westfolk, and it seems that they're the horseherders who saved the Rhiddaer people when they fled the Slavers, all those long years ago."

"That's quite true."

"Ah. And, says Jahdo, these people have the same form as the gods."

Puzzled, Jill glanced Jahdo's way. He nodded a vigorous yes.

"Well, then, I suppose they do," Jill said. "I've never seen one of your gods, so I wouldn't know."

"Huh. I should have thought of that. Of course you wouldn't. No doubt you have gods of your own, and why would mine appear to you? Well, then. That tears that. No offense to you, lad, but I was hoping for another view, as it were, of the matter."

"Oh, I know," Jahdo said cheerfully. "But they be just like the blessed lady who did come to us in our cell."

"Rhodry told me about that, by the way." Jill hesitated, wondering if she should tell him the truth, then decided that if it comforted the boy to think Dallandra a god, well and good. Besides, leaving him his belief was a fair bit easier than explaining. "Meer, I don't know what to think about the resemblance."

"No doubt these Westfolk were formed in the images of the gods for some divine purpose."

"It could well be, for all I know. Or wait, Meer. They're refugees, that's all, from the Seven Cities. The ones your people hold now."

Meer tossed his head back, then muttered something in his own tongue that might have been a quick prayer.

"The Children of the Gods, then," he whispered, awestruck. "Are you telling me, mazrak, that immortals lodge in this very dun?"

"I'm not, because they're as mortal as you or I, though they do live a very long time."

"Ah. If they're not immortal, they can't have lived in the Seven Cities of the Far West." Meer's voice turned tight and hard. "They must just be those horseherders."

"Well, these elves didn't live there, truly. Their ancestors did. I assume they made the images of the gods you know to look like themselves."

Meer growled long and hard.

"What's so wrong, good bard?" she spoke cautiously. "I meant no offense."

"Indeed? Then why do you speak sacrilege?" He hesitated, on the edge of saying more, then merely grunted.

All at once Jill realized that she stood to lose his goodwill.

"Well," she said. "No doubt you're right about their origins. It was all a long time ago now, anyway."

For a moment he sat silently, his hands tight on his staff, his massive head inclining toward her; then he made a sound under his breath that was half a snort, half a laugh.

"And what was your question?" he said. "If it skirts the edge of impious things, as this other talk's done, then I shan't answer it."

"Well, then, I'll hope it's not impious. Do you know any lore pertaining to dragons?"

"A fair bit, truly." Meer relaxed, baring his fangs in a smile. "It's one of the fifty-two required topics for a bard who would be more than a singer at feasts and funerals."

"My grandfather did see one once," Jahdo piped up. "Flying north of our town. And the day after a farmer did tell how two of his cows did get taken, both at once, like, by the beast."

Jill started to make some jesting remark, then realized that the boy was dead-serious. Something about his almost offhand sincerity convinced her that he was speaking simple truth, repeating not some tall tale but an actual incident. Her blood ran cold. This thing is real, she told herself. Only then did she see her own disbelief, that in spite of all her searching for lore, in spite of all the long hours she'd scried and pondered, she'd honestly thought, somewhere deep in her mind and until this very moment, that the creature and its name were merely some peculiar prank or jest of Evandar's.

Somewhere round the middle of the afternoon, Rhodry was walking across the ward when he saw Jill hurrying to meet him. He paused, smiling as he waited, but the grim look in her eyes soon wiped the smile away.

"What's so wrong?" he said.

"Naught. Well, except for everything, of course. Rhodry, I need to talk with you, somewhere we can't possibly be overheard. I think we'd best try the rooftop."

They climbed the spiral staircase to the top chamber of the main broch, a squat and narrow space stuffed with bundled arrows. In the ceiling a trapdoor and wooden ladder led out to the flat roof. Cengarn fell away from them, their view tumbling down the city's hills and spreading out into a pool of green farmland, striped with forest, stretching farther and farther until the mists swallowed their sight at the horizon. Jill walked over to the rim's wall, barely three feet high, and sat, looking down so far and so casually that Rhodry could barely stand to watch her.

"Do you enjoy it when you fly?" he remarked.

"I do, at that. It's a glorious feeling."

"I rather thought you would, knowing you as I do. If ever there was a soul born to fly free, it would be you."

"You can still charm a lass's heart, can't you, Rhoddo? Or an old woman's. Come sit down."

"Shan't, if it's all the same to you. Not there, anyway."

She laughed with a toss of her silver hair.

"Well, mock me all you like, but I've never fancied being up this high. Climbing the Cannobaen light used to turn my guts, not that I would ever have admitted it then, back when I was young. Besides, if I should fall, I couldn't sprout wings to catch myself like you can."

"Well, then, we'll have to get you the loan of a pair. That's why I wanted to talk with you, in fact."

"Oh, ye gods! What now?"

"How gracious you sound."

"It's enough to drive a man daft, having sorcerers jest with him."

"Why do you think I'm jesting?"

"Well, all this talk of wings, of course." He stopped, suddenly wondering if he should be afraid.

"Not a jest at all. It has to do with that word graved inside your ring."

Reflexively he held up his right hand, and the silver band flashed on the third finger.

"Arzosah Sothy Lorezohaz." Jill formed each word carefully. "As far as I've been able to figure out, that's how you should pronounce those written characters, and the pronouncing of them is truly important. Your life's going to depend upon it."

"What? What is it, some kind of spell?"

"It is and it isn't. It's a name, but a name that's a spell by its very nature. The name gives you control over the owner of the name, you see."

"I don't see anything of the sort, my thanks. Who owns it?"

"A dragon, as a matter of fact."

Rhodry started to laugh, but she looked at him so mildly, so blandly, that his mirth spilled and ran.

"There's no such thing as dragons," he snarled. "Except the kind they have in Aberwyn, pretty pictures to put upon a banner or a bit of jewelry."

"Not true, Rhoddo, not true. Up in the Roof of the World there are a few, a very few, of the great wyrms, living in solitude, and they're much like the legends and bard tales paint them, too. Or so I have it on the very best authority."

"Now wait a minute. Whose authority?"

"Er, well." She glanced away in faked indifference. "Evandar's."

"Ye gods! That crazed creature? How by all the hells and their privies can you trust one word of what he says?"

"I had a feeling you were going to be difficult about this."

Rhodry snorted profoundly and began pacing back and forth, his hands shoved into his brigga pockets.

"Will you listen to me?" she snapped.

"I'm listening. Spout away. The bard here's a melancholy man, and I could use a good jest."

He heard her make a sound that was almost a growl.

"Still as pigheaded as always, aren't you?" she said at last.

"I'm *pigheaded*? You drag me up here and start telling me crazed tales, and then when I don't hang on every word like a truckler you call me pigheaded."

"Well, maybe I've been a bit unfair."

It was his turn to growl.

"Will you stop pacing like that? You're driving me daft."

With a melodramatic sigh he sat down on the roof near her feet.

"Very well. Talk away."

"I'll try to make things clear. You remember your father's tale, that a mysterious being gave him the ring, announcing that it was for one of his sons. Well, that person was Evandar in disguise. He's the one who graved the name into the ring, because of a vision he had."

"And can we believe a word of anything Evandar tells us?"

She considered this question seriously.

"I think we can in this case. Besides, Meer's told me much dragon lore, and it matches what Evandar says. They can think and speak, and they put great store in their names. They believe that if a man knows their true name, he controls them."

"I'm not sure if I trust Meer any more than I do Evandar."

"Well, he's the only loremaster we've got who knows one wretched thing about dragons."

"I suppose so. Do you think that's true, about the name controlling them?"

"It doesn't matter if it is, so long as they believe it."

"Sounds a risky thing to me, frankly, hoping they'll believe when the least thing could prove them wrong. But now wait. I don't understand. Why is the dragon so important?"

"Evandar had a vision. He saw the beast guarding Carra's child once it was born, and helping Dallandra in her work, and then at length guarding the ruins of a city he thought to be Rinbaladelan. So he found the dragon of his vision and wheedled its name out of it, somehow or other. I don't know how he managed, but he did."

"Oh, very well. Suppose I accept that. Suppose, for the sake of argument alone, that he did indeed have the vision, find the wyrm, and grave its name on this convenient little bauble. Why give the ring to me?"

She tilted her head to one side and considered him for so long that he began to feel uneasy.

"I'll answer that if you wish," she said at last. "If you truly, truly wish it, Rhodry, I will answer. But I warn you, the answer will tear the way you think about the world into pieces, and the way you look at your life and at other men's lives as well."

He got up and began pacing again, back and forth. To the south the hills dropped away to farmland and the settled kingdoms that had bounded his whole life. To the north he could see with his half-elven sight to a far horizon where hovered white peaks, whether only clouds or the actual mountains he couldn't tell, but a promise of the Roof of the World. The view was beautiful, even alluring, calling him, daring him, even, to risk that distant height. He could climb another height, this one of the soul, if he dared. All he had to do was ask. She would answer. He spun round to find Jill waiting, her hands patient in her lap. All he had to do was ask.

"You want me to go hunt this dragon," he said instead.

She smiled, and the moment broke between them.

"Not to kill it or suchlike. To find it and get it onto our side."

"And how do you expect me to do that?"

"By talking it round. Meer swears up and down that the great wyrms all speak Elvish."

When he rolled his eyes heavenward in disgust, she growled again. He laughed.

"And will you be coming with me?"

"I can't. I've got to stay with Carra, for one thing, and for another, there's trouble brewing here."

He strode back to the north side of the roof. Far away the white glimmerings of mountains danced on the horizon.

"Jill, I've always been a warrior, whether it's been as an honored lord in Aberwyn or a road-filthy silver dagger. In all the battles I've ridden I've never faced a man stupid enough to call me a coward. You know that, and you know it isn't fear that's making me hesitate now. The thing is, what do I know of wild country? Ye gods, all my fighting's been done in armies, with supply trains right at hand. I'm no trapper or forester, to go tramping off through the woods looking for some wild beast."

"Now that, alas, is true spoken."

He walked over to the wall and forced himself to look down. Far below, the stableyard lay tiny, with horses the size of cats and grooms like mice. For a moment he wondered what it would be like to swoop down, free for one glorious moment before the cobbles brought him death. He made himself look up.

"I can see why you didn't want anyone overhearing this story."

"For fear they'd think I'd gone mad?" Jill sounded amused. "To tell you the truth, Rhoddo, I'm rather surprised at myself for believing what Evandar says, but you see, it makes sense of a lot of things I've learned for myself, ties them all up. You will go fetch the dragon, won't you?"

"How can I promise you that? I'll certainly go try." He grinned at her. "Try with all my heart and soul, because it seems a fine way to court my lady Death, if naught else. But to promise you that I'll succeed would be a stain upon my honor and a waste of breath both."

"True enough. You have my heartfelt thanks."

She stretched, cat-lazy in the warm sun, smiling a little, human again for that brief moment—until he realized how casually she took his talk of his lady Death, as if she knew perhaps better than he did how close his suit was to a successful outcome. He hesitated on the verge of asking outright, but she turned away, her smile fading, to look across the uneven rooftop.

"There's somewhat that I've got to teach you," she said. "But I'm afraid of being overheard, no matter where we go in the dun, even up here."

"Is it as secret as all that?"

"Well, it is and it isn't. Every priest in the kingdom knows how to do this, but I don't want the wrong people knowing you know."

"That doesn't make much sense."

"It aches my heart to say this, but from now on, I fear me that not much of what I say is going to make a cursed lot of sense. But for the love of every god, trust me enough to do what I say. Can you do that, Rhoddo? Will you?"

"I'm naught but a silver dagger, riding at some other man's command. Lead away, cadvridoc, and I'll do my best to follow."

She smiled, but briefly.

"Well and good, then. Sit down, will you? If we had time, I'd explain everything, but we don't, and so you'll have to learn this by rote. Meer's lore insists that speaking a dragon's secret name gives you power over the beast, and Evandar swears up and down that the name inside the ring's absolutely correct. But you can't just say it out like you'd say any name—oh, Jill, is that you—or suchlike. Or even like you'd say the king's name, all proper and full of courtesy. There's a dweomer way of pronouncing these things, and you've absolutely got to have it down right. If you don't, and you do face this creature, it's most likely going to kill you."

"I somehow guessed that."

"You don't have to yell and scream, mind, but you've got to bring the sound up from your very heart and soul and make it vibrate like a loosed bowstring. First you breathe very deeply and slowly, to fill your lungs and steady yourself down, then you bring the sound out." She paused, thinking hard. "I can't describe it in words. I'll have to show you, but ye gods, I don't want anyone hearing!"

"We could ride out to the countryside?"

"I don't dare leave the dun, either. Of course, if a thunderstorm or suchlike should come up, we could make all the noise we wanted up here without anyone being the wiser."

Rhodry looked up at the clear and sunny sky.

"Not likely, is it?" he said.

Jill merely smiled.

Some little while before sunset the storm hit. Rhodry was walking across the ward when he felt the wind, whistling up cool and sharp from the west. He trotted over to the outer wall, scrambled up to a catwalk, and watched the sky from this perch with a view free of the encircling dun. Far off to the west the sun was sinking in a huge billow of black cloud, rising above hill and forest and sweeping toward Cengarn. Often out on the grasslands he'd seen storms like this, charging unobstructed over the plains, but never in hill country. The clouds headed for the town so purposefully that for a moment he feared some vast and unnatural fire; then he remembered Jill, and her smile.

Just as the sky was darkening over, and the wind was turning damp, Jill hailed him from the ward below. It was time, he supposed, for his lesson. When he climbed down, she remarked as much.

"If there's lightning with this storm," he said, "we'd best not go up on the tower roof again."

"Oh, we'll be safe enough."

Up on the high tower the wind hissed and whistled round them. Off to the west Rhodry could see the occasional flash, and tardy thunder rolled their way. Down below servants and warriors rushed back and forth, getting horses into the stables, dragging firewood under overhangs, dashing at last for shelter themselves as the first fat drops of rain hit. Rhodry felt one splash on his cheek, then nothing, even when it began to rain steadily all round. When Jill laughed at his surprise, he realized something that his memories of her and their love affair had kept him from seeing until this moment, that she had changed far beyond the woman he once had loved, so far that whether she was a beauty or a crone, or even whether she was male or female, simply no longer mattered. She stood beyond such things, a consciousness that used flesh for her own purposes rather than being bound by flesh, and one that held power over far more than her own flesh.

In a wash of blue glare lightning struck close; thunder boomed and rolled round the dun; she laughed with a toss of her head. Rain poured down like a silver curtain, sheltering them from casual sight, leaving the spot where they stood bone-dry. All at once he was frightened of her. Against the hiss of rain she raised her voice to be heard.

"Remember what I was telling you earlier?"

He nodded yes.

"Listen to me, then. This sound means naught, by the way. It's just a sound, not a dweomer call."

He was glad that she'd told him. She breathed out a long "ah" sound, such as a bard will use to cover a word he's forgotten, but the sound was neither spoken nor sung, more like a hum, perhaps, but strong and deep, resounding from her very soul, as she had said, quivering like a live thing, if indeed a sound can be said to live, vibrating like a harpful of strings. It took a long time to die away, even on the wet, heavy air.

"Try it."

"Oh, here, I could never do that."

"I think you can, Rhodry. For reasons I can't tell you, mind, but I think you can. There's more music in your soul than you might know."

At first he felt embarrassed, as if he'd become some sort of half-wit, standing on a roof and bellowing. Yet for her sake he tried, over and over, making all sorts of yells and hisses and a couple of truly foul remarks as well until all of a sudden something came clear without his truly knowing how it did, just as when a child learns to whip a top, flailing away too lightly, then too forcefully, until suddenly the thing spins. He felt the sound well up deep, seemingly of its own accord, and flood through and out of him, shaking his entire body. Once learned, he knew he would never forget—again, just like that child.

"Splendid!" Jill said, grinning. "You've got it. Now you've got to learn the name."

A syllable at a time she drilled him, over and over till he wanted to scream at her instead of the dragon. He remembered learning how to use a sword, and the endless drills. If she were right, his life depended on this practice more than it ever had on his skill with a blade. As he worked, vibrating each part of the name, he felt that he grew in height, towering up, yet made of nothing more substantial than the clouds round them, weightless, floating up from the stone, trembling yet charged with power stronger than the lightning. Finally, just as the night was growing so dark that he could barely see her face, she pronounced him good enough—for the time being.

"We'll have to do this again and again," she said. "But I don't want you going hoarse on me. Try the whole name, Rhodry. All of it together in one long breath."

He gathered as much air as he could and growled it out.

"Ar Zo Sah Soth Ee Lor Ez O Haz."

For the briefest of moments he felt answered. It wasn't a word, nothing so concrete, more of a touch of mind on mind, a living presence, a soul, hearing his call, turning his way. The feeling vanished, leaving him spent. He felt as if he were falling, shrinking as he fell, tumbling and swooping through clouds and a long way down to hit hard ground.

"Rhodry, ye gods! I'm sorry!"

In the gathering night Jill's pale face swam before him. He realized that he was kneeling on the roof with her beside him. She flung one arm round his shoulders, or he would have fallen onto his face.

"I'm truly sorry," she repeated. "I forgot that you've never done this before."

He nodded, panting for breath.

"It's rather like some townsman who's never ridden a horse," she went on. "And then ends up spending a day in the saddle. You'll feel this on the morrow."

"No doubt." He managed to smile. "But will I pass muster?"

"You will. Oh, that you will! I told you you had a streak of music in your soul, didn't I? Now let's get you down to the great hall, where it's warm. It's a bit damp up here. You need to eat, too. Food's the best thing at a time like this."

Sure enough, after a plate of bread and cold meat, washed down with a couple of tankards of ale in the company of other men in the great hall, Rhodry felt his usual self. Screaming the name into the rain seemed like an odd dream he'd had and nothing more, even though he knew that knowledge was his now forever. As he mulled it over in memory, the entire day turned strange and dreamlike, yet menacing at the same time. Jill and her wretched questions, he thought. A lot of horseshit, thinking that a man might live more lives than one! Couldn't be possible. And what if it was? Just what if? I could have asked her. She would have answered. When he found himself remembering the white mountains, the height at the edge of his view, his mind skipped and shied.

"Somewhat wrong?" Yraen snapped. "You look like you've seen some evil spirit."

"Mayhap I have. Nah, nah, nah, I was just thinking of a shameful thing."

"Some wench, is it?"

"I only wish, but I was thinking of the only time in my life that I've been a coward."

Yraen turned on the bench to consider him narrow-eyed and puzzled. Rhodry had a long swallow of ale.

"And when was that?" Yraen said at last.

"Today, as a matter of fact. This very day." Rhodry slammed the tankard down on the table. "Say one word more about it, and I'll kill you."

"You're drunk."

"So I am." Somewhat unsteadily, Rhodry rose, swinging himself clear of the bench. "I'm going to bed."

But once he was lying in his bunk, the sound of rain kept him awake. He kept remembering Jill, sitting in the sunlight and laughing at him, as merry as a lass over forbidden secrets of the soul.

The rain stopped just after dawn. The sudden silence woke Jahdo, and he lay in bed for a moment with his eyes shut tight, praying that when he opened them, he'd be home. Yet of course, once he succumbed and looked, he saw only the wedge-shaped chamber in the gwerbret's broch, all gray and swimmy with shadows. He sat up, yawning, and realized that Meer's bed was empty. All at once he was wide awake. Why hadn't the bard woken him, if he'd needed to get to the privy or suchlike? The stairs outside would be slippery with damp. He grabbed his trousers, pulled them on, and ran barefoot out of the room.

The dun was beginning to come alive. Yawning servants ambled down the halls or stood stretching and gossiping in the great hall. Jahdo saw old Darro at the main hearth, lifting sods from the coals underneath.

"Have you seen Meer?"

The old man sat back on his heels and considered.

"Just a bit ago, lad, see him I did. Heading for the door, there."

"He shouldn't have gone out without me along."

"Here, here, one of Lord Matyc's riders was with him, talking all urgent like, so he'll be safe enough."

Jahdo hesitated, then decided that he simply had to go see for himself. He dashed out of the great hall, stood looking around the muddy ward for a moment, then heard a smothered giggle from just behind him. He spun round, but not fast enough. A wet and smelly burlap sack flopped over his head, and boys burst out laughing.

"Let me go!" Jahdo yelled. "It's needful that I find Meer."

Although he flailed about him with his hands and screamed in rage, they kept laughing and spinning him round. Later he would realize that with his voice muffled by the sack, they couldn't even make out what he was saying. He could hear them, though, laughing as they began shoving him toward the kitchen hut as far as he could tell. All at once he was falling, hitting dirt hard. A slam and a clang sounded above him. He tore the sack off to find himself in the root cellar, sprawled among baskets of turnips. Above him the barred door, framed by cracks of light, hung closed. He leapt and shoved, but the big iron bar on the outside refused to give way.

"Let me out!"

He jumped again, scraped his hands, and screamed wordlessly, over and over for a good long while. No one seemed to hear. His tormentors, he supposed, were far away by now. He crouched for another spring, then caught himself. Shoving the door like an angry bull was going to do him no good at all. He was going to have to be clever like a ferret instead.

In the light from the cracks round the door he could see reasonably well. He began inching his way along the wooden walls, shoving baskets and sacks out of his way as he went, feeling for weaknesses and cracks that might open into another part of the dun cellars. Finally, in the darkest corner of the back wall, he found a long slit of a hole, probably where two walls came together on the other side. By falling onto his knees he could work his shoulders through. He shoved and squeezed, wiggled and swore, caught his shirt on a nail, swore louder—and heard an answering voice.

"Who's that?" It was Cook. "Who's scrabbling in there like a rat?"

"Me, Jahdo. Please, Cook, the other boys did shut me in the root cellar, and it's needful that I do get out. Meer's walking somewhere without a guide."

"Ye gods! They'll get a smack for that, they will." Massive hands came through the crack and pried, splitting old boards. "It's a cursed good thing that I was down here, isn't it now? Try this."

Jahdo squeezed through and found himself in the little cellar of the kitchen hut proper. With a bowl in one hand Cook stood beside an open barrel of salt; across from her a ladder led up to the light. Shouting thanks Jahdo ran, climbed, raced past startled serving lasses in the kitchen, and rushed, out of breath but too frightened to stop, across the ward. Panting and gasping, he headed for the dangerous wall behind the main broch, where Meer could easily take the wrong set of stairs and end up on the ramparts.

"Here, where's your hurry?"

Rhodry was strolling toward him. Jahdo dodged him and kept running.

"Trouble," he gasped out.

Sure enough, as he rounded the corner of a shed, he saw Meer way up above him on the main wall of the dun and standing next to a broken rail on a catwalk. Behind him stood Lord Matyc. For the briefest of moments Jahdo could have sworn that the lord had his hands raised to shove the bard over.

"Meer!" he screamed with the last of his breath. "Ware!"

The lord suddenly grabbed Meer's shirt just as the bard stepped back.

"Careful!" Matyc sang out. "Ye gods, man, you nearly fell."

Jahdo stopped running, too breathless to do anything but pant as Lord Matyc guided Meer round to the safe direction and led him down to the stairs. Rhodry strolled up and watched the pair with narrow eyes.

"How come you weren't with Meer?"

"The other boys," Jahdo panted, "did shut me in the cellar."

"Oh, did they now? Did you recognize Alli's voice?"

Jahdo nodded yes.

The silver dagger walked over to the wall, just underneath the dangerous part of the broken catwalk, and picked up Meer's staff.

"He must have dropped this. Careless of him."

"Not like him at all," Jahdo said, gulping air. "He knows he needs it."

Jahdo took the staff and trotted over to meet Meer, who was just gaining the solid ground of the ward.

"Here we are, Meer."

"Jahdo, is that you? Good, good." He grabbed the staff in both hands and raised it to his lips to kiss it.

"How did you go and lose it?"

"I was very foolish. I could have sworn that some creature yanked it out of my hand, but I must have merely let it slip. I grow old, Jahdo lad, old. A lax grip is one of the thirteen signs of approaching age. Where's Matyc?"

"Just behind you."

"Ah." Meer turned and made a bow. "Your lordship, I shall consider what you told me very carefully indeed."

"My thanks, good bard." But rather than pleased, Matyc looked as sour as a Bardek citron.

His lordship trotted off one way as Jahdo led Meer another, but Rhodry came along with the pair of them. He waited until Matyc was out of earshot before speaking.

"Meer, it's Rhodry. What was all that about?"

"I'm not sure, silver dagger. He fed me some strange story about a man who hated the gwerbret because of old judgments that his grace had handed down in malover. Said he was sure that this fellow was planning treachery of some sort. Now, what I want to know is this: why was our Matyc telling me such a peculiar thing, and with all this secrecy and privacy abounding, too? He insisted that he had to speak to me as soon as soon, but there's naught that I can do about some ancient court ruling."

"Of course there isn't. Why didn't you take Jahdo with you?"

"Well, I thought of it, but the lad slept so soundly I hated to wake him. One of his lordship's men came into the chamber, you see, to fetch me, and so I thought I was safe enough."

"How could I have slept through all that?" Jahdo burst out. "Him coming in, and you getting up, and the door opening and stuff."

"I wondered, lad, I wondered, but sleep you did."

"Stranger and stranger," Rhodry said. "I think we'd best go find Jill."

"Jill?" Meer rumbled. "What does the mazrak have to do with this?"

Rhodry never answered. Jahdo noticed the silver dagger staring up at the broch, and when he looked in the same direction, he saw a leather curtain fall back over one of the windows above, just as if someone had been watching them.

Rhodry found a maidservant who told him that Jill was attending upon the princess in the women's hall. He sent the lass in with an urgent request while he, Meer, and Jahdo waited outside on the landing by the spiral staircase. Meer glowered, clasping his staff tight, while Jahdo examined his bruised and bleeding hands.

"We'll have to have Jill take a look at those cuts," Rhodry remarked.

"I certainly will." Jill came out at that moment. "Jahdo, what happened?"

"Nah nah nah!" Rhodry hissed. "He'll tell you when we've got a bit more privacy."

"Then come up to my chamber. I'll make up some herbwater, and he can give those hands a good soak."

They all went down and crossed over to the side broch, then panted up the winding stairs to the very top floor, where Jill ushered them into her quarters. Jahdo helped Meer sit on a carved chest near the door, then at her order took the one chair by the rickety round table. Rhodry perched on the windowsill, but he kept himself from looking out and down.

"Nevyn always used to lodge on the top floor of brochs, too," he remarked. "What is it about you dweomermasters and heights?"

"He mostly enjoyed having a view. For me it comes in handy."

Meer shuddered and growled, just softly under his breath.

A charcoal brazier stood near the stone portion of the wall. When Jill snapped her fingers in its direction, pale flames sprang up and lighted the sticks and coals. Jahdo yelped.

"Haven't you ever seen that before?" she said.

The boy shook his head no.

"It's the elemental spirits of fire who do the actual lighting," she said, smiling. "I just show them what I want lit. Now, how did you hurt your hands, and why is Rhodry being so secretive about it?"

While Jahdo told her, Jill kept working, pouring water from a pitcher into a metal pot, stirring in herbs and suchlike, but Rhodry knew her well enough to see that she was paying strict attention to the boy's tale. When Lord Matyc's name was mentioned, Meer interrupted and took over, repeating the conversation they'd had up on the wall. Jill poured the steaming, mint-scented herbwater into a pottery bowl and made Jahdo put his hands into it, even when the lad yelped and whined.

"All sorts of molds and dusts collect in root cellars," she said. "I know it stings, but we've got to get those cuts clean. Meer, I wonder if you're thinking the same thing I am, that the disgruntled man Matyc was talking about was actually himself."

"The thought did cross my mind. Just a feeling, like. Huh. But what was he doing, then? Sounding me out to see if I felt like coming over to his side?"

"Actually," Rhodry broke in, "he was trying to kill you."

Meer swore in his own language.

"He needed to distract you so he could push you over the edge," Rhodry went on. "I'll wager every coin I have that he's the one who pulled your stick away, too. But our Matyc's not a man of much imagination. I doubt me if he could invent an interesting long story, like, so he had to tell you his own. Didn't matter, since he was planning on murdering you."

"A good guess, and mine as well," Jill said. "Jahdo, I suspect that Alli was only following orders when he shoved you into the cellar."

"I saw Matyc giving the lad a coin last night," Rhodry put in.

"But the pages do tease me all the time." Jahdo looked up, his eyes brimming tears.

"True spoken," Rhodry said. "But why did they choose this particular morning, and it so early and all, to play a prank that they must have known was dangerous, stealing the guide of a blind man away? What if someone put them up to it, knowing that they were the noble-born sons of powerful men and beyond hard questioning in the death of a stranger? And what if that someone lured Meer up to a rain-slick wall and tripped him? Easily enough done, easily enough indeed."

"I agree," Jill said. "If you'd been the usual sort of lad, Jahdo, you would have stood there yelling and banging on the door for a long, long time. They weren't counting on you being so clever, to think of a faster way out." She glanced at Rhodry. "But we don't have any evidence for any of this. Naught that would sway the gwerbret's mind in full malover, anyway."

"Do you think you'll ever find aught that'll convince his grace?"

Jill shrugged to say she didn't know, but Rhodry could see the hopeless look in her eyes. Convincing the gwerbret that one of his sworn lords was a traitor would take the word of a priest, no doubt, or maybe a templeful of them. His grace wouldn't be listening to a silver dagger and a common-born boy.

"Why?" Meer snapped. "Why kill me?"

"I don't know," Jill said. "But I wonder if our lordship worships those false gods you've told me about, and if he thinks you might recognize him for the traitor he is."

"Hum." Meer considered this for some moments. "Could be. Again, we'll not be having an easy time finding out for certain."

"And in the meantime, who knows what Matyc will be doing," Rhodry said. "I think me I'd best keep him from working harm."

"Rhoddo!" Jill turned to him with a snarl. "This is a matter for the laws, not for murdering."

"And did I say I was so much as thinking of murdering the man?"

"You didn't, but I know you cursed well. The first thing you always think of is blood."

"I'm not about to get myself hanged for killing one of the noble-born. Don't trouble your heart over it. What I will do is stay close to Meer and Jahdo for the next few days. And I think I'll just have Yraen keep an eye on our fine lordship."

"Now that's a splendid idea." Jill turned back to her patient. "All right, lad, you can take your paws out of the water now. Let's see what they look like clean."

Time, Rhodry knew, was their ally and Matyc's foe. Now that the gwerbret had given his vassals leave to return to their own lands, Matyc quite simply couldn't dally in Cengarn without some good reason. With his lack of imagination, reasons would be hard to come by. As he told Yraen, while they lingered at table after the evening meal, Matyc was going to have to make his move fast, if indeed he did strike again.

"I'm going to stay in the bard's chamber tonight," Rhodry said. "Having a silver dagger sleeping in the doorway does wonders for keeping trouble out of a room."

"True spoken. Where are the lad and Meer now?"

"Up in Jill's chambers. I figure they'll be safe enough there for a bit."

"I wouldn't cause trouble where Jill could see me, not on your life." Yraen paused, chewing on the ends of his mustache. "Now, as for Matyc, I might be able to bribe a servant to give me a place to sleep near his lordship's apartments. Worth a try."

Only half consciously they both turned to look across the great hall, laced with a strand or two of blue smoke from the secondary hearth, to the table of honor. Although the gwerbret and his lady had retired, and the prince and Carra were nowhere to be seen, the two vassals lingered over goblets of mead. Matyc listened, his face its usual mask, while Lord Gwinardd told some long tale that, judging from the way he laughed as he told it, was meant to be humorous.

"I've never seen a man so sour as Matyc," Yraen remarked. "You think he'd at least feign a smile for the courtesy of the thing."

With his story fallen flat, Gwinardd lingered but a moment longer. He rose, bowed briefly to Matyc, and stalked out of the great hall. Without a trace of expression on his face, Matyc watched him go, then reached for the flagon of mead. Yraen stood, considering.

"I'll just go have a word with Matyc. One of his riders was telling me that his lordship dearly loves to gamble on a good game of carnoic, and the gwerbret keeps a set right there, in that chest in the curve of the wall. I'll see if Matyc will take a challenge from a silver dagger."

"Good thinking." Rhodry stood, too. "I'm just going to take a walk out in the ward."

By then the sun had all but disappeared, and the first few stars were coming out over the towering walls of Dun Cengarn. Out by the kitchen hut servants scurried round, and the scullery boys lugged bucket after bucket of water from the well, but otherwise the ward stood empty. Rhodry made a tour round, looking for places where a man bent on murder might hide, and finally strolled down to the main gates, which still stood open with a guard on either side. The town spread out downhill, dark except for the occasional crack of firelight from an open window. Far away in some temple or other a bronze bell clanged.

"A friend of yours rode in some while back, silver dagger," a guard said. "That dwarven merchant, Odo or Thoto or whatever his name is."

"Ah. I wonder if the little bastard's finally come to pay me what he owes me?"

"He said he was headed for the great hall, but good luck. Squeezing coin out of a dwarf's a hard day's work."

Rhodry trotted uphill to the main broch and slipped into the great hall by the back door. The riders' side stood empty, while up at the honor hearth a small crowd flocked round the table, watching and wagering upon the game of carnoic. Judging from the silence in the hall, it was running close. Rhodry saw Otho, standing back a bit by the hearth itself and looking as irritable as if he had a thorn in his breechclout. As Rhodry was walking over to join him, he heard Lord Matyc swear. Scattered groans and whoops broke out in the crowd.

"Good move, silver dagger," Matyc said, and never were fair words so grudgingly sounded, not that Rhodry had ever heard. "Let's have another, shall we?"

"Now here, I can't hang about with you louts all night." Otho shoved himself forward. "Yraen, I need a word with you."

"It'll have to wait." Matyc snapped out the words before Yraen could answer. "We're in the midst of a gamble."

"I don't give a pig's fart," Otho snarled. "Can't find Rhodry, so I need to talk to Yraen—here!"

Otho dodged back just in time as Matyc slapped at him in lazy contempt. So! Rhodry thought, losing is one thing that goads our lordship.

"You impacted pusboil from the hind end of a leprous mule!" Otho snapped.

"Don't you insult me, you stub-legged excuse for a man."

"Very well, I retract that. You're a running sore on a leprous she-mule's cunt."

Matyc leapt up so fast that he tipped the bench over behind him. Yelping, riders and dogs alike scattered out of his way. The lord slammed both hands palm down on the table and glared at Otho, who stood his ground and glared right back.

"Draw that knife of yours," Matyc said, and his voice rang dangerously level. "If you dare."

"Hold." Rhodry stepped in front of Otho. "We're in a gwerbret's hall."

Matyc let out a long breath in a deep sigh.

"So we are, silver dagger, and you have my thanks for reminding me of that."

If Otho had held his tongue or muttered something conciliatory, the matter would have died, but Otho had never been much for keeping his lips together.

"Very well," the dwarf snapped. "If that piss-proud excuse of a noble lord apologizes to me, I'll accept."

"Me apologize to you?" Matyc's voice cracked. "I'll see you dead first."

At that the captain of Matyc's warband grabbed his lord's arm. Matyc shook him off, his face as cold and blank as a stone.

"Fear not," he growled. "His grace's hall is safe from my spilling blood in it. But come the morning, dwarf, you'd best be here, because I'm bringing this matter to justice in malover."

Matyc spun round and stalked out, his captain and his men filing out after him. Yraen, who'd been sitting on the other bench all this time, shook his head and began putting the carnoic stones back in their tiny coffer.

"This is going to cost you a grand lot of coin, Otho old lad," he said, grinning. "Rhodry, we'd best get the hire he owes us out of his hide before Matyc drags him into court."

Otho howled in sheer anguish. Although the other riders in the hall began to laugh, Rhodry turned and snarled them into silence.

"This is a fair bit more serious than coin," Rhodry said. "His lordship feels his honor's been insulted, and I doubt me if that's a laughing matter, lads."

Rhodry was proved right on the morrow morning. Since Gwerbret Cadmar could refuse no request for a judgment from one of the noble-born, he convened malover and sent a couple of servants trotting down into town to fetch Otho from his inn and a priest of Bel from his temple. Everyone in the dun who would fit crammed into the great hall, even Meer and Jahdo, way off in the back, while the latecomers stood just outside at door and window. To prevent trouble, Matyc's warband was forced to stay in the barracks, but when Otho arrived, he brought his three kinsmen with him, to stand beside him as was his and their right under the laws. As witnesses, Rhodry and Yraen knelt on the floor up at the front of the hall. The best view, of course, was reserved for the noble-born. Off to one side but close at hand sat Lord Gwinardd, Prince Daralanteriel, the gwerbret's lady, and of course Carra, pale with worry.

After the servants turned the honor table sideways and placed his grace's chair, Cadmar sat in the middle of one long side with a priest at one hand and a scribe at the other. Before him on the nicked and scratched oak slab lay the golden ceremonial sword of the gwerbrets of Cengarn. 'Twixt table and witnesses, Otho knelt toward the gwerbret's left and Matyc, to his right. Cadmar took the sword and raised it high, point upward.

"I hereby declare this malover open," the gwerbret called. "Let the gods strike dead any man who lies during its course."

He knocked the pommel of the sword three times upon the table, then laid it flat.

"Lord Matyc of Brin Mawrvelin will speak first and lay his grievance. Then Otho the dwarven merchant will speak to answer him. Then the witnesses will tell me what they saw."

Lord Matyc rose in icy calm, his voice flat as he recounted his version of the incident.

"I'll admit that I raised a hand to the man, Your Grace," he finished up. "But I never meant to land a blow. It was just a stupid sort of slap, like brushing away a fly."

The scribe wrote something down.

"And what did he call you, Lord Matyc," Cadmar said, "that makes you feel your honor's at stake here?"

Matyc hesitated, his face turning just the slightest bit pale.

"Unless you give out with the insult, I can hardly judge it, can I now?"

"Very well, Your Grace. He called me a running sore on a leprous she-mule's cunt."

Carra laughed. No doubt she was merely anxious, but she giggled so loudly that most everyone could hear, and way in the back of the hall some maidservant or other answered with a snicker of her own. It was too much for human nature to bear. The hall broke, man and maid alike snorting, tittering, guffawing, and outright howling. Cadmar hauled himself up and pounded on the table.

"We will have silence in this hall!"

The laughter abruptly died. Matyc was trembling with shame and rage, his lips bloodless, his face red, his fists clenched at his side. That's torn it, Rhodry thought. When he glanced at Otho's kin, he saw them rolling their eyes heavenward, as if in prayer.

"Otho the dwarven merchant," Cadmar intoned. "Do you deny this charge?"

"I don't, Your Grace, because he deserved every word of it. How was I to know he never meant to hit me, eh? When a hand as big as your face comes flying your way, you've no mind for subtleties."

The wrangling went on, back and forth, while the great hall grew hot and fetid from the bodies packed into it. Although Otho turned furious, growling each word, Matyc stayed dead-calm, his entire face bloodless by then. Cadmar started scowling, then finally leaned forward.

"I find both of you equally at fault," he snapped. "This is a stupid wrangle over naught."

"Naught, Your Grace?" Matyc stepped forward. "He insults me in front of you, my peers, my captain, my men, the common-born servants, these silver daggers. His words shame me here in your very hall and expose me to the mocking laughter of my peers as well as my inferiors. And you call that naught?"

Cadmar hesitated, glancing at the priest.

"A lord's honor is more precious than gold." The priest began quoting from the laws. "Without honor in the eyes of his people, how may a lord rule? Will men who mock him in secret obey him in the open? Thus a lord must seek redress for the slightest stain upon that which he treasures."

"Well, true enough," Cadmar said, sighing. "But, Matyc, I can't find you blameless. A slap at a man's head is a threat. What redress would you have me assign you?" He glanced at the priest again. "What's the usual price for this sort of thing?"

Before his holiness could speak, Matyc stepped forward.

"I want no coin nor cattle, Your Grace. I demand a trial by combat to let the gods assign the shame and blame for this."

"That *is* his lordship's right under the laws," the priest said. "But I would counsel against it."

"I demand my right," Matyc snarled.

Otho sat down heavily on the floor, his mouth flopped open like a landed fish. Carra clasped both hands over her mouth to stifle a scream. The crowd began to murmur as the gwerbret bent close to the priest to whisper. Suddenly Rhodry saw the way to solve the little problem of Lord Matyc once and for all. He stepped forward with a low bow toward the table of honor.

"My lords, Your Grace, and all you assembled here." Rhodry turned to look significantly at various members of the crowd. "Even by the standards of his people, Otho's an old man. Even if he were a young one, he'd still have a bare half the reach of Lord Matyc here. And even if he had Matyc's height, he's never fought with a sword in his life."

The crowd began to murmur, and Matyc looked Rhodry's way with poison in his eyes. Cadmar let the talk go on for a moment or two, then yelled for silence.

"The silver dagger's right enough," the gwerbret said. "A trial by combat in circumstances like these would be an affront to the gods and naught more."

"Your Grace!" Matyc howled. "Then where's my redress?"

"Your Grace." Rhodry knelt in front of the gwerbret. "I offer myself as a champion for the justice of the thing."

The crowd started to cheer, then bit it back. Trapped in a rat cage of his own weaving, Matyc made a choking sound deep in his throat.

"Ye gods!" Cadmar snapped. "How has this stupid incident got itself so overblown? Your Holiness, I can't countenance this."

The priest shrugged with a little fling of his hands.

"I have no say in the matter, Your Grace. Matyc's called for formal combat. There's not one thing I can do to stop it now. When a man speaks in front of the gods, he speaks but once."

Cadmar turned to Matyc.

"Will you withdraw your request?"

"How can I, and have a scrap of honor left? Do you think I could ever hold my head up again if people thought me frightened of a silver dagger? The god will aid me, Your Grace, and then we'll see who's acting for the justice of the thing."

Otho sighed and wiped his sweaty forehead on his shirt sleeve.

"So be it," pronounced the gwerbret. "You shall fight with the ritual arms: neither mail nor shield shall come between you, but you shall have a sword in the right hand and a dagger in the left. Lord Matyc, son of Arddyr, do you accept these terms?"

"I do, Your Grace." To give him his due, his voice was rock-steady. "I submit to the arbitration of the gods."

"And you, Rhodry, son of—my apologies, silver dagger. I don't know your father's name."

"Devaberiel Silverhand, Your Grace."

Whispers rippled through the great hall. Cadmar sat stunned for a moment, then lifted the sword for silence. It came promptly.

"Very well, Rhodry, son of Devaberiel Silverhand, do you submit to the arbitration of both the gods of Deverry and those of your father's people?"

"I do, Your Grace."

Cadmar turned to the priest.

"Your Holiness, I have called you here on a matter of justice, and justice we shall have. Will you preside?"

"I will, Your Grace, but Great Bel will do the judging, not me or any other mortal man."

Without waiting for another word from lord or priest the assembled warbands began to file out of the great hall. Although the crowd murmured as it fell back to let them go, the riders themselves walked in dead silence. They saw the rite of combat as a seal on their warriors' lives, an outward and visible sign that their death-dealing stood holy in the eyes of the gods. Rhodry was enough one of them to know that they were at heart grateful for the chance to witness this rare act of worship. He followed them out, walking alone, with a little space around him that seemed as impenetrable as a dun wall, judging from the way none dared approach him.

Outside the many-towered dun, in a grassy stretch of meadow, the priest of Bel paced out the long rectangle of the combat ground and cut the turf with his golden sickle to mark it. Matyc's men ranged themselves along one side, Otho and his kin on the other, and the gwerbret's men stood all round to prevent trouble. In shirts, brigga, and bare feet Rhodry and Matyc walked to the center of the ground and handed their weapons to the priest, who kissed each one and prayed over it as well. When Rhodry and Matyc knelt before him, he laid his hands on their heads and offered up a long prayer, asking Bel to judge the true man from the false. Bel was the High King's god, and all his life, whether as silver dagger or great lord, Rhodry had considered himself the High King's man with a devotion greater than any Deverry man would ever pay to one of the deities. As he knelt on a matter of justice, Rhodry felt the touch of another hand, this one cold and hard upon the back of his. The god had come.

The prayer wound on and on through the assembled silence. Rhodry's blood ran cold; the hairs on his nape and on his arms prickled and rose; he felt a profound stillness deep in his heart. Round him the sun turned hard and sharp and brighter than any sunlight he'd ever seen before. Rhodry was aware of Matyc, kneeling next to him, trembling a little, but in rage, not fear. Rhodry was sure of that. When the priest finished his prayer, they rose and took their weapons from the gwerbret, standing nearby like a page. Cadmar looked at Rhodry and stepped back involuntarily in sudden fear. Rhodry merely smiled and strode down to his edge of the ground.

"Begin!" called the priest. "May each man's Wyrd fight with and upon him."

Rhodry stepped across the sacred border and walked slowly toward the center of the ground. Matyc hesitated, started to meet him, then hesitated again and began to circle. If he wanted to make a game out of it, Rhodry decided that he'd oblige and turned to match his moves. Spiraling round and round they came closer, feinting in, dodging back, the silver dagger winking and flashing in Rhodry's left hand, Matyc's dull steel quivering on guard. All at once Matyc charged. Rhodry danced away and struck, dodging in as his enemy instinctively flung up his left hand to parry with a shield he didn't have. As the blood bloomed on Matyc's sleeve, Rhodry burst out laughing. The berserker fit sank cold claws into his heart and took him over. With a yelp Matyc threw his dagger straight at Rhodry's head with the last bit of strength in his broken arm.

Rhodry ducked and let him get away, stumbling back with death in his eyes, then laughed and charged and laughed again, slashing in from the side. Steel rang on steel as Matyc parried, sobbing for breath, twisting back and forth, then trying a desperate lunge that was a sheer mistake. Rhodry caught Matyc's blade on his and let the momentum send it sailing into the grass. Panting for breath, Matyc drew himself up straight to face his death.

"Go fetch it." Rhodry pointed with his own sword. "No one's ever going to say I killed an unarmed man."

For a moment Matyc stared goggle-eyed; then slowly, moving backward, keeping his eyes fixed on Rhodry like the proverbial rabbit watching a ferret, he angled off. While he picked up the sword, Rhodry sheathed his silver dagger to even the fight. He could feel that the god was pleased with him. Armed and ready, Matyc came back, circling again to Rhodry's left, aiming for his unprotected side. Rhodry scorned to follow him. He laughed in one cold sob, lunged, and caught Matyc's blade again. With a howl of laughter he twisted it to one side and stabbed in hard. Matyc grunted and spasmed, slashing back. Rhodry felt the wound opening on his left shoulder as a line of cool fire, naught more, as Matyc coughed blood, crumpled, and fell at his feet. He looked up, mouthing some word, a name—Alshandra's name, Rhodry realized with cold horror—then choked up clots and died.

The priest flung his arms toward the sun and shrieked a long, wordless cry to great Bel. With a toss of his head Rhodry howled in echo.

"The god has given judgment!" Cadmar called out. "Otho the dwarven merchant is innocent of all harm and insult toward Matyc son of Arddyr and his kin and clan. Let no man perpetuate the feud that the gods have ended here upon this holy ground."

As the assembled warbands cried out their agreement, Rhodry felt the god leave him. Suddenly icy cold, panting for breath, he fell to his knees and clutched his wounded shoulder with his right hand. Warm blood welled between his fingers. Laughing and howling, half-berserk themselves with relief, Otho and his kinsmen came rushing over.

"Can you walk, silver dagger?" Jorn said. "Here, let me help you. We owe you all the help we can give."

"My thanks, but it's a shallow enough cut." Leaning on the dwarf, Rhodry got to his feet. "What I need is drink."

"You shall have mead from my own table for this fight, silver dagger." It was Cadmar, hurrying over. "It's your right as the victor and the favorite of the god."

"No matter how much grief I've brought you, Your Grace? I'll not ask you for that cup."

The gwerbret sighed and looked away, his face hard set against showing the grief he must have felt for a man he still thought loyal to him. His warband, however, and Lord Gwinardd's crowded round to stare at Rhodry, a god-touched man now and forever in their eyes. The bolder men reached out to dabble a forefinger on his gore-wet sleeve so they could mark their foreheads with a spot of his blood. Jill came pushing her way through the crowd.

"Otho, Jorn, take Rhodry back to your inn. Your Grace, I think me it would be very unwise to give the silver dagger his due in your hall. Matyc's clan worries me a fair bit more than the gods and their penchant for detail." She glanced at Rhodry. "I'll just get my medicinals and join you there. That cut's not so bad you can't walk, not for a man like you."

"I think I said somewhat like that myself." Rhodry grinned at her. "Done, then."

With the help of the dwarves, Rhodry made his way, though slowly, through the twisting streets of Cengarn. By then it was full noon, and the hot sun beat and danced upon the cobbles. Rhodry suddenly realized that the view swam round him, as if he looked through blown glass. Sweat stung his eyes. Dimly he was aware of townsfolk, stopping in the street to stare at their strange little procession. Every now and then he caught a murmured word, a guess about tavern brawls, mostly. At last they came to a hillside so steep it was half a cliff. Set right into it, between two stunted little pines, stood a wooden door with big iron hinges. Fussing and fuming about his wound and Matyc's clan both, the dwarves led him inside to a stone hallway, lit with the eerie blue glow of phosphorescent fungi gathered into baskets and hung along their route.

The air, startlingly cool, blew around them in fresh drafts. After a couple of hundred yards, they came at last to a round chamber, some fifty feet across, scattered with low tables and tiny benches round a central open hearth, where a low fire burned and a huge kettle hung from a pair of andirons and a crossbar. Reflexively Rhodry glanced up to see the smoke rising to a stone flue set in the ceiling as well as a vent or two for fresh air. At one of the tables, a yawning innkeep stood polishing tankards with a rag. When Otho spoke to him in the dwarven tongue, he answered with a shake of his head and rushed off through one door.

"Just sit down, lad," Jorn said. "Here. If you sit on the table, like, Jill will be able to work on you better."

By then Rhodry was more than glad to do what he was told. His entire sleeve and the side of his shirt were soaked through with the slow ooze of blood. Carrying a silver flask and a tiny glass stoup, the innkeep came hurrying back.

"Drink some of this," he said. "Warms a man's heart."

The pale gold liquor warmed Rhodry's entire body, or so it seemed to him, with the bite of bitter herbs in raw alcohol, but he had to admit that once he'd choked it down, it left him feeling clearheaded and re-markably comfortable. In a few minutes Jill hurried in with a big burlap sack of medical supplies. She perched next to him on the table and sniffed the air.

"Well, no need for me to fix you herbwater if you've been drinking that," she pronounced. "Let me cut that shirt right off you. Carra sent a new one for you as a thanks for aiding Otho, and it's a good thing she did. She said to tell you that it's one she sewed herself."

"Then I'm twice honored," Rhodry said. "And tell her I said that."

Otho looked away fast, but there was no hiding the tears in his eyes.

Rhodry submitted to having Jill wash and stitch the wound while Otho and Garin talked urgently in Dwarvish. The innkeep took the bloody shirt away and returned with a big flagon and some goblets, full-sized this time. Mic poured mead all round, except of course for Jill, who waved the drink away.

"I think I'd best keep my wits about me," she remarked. "Rhoddo, can you get this new shirt over your head?"

With her help, he could, but the effort left him gasping. The thin and leathery Jorn insisted that Rhodry sit in the best chair, all propped with pillows, since it was a low thing indeed for a man of his height, while they drank yet another toast and Jill packed up her supplies.

"Never did I think I'd live to see the day when an elf would do me a favor," Otho said at last.

"Ye gods," Jorn snarled. "Will you mind your manners? It's that kind of talk that nearly got you sliced into shreds and snippets by the late and unmourned Matyc."

"He's got a point," Garin said. "Apologize."

"None needed," Rhodry broke in. "I've known Otho too long to expect courtesy."

Otho actually smiled, a quick and quickly over draw of his lips.

"Good. Don't." Otho raised his goblet in Rhodry's direction. "All right, silver dagger. Name your debt price. I know you've got one, and I know it's going to be high."

"Of course. Look, Otho, I don't want gold or suchlike. I need help in finding somewhat up in the northern mountains, and I've got to find it fast. It's summer now, but winter does tend to come before you want to see it."

Otho groaned and rolled his eyes ceilingward.

"What is it?" Jorn said. "A vein of metal? Jewels or suchlike?"

"Naught like that. A dragon."

Jorn sputtered. Garin whitened. Mic sat down hard on the floor. Only then, seeing their terror, did Rhodry believe that a dragon truly existed for him to find. When he glanced Jill's way, he found her watching him with a certain admiration.

"Worms and slimes!" Otho spat out. "Why don't you ask for the moon, silver dagger? We could make a ladder long enough for you to climb to the heavens and fetch her down."

"I've always heard that the Mountain People pay their debts. Isn't that true?"

There was a beat of silence in the room as loud as any drum. Rhodry had attended enough royal courts to know that he'd committed a discourtesy and a major one, but whether he'd thrown a challenge or simply been insulting he couldn't tell. At length Garin looked daggers at Otho, snapped a few words in Dwarvish, then turned to Rhodry.

"I'd ask you not to judge us all by my kinsman."

"Now, here, I meant no insult. I was just speaking offhand."

"There's naught offhand about debt and the paying of debt." Garin paused for another significant glance Otho's way. "And since we owe you Otho's life, then the dragon you shall have in return."

"It'll take us a while to raise the army," Jorn put in. "I hope you're not in a hurry or suchlike."

"I don't need an army," Rhodry said. "All I'm asking you is to help me find the beast. I'll do the capturing and suchlike."

The dwarves all looked back and forth at one another for a long moment, then stared at Rhodry. He didn't need dweomer to hear them thinking "half-witted dolt" and "madman." Garin turned to Jill in mute appeal.

"If anyone can tame the beast," she said. "It'll be Rhodry."

"Oh," Garin sighed. "Well, then. If anyone can, you say? If. Well, then."

"Humph." Otho considered, combing his beard with nervous fingers. "I'm sorry now I didn't let Matyc cut me into pieces. It would have been a faster and a lot more pleasant way to die."

"Some of us have been having similar thoughts," Jorn remarked absently, as if to the ceiling. "But kin is kin, and debts are debts, and there we are and here we are."

"Just so," Garin said. "We'll have to go to Enj."

"Where's that?" Otho broke in.

"Not a where, a who." Garin nodded in Otho's direction. "He was born some years after you—er, well—left us so sudden, like."

"The where's not such an easy thing, either," Jorn said. "The trip to Haen Marn's somewhat of a trial in itself."

"We'll have to suffer it, then." Garin shot him a dark glance, as if in warning. "No one knows more about dragon lore and fire mountains than Enj. If anyone can find this beast, it'll be him."

"But he's mad," Mic wailed. "Stark raving."

"Oh, splendid!" Jill laid her sack on the floor and turned toward the dwarves. "That's all Rhodry needs, a madman for a guide. And what do you mean, volcanoes?"

"That's where they live," Jorn said. "Dragons, I mean. They're cold-blooded creatures, the great wyrms. They'd die in winter without some source of heat. And I wouldn't call Enj mad, exactly. All of his clan are a bit—well, er—unusual-minded."

"Mad is what I calls it," Mic snapped. "Starkly, ravingly, babblingly daft."

"Otho, you know the dragon hearth in his grace's hall?" Jorn turned on the bench to present Mic his back. "Well, Enj's people carved it."

"Ah, I see." Otho nodded sagely. "Well, then."

"Well then what?" Jill said. "It's a beautiful bit of stonework, but what does that prove?"

"You wouldn't understand, Jill," Garin broke in, "for all your dweomer. It's a thing that only the Mountain People would understand."

Jill rolled her eyes heavenward, but she held her tongue. If Rhodry hadn't been so tired, he would have howled in berserk delight. As it was, he found himself grinning.

"Fire mountains, vicious beasts, dwarven madmen—oh, it all sounds a splendid little journey you're sending me on, Jill."

She made a sour face in his direction.

"Hah!" Otho snorted. "Smirk all you want, silver dagger, but think of this, will you? If we take you on this fool's errand, you'll have to walk."

"Walk?" Rhodry felt his grin disappear. "What do you mean, walk?"

"Just that. How do you expect horses to survive a trip like this? We might even end up traveling underground." Otho held a hand upside down and made striding motions with his fore and middle finger. "So walking it is. I know what you elves are like. Tender little feet, all of you. Lost without a horse."

"Otho, will you hold your ugly tongue?" Garin snarled. "You owe the man your life!"

"And it sounds to me like he's asking me to give it right back to him, traipsing round the mountains, hunting dragons." Otho drew himself up to full dignity. "Not much of a bargain, is it now?"

"You could pay Enj and his clan to accept your blood-debt for you," Jorn said.

"Hah! And what will they want for that? Every gem I own, no doubt. I'd be beggared!"

"Better than being dead, isn't it?" Rhodry said, grinning.

Otho merely snorted in contempt at the very idea. Jill picked up her sack.

"I'd best get back to the dun. Things are bound to need some straightening out. Rhodry, I suggest you simply stay where you are, if our friends agree?"

All the dwarves but Otho nodded a yes.

"Splendid," Jill went on. "I'll have Yraen bring you your bedroll and suchlike later. Lord Matyc has a brother who's honor-bound to look into this whole affair, you know. Which reminds me. Can you walk? I want a word with you, privatelike."

Instead the dwarves withdrew to the far side of the big room to argue among themselves about the best way to approach this mysterious Enj. Jill hunkered down by Rhodry's low chair.

"I asked you not to let this come to murder," she hissed.

"Murder? You asked me to let it come under the laws, and that's exactly what I did. A priest of Bel himself judged the affair, didn't he?"

"True, but you leapt at the chance to have at Matyc with cold steel."

"So? The man was a traitor."

"We all thought the man a traitor. That's not necessarily the same thing."

He would have argued more, but his head was swimming from the drink, to say nothing of the wound. Jill stood up with a little shake of her head.

"Well, no use in discussing it now. I've got to get back. I'll be back tomorrow, say, when you've had a chance to sober up."

"Do that. Ye gods, you could at least thank me."

She started to speak, then merely set her mouth in a tight line and turned away.

"Otho," she called out. "See if the innkeep can find your savior here a bed that fits him, will you?"

Before Rhodry could think of what to say to her, she'd slung the sack over her shoulder and marched off. He yawned, yawned again, and fell asleep where he sat.

When Jill returned to the dun, she found the ward a shouting, surging confusion of men and horses. She slipped in the gates without being noticed and made her way along the curve of the wall until she could get round the mob and cross safely to the broch complex. In the doorway to the great hall Gwerbret Cadmar was standing and talking to a kneeling rider while just behind the pair the chamberlain and equerry hovered. All of the men looked deeply worried, especially the kneeling rider.

"If his grace orders us to stay," the fellow was saying. "We'll have to try to leave anyway. You might as well just hang us all straight off, Your Grace, and spare the dun the fighting."

"I'll do no such thing, lad, and I've not ordered you to stay, either. I asked you to consider staying, that's all."

"But, Your Grace, I can't—"

"I know." Cadmar held up a hand flat for silence. "The situation has an honor of its own, and that honor demands that you take your lordship's men home. Here, get up."

All at once Jill understood—the rider was Matyc's captain, and the pack in the ward, the warband the lord had brought with him. Mentally she cursed Rhodry with every oath she could think of. The captain rose, dusting off the knees of his brigga.

"I've written a letter to your lord's brother." Cadmar held out a hand, and the chamberlain put a silver message tube into it. "Will you deliver it for me?"

"I will, Your Grace. After all, he's our lord now, isn't he?" The captain glanced the chamberlain's way. "He will inherit, won't he?"

The chamberlain groaned and ran both hands through his thinning hair.

"That's up to the priests. But by all rights the lands of a lord who loses a trial by combat are forfeit, to be reassigned by his overlord."

"Well, then," Cadmar broke in. "I'll just see to it that the brother—"

"Your Grace!" The chamberlain tugged on his sleeve. "By tradition though not law the lands go to the temple."

The captain threw up his hands with a jingle of mail.

"This legal wrangling's beyond the likes of me," he said. "Your Grace, we've got to ride out of your city before sunset."

"Then go now, and with my blessing." Cadmar handed him the message. "And for the love of every god, get this to Lord Tren straightaway, and tell him what you've heard here, too."

The captain slipped the tube under his mail and into his shirt, settling it against his belt, then hurried back to the waiting troop. Yelling orders, he mounted. When a page tossed him the lead rope of a particularly fine gray gelding, Jill noticed an ominous blanket-wrapped bundle slung over its saddle. In utter silence Matyc's men gathered round their captain and the body of their dead lord. Together they turned their horses and began filing out of the gates. Shaking his head from side to side, Cadmar watched them go.

"Your Grace?" Jill said.

The lord and his councillors yelped or swore in surprise.

"Ye gods, Jill, I didn't even see you walk up," Cadmar said with a grin. "You didn't just pop out of thin air, did you now?"

"Your grace was much distracted, that's all. How much trouble is there going to be over Matyc's death?"

"I don't know. It depends in large part on whether or not Lord Tren inherits his brother's holdings, I suppose. If he does, no doubt we can smooth things over. If the priests demand the land and taxes for themselves, well, now, I don't know what to predict."

"I see. I've settled the silver dagger down in town, anyway. I figured he'd best be out of your dun."

"I suppose so." Cadmar glanced at the chamberlain, who nodded a yes. "But it gripes my soul to turn him out. By rights I should be honoring him at my table, just as the gods honored him on the combat ground."

The chamberlain groaned in some distress.

"I'm not going to do it," Cadmar snapped. "Don't trouble your heart. Here, everybody, let's go inside and sit down. I hate hovering round like this in doorways!"

At the table of honor Labanna stood waiting, one hand resting on the back of her husband's empty chair. Behind her, the serving women hovered in the shadows at the foot of the spiral staircase. Cadmar raised a questioning eyebrow in her direction.

"I've just told the servants that there won't be a feast after all," she said. "It wouldn't be appropriate."

"Of course not, my dear, and my thanks. I'd forgot about that." Cadmar sat down and reached back to pat her hand. "You're welcome to join us."

"My thanks, my lord, but I'd best be about my business. There's much to settle and settle down."

He nodded, smiling wryly, and she hurried upstairs, sweeping her women with her. Servants rushed over with tankards of ale for the men, though Jill waved hers away. The servitors sat down at Cadmar's right, but Jill chose to stand.

"Your Grace," she said. "Answer me honestly. Is it a burden upon you to have me, Carra, and all the trouble we've brought with us here in your dun?"

"Where else would you go?"

"I don't know, Your Grace, but—"

"I refuse to send anyone away from the safety of my walls when they might meet with danger on the roads. It would ache my heart as well as shame it if the slightest evil befell the prince and his lady."

"Not half as much as it would ache mine. Well, I need to give the matter some thought. This whole thing happened so suddenly."

"So it did, but here, Matyc brought it upon himself. You heard him, there in the malover, insisting on his right to combat."

"True spoken, but will his kin see it that way?"

Cadmar shrugged to show his ignorance.

"If I may speak boldly, Your Grace," Jill went on. "You need that alliance, and badly. I would most humbly and with all deference to the gods ask you this. In a war which would be of more use to you in keeping your people safe, the temple or Lord Tren?"

"Your Grace?" the equerry broke in. "The only person whose pres-ence should influence the matter at all is the silver dagger. If he stays in town . . . "

"Better yet, my lord"—Jill glanced at him—"I'm sending him away. I have a crucial errand that needs running, you see. Once he's healed, he'll be leaving Cengarn."

The equerry bobbed his head in her direction, the best bow he could muster seeing as he was sitting down. Cadmar considered, running the palm of his hand round and round the tankard's lip.

"Do as you think best about the silver dagger," he said at last. "But may the gods forgive me for slighting the winner of that combat!"

"I think me they will, Your Grace."

"As for the other matter, I'll have to see how things develop. Lord Tren's warband won't do us much good if the gods are turned against us by the priests."

Jill held her tongue with difficulty.

"But it'll be some days before Tren even answers my message," Cadmar went on. "I don't suppose you've seen any more raiders coming our way?"

"Not yet, Your Grace. As you say, we'll have to see how things develop. May I have leave to go? I need to find Yraen and have him take Rhodry's gear down to him."

"Of course. As I say, do as you think fit."

"I will, then, Your Grace. Consider the matter decided."

As she made that near casual remark Jill felt a peculiar sensation, as if she were suddenly being watched. She felt that from some great distance eyes had turned her way, powerful eyes with strong dweomer behind them. Although she managed to smile pleasantly and take a civil leave of the gwerbret, she hurried up to her tower room to be alone rather than sending a page for Yraen.

Her chamber swarmed with Wildfolk, darting this way and that in the air or on the floor, clustering on the furniture, huddling together in the curve of the wall. When she walked in, her gray gnome leapt into her arms.

"Oho, you felt it, too, did you? Someone's found Cengarn, I think. The question is, are they looking for Carra or for me?" She thought back, remembered that she'd felt the sensation at the exact moment when a possible course of action had been decided into reality. "Or, come to think of it, is it Rhodry they find so interesting?"

With the gnome riding on her shoulder, she went to the window and looked out. She could see over the dun wall to the town, but the market hill blocked her farther view. Why would some enemy be searching for Rhodry? Unless, of course, they knew that he'd been guarding Carra and thought he still was. She turned her head to catch the gnome's attention.

"Go fetch Dallandra for me, will you? All you have to do is find her, and she'll know what it means."

The gnome grinned, revealing an uneven mouthful of pointed teeth, then disappeared. She could only hope that it had understood, and that Dallandra would come promptly—as the physical world measured Time.

As she often did in these situations, Jill found herself thinking about her master in the dweomer, dead these many years now, and wondering what he would have done. She particularly wished that she had his influence with the priesthood of Bel. If she'd been Nevyn, she could have gone to the temple and perhaps worked them round over the matter of the late Lord Matyc's lands, but they would never listen to a woman, especially not to one they barely knew. That particular matter lay in the laps of the gods, she supposed, such as they were. It occurred to her that the priests stood to lose a great deal if Alshandra's forces conquered Cengarn and overthrew their god. That grim possibility, at least, might give her some sort of weapon.

She studied the shadows in the ward, making mental notes of their position to give herself a starting mark for the passing of Time. Since her window faced east, she could measure by the shadow of the broch itself, which was at the moment about halfway across the ward. Although she stood there until it touched the main wall of the dun, Dallandra never appeared.

Rhodry slept most of that day curled up on a short bed in the dwarven inn. When the pain of his wound finally woke him, it took him a long time to remember where he was and why. He sat up, stretching cramped muscles, peering round him at what he could see of the tiny chamber in the dim blue light from the half-spent basket of fungi. Only his elven eyesight made it possible for him to see anything at all. As it was, he could make out the walls, the shape of a plain chest, and a door. He got up, grabbing a wall to steady himself as the chamber spun.

"Worse off than you thought, are you? You're getting old, Rhodry lad."

He sat down again rather fast, rested for a moment, then found his boots and pulled them on. This time when he stood, he did so slowly and managed to stay standing.

The hallway outside was better lit but utterly featureless, giving him not one hint of which way to go. He choked back an oath, then merely listened. Sure enough, he could hear faint voices far to his left, and following them did indeed lead him to the common room of the inn. Seated round the table were Otho and all his kin, while at the hearth the innkeep tended the iron kettle, which smelled of stew.

"Come sit down," Garin called out. "You shouldn't be up this soon."

"Oh, I'm healing already."

Still, Rhodry was glad enough to sit, even though the bench was much too short for his legs. The only way he could get comfortable was to perch forward on the edge and cross his legs loosely, so that he was almost resting on his knees, but it was better than hunkering down on the cold stone floor.

"Want some stew?" the innkeep called out.

"None at the moment, my thanks. I was hoping for another drink of that medicinal you gave me earlier."

"Good idea. I'll just go fetch it."

The innkeep had no sooner disappeared down the corridor when they heard a faint pounding that must have come from the outer door. With a sigh Mic rose and trotted off to answer it. He came back with Yraen, carrying a mound of gear, a bedroll, saddlebags, even Rhodry's winter cloak.

"Oho!" Rhodry said. "So I've been banished from the dun?"

"More or less." Yraen dumped the mound unceremoniously on the floor near Rhodry's feet. "Jill did mutter somewhat about it being safer for you here, like, but I know it aches the gwerbret's heart to turn you out."

"His grace is the very soul of honor. What about my horse?"

"Jill said to leave him be in the stables. Young Jahdo said he'd tend him."

"Thank him for me, will you?"

"I will." Yraen squatted down beside him. "How do you fare?"

"Not too badly. It was a shallow enough cut."

The innkeep returned with the tiny glass of medicinal liquor, handed it to Rhodry, then trotted off again for more ale all round. Garin leaned forward to speak to Yraen.

"Any news from the dun? About more raiders and suchlike?"

"None yet, though Jill's shut herself up in her tower room again. Creeps my flesh when she does that. I'm always afraid to look up when I'm walking in the ward for fear I'll see that cursed falcon flying about."

The dwarves all nodded grim agreement.

"It's beginning to get on my nerves, all this waiting," Yraen went on. "And the rest of the men are as jumpy as cats in a bathhouse, especially now that it looks like his grace might lose Matyc's brother's loyalty."

Rhodry winced. He'd rather forgotten about affairs of state when he'd been challenging the lord. But what was I supposed to do instead? he asked himself irritably. Let him cut down an old man in a piss-poor excuse for a combat? Yet all at once he could see an entire web of politics that he'd slashed when he'd killed Matyc. Perhaps he should have tried to talk the lord round?

"You all right?" Yraen was saying to him. "You've gone as white as snow."

"Have I now? I think I'll go back to bed. My thanks for bringing me my goods."

"I'll carry them down for you. Where are you sleeping?"

Once Yraen had dumped the gear into the chest and gone again, Rhodry lay down and fell asleep, boots, belt, and all. All night he had strange dreams of dragons and of eyes, disembodied elven eyes, floating in clouds and watching him from far away. When he woke again, he was soaked with sweat. The chamber was pitch-dark; he could guess that the fungi had given up the last of their stored sunlight some time before. He staggered up and flung open the door. Merciful light, dim but adequate, bloomed in the corridor outside. Leaving the door open, he went back in and found on the chest a pitcher of water and other necessary items.

Apparently someone had come in during the night, and he'd never even woken.

He considered sleeping again, but he was afraid of the dreams. He cleaned up a bit, then returned to the common room. Only Otho and young Mic were sitting at the table, which was spread with a variety of oddments—two oblong wooden trays, a sack that seemed to be filled with sand, some pointed sticks, a bone object that looked like a small comb, and part of a split cowhide, all painted over and written upon.

"Morrow, Rhodry," Mic said. "How do you feel this morning? It is morning, by the by."

"A good bit better, my thanks. The cut aches, but it's mending."

"Come sit down." Mic gestured at a bench. "Uncle Otho's going to cast us an omen."

The innkeep came bustling across from the fire and handed Rhodry a bowl of porridge, glistening with butter, and a wooden spoon.

"My thanks," Rhodry said. "Has there been any word from Jill?"

"None, but it's not long after dawn now. Mayhap—"

"Will you two hush?" Otho snarled. "I'm trying to prepare my mind, and I don't need anyone nattering round me."

With a choice oath the innkeep retreated. Rhodry ate his porridge in silence and watched while Otho poured pale white river sand into the trays, then used the comb to smooth it out as flat as parchment. With a stick he drew lines on one surface from corner to corner to divide the tray into four triangles. Then, on the outer edges, that is, the bottom of each triangle, he found the midpoint and connected those, overlaying a square to divide the area into four diamonds and eight smaller triangles.

"The lands of the map," Otho announced. "See, each one is the true home of a metal. Number one here is iron, two copper, and so on. The third is quicksilver, and the twelfth is salt, and I suspect that those two lands are going to figure large in this map."

"Salt's not a metal," Rhodry said.

"I know that, silver dagger. That's why it stands for all the hidden things in life, feuds and suchlike, and the dweomer."

"All the things that brighten a man's day, indeed. How do you tell fortunes with it?"

"Watch. I'll show you."

Otho took the second stick, held it over the second tray, then turned his head away and began to poke dots into the sand, as fast as he could. When he was done, he had sixteen lines of dots and spaces to mull over.

"Now, these are the mothers, these rows. You take the first lines of each to form the first daughter, and the second lines for the second, and so on. I won't bother to explain all the rules. It'd take me all day, and you'd find it tedious, no doubt."

Mic was studying the painted hide. When Rhodry craned his neck for a look, the young dwarf slewed it round so he could see, but the alphabet was utterly foreign to him.

"My apologies, but I don't know how to read that," Rhodry said. "What is it?"

"An omenbook, or part of one, I should say," Mic answered. "It's a chart, like, of the basic meanings of the figures. Otho knows it off by heart."

"I do when no one's flapping their lips," Otho snapped. "Now. Let me think. Hah! Just as I suspected. Here's the Head of the Dragon, all right, falling into the first house again." Deftly he poked a figure into the waiting sand, two dots close together and below them three dots vertically for the dragon's body.

"Again?" Mic said.

"I did a reading a fortnight or so past, and that same figure fell into that same place." Otho paused for a profound sigh. "You can be certain it's a true reading, when a thing comes up twice, and so we're stuck with this wretched wyrm whether we want it or no."

Otho brooded over the lines of dots for a few moments more, then poked figures into the map, one each for each land. When he came to the twelfth he hesitated.

"Last time I had a bit of luck fall in here," he announced. "I hate to think what lies in store, this time around." With a sigh he turned back to his lines, then howled. "The Red One! I knew it was going to be bad, I just knew it." He poked some savage dots into the Land of Salt. "Never do business with an elf, my father said, and I should have listened to him."

"According to this, Uncle Otho"—Mic flapped the hide in his direction—"the Red One's not as bad as it might be if it falls into the twelfth."

"Hah! That's all I have to say to that, young Mic. Hah!" Otho snorted so hard that his beard fluttered. "Look at that! The Road lies in the Land of Tin."

"And?" Rhodry said.

"Well, tin usually means the gods, but this time I think me it means long journeys."

"Gods!" Rhodry snapped. "I've been a dolt!"

"It's good to see you realize the truth about your essential nature."

"Hold your tongue! I've got to go talk with Jill."

"She told you to stay here," Mic broke in. "Can't I take her a message?"

"Well." Rhodry considered. "Truly, it would be best. Do you have a thing a man could write on, and a pen and ink?"

"Don't tell me you can read and write!" Mic sounded honestly awed.

"I can indeed."

"There's more to this wretched elf than one might suppose," Otho said. "Not much, but more than one might suppose."

Rhodry ignored him and called over the innkeep, who'd been shamelessly eavesdropping nearby. The writing materials available turned out to be a pair of wooden tablets, hinged with leather on one side and covered thickly with wax. In the frugal dwarven way, the writing could be smoothed off once a message was read, and the tablets used many times over. Rhodry found he could write well enough with the thin bone stylus the innkeep gave him. Once he was finished, he tied the tablets together with a thong.

"Want to put a seal on that knot?" the innkeep said.

"I don't. If someone steals it, they'll break it anyway, and I trust Mic."

The young dwarf smiled with a bob of his head and took the tablets. As he watched Mic hurry out, Rhodry felt profoundly relieved. He'd had every right to kill Matyc after all, or so it seemed to him.

When Mic arrived in the great hall, Jill had a servant fetch him a tankard of ale for his trouble, then took the pair of tablets just outside the door, where she could read them in relative privacy. As much as it griped her soul to admit it, she was pleased that she no longer had to worry about

Matyc popping up like a witch's curse every time she was trying to keep something secret. The message was brief enough, anyway.

"Matyc's last word was Alshandra's name."

Jill whistled under her breath and shut the tablets fast. For a moment she considered sending a message back, then decided that she needed to talk to Rhodry outright. While Mic finished his ale, she told Yraen where she was going, then accompanied the young dwarf back to the inn.

In the common room Rhodry was sitting on his bedroll on the floor with his back against the wall and his long legs stretched out in front of him. At the table Otho brooded over his geomancy figure while the innkeep consulted the painted cowhide.

"So," Rhodry called out. "You thought that message important, did you?"

"You knew I would. I'm glad you finally remembered this." She waved the tablets vaguely in his direction. "We need to talk in private."

They went down to his tiny chamber. With a snap of her fingers Jill summoned Wildfolk of Aethyr to spread their silvery light. Rhodry tossed his bedroll down in a corner and sat upon it again, but though tall for a woman she was still short enough to be comfortable sitting on the bed. She opened the tablets and laid her hand upon the message, letting the wax warm.

"You're certain of this?" she said.

"As sure as sure. He looked right up at me, coughed out her name, and died."

"Well, and grim news that is. I've had a singularly unpleasant thought, and this one's got naught to do with dweomer. If you're right about Matyc being a traitor, and it certainly looks like you are, who's to say that his brother isn't one, too?"

It was Rhodry's turn for the surprised whistle under his breath.

"I was asking the Lady Labanna about Lord Tren—that's Matyc's brother, you see—earlier. She tells me that their entire clan tends toward brooding, them being all alone up there on their ancestral lands. Their nearest neighbor's some fifteen miles away."

"A bit far for a casual ride over of an afternoon, truly. Huh, sounds like they're the most northerly dun in the entire kingdom."

"They are. The most northerly one that claims allegiance to the

High King, anyway. But Matyc's dun and his brother's manse would have been good places for some of these prophets that Meer tells me about to fetch up."

"I suppose so." Rhodry paused for a long moment, thinking something through. "I don't understand this business of new gods. What good would worshiping someone do you, if it weren't a god of your own people and your ancestral lands? I mean, you'd need to propitiate a foreign god, but worship it?"

"Well, I don't know, but I suspect that Alshandra's become a goddess that men can see and touch, no doubt the first one ever in their lives. And from what Meer says, she performs mighty dweomers in front of her worshipers and promises things to them."

"Promises? What sort of things?"

Jill smiled thinly.

"New land and new slaves, Rhoddo. Us, in short. The lands and people of Deverry."

Rhodry swore in a mix of several languages.

"Just so," Jill said. "Now, Alshandra has no idea of the extent of the kingdom. I doubt me if she even knows the High King exists, much less how large an army he can command in times of need. But then, neither do her followers, do they? If she raises enough of them in holy war, things are going to go very badly for those of us on the border, before the king marches west to put a stop to it."

"Badly indeed. Now here, Cadmar's going to need every sword he can find. This is no time for me to run off hunting some beast."

"Very clever, Rhoddo, but you're not slipping out of this noose as easy as all that."

When he made a sour face at her, Jill laughed. Under her hand the wax moved as it turned soft enough for her to efface the writing. She rubbed it smooth with the heel of her hand.

"Besides, you've got your own affairs to consider," she went on. "Lady Labanna and her women have begun asking me pointed questions about you, with your fine manners and courtly ways. It's been a long time since you rode away from Aberwyn, but not so long that someone might not recognize you, some noblewoman who was but a lass then but has a long memory. Alliances get sealed by marriages all the time, and they take women long ways from their homes."

Rhodry winced, remembering, no doubt, his own lady, who'd been less than happy with the disposition her brother had made of her life.

"That's true spoken," he said, "and for more reasons than one. It was all very well down in Eldidd to assume that no one would ever believe me to be as old as I am. Look how young he seems—he couldn't be the old gwerbret, they'd say. But up here in Cengarn they know how long an elven half-breed lives, and thanks to the malover, they know my father's name. If someone were to accuse me, if it ever came out that I was once Rhodry Maelwaedd, Gwerbret Aberwyn, but yet no true Maelwaedd at all—well, then. Will my son have a claim to the gwerbretal chair any longer?"

"He won't, truly, and it would be a pity to see him deposed. He's been a splendid ruler, you know. You raised him well."

"My thanks. I tried to."

She considered for a moment.

"Tell me somewhat," she said finally. "Do you miss your kin and clan?"

"Miss them? You mean long to see them or suchlike? I don't, truly, not after this lapse of years. News of them is welcome, though, and it gladdens my heart to hear that they're doing well. And it would ache that heart bitterly if I were the cause of doing them harm."

"Nicely put. Then I think, my friend, you'd best take yourself out of Cengarn, whether you want to go or no."

"So it would seem." He got up, wincing as he moved his wounded arm.

"I should have a look at that while I'm here. I'm not sending you off anywhere till it heals."

"It feels a fair bit better today than it did yesterday, I tell you."

With his good hand he picked his sword belt up from the chest and slung it onto the bed next to her, then raised the lid to rummage round.

"I've got somewhat to show you," he said. "Ah, I think it's in this one."

He brought out a leather saddlebag, set it on the floor, then closed the chest so he could sit on top of it. Jill had to untie the toggle on the bag, but once she had, he reached in himself and brought out something wrapped in a bit of old rag. This lump proved to be a leather sheath carrying a knife of sorts, a crude wedge of bronze stuck into a wooden handle, bound round with thongs to keep the blade in place.

"What do you think of that?" Rhodry said.

"I hardly know what to think. It's no ordinary knife. It looks like it was made long before the Dawntime, and I feel dweomer upon it." Jill took it, hefting it cautiously. "Where did you get it?"

"From Evandar. Do you remember me telling you about the whistle and the badger-headed creature?"

"Of course."

"Well, this is the blade that killed it. I doubt me if an ordinary one would have done the job."

"I see." She held the knife in one hand, looked absently away, and let its impressions flood her mind. "I don't think this blade is really here, you see. It exists on another plane of being, and this, the thing you feel, is more of an image of it, though an image made of matter, just as that badger creature probably was only an image of his real existence. So when you stabbed him with this, you were stabbing his real body, back on its own plane. An ordinary blade would only have stabbed his image to no lasting ill effect."

Rhodry tried to speak and failed.

"I know that doesn't make much sense," she went on. "I'm sorry, but I don't know how else to explain it. Consider this knife a shadow, like, thrown by the real one, which has its true home elsewhere."

Still he said nothing, merely shook his head, half-angry, half-baffled. When she handed the knife back, he started to wrap it up, then hesitated.

"Do me a favor, since you've got two good hands. Put this on my sword belt for me, near the silver dagger. I think me I'm going to need it."

After she'd taken care of the knife, Jill took a look at his wound, which was healing cleanly and far faster, of course, than a cut would have on a full-blooded human being. Even so, she made him promise to be careful of it for some days yet. As he was walking her back to the inn's door, she paused for a moment to glance at Otho's earthen omens.

"It looks clear as clear," Otho said, sighing. "There's no way out of going to fetch the dragon."

"I could have told you that," Jill said, grinning. "That dragon's calling to you, Otho lad."

The dwarf groaned with a roll of his eyes.

"Gods!" Rhodry snapped. "I nearly forgot another thing. All last night, Jill, I dreamt that someone was watching me. It was like a huge eye, floating above me. Does that mean aught?"

Jill felt her blood run cold.

"It does, indeed. Be careful, will you? On guard, every moment. Especially since there might be someone here to work you harm."

"There's not," Jorn broke in. "If you mean the fellow who tried to kill young Carra, he's dead. We found him out, you see."

"Oh. You might have told me."

"Well, truly." Otho looked embarrassed. "In all the excitement, it slipped my mind, like."

Jill waited, expecting more of the tale. The dwarves merely looked at her.

"Do you mind telling me why he tried to kill the lass?"

Jorn and Otho exchanged a glance first with each other, then with the innkeep, who looked down at the floor. No one spoke for some minutes.

"Er, well," Jorn said at last. "It's a dwarven matter."

Jill considered both threats and invective, but she knew them useless. When Rhodry started to speak, she waved him into silence.

"Well, keep Rhodry safe for me, will you? And send Mic with a message if you need me for aught."

When Jill got back to the dun, she hurried up to her chamber in the hopes of finding some message or token from Dallandra, if not the elven dweomermaster herself, but her room was exactly as she'd left it. In a fit of irritation she went down to the ward to pace back and forth where she had some room. Whenever she came to a place with a good view of her chamber window, she would stop and peer up, but she never saw anyone in it.

During one of her rounds, just as she passed the stables, she heard voices behind a nearby shed, nothing unusual in itself, but there was something oddly furtive about these, an old man's voice, a woman's. Such was her mood that she sidled close to hear.

"They don't look worth the fart of a two-copper pig," the woman was saying. "No wonder they got left behind!"

"Well, I don't know about that. There's a pretty pair of blue beads, and then this here bit could be silver, couldn't it now? Looks silver. And a nice bit of bronze with a design, like, on it. I deserve somewhat for all the trouble I went through with them prisoners. That worm-gut silver dagger ordering me around!"

Jill walked round the hut in her usual quiet way, raising a shriek from the pair—one of the kitchen maids and the elderly jailor, who was holding a cluster of thongs and amulets much like the ones Jahdo wore.

"And what have you there?" Jill said.

"Naught, naught." The jailor started to shove them into his pocket, then paused, caught by her stare. "Er, well, now, don't you be putting the evil eye on me!"

"I'm doing naught of the sort. All I did was ask you a question."

He licked dry lips and looked this way and that. The kitchen maid began to move backward, one cautious step at a time.

"Well?" Jill said.

"Er, I found them, like, in the straw in the cell where that hairy creature and his lad were kept, and I've been wondering what they were, like, for days now. You can't say I stole'm, can you now? They left 'em there, threw them away, and you can't say I stole'm!"

"I never said you did. I merely asked you what they are."

"Take'm, then, take'm! They creep my flesh, anyway."

He tossed the thongs her way, then turned and bolted with the kitchen maid right behind. Jill caught them in one hand. As soon as she got a good look at them, she realized that they were Gel da'Thae work. When she glanced at the sky, she realized that it was about the time of the afternoon when Meer took his nap and that, therefore, Jahdo was likely to be outside somewhere.

She eventually found the boy out behind the stables, rubbing down his mule with a brush braided from straw. She made sure that they were alone before she took the thongs and charms out of her pocket.

"Oh, Thavrae's amulets," he announced. "Where did you find them?"

"The jailor just gave them to me, I suppose you could say. Had he stolen them from you?"

"He hadn't. I did cut them off—well, we found Thavrae dead, you see." The boy's voice shook badly. "I did cut the thongs so I could get them free from—well, anyway, I did think Meer would be wanting them.

But he said Thavrae were no brother of his and did throw them against the wall. When we were in the cell, I mean. So I guess the old man found them there."

"I see. The old man could have kept them, then. Meer certainly didn't want them." Jill glanced round, but there was no sign of the jailor. "Though I don't know, if any of these have real dweomers laid on them, he shouldn't be carrying them about, for his own sake, like." She began to look through the handful of charms and immediately spotted a pewter disk with a sigil she recognized.

Now that's odd! Jill thought to herself. The Gel da'Thae dweomermasters would never use the same sigils and suchlike as we do, would they? But here's the sigil of the Lord of the Fire of Air, plain as plain.

"Jahdo, do you have a talisman with this kind of picture on it?"

"I don't. But I've seen one like it before." All at once the boy's eyes seemed to cloud over. "Somewhere. I don't remember."

Jill hesitated, wondering if she should test him for ensorcelment then and there, but the ward was as usual full of people coming and going on their various errands.

"Well, it doesn't matter." With a deliberately casual gesture, because she wanted to spare Jahdo worry, she shoved the handful into her brigga pocket. "I might ask Meer later, if I remember it."

What she did instead was go to Meer's chamber, wake him up, and ask him there and then. Although just describing the sigil told him nothing, when he felt it with a fingertip he could form, or so he said, a good idea of its shape.

"I can tell you this," he rumbled. "It's naught that he received from his mother or from one of the priestesses of the Gel da'Thae. I've never come across this mark before, and as a loremaster, you learn a good bit about the sacred symbols. Beyond that, I have no idea of what it might be. As for the rest of these holy marks and symbols, ask me not, because those secrets, mazrak, I will not betray."

"Very well, then. Well, my thanks, good bard, for what you've seen fit to tell me."

Jill left him, then stood hesitating by the staircase, considering what she needed to do next. All at once she felt the touch of Dallandra's mind on hers, a sign that the elven dweomermaster was back on the physical plane. When Jill went up to her chamber, she indeed found Dallandra there, sitting at her table and leafing through the book of elven chronicles that Jill had brought back from the Southern Isles.

"My gnome found you, then?" Jill said.

"He did." Dallandra looked up with a smile. "Have you been waiting long?"

"Two days."

Dallandra made a small irritated sound and shut the book.

"It seemed but a few moments to me."

"Oh, I know. I'm not blaming you or suchlike."

"I need to come back to this world, don't I? I simply can't keep traveling back and forth, trying to skip along the river of Time the way a child skips a rock on water. A delay like this could be a disaster if you needed me badly."

"Just so, but what about your own work? What about Evandar's people?"

"Well, I could stay here months, and it would be but a single day in his world, wouldn't it?"

Jill laughed, in relief, not merriment.

"Of course. I'd quite forgot that the differences run both ways. I'm getting worried, Dalla. Alshandra's already sent one pack of her worshipers here, trying to kill Carra and the child. Now that they've failed, she's bound to raise another. She's determined to get Elessario back."

"So she is. Naught can make her understand the truth, Jill. She honestly believes that I've stolen her daughter, and that if she kills Elessario's new body, then her daughter will be free of some sort of trap and come back to her."

"In a way you have to pity her, but I keep thinking of those other women, the ones her dogs of war killed, and their men, too, dying trying to defend them."

Dallandra shuddered.

"I do have to return to make my farewells and to make sure Evandar realizes that we're going to need his help and most likely soon. But I'll be back as soon as I can, and this time I'll stay until this matter's settled, and the child is born." Dallandra rose and picked up the chair in both hands. "We have to stay on guard if we're going to protect Carra from Alshandra, and you do have to sleep."

"Every now and again, truly. My thanks. And I've got a lot of information for you, too, that we'll need to sort out."

Jill was on the verge of asking her fellow dweomermaster just what she might be doing with that chair—she had a brief wondering if Dallandra was so distracted that she'd forgotten she was carrying the thing—but Dalla put it down in front of the window.

"Stone and air and the antagonism between them," Dalla remarked. "Gates are where you find them, you see."

She stepped upon the chair, stepped up onto the windowsill, stepped again, and disappeared. Jill rushed to the window, half expecting to see her sprawled on the cobbles beneath, but she was quite simply gone. Jill let out breath in a sharp sigh—she hadn't really realized that she'd been holding it. For all her own great power, there were some magicks she found hard to get used to.

When first Dallandra had learned the dweomer of the roads, she'd been forced to depend on the obvious sites of possible gates between worlds, such as the meeting of three streams or a thicket where hazel and rowan grew mingled together, but now after so much practice she could sense the fine edges where planes of energy met and rebounded from each other again, leaving a short-lived gap 'twixt one world and another. She slipped through this particular gate just as it was closing and found herself on the hill overlooking the astral river.

From behind her she heard singing and turned to see women walking back and forth in her formal garden. Wearing long dresses of fine cloth, red and white and gold, they strolled among the roses and clustered round the fountain, blond heads, dark heads, bent together as they talked. At times it seemed that perhaps a mere dozen souls walked among the green; at others, a huge throng swarmed there, just as a fire will flare up and flames multiply, only to fall back again when the draft that fanned it dies. As she hurried to join them, she heard them mention Elessario's name.

"You could join her, you know," she called out.

All attention they flocked round her, chattering and laughing, but the laughter vanished and the chatter turned to sighs when she repeated her oft-given message about the world of matter and Time. The woman she always called the night princess, who had modeled herself on the dark-skinned folk of Bardek, shook her head with a rustle of black curls.

"Why did she go there? I don't understand."

"To know life. What you have here is only a semblance of life, colored shadows thrown upon a wall."

They considered, looking at each other, looking at her, dark eyes, yellow eyes narrow and puzzled. With a shrug the night princess turned away.

"Dancing," she cried. "Let us go to the lilac arbor and have dancing!"

Their laughter turned to cries and chatter as they themselves mutated into a flock of bright-colored birds, parrot and cockatoo, gold and red and pink with here and there a flash of turquoise feather, and one black macaw with pink-trimmed wings and golden beak. On a wave of calls and rushing wings they flew away, circling once overhead, then flying steadily off toward the west. Dallandra said something foul in Elvish. Would she ever get them to understand?

Shaking her head she walked back over the hill to the astral river, which like quicksilver oozed through the dark green reeds and sparkled in the noontime sun. Nearby in the meadow the golden pavilion stood empty and silent. When she called Evandar's name, only his page came running.

"He's still gone," the boy said. "Riding the border still with the warriors. Do you want mead?"

"None, my thanks. But fetch me some bread, will you?"

The boy darted off again into the pavilion. Dallandra was just wondering whether to join him inside when she heard him scream. Without thinking she rushed for the pavilion entrance, but before she could reach it warriors sprang into being all round her, warriors in mail and helms of black, wolf faces leering, bear faces grinning, paws and claws reaching out to grab her. She flung up her hands to summon fire, but a familiar voice stopped her.

"Hold!" the fox warrior called out. "Or I'll kill this child."

He came strolling out of the pavilion carrying the page, trussed and sobbing, slung upside down over one mailed shoulder, the boy's head dangerously close to the sharp wedge of bronze knife that the warrior held in one gauntlet. Dallandra let her arms drop.

"What do you want of me?"

"Hah! I knew it would work." He was looking round at his men, if such you could call them. "She's weak, this woman. She pities things."

They howled and pressed close round her. She could smell bear and wolf, too, grease and blood and musk, mingling with an all too human sweat. Fur poked through their mail in tufts.

"You come with me," the leader said. "And you work no magic, or I'll fray and tear every weaving of this lad's body, and his spirit will spill and die."

The page wept the louder.

"Hush, child, I won't let them hurt you."

"Hah! She takes our bargain." The fox warrior pulled back dark lips in a fanged grin.

"What do you want of me?"

"Of you, naught. Of Evandar, everything. He's weak, too, giving me the whistle when he didn't have to. Losing a woman brings pain, he said, and so I got my idea. Ransom you are and ransom you'll be, until he saves my dying country."

Dallandra spat on the ground.

"You have the soul of a maggot, not a fox."

"She sees things, this woman! Maybe I'll trick Evandar and keep her forever!"

His soldiers growled and roared. A clawed hand cuffed her cheek and left her dizzy.

"Scoop her up, bind her, carry her off! We'll slip out the way we came in."

Ropes as rough and abrasive as straw circled her round, yet at the same time she felt as if she were falling, fainting, swooping nearer and nearer the ground yet never hitting against it. As her head cleared she saw round her huge flies and beetles, all shiny black bodies and green wings, with mandibles and mirrored red eyes—and realized that this insect horde was a normal size, but that she herself had shrunk to match them. Two massive black wasplike creatures with golden wings held her sling of ropes in their mandibles. With a buzz and drone of wings they flew, a horrible grating sound that combined with the pain in her head to drive her half-mad. She thrashed and kicked, but nothing she could do freed her from the web that dragged her along after them through the air.

On and on they flew over a huge green confusion, a swelling of trees that filled the world and reached up brown claws as if to grab them as they sped past. By twisting round and straining her back to look up she could just see the white clothes of the page, who dangled ahead of her like a crumb of bread in the grasp of an enormous and glittering blue-black fly, but a crumb that kicked and fought on occasion. At least Evandar's brother had had the sense to keep his hostage's hostage alive. All at once the green below started to rush up to meet them, or so it seemed to her, rushed and swelled and spun round and round. She would have screamed but it seemed that her tongue and mouth had fused together, that her throat swelled, that her body bloated and puffed up till pain seemed to burst out through her skin.

The ground smacked her hard. Light spun round her. The last sound she heard was the screaming of the page.

For a long time it seemed to her that she lay dead. Although she could not move nor hear nor see, her mind did exist, a floating point of consciousness on a black sea. She waited calmly for the light to rise and float her onward while she thought over the fall. It must have disrupted her etheric double, she supposed, and killed her that way, being as she had no body at the time. She felt profoundly sorry for Evandar, much more than she was worried about herself. In time she would be reborn, and she planned on begging that her rebirth take place as soon as possible, so that she could return to her work—if, of course, she could keep the memories of her work alive long enough to remember to beg.

All at once she realized two things. First, she was thinking too coldly, too calmly, to be actually dead. Second, she ached all over, a mere distant throb now that she'd noticed it, then a rather present throb, then an ache, and finally a burning like fire. Light like fire danced before her eyes; it seemed that she swam through fire, upward to a distant, cooler light. When she opened her eyes she found the vulpine face of Evandar's brother leaning close to hers.

"Good," he grunted. "You live. Dead you'd have been of no use to me."

She tried to speak and mock him, but the pain overwhelmed her. Once more she sank away from consciousness, but this time her last thought was that at least she was still alive—for at least a while.

• • •

Since Jill was of course used to the warped seams of Time between the physical world and Evandar's country, she thought nothing of it when Dallandra failed to return straightaway. Over the next few nights she spent long hours scrying, ranging as far from the dun as she dared, whether in the falcon form or the body of light, in the hopes of bringing the gwerbret some advance warning of an attack. Every morning she would join Cadmar at breakfast to make her report. Since Lord Gwinardd had taken his men and gone back to his own dun, the great hall echoed half-empty and strangely silent. On the far side of the hall, the warband would strain to hear what she might be saying to their lord. Rumors had spread, as they always do, and every man there knew that war was on the way. The only question was when.

After her meal Jill would walk to the dwarven inn to tend Rhodry's wound and ask him about his dreams. Never again did he see the eyes, watching him, but she assumed that the enemy, who or whatever it might have been, was continuing to scry, merely more deftly. She was faced with an evil choice. She could easily have put astral seals over Rhodry—over the entire town and dun, for that matter—that would have prevented any dweomerworker, no matter how skilled, from scrying out a single detail. If she did so, though, she might as well have hung out huge banners announcing the presence of a master sorcerer. Since she had no reason to assume that their enemies knew either who she was or that she was in the dun, she preferred to keep them wondering about Cengarn's strength.

After her visit she would return to her chamber and sleep for a few hours, waking before sunset to eat a meager meal before resuming her night watch. On the fourth afternoon of this routine, Jahdo came to her chamber just as she was finishing a chunk of bread and cheese. One sharp glance at the boy told her that something was badly wrong. She ushered him in, then called upon the Wildfolk of Aethyr, who materialized in a flicker of silver light.

"Are you ill, lad?"

"I'm not, my lady. I did hear that Rhodry would be leaving Cengarn with his small friends and that none did know when he would return."

"Where did you hear that?"

"From Yraen. He did tell me not to tell others, and I have not, only you, being as I were sure you knew this well already."

"Just so. Well, now, are you going to miss Rhodry? Is that the trouble?"

"I do want to go along with him."

Yet his voice had such a false ring that Jill gave him a sharp looking over. She found agony in his eyes.

"Jahdo, are you sure you don't feel ill? Fevers give us strange thoughts at time."

"I be well, truly." He began to tremble. "I just did want to ask if I could go with Rhodry and the dwarves."

She knelt on one knee so that she could look him in the face.

"You really want to leave Cengarn?"

The trembling turned to a shake like palsy. He made a guttural noise deep in his throat, swallowed hard, and finally spoke.

"I want to go away."

"I don't believe you. Is it really true that you want to go away?"

"It is." But his head shook in a convulsive no.

Jill whistled softly under her breath.

"You don't want to say those words you've been saying, do you?"

"I don't." He forced the words out. "It's needful."

"Indeed? Interesting. Now, just stand there quietlike for a moment. Don't move and don't speak."

Jill opened up her dweomer sight to take a look at the boy's aura. As is the case with most children, his formed a lopsided, ever-changing cloud of energy, at moments shriveled, at others billowing out to one side or the other. Yet spiraling round the aura ran a dark smear or line, ineptly drawn, but no doubt effective. Jill grunted in distaste, then sent a line of light from her own aura and wiped the dark away. She shut down the dweomer sight to find Jahdo watching her, his head cocked to one side like a puzzled dog.

"Now tell me, lad, do you want to go with Rhodry and the dwarves?"

"I don't! Oh, please, mayn't I stay?"

"Of course. And as soon as ever we can, we'll take you home."

He broke into a grin, started to skip a few steps, then stopped, letting the grin fade as he stared off in thought.

"Jahdo?" Jill kept her voice very soft. "Someone told you to ride with Rhodry. Who was it?"

"No one did tell me. I did but know that it was needful for me to keep going onward."

"Indeed? 'Onward,' is it? Try answering this. Who told you to go with Meer?"

"I—I don't remember."

"But someone told you."

"Not exactly. I just did know it was needful. I couldn't say I didn't want to go when Meer asked."

"And Yraen asked if you wanted to go with Rhodry?"

"He did, but it were a jest, like. I did see in his eyes that it were a jest, and yet I couldn't say no. It was needful for me to travel onward."

Jill growled under her breath. Whoever had ensorcelled the child was a clever little scoundrel. Since he'd never given Jahdo a direct order, the boy wouldn't remember him directly, either, unless Jill could think of perfectly apt questions. Until she knew more, those lay beyond her. It was at least obvious that this amateur sorcerer lived in Cerr Cawnen, where Jahdo had started his journey. She would simply have to wait and deal with him there, providing, of course, she did manage to get the boy home again someday.

That night Jill risked traveling in the etheric a little farther than usual. Normally she went north and west, searching in the general direction in which an attack was likely to come, but this time she headed straight west, wondering if perhaps the enemy was outfoxing her by marching from an unexpected direction. Again, she found nothing, returning exhausted at dawn to her body and the dun. Before she went down to the great hall she rested, wondering if perhaps Alshandra had given up her mad plan of releasing her daughter's soul by killing her growing physical body. It seemed unlikely that a spirit so single-minded, so lacking in the breadth of experience and the compassion that incarnation brings, would abandon her obsession so easily. Certainly Dallandra had always considered her implacable.

Dallandra. All of a sudden Jill was wide awake, realizing just how long it had been since Dalla had gone off, promising to come right back. Yet even though she worried, she could explain her fears away. With Time's flow so uneven between the worlds, Dalla might very well have

been experiencing but a few moments passing. Jill had no way of finding
her. Evandar's country was so foreign to her nature as well as so distant
on the astral that Jill could never scry into it. She put the matter out of
her mind, for that while at least, and went on down to breakfast with
Cadmar and, of course, his lady as well as Carra and her prince.

Dar had apparently been doing some thinking of his own about their
situation. He waited until the serving lass had set down the bread and
porridge and was gone before speaking, then leaned forward to address
both Jill and the gwerbret.

"Your Grace, good sorcerer, if Cengarn's going to be sieged, what
we need is archers, and my people can easily raise five hundred of them,
all armed with good yew bows. All I have to do is send out some of my
men to find Calonderiel, Banadar of the Eastern Border. Well, it's east
to us, anyway. It would be your western border, of course."

"Now that's a splendid thought," Cadmar said. "How long will it
take to find him, though? I know that you people wander with your herds
all summer long."

"That's true, Your Grace, but in the fall we all move south, and
there's one particular winter camp where Calonderiel always goes, and
he always heads down that way early, so people will know where to find
him if they have some dispute or suchlike for him to settle. It'll take
some weeks, truly, but the task's not impossible. And then, once they
find him, the company will have to ride here. It'd be two full turnings
of the moon, all in all, before they could arrive."

Cadmar glanced at Jill. She could see he was worried, caught between
courtesy and grim realities.

"Well, Dar, the problem's going to be feeding them," Jill spoke to
spare the gwerbret's sense of gratitude. "That's why his grace sent Gwinardd back to his own lands, and why he hasn't called in all his other
alliances yet. Arcodd's not a very rich place, you know. The hay for all
those horses alone would be hard to come by, to say naught of the room
to stable them."

"Oh, of course." Dar did understand, fortunately, rather than being
insulted. "I'd forgotten that. Well, Your Grace, what shall we do, then?
Wait till we know the army's on its way, and then send out the
messengers?"

"That would be best, Your Highness." Cadmar sounded relieved.

"We could stand a siege better than we could provision so many men for month after month. I'm sure Jill will be able to give us a few days' warning, eh?"

"I hope so, Your Grace," Jill said. "I'm trying my best to scout them out."

"Let's just hope that they hold off till the first harvest's in, and the dun fully provisioned," Cadmar went on. "It's likely. They'll want to see their own winter wheat brought in, no doubt. The bards like to sing about armies living off the country and all that, but hah! it's a risky business. Never know what you'll find, or how much, and foraging takes forever, when you need to make a fast march. Besides"—and here he paused for a grin—"if they're coming from the north and west, it's cursed few farms they'll find along their line of march, and some wretchedly sparse provisioning. The only supplies out that way are the fat on the bears."

Everyone dutifully laughed at the jest, but Carra and Labanna exchanged glances full of anxiety. Even though Jill agreed with the gwerbret's line of reasoning, she intended to keep up her nightly scrying. Thinking of the scrying did, however, remind her of another grim reality.

"Dar, I do have one rather nasty thought. When our enemies arrive, they'll have dweomerworkers with them—at least one, maybe more. I'd just as soon they didn't know your men were on their way. Why don't you send messengers now to find Calonderiel, tell him the situation, and ask him to gather his company and keep them ready? We can send other men when I see the army approaching, for the final warning, like, but this way the banadar will know our situation."

"Good thinking," Dar said. "And he'll know to march anyway if he never hears any more news. What shall we tell him? We have a festival, Delanimapaladar, to mark the day when the light and the dark are an equal length. What about then?"

"Sounds a good choice." Cadmar smiled all round. "Jill, you've got a good head for war, I must say."

"I've seen more than a few, Your Grace. Too many, truly, far, far too many, all in all."

"So have I." Cadmar looked away, suddenly troubled. "Huh. All this waiting's bad for a man, gets on his nerves. Which reminds me. I wonder why Lord Tren hasn't sent me a message about that letter I sent

him? Sure enough, the priests down at the temple are putting in a claim
for his brother's lands. I sent another man off to Tren with that news
just yesterday, so maybe it'll jog him into some action."

Everyone nodded, looking back and forth at one another. In her
worry over Alshandra, Jill had almost forgotten that there was more than
one kind of trouble brewing, this one from an all too human source.

That very morning Daralanteriel sent his pair of messengers off with
letters and tokens for Calonderiel. From her tower room Jill watched
them ride out, leading a packhorse, carrying their short, curved hunting
bows strung at the ready and slung over their shoulders. She would scry
for them, too, off and on over the next few days, until she could be sure
that they were safely out in the grasslands and on their way south
unharmed.

More and more she believed that some enemy was scouting the dun
just as she was scouting the surrounding countryside. Although she
doubted very much if another shape-changer lurked physically round
Cengarn, such a sorcerer might well have been scrying by more conven-
tional means or prowling out on the etheric plane. Every now and then,
when she was traveling in the body of light, she would peer round her
through the billowing blue waves of etheric energy and see hints that
someone else had passed the same way. Occasionally as well she would
run across the Wildfolk, who in their true home were beautiful creatures,
all geometric shapes and lines of colored light. At times they would flock
round her in an exhalation of rage, perhaps caused by an interloper in
their world, at others of terror, as if that interloper had frightened them.

Besides, she and Rhodry both still had the sporadic feeling that they
were being watched. Of course, many people who have no dweomer of
their own suspect it everywhere and in the most normal of occurrences,
a thing true in Jill's time just as nowadays. Not only was Rhodry half-
elven, however, with that race's natural sensitivity to magic, but dweomer, for evil as well as good, had touched his life many times in the past.
When he said that he felt it now, she believed him.

"But you know what's strange about this, Jill?" he remarked one
morning. "I don't feel any malice when this mind or whatever you'd call
it turns my way."

"You don't? Interesting! I've felt malice in good measure, myself,
and so have the Wildfolk. Somebody's terrified them."

"Stranger and stranger."

"Well, I'll make a guess that we're dealing with two different dweomerfolk, but that's only a guess." She hesitated, then decided that there truly was naught more to say until she had more evidence. "What I do know is that this wound of yours is healed up nicely. I think me it's time for you and the dwarves to get on your way."

"Are you sure I wouldn't better serve the gwerbret by staying here? If there's a war coming—"

"Soldiers the gwerbret has. You're the only man on this earth who can find that dragon and unravel Evandar's tedious little riddle."

"And you think it's truly important that the dragon get itself found?"

"I do. I can't tell you why, but I do."

"No hope for it, then." He flashed her one of his lunatic grins. "I shall do my lady's bidding and walk strange roads, climb high mountains, freeze in the snows, and deal with dwarven madmen, and all of this shall I do with cheerful heart and—"

"Will you hold your tongue? This is no time for daft jests."

"On the contrary, my lady." Rhodry bowed low to her. "What better time for a daft jest than when the times themselves are mad?"

She started to snap at him, then decided he was right enough.

"Let's go out to the common room. I want to talk to Otho about provisioning this expedition. By the by, did he ever hand over the coin he owed you?"

"Of course not. It's all gone to the innkeep for my bed and board."

"The gall! I'll speak to him about that."

"No need. We're doubtless all about to die, anyway, gulped down for a tidbit by this wyrm, so what does a handful of coppers matter, anyway? Of course, it might give the beast indigestion, if it ate my pockets with me, and so we'd have a revenge of sorts."

"I wish you wouldn't jest like that."

He hesitated, then turned away with a shrug.

"As my lady commands, then."

"And the paying of that coin's important, Rhoddo. He should pay and maintain you as well."

"At the moment I can't much worry about a handful of coin."

"Nah nah nah, I didn't mean important to you. Important for Otho."

Rhodry blinked at her.

"Haven't you ever wondered what got him exiled?" she went on.

"Many a time. I never thought it my place to ask."

"Right you were, too, and if you ever tell anyone you know this, I'll be displeased."

Rhodry shuddered, but it was only half a jest.

"He wouldn't pay a debt." Jill ignored the gesture. "I don't know all the ins and outs of it, but he owed a man some steep fee, and he wouldn't pay. He had it all worked out why he shouldn't pay in his own mind, like, but no one else agreed, and he had to go into exile."

"Go into exile for a debt of *coin?*"

"Just so. The Mountain People take their obligations very seriously."

"So that was it." Rhodry winced at the memory. "When Garin asked me not to judge them all by their kinsman, I knew I'd made some sort of botch of my courtesies. Well and good, then. Let's go torment the old man a little."

They found Otho sitting in the common room with his kinsmen, drinking and playing at dice. At the hearth, the innkeep was adding chunks of some indefinable vegetable to the stew pot, but he stopped to listen in.

"Otho," Jill snapped. "You owe Rhodry and Yraen coin."

The elderly dwarf howled and turned his face to the distant sky, perhaps asking it to witness his sufferings.

"Is this true?" Garin snapped.

Otho moaned, muttered, moaned again, but when every dwarf in the room stared at him, arms crossed over their chests, he reached for the pouch at his belt. Jill took half of what he handed over to give to Yraen.

"Will you all be going with your kinsman?" Jill said to Garin.

"I will, at least as far as Haen Marn, though Jorn here won't. If Enj won't take our clan's coin, I'll go a-hunting the wyrm instead, but a weak reed I'll be to lean upon, I tell you. I'm sure that loremasters spend years memorizing all the things I know not about dragons."

"I'll go," Mic broke in. "May I, Uncle Otho? I've never been any-where nor done anything."

"Hah, and no doubt you'll wish you'd stayed in that blessed condition before this little walk is over," Otho said. "But come along you may, if your father allows." He glanced at Jorn and raised an eyebrow. "Think he will? My brother was always the most stubborn man on earth."

"Until his son was born and took the title from him," Jorn said, grinning. "Well, ask him. You'll have to go home first before you head out to Haen Marn. He'll probably want to set a blood price for young Mic, though, in case he never returns."

"A blood price? The gall!"

"Otho!" Jorn and Garin spoke in chorus.

Jill left them squabbling and went back to the dun.

Yraen she found in the great hall, sitting and drinking at a table near the back door. When she gave him the coins, he grinned, a rare thing for him, and slipped them straightaway into the pouch he wore round his neck and under his shirt.

"Rhodry taught me to do that," he remarked. "Keep your coins out of sight, I mean. He said he learned it from you."

"So he did, when we were both a fair bit younger."

"I'm glad old Otho finally came across. I was wondering if he ever would. Here, is he daft?"

"Not that I know of. Why?"

"Cursed strange thing, a few nights past. I happened to run across him in the ward. Come to pay me, have you? says I. All in good time, says he, I've been to visit the princess. And all at once he fixes me with this look. You owe her a debt, says he, though you won't remember it, and if ever a debt should be paid, it's that one. And then he stumps on by without so much as another word."

"Well, um, odd indeed." Jill fished round and came up with an evasion. "Maybe he thought you were someone else. He's getting on a bit."

"True enough, true enough. That's probably all there was to it, then."

Jill left the matter there, but she was honestly surprised that Otho would recognize in their new bodies souls he'd known so long ago, in his youth but when they were living out other lives, turns of the wheel of birth and death that had long since ended. It was all because of Carra, or so Jill assumed, who back in that other long-gone existence had been the only person in the dwarf's entire life whom he had ever loved. Jill wasn't about to probe that old wound, however, and ask the old man for details.

Over the next few days, Cengarn began to prepare for war. The gwerbret took to spending much of the day riding his lands, with his servitors in attendance, going from farm to farm, sizing up the harvest and having a word here and there with various yeoman farmers who could be counted on to join the muster. Messages went back and forth between his various vassals, too, discussing plans. The townsmen began making preparations of their own, gathering in what supplies they could, meeting together to discuss mutual support and to choose the men and wagons they owed the gwerbret in times of war. Yet in all the flurry of hard work and messages, no one ever heard from Lord Tren, not the gwerbret himself, not his loyal vassals. Whenever Cadmar sent him a messenger, the man was always well treated, told that an answer would follow, and sent away empty-handed. No answer ever did come.

During these days Jill spent more time at her scrying than ever, yet never did she find one sign of military action along the gwerbret's borders. More and more, too, she worried about Dallandra. It had been close to a fortnight since she'd seen her, but of course, as she reminded herself, that lapse of time could have been a mere afternoon up in Evandar's country. As she often did, she sent her gray gnome, who was beginning to form a seed of true mind, to find Dallandra. Although the gnome couldn't give her a concrete message, often his arrival was enough to remind Dalla that Jill wanted to see her. Yet every time, the gnome came back without her. When Jill tried asking him simple questions, he would shrug and wander round her chamber, peering into things, shrugging again. She could figure out that he meant he simply hadn't found Dalla anywhere he'd looked.

Finally Jill decided to try contacting with Evandar or his people herself. When Prince Daralanteriel took his men out hunting, she rode with them until she found a place where two streams joined and a farmer's fence ran to meet them. It was just this sort of contrast on the one hand and a mingling of disparate natures on the other that seemed to harbor those mysterious gates Dallandra had discussed with her.

Jill waited until the prince and his men were out of earshot, then dismounted, tied her horse to a fencepost, and walked over the three-way join. She could indeed feel a slight difference in the place, a certain stirring of the energy of the earth, a tension in the air, a scurrying in the water. No doubt if she'd been carrying a torch, it would have burned the brighter on this spot. She glanced round—no one in sight but a white cow, drinking at the stream.

"Evandar!" Jill called out. "Dalla! Can you hear me?"

Nothing, not a sound, not a change of energy, not a ripple in the etheric forces to count as an answer. She sat down, leaning against a post, and allowed herself to slip into a light trance so that she was half-aware of the etheric, half of the physical. She could see in the blue light a sort of shimmering plate or shape, but she had not the slightest idea of what to do with it. With a shake of her head she brought herself back and abandoned the attempt.

When she caught up with them, not one man of the Westfolk asked her what she'd been doing. They had had too much experience with dweomer to question a Wise One. As the warband let their horses walk slowly back to the dun, Jill rode beside Dar. The hunting had been good; they were bringing three deer back with them.

"I've heard these sieges can last for months," Dar remarked.

"That's true. Do you think you and your men can endure it? Being shut up, I mean."

"If it's not safe to take Carra away, I'll have no choice. I can endure what I need to. We all can."

"Good, because she won't be safe out on the grass. I've thought of calling to other Wise Ones—you know that we have ways of doing so—but frankly, Dar, I've been afraid to. It's possible to be overheard, when you send thoughts through the fire and on the winds. And if it's enemies that hear us, it won't be a good thing."

"I'd wondered about that." He turned in the saddle to look at her. "I assumed you knew your own affairs best."

"My thanks, but I felt I owed you an explanation. One other thing I wanted to tell you. Rhodry will be leaving Cengarn on the morrow. I've sent him on a dangerous errand indeed."

"I see. He's not going alone, is he?"

"Some of the Mountain People will be traveling with him. Why?"

"That shape-changer worries me, the raven that he and Carra saw when he was escorting her to Cengarn. Does he have a bow with him?"

"Not that I know of. Does he know how to use one?"

Dar grinned.

"You could say that. Oh, he'll make light of his skill, and he's got nowhere near the fine eye that, say, Calonderiel does, but all in all, he's a man I wouldn't mind having with me if I needed an archer."

"Ah. Do you have a spare bow I could take him, then?"

"I do. I'll bring it to your chamber when we get back, and a quiver of arrows as well."

It was late that day, close to sunset, when Otho came up to the dun to consult Jill about their plans. Although she'd been hoping that the dwarves had built some sort of hidden exit or tunnel out of Cengarn, no such thing existed—the bedrock was too close to the surface, or so Otho said, and such tunnels were dangerous to a town built to withstand siege if a traitor should betray their existence to any enemy.

"Now, don't you worry, though. We'll stay in the wild hills. There's a road there that only we know."

"It'll have to do, then."

"No one's going to spy us out, well, not unless they're using dweomer, that is, and such would find us no matter how deep under the earth we were. There's one good thing about Rhodry being half an elf. He can see well enough in the dark to travel at night, same as us, and that's what we'll do, travel at night and hide ourselves in the day."

"Splendid! You have my thanks, you know, for what it's worth."

"Worth a great deal." Otho sighed with a shake of his head. "Ah, it's strange how things turn out! I keep thinking of you as that golden little lass you were when first I met you, years and years ago now, when you were just a silver dagger's brat, trailing along behind your da. Do you remember the riddle I told you?"

"About how 'no one' could tell me what craft I'd learn?" Jill smiled, remembering herself as a child standing in his silversmithy. "I do, at that. Nevyn and I both got a good laugh out of it, once I'd sworn myself over to study the dweomer, because 'nev yn' had told me, indeed."

Otho nodded, looking away with one of his rare smiles. Then he sighed, turning sad.

"I'd best be making my farewell to the Princess Carramaena," he said. "Doubtless I'll never—ah well, I'm not going to weave myself a bad omen by saying that aloud. You'll be down at the inn to see us off?"

"I'll go down now. I want a word with Rhodry." She patted the quiver of arrows. "And I've got to give him Dar's gift."

Jill found Rhodry pacing back and forth in the common room of the dwarven inn, and all alone, as if the innkeep and the other dwarves had fled to leave him to his brooding. By human standards he was a tall man, anyway, and in the midst of dwarven-sized furniture he seemed enormous, looming over everything in the pale, uncertain light, part blue phosphorescence, part fire's glow, that danced about the stone chamber. He was in a somber mood—she could tell by the way he laughed one of his crazed peals at the sight of her. At times she found herself wondering if he'd been possessed by one of the old gods of war, Gamyl, perhaps, or even Epona, Mistress of Horses. She was afraid to probe his mind and find out.

"What's that you're carrying?" Rhodry said. "Looks like a hunting bow."

"It is, and a present from Prince Dar himself. He says you've a fair hand with it."

"Only fair, I'm afraid, but if we're going to have shape-changers flapping round us, better to arm me than give us no archer at all."

Rhodry laid the bundle on the table and began to unwrap it, whistling a little at the sight of the painted doeskin quiver and the golden buckles on its baldric. He laid that to one side, flipped the cloth one more time, and freed the unstrung bow itself, a graceful curve like the ridge of a man's eyebrows, and made of two kinds of wood and horn, trimmed with silver round the handgrip. As he ran one finger along it, his eyes filled with tears.

"Dar's sent me his own bow," he said. "Now that's an honor I never thought to have."

"Well, it seems the least he can do. It's his lady you're risking your life for."

"Jill, ye gods! You have a way of taking the bloom off a fine gesture, I must say."

"It comes from having been born a silver dagger's bastard."

"Well, no doubt. Now that I've spent many a long year at the bottom of things, as I'd suppose you'd call it, I begin to see your point. But still." He ran a loving hand along the bow's shaft. "I appreciate this stick of wood. Tell my prince that I'm honored."

"I will, then."

They hesitated, looking at each other in the bizarrely colored light.

"This is farewell, isn't it?" Rhodry said. "Think we'll ever see each other again?"

"I hope so. If we don't, somewhat will have gone badly wrong for one or the other of us."

"That's what I fear, sure enough. Ah, well, if my lady Death snatches me away from you, it'll only be retribution for the way the dweomer took you from me, all those years ago."

"Rhodry, I had to go."

"Do you want to know a strange thing? I see that now. Now. All these years later." He smiled briefly. "Do young men ever see the truth of their women's lives? I doubt it, I doubt if they can, I doubt if we could and go on being the men our fathers and our king expect us to be, truly. But now, well, I don't remember how many years I've lived, but it's getting close to four score, isn't it? Must be by now, if not more. And I do see things a bit more clearly." He turned away and busied himself with wrapping the bow back up. "I just wanted you to know that. I don't know why."

"My thanks. It means a great deal to me, a very great deal indeed. It's ached my heart, all these years, knowing you'd never forgiven me for riding away with Nevyn."

He shrugged and tucked the last corner of cloth round the quiver, as lovingly as a mother swaddling her baby.

"One last thing," he said. "Do you remember when you came to fetch me from Aberwyn?"

"I do."

"I'd hoped that we could ride together again."

"I knew it."

"You were cold enough to me, cold as a winter storm."

"I had to be, you dolt!"

"Your Wyrd again?"

"Not mine; yours. You no more belong to me than I do to you, but I knew that you'd never listen to simple reason. You had to find a new road, Rhodry. I honestly thought you could live in peace out on the grasslands, find a new love, no doubt, and a new life. I never dreamt that the dweomer had its claws in you so deep."

He spun round, startled.

"So." He managed a grin. "You dweomermasters don't know everything there is to know, do you?"

"Of course not. If we did, you and I and Carra and everyone else wouldn't be in this wretched mess now."

He laughed his berserker's howl, and hearing him sound so daft ached her heart. As if he'd picked up her change of mood he choked the laugh off. For a moment they looked at each other in a silence that rang loud.

"But, Jill," he said at last, "if the worst happens, remember how I loved you, will you?"

"Always, Rhodry. And remember that before my Wyrd tore me away, I loved you."

She turned on her heel and hurried out of the chamber, headed for the door and fast, because for the first time in some forty years, she was afraid that she would weep. As she walked back to the dun, she was remembering the hideous omen of a few days past, when she'd seen his Wyrd devour him. No one, not dweomermaster nor king nor priest, can turn a man's Wyrd aside, but Jill vowed that night that if ever she could undo Rhodry's fate after it had come upon him, she would risk whatever needed risking to do so.

Just at dawn Yraen woke up in the barracks to gray light, falling in squares through unshuttered windows. For a moment he lay awake, hands under his head, and listened to the sounds of other men sleeping in long rows, a noise that had become familiar, a mark of the only home he had left, during the four years since he'd left his father's holdings and ridden off to become a silver dagger. Out of long habit he turned his head to see if Rhodry was awake, but the bunk next to his was of course empty. Bastard, he thought. I'm going to miss him. He lay still a moment longer, then rolled out of bed, dressed, and, cradling his sword belt against his chest to keep it from jingling, crept out before he woke anyone.

Out in the ward he paused, buckling on the heavy belt, sword to the left, silver dagger to the right. It was hot that morning, with a sweep of mackerel clouds across the sky that promised coming rain. As he headed for the gates, the wind picked up, sighing across the ward in a rustle of thatch and a banging of shutters. Spring had turned into full summer.

The days were growing longer and longer, and he'd heard the servants talking about the first harvest of winter wheat and short hay. If you had to send someone off on a fool's errand, it was as good a time as you were going to get, he supposed. At the gates a sleepy guard greeted him with a yawn.

"Where are you off to so early?"

"Oh, Rhodry's leaving town today. He owes me money."

"Better get it while you can, then."

Yraen smiled and strode on, wondering why he'd lied, why he had to pretend to some cold reason for saying farewell to a friend. All round him the town was just coming awake, with much banging of shutters and the smell of newly lit fires. He walked down the middle of the streets, ready to dodge slops as he made his now-familiar way to the dwarven inn. In the brightening light Rhodry stood outside, yawning and leaning against the stonework round the open door. He was wearing a strange pair of boots, cut from sheepskin with the fleece inside and bound to his ankles with strips of dirty cloth, like a peasant would wear, a strange contrast to the gold-trimmed baldric across his chest and the painted quiver slung at his hip. Leaning next to him was a big peddler's pack— stiff canvas sacks and a bedroll, lashed to a wooden frame—and beside that a curved elven hunting bow, loose-strung for carrying. When he saw Yraen he grinned and strode over to meet him.

"You're up early," Rhodry said.

"So everyone tells me. Ye gods, you look like a cursed woodcutter!"

"At least do me the honor of calling me a gamekeeper." Rhodry patted the quiver. "Please note the drinking cup at my belt, and the ax hanging from the pack. Our generous Otho has hung me with trinkets, all suitable to my new life as a creature of wood and heath."

"Imph. Where are the Mountain Folk?"

"Squabbling inside. I'm cursed glad Garin's coming with us. He's the only one Otho'll listen to."

"And what are they fighting about?"

"I wouldn't know. They're talking in their own tongue." Rhodry paused for a laugh, but mercifully just a normal one. "This is going to be a journey fit for a bard to sing about, Yraen my friend. The question is, will it be a noble tale or a satire on men's folly?"

Yraen tried to think of some jest and failed. Rhodry grinned, looking away toward the east, glancing up as if he were watching the sun brighten on the town wall.

"Are you supposed to carry that thing, by the by?" Yraen pointed to the peddler's pack.

"I am, and so I will." Rhodry looked at it with grave doubt. "Well, it's going to be the strangest road I've ever traveled, but who knows? Maybe it'll lead me at last to the bed of my one true love, my lady Death."

"Will you hold your ugly tongue?" Yraen realized that he'd shouted and reined in his voice as he went on. "I'm sick as a man can be of you indulging that wretched daft fancy."

"It's not daft. She'll have us all in the end, she will."

Again, Yraen found that he had nothing to say. Suddenly solemn, Rhodry turned to him.

"My apologies. Keep yourself safe, will you?"

"I'll do my best. And the same to you, you berserk bastard."

Rhodry smiled briefly. There was, Yraen decided, nothing more to say. With a wave he turned and headed back, walking fast for the dun.

By the time he got back to the ward, the sunlight had topped the walls. Outside the barracks, the men of the warband were up and moving round, some ducking their faces in the water of the horse trough, others standing in a clot near the privies, a few straggling toward the great hall and breakfast.

"Yraen!" Draudd called out. "Jill was out here looking for you. Better be careful, lad. She'll be putting the evil eye on you or suchlike."

"Oh, hold your ugly tongue! Does she want to see me?"

"She does and right away. She'd be in the great hall, she said."

When Yraen walked into the hall, he saw Jill sitting at the table of honor. Since the gwerbret and his lady were also there, he hesitated, wondering if he should approach, but Jill saw him and hailed him, waving him over. With a bow to the gwerbret he knelt beside her.

"Yraen, I've a task for you," Jill said. "I want to put a guard near Prince Daralanteriel's chamber. The chamberlain tells me that right next to it is a little room, for a servant, like, where you can sleep from now on. You'll be right at hand if there's trouble. And then, during the day, I want you to keep a watch on Princess Carramaena whenever she's not in the women's hall or with her husband."

Yraen felt as if she'd slapped him across the face. He wanted to scream at her and tell that he was the worst man in the world for this duty, but how was he going to explain that being near the princess was a dagger in his heart, that he'd been fool enough to fall in love with a married woman? Jill hesitated, considering him with her piercing blue stare.

"What's wrong?"

Nearby the gwerbret and Labanna had paused, as if to listen.

"Naught," Yraen said. "It's just—ah, it's naught. I've just been saying farewell to Rhodry, that's all, and wondering if ever I'll see him again."

"I see. I'd love to ease your mind, but frankly, I've been wondering the same thing myself. These aren't the best of times, Yraen, which is why I need a guard over the princess. You're as courtly as any man in the dun, after all, and I know I can trust you."

"My thanks." He swallowed hard. "I'll do my best to deserve your trust."

"Good. There's the chamberlain now. Go get your gear from the barracks, and we'll get you moved over to the broch."

Yraen rose, bowed again to his grace, and hurried off. He felt much as he had when he'd once been wounded in battle, a stunned disbelief that such could be happening to him, a cold shock that had left him feeling light-headed, as if he were going to drift into the sky. When he'd been wounded, however, the pain had started right after, giving him something to fight against, to focus upon and use to pull himself together and ride to safety. Now he had nothing to fall back on but his honor, a tarnished commodity, a dull blade indeed after so many years on the long road, and there was no safety, none, from the treachery of his heart. As he was cursing Jill and his luck both, Carra came down the staircase with her maid and a page hurrying after. For a moment he couldn't breathe, just from a hunger like fire.

When Dallandra woke again, she found herself trapped in a cage. For a moment she lay still, staring in disbelief at the view round her. Not only was she penned in a cubical cage made of branches lashed together, but this entire rickety structure was hanging from the limb of an enormous leafy tree. She could see it quite clearly through the slatted roof, an arch of branch, a canopy of leaves. Automatically she laid her hand on her throat and found the amethyst figurine still safe and present. When she sat up, aching in every muscle and tendon, the cage swayed. She grabbed the nearest bar and steadied herself while she looked round. Not far away hung another cage, made of the same roughly trimmed branches, confining the young page, who was sitting all curled up with his head on his knees and his arms round his head, as if he were trying to make the world go away by pretending it didn't exist.

She looked down, through cracks between the tightly lashed branches of the floor, and saw a rough sort of camp on the bare ground below and off to one side. Apparently her tree stood at the edge of a clearing. In the middle round a fire sat Evandar's brother and some six of his men—well, six of his followers, all of them as much animal as man, the wolf warrior with his long snout, the bears with their huge clubs of paws at the ends of human arms, another vulpine creature with a roach of hair like his leader's but purple elven eyes, a fellow with a human head but a bloated, misshapen body. They'd laid aside their armor and were dressed only in tunics of green cloth, bound at the waist with weapon belts, and low leather boots, so she could see the variegated fur they sprouted and sported on their legs and thighs. Nearby sat a being that Dallandra recognized. Hunchbacked and bald, he clutched a long staff, wound with ribands, that lay across his lap. His face was grotesquely distorted, all swollen and pouched, his skin hanging in great folds of warty flesh round his neck.

"Good herald!" Dallandra called out. "Tell your lord that his prisoners require water."

All of the men jumped and swore, slewing round to look up at her. Leaning on the staff, the herald hauled himself to his feet. The folds of flesh round his neck swung and rustled like dead leaves in a wind.

"My lord," he said, and his voice creaked and rustled as well. "Well-treated prisoners make for a better bargain in the end."

The fox warrior grunted, considering, then snapped his fingers in a clear imitation of Evandar's gestures. At his command a bronze flagon appeared, but it was all lumpy and distorted, as if the mold had been carved by the rawest apprentice at the smithy.

"Haul them down," he said to one of the bearlike figures. "Her first."

The rope suspending the cage turned out to be lashed round the trunk of the tree. Growling and sweating the ursine fellow untied the knot, picking at it with clumsy claws, then reeled her down fast. When the cage smacked into the ground, and Dallandra yelped and grabbed the bars to save herself a fall, the warriors screeched and cackled.

"Oh, she's a fair one." The ursine fellow shoved his stinking face close to the bars. His lips and nose were human under a dusting of brown fur, but his black eyes were tiny and seemingly lidless. "Can we have her, my lord? Can we take her out and pass her round like wine? She'd be sweet, my lord, to soothe a man's itching with."

Dallandra spat full into his face. When he snarled and swatted at the cage, the fox warrior grabbed his arm, hauled him round, and threw him down onto the ground, where he howled curses until his lord kicked him in the head.

"Why would Evandar bargain for a broken thing?" the fox warrior snapped. "Leave her alone! Do you hear me? If I find anyone's meddled with her, or with the page either, then I'll kill him. We want them whole and pretty for our bargaining."

Moving sideways, keeping his lord's temper always in view, the herald sidled up to the cage and passed the misshapen flagon through the bars.

"Keep it," the fox warrior snapped. "I'll make another for the lad. Huh, I can match your fine Evandar, I can, and call things from the air and weave them from the light, just as he can. Haul her up, and bring the page down."

Dallandra clutched the flagon to her chest to keep it from spilling as the cage made its jerky way back up. Once it had stopped swaying, she drank in greedy swallows. They hauled the boy's cage down the same way, handed him in a flagon of water of his own, but at the fox warrior's order they left his sitting on the ground.

"You! Elven witch!" The warrior strolled under her cage. "The lad stays down here, closer to me than to you. One hint of your wretched magicks, and I'll haul him out and torture him to death right in front of you. Do you hear me?"

The boy burst out sobbing and screaming. The wolflike creature stuck a paw through the bars, grabbed him by the hair, and shook hard, which made him scream the more.

"Leave him alone!" Dallandra yelled. "I'll do what your leader says."

The wolf-thing threw the boy to the floor, but he did stroll away and let him be. When the fox warrior joined the others at their fire,

Dallandra sat down on the floor of her cage and tried to think. How long had she been lying unconscious, first from the return to her normal size, then in her faint? She had no idea, none. She couldn't even begin to guess how much time had passed on the physical plane since she'd left Jill. She rose to her knees, then wedged the flagon between two branches so that it wouldn't spill.

"Herald!" she called out. "Has my lord Evandar been notified of this outrage?"

The old man trotted closer, looking up with pink and rheumy eyes.

"I've not been sent to him, my lady," he said. "My lord believes that he should find us."

"In other words you've set a trap for him."

The herald moaned, wringing his long and clawlike hands together.

"Get over here!" the fox warrior called out. "You've naught to say to her."

Bowing, cringing, moaning under his breath, the ancient creature scurried away, but as he did so he shot a glance back Dallandra's way that she could only call apologetic. She crouched in the middle of the cage floor, to keep the structure balanced and level. She wondered if Evandar would realize that she'd been taken by his enemies or if, when he found her gone, he would simply assume that she'd gone to help Jill. Perhaps the night princess would remember that she'd seen her and tell him so? Dallandra doubted very much that one of Evandar's folk was conscious enough for putting a memory together with a present danger and drawing a conclusion. She could only hope that his brother's ugly crew had left some clue behind them. Otherwise, she might rot there, bait in an unsprung trap, for aeons as men and elves measure Time.

4

VIA

*A figure most mixed in its influences, inju-
rious to those figures it does fall between upon
the map, but good in all manner of journeys
and most beneficent indeed in the Land of
Gold. Yet if it fall into the Land of Silver, it
bodes great evil in matters of Love.*

The Omenbook of Gwarn, Loremaster

WHEN RHODRY AND THE THREE DWARVES finally left Cengarn, closer to noon than dawn, they headed northeast on a narrow dirt road that climbed and twisted its way round sheep pastures and coppiced woods. It took climbing only two of those hills for Rhodry to start wondering if he could endure this journey. Although he was more than used to wearing mail and carrying its particular pattern of weight, he'd never hauled a pack on his back before. Garin had fitted a sheep's skin across his shoulders before loading him up, but even so, the wood and canvas chafed, dug, and shifted position constantly. Since he was carrying Dar's bow, he couldn't hook his hands in the pack straps to steady the load as the dwarves were doing. Under the hot sheepskin he began to sweat, which made the chafing worse.

The real problem, though, was the walking. Rhodry had started learning to ride when he was three years old, on a little Eldidd pony, and from then on the major part of his waking life had been spent on horseback. His warrior's code, in fact, labeled walking as something fit only for peasants and other such inferior beings. By the time he'd grown into manhood, his legs had grown into the shape of a horse's barrel.

Now the uphill walk made his turned-out knees ache first, but his hips soon followed, especially when the pack began to rest heavy on his kidneys. While the dwarves strode on ahead with their short but straight and sturdy legs, he waddled after them, blistering his feet on the road and his back muscles on the pack as he fell farther and farther behind. Finally, when the dwarves were halfway up the third hill and Rhodry was just starting it, Garin called a halt. The dwarf waited until Rhodry staggered up to them before speaking.

"This won't do, Otho. It's unjust to expect our silver dagger to learn the ways of the road all at once, like. When we stop at the farm to pick up the supplies you bought, we'll have to bargain for a mule as well, to carry his pack and the extra food and suchlike. You can always sell it later on, when he's used to trekking and ready to try the pack again."

Otho made a sputtering noise, but Mic nodded, agreeing with the leader. Rhodry felt like kneeling at Garin's feet and singing his praise like a bard.

"How much farther to this farm?" he said instead. "I don't mind admitting that this mile or two's been a humbling experience."

"Then it was worth somewhat, eh?" Otho said with a grin. "Not far now, lad. Just keep putting one tender elven foot in front of the other, and you'll get there, sure enough."

Rhodry said nothing, but the silence cost him.

Fortunately the farm turned out to be reasonably close by. While Otho haggled for the mule, Rhodry sat down in the muck and swarming flies with his back against the cow barn and fell straight asleep. The sun was a fair bit lower when Mic shook him awake.

"Time to get on the road again," the young dwarf said. "We've finally got the mule loaded up the way Uncle Otho likes."

Walking without a fifty-weight of gear and pack turned out to be a good bit easier, but even so, every muscle in Rhodry's legs ached by the time they were among the wild hills. He was honestly taken aback by how thoroughly his body had shaped itself to ride horses, by how unfit he was to travel any distance on his own two feet. The surprise turned him stubborn, and he forced himself onward, refusing to ask for a rest even when Garin glanced his way as if offering him the chance. As the road dwindled to a goat track, the pace slowed anyway, because they had to pick their way through rocks and brambles. When they paused to rest, Garin cut Rhodry's old sheepskin into strips and tied them round the mule's pasterns.

"This wretched mule is going to make it hard to travel at night," Otho growled. "I wish we'd never acquired the thing."

"Hold your tongue," Garin said. "Killing the man you're trying to repay is no way to settle a debt, and that's that."

Otho snorted once, then devoted himself to his bread and cheese. Rhodry wondered all over again where Garin's obvious authority had its roots; he'd never heard of the Mountain People having gwerbrets and lords, but there was no doubt that Garin expected to be obeyed like one. About average height for a dwarf, broad in the shoulders, narrow in the hips, with the dark, full growth of beard so prized by the men of his people, he stood with authority as well as spoke with it.

When they started off again, in the fading twilight, Garin took over leading the mule. By walking a bit ahead of it and kicking the bigger rocks and obstacles out of its way, he managed to keep them all moving for some hours after dark, but they were traveling much slower than any of the dwarves liked. When they made their camp, in a little valley between two hills, Garin and Otho walked a ways away from the others and stood squabbling in their own language for a long time.

"They're arguing about whether it's safe to travel during the day," Mic said. "What do you think?"

"I don't know. One thing, though. It'll be a fair bit easier to use this bow I've been carrying in the daylight. I can't see as far or as finely in the dark."

Mic trotted off to add this piece of information to the argument among the rocks. Rhodry unstrapped the baldric, placed the bow and the quiver beside his blankets, and sat down next to them to untie the bindings and pull off his boots. Garin had stressed the importance of airing out one's boots and keeping one's feet dry on these long marches. After he was done, Rhodry lay down, planning on a mere moment's rest, but he fell asleep, too tired even to eat. He did wake once, when the dwarves began tramping round the camp and spreading out their own blankets, but drifted off again straightaway. Yet in his dreams he felt eyes watching him, dragon eyes, human eyes, and he kept hearing a peculiar screech or cry that came from too great a distance for him to identify it. From one particular dream of a ruined city he woke just after dawn and found himself in a cold sweat.

All round him the dwarves were rolled up and snoring in their blankets. The mule, tethered out in a grassy spot, stood head down and drowsy. The sheltering trees round about rustled as the wind picked up, cool and welcome in what promised to be a hot bright day. Rhodry sat up, laying an automatic hand on the bow. Although he was wide awake, he could still sense the eyes from his dream. Or rather, he could sense one pair. Over the past week or so, he'd come to realize that there were two dream watchers. The dragon eyes considered him with curiosity, certainly, but it seemed an indifferent, utterly neutral gaze. The human eyes carried malice. It was malice he was feeling now.

He threw back the blankets to sit up and look round—no one there, and he realized that he'd never truly expected to see anyone, either. All at once the mule tossed up its head and snorted, turning on its rope to sniff into the wind. Rhodry grabbed the bow and strung it, looping the bowstring into the notch at one end, hooking that end under his outstretched foot, and pulling back against the brace of his own leg to shape the bow as he finished stringing it. That done, he stood, nocking an arrow and taking a few steps away from his bedroll. Slowly he turned round in a circle, looking everywhere for signs of a hidden enemy. He saw nothing, but the mule snorted again, dancing a little.

This time, when Rhodry looked among the trees he saw a figure watching him. At first he thought it a shepherd, because it wore tattered brigga and a rough shirt, all greasy and torn, but then it stepped out into the sunlight. Although the face was recognizably human, its body perched on a pair of legs as long and skinny as a stork's, its back bowed out, and its arms hung tiny from its sides. Its head rose long and narrow from a skinny neck, so that the warty, wattled face seemed to float in front of the rest of it.

"What do you want?" Rhodry hissed.

Its eyes glittered bright, and it grinned, exposing long yellow fangs of teeth. There was malice a-plenty in that smile, a twisted urge to rend and tear, perhaps, just for the joy of the bite. Rhodry swept up the bow and loosed. The bowstring sang; the arrow hissed and flew directly through the creature to rattle onto the rocky ground. Yet even though the arrow did no visible harm, the creature shrieked in agony as the steel-tipped shaft pierced it.

"Stay away, then," Rhodry snapped. "Be gone!"

It bared its fangs in a snarl and disappeared. For a moment the snarl seemed to hover on the air like a greasy stain, then hurried after the rest of it. Rhodry shuddered convulsively, then carefully, one step at a time, walked over to retrieve his arrow. When he knelt down he examined the ground round about, but he saw no footsteps in the dust.

He walked back to the camp to find the dwarves awake, throwing back blankets and scrambling up.

"What was that thing?" Mic burst out. "I've never seen one of the Wildfolk like that before. It was so big."

"Well, I doubt me if it was one of the Wildfolk." Rhodry hesitated, wondering how to explain. "But it wasn't really there, either. My arrow sailed right through it."

"We saw that."

The others waited, looking at him expectantly.

"I told you about Alshandra, didn't I?" Rhodry said. "I'd guess it was one of her people."

"What do they want with you?" Garin said.

"Cursed if I know."

"We might all be cursed," Otho broke in, "if we can't figure it out."

All at once Rhodry felt dishonorable. For all his squabbling with Otho, he'd known the old man practically all his life, and he honestly liked his kinsfolk.

"Why don't you all turn back?" Rhodry said. "Garin, tell me how to get to this Haen Marn place, and I'll try to find it on my own. This whole thing's just gotten a good bit more dangerous, and I feel like a shamed man for dragging you into it."

"Hold your tongue, you stupid elf!" Otho snapped. "Don't go dousing the wound with vinegar. You could have thought of that before we drove a bargain."

Rhodry stared, utterly uncomprehending.

"Otho, one of these days I'm going to sew your lips shut, and life will turn much sweeter," Garin said. "Rhodry, listen. You saved Otho's life. We promised that in return we'd find you this wyrm. There's an end to it. We have a debt bond between us."

"Well, what if I release you from the debt?"

"There is no release. A debt is a debt until it's paid."

All at once Otho got up and strode off, muttering something incomprehensible. When Garin and Mic exchanged significant glances, Rhodry remembered the story of their kinsman's exile.

"Well, you have my thanks from the bottom of my heart," Rhodry said.

Garin smiled briefly, then turned to Mic.

"Get some food for all of us, will you? We've got a lot to do before we get on the road today."

Rhodry decided that indeed there was nothing more to say and went to lead the mule to water.

Over the next few days' worth of traveling, the land rose higher and higher in broken hills, gashed by steep ravines and white-water creeks. Through the thin soil huge black boulders pushed like knuckles on a fist. In narrow valleys they found farmsteads, round thatched houses and barns barricaded inside earthworks, where dogs rushed to throw themselves against the gates and bark savagely as they passed. Now and again they saw a farmer or his wife, too, standing guard with flail or cudgel clasped in work-gnarled hands while these strangers walked on by. Grazing in what grass there was they saw goats, never cows, rarely sheep, and each flock was guarded by two and three boys, never a single lad alone, and a pack of dogs.

Late on the second day they passed an entire fortified village, some twelve buildings surrounded by stone walls laced with timber. Brown and white goats grazed on the tops of the walls, which were covered with sod. At the gates stood armed guards, two young men dressed in the omnipresent coarse brown cloth of this part of the world. One carried a sword, the other a dwarven-style battle-ax, with a long shaft and deep-bitten curved blade. As the dwarven party passed by, the pair went tense, ready to sound an alarum, no doubt, at the least sign of trouble.

"Did these people pay fealty to Lord Matyc?" Rhodry asked.

"Hah!" Garin snorted. "I doubt me if they know he existed. You find people like this all along the Deverry border, a tough lot they are, hating lords and foreigners alike. My people do a little trading with them, now and again, but they don't have much we want, and they don't much like us, either."

It was then that Rhodry realized they'd crossed the border between his native kingdom and the dwarven lands. Even though he'd known better in his mind, in his heart he'd always assumed that Deverry went on and on, right to the edge of the world, perhaps. He looked round at the glowering hills, dark with twisted pines, gashed with tumbles of rock down ravines, and realized that indeed this was a foreign land.

"But you know, that village, from what I can see of it, anyway, looks like a Deverry village, or more like a dun, with that big broch in the middle and all."

"Well, these border folk, they came from Deverry, after those wars you had over the true king and all that," Garin said. "They were on the losing side, I think."

"They were," Otho chimed in. "After Maryn took the throne, a lot of the Cantrae lords fled to what you people call Cerrgonney, and when Maryn's grandson—I think he was a grandson? Well, one of Maryn's descendants, anyway, but eventually he followed them to Cerrgonney to impose his peace, and some of them, the most stubborn ones, like, fled here."

By then they were climbing a hill just beyond the village, and Rhodry paused for a look back. He could see clearly from this height into the compound, a thing of mud and pigs, small children running round half-naked among the chickens, wood houses with mangy thatch clustering round a broch built of piled stones caulked with mud. Yet flying from the broch was a crude pennant, whipping this way and that in the wind. Finally he got a look at it—a boar device.

"The final end of the enemies of the king," Otho said with obvious relish. "Stinking whoreson bastards."

"You sound like you remember them," Rhodry said.

"I do. I was a young man then and just come into your country." Otho seemed to be about to say more, but he let his voice trail off and looked away. "Well, no use in standing round here, flapping our lips. Let's get on our way."

The longer they traveled, the more Rhodry grew inured to hiking in rough country, but still he tired early, stumbling along after the dwarves on blistered feet by the end of the day. Their route kept climbing, higher and higher toward the white mountains, which grew larger at the edge of the view. Finally, too, their luck with the weather broke, and it rained. Late one afternoon a storm came blowing up so fast that he first thought it dweomer, but the dwarves explained that the mountains spawned fast storms.

"It'll blow over soon enough, too," Garin said. "But we'll make an early camp."

Although tents were too heavy and bulky a luxury to bring on a journey like this, the dwarves did have lengths of coarse-woven linen canvas, smeared heavily with grease from sheep's wool, that could be laced together and pegged out as a lean-to of sorts. Just as the clouds were piling black and swollen overhead, they found a rise of boulders with a couple of scraggly, twisted pines growing among them where they could sling their canvas and weight the edges with loose stones against the gathering wind. In among the boulders was a narrow space where they could cross-tether the mule as well, and give the poor beast a bit of shelter. Nearby a river, narrow but cut deep, threaded its way between rocks.

"Going to be dark, and it's going to be noisy," Garin announced. "What if that storklike creature comes snooping round? Or somewhat worse? I say we stand watches, lads."

Even Otho had to agree to that. Just as the first drops of rain began falling, in a round of broken twigs for want of straws Rhodry drew the longest and the last watch with it. Huddled under the scant shelter, they all spent a cramped and miserable night of it, but Rhodry managed to sleep, no doubt more than the others, simply because he was so tired. Even so, he was glad when Mic wakened him for his turn on guard. It was a chance to stretch and to get away from the smell of other people's damp bodies and clothes, to say nothing of the rancid lanolin of sheep long gone.

Although the rain had stopped by then, the air was cold, and he was shivering as he picked his way down to the stream over the wet and uncertain footing. Since he was thirsty, he squatted down, fumbling for the tin cup tied to his belt. From behind him he heard a sound that might have been a footfall. Sheer warrior's instinct brought him to his feet and spun him round just in time to see a gray shape rushing for him. As his hand went for the bronze knife at his belt, the thing stopped and hovered some ten feet away. It was roughly man-shaped, but its head was a lumpish affair with no features that he could pick out, elven sight or no. When Rhodry drew the bronze knife and flourished it, the creature snarled like a wolf and disappeared. Well, fancy that, Rhodry thought. Someone just tried to drown me. Behind him the river raced fast and swollen, with the occasional gleam of foam or bubbles in the broken light. He decided that his thirst could wait till the others woke.

Garin was first up, squirming out of the shelter just as a pale streak of silver in the east announced the rising sun. When Rhodry told him of the attack he considered for a long moment, running his hand through his beard.

"Well, now, I don't know what to do," he said at last. "So they fear that bronze knife of yours, do they?"

"They always have before. Jill told me it has dweomer upon it."

Garin nodded, combing busily.

"Don't know what to do," he said again. "Well, the thing is, we're almost home. To Lin Serr, that is, the town where Otho and I were born and all that. I say we make a quick march there, fast as we can in this rotten weather."

Rhodry glanced round at the silent, empty hills. Up among the pines anything could have been hiding, waiting.

"If we'd only gone by the main road," Garin went on. "We'd have been there by now, but Otho insisted we come skulking about to the back door, like. Jill put the wind up to him, I gather, saying he'd best be careful as careful."

"And here enemies went and found me anyway, for all our caution."

"So they did. You're quite right. Well, then. We'll leave this wretched back road, since there's no use in hiding. We're bound to be safer, once we reach a proper town. It's the cursed dweomer at work in all of this, I suppose. We dwarves mostly leave such things alone, you know, except for a few spells and suchlike for our metals. Well, the women make a talisman or two, but that's them, not us. I don't trust dweomer, never have, either. A man starts mingling the natures of this world with some other one, or traveling round to peculiar places and messing about with what he finds there, and who knows where that'll end up, eh? With trouble, usually, so there you are."

On this flood of platitude Garin sailed away to wake the others.

When they set out that morning, they left the road they'd been following—such as it was—and headed across wild country, following a stream that wound between two hills. The footing there ran narrow and slick, a mere ridge bitten into the hillside in places, a series of rocks and puddles beside the stream at others. Garin spent most of his time and attention fussing with the mule, encouraging it where he could, giving it a good whack when it balked. Mic helped him, Otho hiked along wrapped in some black mood of his own, which all left Rhodry as the only man on any kind of guard. Although he considered carrying the bow strung and ready, its arrows had already failed him once. He slung it across his back and trusted in the bronze dagger instead.

The hills on either side of this difficult trail had once been forested, it seemed, because stumps and straggly saplings poked up among the tangled ferns and grass that covered them now. While they would have provided no hiding places for a man or even a dwarf, Rhodry could never be sure what size his peculiar enemies might take. As they picked their way along he kept his eyes moving, watching endlessly, searching both hillsides for unnatural motion, a possible threat. Since the storm was breaking up, the light kept changing, too, dark one moment, sunny the next in a dance of confusing shadows.

They had just cleared the first hill to the slightly better footing of a valley when Rhodry heard the sound, something like a whistle, more like a screech, and very familiar. He stopped dead, cocking his head to listen. Faint, very faint it sounded, and yet he could have sworn that it emanated from a spot nearby.

"Come along, you stupid elf!" Otho called out. "Don't go falling behind. It's dangerous."

"Oh, hold your ugly tongue! Didn't you hear that?"

The sound whispered again, a little trill of three sour notes.

"Hear what?" Otho said.

The other dwarves had stopped to listen as well, but they merely shrugged in puzzlement. For a moment Rhodry wondered if he were going daft. Yet again the whistle sounded, a little louder, a little nastier.

"That!" Mic said. "I do hear it."

So, apparently, did the mule, because it flattened its ears and kicked out, rather randomly, with one hind leg. Rhodry spun round, staring at the hillside, examining every bit of the view. The whistle sounded a four-note melody, all warped and rasping, as if to mock his efforts.

"No one's there," Mic whispered. "But we hear it."

"Let's get marching, lads!" Garin snapped. "Hup! Forward! Let's get out of here!"

Even the mule agreed, striding along briskly from then on. All that day they heard the whistle, sounding at random intervals, sometimes a screech, sometimes an ugly little tune. Whether they trekked through open valley or wooded hill, Rhodry never saw who was playing it. Early on, though, he recognized the sound as being like that of the whistle made of bone that he'd once carried round himself. He'd even played the thing once or twice, a bare few notes out of idle curiosity, though he was rather sorry now that he had. Since he had no way of knowing then that Evandar had given the whistle away, he assumed that there was a fashion for such things among Alshandra's ugly followers and left it at that.

Late in the afternoon they reached what Garin called the "proper road," narrow but banked and covered with sod, perfect footing for the mule and the men alike.

"This will get us home by tomorrow," Garin remarked.

"Huh," Otho snorted. "If we're not snatched and carried off to the Otherlands by these misshapen louts that keep following us."

Although he was only grumbling, his choice of words gave Rhodry pause. Until then, he'd been assuming that their enemies were doing what he would have in their situation—trying to kill them. He'd forgotten about that mysterious other country where beings like Evandar lived. They could travel back and forth with great ease, it seemed, judging from his one brief experience with it. What if they were after prisoners?

"You know," Rhodry said. "I think we'd best march late, and stand watches again once we camp."

Otho snarled a few words in Dwarvish.

"He's right." Garin spoke in Deverrian. "Hum. I wonder. If we had a bit of a rest now, could we do a forced march all night? The mule's not carrying much, being as we've eaten most of the food."

Everyone looked to Rhodry for an answer.

"I don't know," Rhodry said. "I've got a dread in my heart that marching at night could well be more dangerous than staying in one spot. We can all see in the dark, truly, but not all that far ahead. I'd hate to mistake the road."

"Listen, elf-wit," Otho snapped. "We're on the home road now. We're not going to be wandering off it—"

"You don't understand. These creatures can cast dweomer on roads. You think you're walking down one path only to find yourself on another, and heading somewhere you never wanted to go."

"Oho!" Garin put in. "Makes me wonder about that whistle. I wouldn't mind guessing that they were hoping we'd follow the sound, like, just to see what we could see."

Rhodry shuddered, just an involuntary twitch.

"I wouldn't mind agreeing with you. We'd best be good and careful from now on."

"Sharp eyes, lads, and no leaving the road." Garin looked at Mic and Otho in turn. "There's a shelter not far ahead, and we'll camp there."

The shelter turned out to be a peaked roof of slates and beams, supported on stone pillars, over a wooden windbreak and floor. The pillars were amazingly slender for the weight they were bearing; Rhodry had to marvel at them, delicately carved in a vertical pattern of chained links. Garin noticed his interest.

"There's iron bars inside them. That's how they hold all that weight."

"Interesting idea, that. You know, I was thinking. We'd best tether the mule close, in here if that's possible. I don't want it being chased away in the night and having Otho insist on chasing after."

"Good thinking. We'll do that."

Although Rhodry drew the second watch, he was wakened long before by the sound of Mic yelling and the mule braying. Half-asleep as he was, he grabbed his sword rather than a knife and rolled free of his blankets. From nearby Otho and Garin were waking in a flood of Dwarvish curses. Rhodry got to his feet and ran down the length of the shelter to help Mic, who was hanging on to the panicked mule's tether rope as the animal kicked and bucked, braying all the while.

"I've got the mule," Mic yelled. "Look outside!"

Circling round the shelter were misshapen beings, mostly human but never quite, dressed in bits of bronze armor and waving bronze knives— a jumble of human bodies or animal torsos on human legs, human heads, cat heads, dog faces, braided manes like the Horsekin, dwarven hands, elven hands, ears like mules, fangs like snakes swirling round in a whirlpool of malice. At the sight of Rhodry they began to curse and shout in a babble of languages, but though they threatened, they never came closer. Rhodry was never far from going berserk, and as he listened to their insults something snapped in his mind. Half-dressed and barefoot though he was, he screamed out a battle cry and charged, swinging the flat of his sword from side to side. Dimly he was aware of Garin's voice, ordering him back, but he ran straight for the clutch of creatures.

Bird-headed, human-headed, clawed and pawed and handed, the screeching pack howled with terror and pain at every whack of his good steel sword. Although a few of the bolder ones darted his way, they fell back screeching the moment the blade touched them, even though it seemed to leave no wounds, merely passed right through their illusions of flesh. Slashing back and forth he drove them round the shelter. As they raced away from him, they began to disappear, a few at first, winking out like sparks flying up from a fire, then more and more, until all of a sudden he stood alone and panting for breath in the middle of the road. His red berserker rage lifted like fog, leaving him feeling more than a little foolish.

"Rhodry!" Garin was howling. "Get back here!"

Rhodry took two steps to follow the order and realized that he was no longer alone, that facing him in the roadway stood Alshandra. That night she appeared as the beautiful elven woman he'd met before, years past, standing almost as tall as he was, but slender, with honey-blond hair that cascaded round her shoulders and down to her waist. She held out delicate hands and smiled at him.

"Rhodry, Rhodry, come help me. I'm so alone now, and my poor daughter, I must save my daughter. Won't you help me, Rhodry Mael-waedd?" All at once tears ran down her cheeks. "There's naught I can do to save her, all alone as I am."

Even as well as he knew her, her sobbing touched him, the silent way her shoulders trembled, the sincere pain in her golden eyes.

"Oh, Rhodry," she whispered. "You'll have a reward, the best I can offer. I could love a man like you, easily, easily. Come with me and let me love you forever. In my country you'll never grow old, you know. Just put down that sword and come with me. I'll give you a better sword, all made out of silver like the dagger you carry."

All at once he found it hard to speak, to put rational thoughts together. When he glanced round he found that the road, the shelter, and the dwarves had disappeared into an opalescent mist.

"Take just one step forward, Rhodry," she whispered. "Please, please, help me, and then we'll be happy forever. Just drop that ugly sword and take but one step forward."

With a wrench of will he swung the sword and held it straight up, a barrier between them. She shrieked and leapt back out of his reach, but though every muscle in his body ached to charge after for the kill, he made himself stand where he was, on his own side of the invisible border between their worlds. As she moved she changed, a huntress now, towering up huge, a gleaming bronze battle-ax clasped in her hands. She swung it up high, her face contorted in pure rage, as Rhodry tensed, half-crouched. Since attacking would take him forward, his one desperate chance lay in a dodge when that ax began to swing down. The mist dissolved; light gleamed all round them; a shout echoed.

Alshandra screamed and bent backward, the ax flying from her hands and dissolving in midair. Her entire body seemed to ripple and waver, her image flapping like a sheet of cloth in the wind. With her magic broken, Rhodry risked leaping forward, sweeping his steel blade through her. With a scream she disappeared.

He was standing back in the road, and round him towered the mountains he knew as part of his own world. In a gray dawn Garin stood facing him, holding a woodsman's ax. The dwarf was grinning.

"From the look of things, those friends of yours couldn't abide the touch of iron," he said. "You hear of such, in the old lore. So once I could see her again, I just ran up and tried it out. Worked like a charm." His smile disappeared. "Well, that's an ill-omened way of speaking."

Rhodry laughed, a bubbling howl of his berserker's mirth that made Garin turn pale. He choked it off.

"My apologies and my thanks. The apology's because I didn't follow my own advice, and the thanks are for my life."

"Think that ax would have killed you? I wasn't sure if it was real or not."

"Oh. I hadn't considered that, truly. Well, let's just say that I prefer the wondering to the finding out that it could cut me in half."

"Now that's true spoken."

"But I tell you, Garin, I owe you a debt."

"Maybe someday I'll call it in, silver dagger. I'll keep that in mind."

Together they walked back to the shelter, where the other dwarves stood gaping. Mic had a chunk of bread in his hand, Otho some cheese, and the mule was grazing peacefully nearby as the sun brightened.

"Ye gods," Rhodry said. "It's dawn."

"It is," Mic said. "What was happening to you, all that time when you were gone?"

"It was only a few moments to me. Just time enough to have a bit of a chat with her."

"Indeed?" Garin rolled his eyes. "I take it that she was this Alshandra female you've been telling us about."

"She was, and I hope to every god and his wife that we've scared her off."

"Scared—you mean she isn't dead?"

"Jill says she can't be killed, not in any ordinary way. She's gone back to her own country, I'll wager, to nurse her grudges."

Garin started to speak, then merely shook his head. Mic made a strangling sort of sound, deep in his throat.

"Let's hope she stays there, then," Otho snarled. "An elf, that's what she was. All at once Garin here swears and drops his breakfast, and the next thing I know he's grabbing an ax and running out into the road to attack some elven sorceress."

"Nah nah nah," Rhodry said. "She may have looked like an elf, but she's not true flesh and blood. Jill says she can take on any form she wants."

Otho silenced himself on the edge of some other nastiness.

"Get yourself somewhat to eat, silver dagger," Garin said. "I want to get on the road soon. If the iron bothers her as much as all that, we'll be as safe as safe in Lin Serr."

Whether their enemies had spent themselves the night before or whether the sunlight hampered them, Rhodry didn't know, but whatever the truth of it, they traveled all morning in peace. Toward noon the road climbed hard and fast, but that last effort brought them to the top of a summit. Far ahead of them unrolled a broken plateau toward the distant rise of the white mountains. Rhodry could see forests ahead, striped with open land, but nothing that looked like a city to him.

"Is Lin Serr under the mountains?"

"It's not," Garin said. "You'll see soon now."

For some miles the road climbed and fell over a series of hills like vast ripples in the earth. They passed through a woodland and across a wild meadow, then climbed to the top of one final ridge to find themselves standing on a raised tongue of grassland, stretching about a mile in front of them. Ahead, at the end of this obviously artificial formation, the land sloped down fast to a huge basin, mostly grass-covered though Rhodry could see a few trees. On the far side pale gray cliffs rose, their tops level with the ground on which Rhodry and the dwarves were standing. At the sight, Otho burst into tears and stood sobbing with his arms hanging helpless at his sides.

"Lin Serr," Garin said. "Home."

He clapped his hand on Otho's shoulder in silent comfort, then walked on with Mic and Rhodry, all of them moving slowly to allow Otho time to recover himself. The view was one to be savored, anyway, Rhodry felt. A horseshoe of cliffs embraced the parklike basin, with the tongue or spit of land upon which they walked entering it in the center of the open side. Off to the right ran a river, sparkling in the clear mountain air as it curved round the tongue to continue downhill in a deep-cut channel. Off to the left, in the basin but even with the end of the horseshoe, stood a tall structure that at first seemed a natural spire, freestanding with the cliff to one side and the vast open basin to the other, though it towered a good fifty feet higher than the cliff tops. When Rhodry shaded his eyes for a better look, it proved to be worked stone, carved like a statue from one living rock, even though it must have been well over two hundred feet tall. The main shaft rose as straight as a column but so smoothly it almost shone, except for that portion extending higher than the cliffs, which had been added on with masonry. Here and there a window indicated that the tower inside was hollow.

"The old watchtower," Garin said to Rhodry. "You can just see the gap 'twixt it and the cliff. That gap used to be the only way into Lin Serr."

Blowing his nose on an old rag, Otho stomped up beside them.

"Humph. The place looks a bit bigger than I've been remembering it."

"Well, the clans keep growing, and so we keep digging it out, a bit here and there," Garin said. "Let's go round and walk through the old gate. No need, but we all do it, somehow, for the ritual of the thing. Silly, I suppose, but there you are."

Once down on the basin's level floor, Rhodry realized that the circling rise of cliff had to be a constructed thing, not some natural phenomenon. Looking up he could tell that the tops of all the cliffs were perfectly flat and all the same height. As they came closer, he saw that the vertical formations he'd taken for the natural cracks and outcrops of a cliff were actually sculpted corrugations and pyramidal bays marching at regular intervals all round the basin. What he'd taken for caves and erosions seemed to be air shafts and doors.

"You dug the basin out," he said, and his voice shook a little. "Your people dug this whole thing out, and those cliffs are what? Exposed bedrock?"

"They are." Garin was grinning at his amazement. "We dwarves are patient sorts. We keep chipping away, a bit here, a bit there, and soon enough, it all adds up."

"But the river—"

"Flowed underground once, that's all. No doubt it's happier, here in the light of the sun." Garin waved his arm vaguely in the direction of the meadow—no, the lawn really—that covered the basin. "We saved the topsoil, of course. We do like a bit of green and all in a view."

"Ah." Rhodry could manage nothing more.

"Digging the first shaft was the hard part," Garin went on. "Once we had a good start made and room for a good many families to live, well, then! It all went forward smoothly. By the time we had the tower chipped away, the basin was about—" He glanced at Otho. "I was just a lad, then, and I don't remember it so well."

"About half a mile across and some thousand people lived round it. The only way in, then, was this." Otho waved at the ten-foot gap between the spire and the cliffs. "The spire didn't stand free in those days. It was connected on the other side to rock long gone to make a gate, like."

As they approached, they were looking at a side of both spire and cliff that was perfectly smooth, offering not the slightest handhold to an enemy. They walked through the deep shadow of the cleft and came out again into the sunlight. Rhodry paused to look back and found that here on what had once been the inside of a fortress the spire sported ramparts, stairs, and little towers, all sculpted out of the rock.

"Look up at the cliffs." Garin pointed in the general direction. "See how the top fifty feet or so is smooth as glass? Any invaders who thought they could just go up top and avoid the gate would have to climb down on ropes. And if they did, well, then, we could send archers out onto the flat. It would have been less sporting than those contests your people hold at fairs, the ones where they tie chickens to poles for a target. Now, of course, Lin Serr's open, as you can see."

"This was dangerous country, then, when you started building it."

"Any new country's dangerous."

"Hah!" Otho snorted. "The very soul of diplomacy, aren't you, Garin? Why not tell him the truth?"

"Curse you and your ill manners both." Garin sounded more weary than enraged. "The man's our guest."

Rhodry thought he saw the answer to the question of Otho's ill will toward the elven race.

"You can tell me," he said. "What was it? Some sort of war between you and my father's people?"

"Not your father's people. Your mother's. We used to live farther west and to the south, but when the invasion started, we moved here."

"Invasion?" But Rhodry was remembering Jahdo's tales as well. "From our old Homeland, you mean."

"Just that," Garin went on. "Gallia or whatever you called it. But it was the Horsekin who were the real trouble. I don't understand all of it, but it seems plain enough that your ancestors fell upon the Horsekin first, and they fled any way they could to get out of danger. One of those ways was ours. They don't make good neighbors, you might say. We had some warning, time enough to retreat to the mountains and hide out till the worst was over. Then we fled here. We thought your ancestors would be marching upon us next, but they never came."

"Luck and naught more," Otho sneered. "Sheer luck that dwarven heads weren't decorating their cursed walls. Oh, it's a lovely lot your people are, Rhodry Maelwaedd. Is it any wonder that everyone hates you? You never belonged here, and it's a pity you don't all go back where you came from."

"Otho!" Mic and Garin barked in unison. "Hold your tongue!"

Rhodry felt as if someone had kicked him in the stomach. Not from the elderly dwarf's venom—he was used to that—but from the shock of this new view of a history he'd barely considered before.

"Oh, ye gods," he whispered. "And the Hordes fled south, didn't they? That's when the Great Burning—oh, ye gods! They destroyed the elven cities because they were fleeing us."

"Just so." Otho grinned, all smugness. "It's your people behind that, just as sure as if you'd lit the torches yourself."

Garin snapped three dwarven words that wiped the smile off Otho's face, then continued for another sentence that had the old man turning pale.

"You didn't know," Garin said to Rhodry. "There was no way you could have known, and from what I understand, your people came here because you'd been driven out of your home, too, conquered and slaughtered by some stronger enemy."

"We were. The Rhwmanes they were called, and a ruthless lot they were, but still! Ye gods! How can I ever go back to my father's people now, knowing what I know?"

Garin merely shrugged, waving helpless hands in the air. Rhodry reminded himself that his living to see the Westlands again was too unlikely for him to be vexing himself with the problem. If he did live to see his father once more, he decided, then he'd tell that learned bard what he'd discovered and let him deal with it. Until then, like the warrior he was, he put the past out of his mind, but the surprise lingered for a long time, and with it a real unease.

They'd come well out into the lawn in the center of the horseshoe of cliffs. All the way across, at the deepest bend of the shoe, Rhodry could see the gleam of white water where the river poured out of a cavern and, beside that, marks that seemed to be stairs, marching up the cliff face toward a dark slit. When Garin saw him looking that way, he pointed it out.

"The public entrance. Rhodry, I'm sorry, but we'll have to leave you in the envoys' quarters for a while. That's what they're called, that is, a couple of houses, and quite nice they are, too, for visitors. We dwarves don't let strangers into the deep city, no matter how well we know them."

"Fair enough, especially for a bloodthirsty barbarian like me." Rhodry flashed him a grin. "How long before we get on the road again?"

"Er, well, that depends." Garin hesitated, glancing Otho's way, then smiled in a rather unpleasant manner. "Well, Otho, since you're so keen on throwing the truth into people's faces, surely you won't mind if I tell our guest yours."

Otho made an inarticulate howl, but it was only halfhearted, as if he knew defeat when he saw it.

"Otho's got to stand trial, you see," Garin went on. "There's a certain matter of the old fault that got him exiled, and a fine will have to be assessed. I hope that it doesn't take too long. Things like this have been known to drag on for months at a time."

Otho snarled, but feebly.

"I hope it doesn't indeed," Rhodry said. "Far be it from me to stand in the way of justice, but Jill seemed to think we'd best hurry and all that."

"A postponement!" Otho said, and he actually smiled. "We might be able to ask for a postponement. And then if this dragon eats me, well, then."

"Then what?" Garin snapped. "You'll be able to count your gemstones in the Otherworld rather than paying them over here? But truly, I suppose you're right enough about getting that postponement. With a life debt to be paid, and a geas laid on by a dweomermaster as well, the judges might listen to reason."

As they walked on, Rhodry noticed a group of figures down by the river near the cliffs. They were kneeling on the bank, and all round them on the grass, like pale flowers clothing lay spread out to dry. Women doing laundry, he assumed, but he was surprised to find that while they were washing clothes, all right, the launderers were all young men and boys. When they recognized Garin, they rose and came running, damp and soapy as they were, to cluster round the leader and all talk at once in Dwarvish. Otho tossed Mic the mule's lead rope and hurried over to join them. Since Rhodry was part elven and the son of a bard as well, he had a good ear for languages; he'd already picked up a word or two of Dwarvish merely from listening to his companions on this journey.

"While I'm here?" he said to Mic. "I should try to learn somewhat of your speech. Think I could find someone with the leisure to teach me?"

"I doubt that." Mic turned guarded, looking away. "Um, well, it's not likely."

"Oh. Is it against your people's custom to teach others your tongue?"

"Couldn't say." Mic began studying the grass. "You might ask Garin."

Rhodry let the subject drop. He was remembering Otho's remark, "everybody hates you," and he wondered if the dwarven folk had left some splendid city behind when the invasions forced them to build Lin Serr. He became aware, too, that the men clustered round Garin and Otho kept turning to look at him, blank-eyed, carefully neutral, never offensive, but never friendly, either. Garin seemed to be making hard points, stabbing the air with one finger while he spoke.

"He's telling them how you saved Uncle Otho," Mic said. "And that you're our guest. That means a lot, you see."

"No doubt. Here, if they don't want me inside, the mule and I can just camp out here."

Mic grinned and called that information out to Garin, who nodded to acknowledge he'd heard and went on talking.

"You'll never get that mule up those stairs, anyway," Rhodry said.

"True enough. We'd have to tether him out here till I get the chance to sell him for Uncle Otho." Mic waved vaguely to the north and beyond the cliff tops. "Some of our people are farmers, of course, out on the plateau."

Carved from living rock, the stairs in question zigzagged up the side of the cliff, heading first left, then right, then left again with about twenty stairs to a flight, over and over. Although they weren't as steep as the flights in Cengarn, they were much longer, leading up to the main entrance, that a good hundred feet above the ground. From where Rhodry stood the stairs seemed to debouch onto a landing under an overhang of raw rock. In the shadows he could just pick out the form of massive doors.

"Rhodry?" Mic said suddenly. "I owe you an apology. You saved my uncle's life, and here everyone's treating you like you're carrying plague."

"Well, I appreciate it, lad, but don't vex yourself. I've always heard that the Mountain People stick to their own, and now I know they've got good reason to. Certainly the fellows down in the inn in Cengarn treated me decently enough."

"True. It's easy to be friendly and suchlike in Cengarn or one of the other towns where we know we're welcome. When you get near home you get protective, like. But I don't know. Most of the men won't even go to a human town, anyway. That's why Garin's so important. He can get along with anyone."

"Even a wretched elf like me?"

"Oh, that's just Uncle Otho! Most of us young men have never even seen an elf. I mean, there's some old story about during the invasions. A band of dwarves tried to take shelter in some elven city or some such thing like that, and the elves wouldn't open the gates because they were afraid of Horsekin, and so all the dwarves got killed." Mic shrugged with the profound indifference of the young. "But that was over a thousand years ago. Who cares anymore about a thing that long gone?"

"Well, old grudges die hard and all that."

Yet Rhodry found the story disturbing, as another dishonor that his human kin had bred in their passing.

Eventually Garin came back, shaking his head in disgust.

"Rhodry, lad, my apologies. I'm afraid my people are a stubborn lot all round, but I've made them see reason in the end."

"Well, here, I can always just camp—"

"With those creatures prowling round after you?"

"Er, well, truly, I'd forgotten about that."

"Imph. I haven't. Mic, Larn and Baro here are going to take the mule up top and find a farmer to stable him till we see what's going to happen. We may need the creature again, for all I know."

With extra hands to help they got the mule unloaded and the packs distributed. By then their supplies were so low that the packs were light, and Rhodry could just sling his over one shoulder for the climb up. As they all puffed and panted up switchback after switchback, he was glad of it, too. Finally they reached the top and a landing of worked pale stone, long enough for a warrior troop of some hundreds to assemble if they needed to. Garin walked over to a big bronze gong hanging in a wood frame near the doors, picked up the stick chained to it, and struck hard. The boom echoed round the silent basin for a long time.

"The doorkeeper will get round to letting us in sooner or later," Garin remarked.

While they waited, Rhodry had a chance to study the stone doors, firmly shut, that nestled under the overhang of living rock. Some twelve feet high and eight wide, both doors were divided into panels, each a bas relief portrayal of some event in the building of the city. He found the earliest one at the bottom right-hand corner of the right-hand door and hunkered down for a better look. A band of ragged refugees stood on the plain that would become the city. He realized that he'd been half hoping for, half dreading, a portrayal of his own ancestors.

Suddenly from deep inside came an answering stroke of a gong. Rhodry got up and moved out of the way just as the doors opened smoothly outward, with not so much as a creak or groan, to reveal a vast natural cavern, stretching on and on into a blue-lit dimness.

"Well, here we are, lads," Garin said briskly. "Come along."

As they walked into the dimness of the entry hall, it took Rhodry's eyes some moments to adjust. Off to either side he could see worked stone openings, the mouths of tunnels, apparently, leading various ways, and he could hear water running over rock at some distance. In the spill of sunlight from the open doors he could see that the floor was paved in slates and that directly ahead lay a huge decorative roundel, worked in different colors of slate into a complex and coiling maze. All at once Otho strode forward and stepped onto the beginning of the maze. While the others watched in dead silence the elderly dwarf began to walk, weeping convulsively as he did so, quickly and without the slightest hesitation, as if even after hundreds of years of exile he still remembered the pattern.

When he reached the center he fell to his knees, kissed the floor, then sat back on his heels, flinging out his arms as he cried out one phrase or sentence in Dwarvish. Garin answered him, other voices answered as well, shouting from the tunnels, echoing from the far side of the entrance hall. As the outer doors slid shut, the blue light of phosphorescence brightened in the cavern. Figures emerged out of the murk, standing quietly round the edge of the cavern, huddling in tunnel mouths, hundreds of them, Rhodry realized suddenly, all come to see their kinsmen come home.

Otho rose. While he retraced the path out of the maze, Garin caught Rhodry's arm and whispered to him.

"His brother—Mic's father—is the fellow over there in the white tunic, waiting to receive him. They'll have a lot to say to each other, I wager, and then of course we'll have to go talk with the judges soon enough. Here, come with me."

They slipped away from the gathering crowd and into a side tunnel, which traveled only some ten yards before dead-ending into a wooden door, carved with a vertical design of chained links, much like the one on the stone roadside shelter. Garin opened it and ushered Rhodry into sunlight.

"I asked the lads we first met what was available, you see. Welcome to one of the envoys' quarters."

Although the stone-faced room was small, it had a high ceiling and a big window that opened directly onto a view of the grassy basin, far, far below. A pair of wooden shutters hung to either side in case of rain. For decoration, there were panels of steel, engraved and chased in various patterns and pictures, that ran from floor to ceiling at intervals down the walls.

"Alshandra and her followers are going to have a hard time troubling anyone here," Rhodry said with a grin.

"Just so." Garin was looking with some satisfaction at a steel plate engraved with stags' heads. "Lin Serr is full of this sort of thing. It's been popular, like, for hundreds of years now. That and thin ropes of wrought iron, twisted into a sort of filigree. We like our baubles to last, we do."

The bedstead, in fact, was just that sort of ironwork, forming a pattern of iron vines and flowers all down the side. The bed itself was low but long enough, no doubt designed with one of these mysterious "envoys" in mind. A low round table and a wood chest, both carved in a pattern of spirals, stood against the other wall. Rhodry dropped his pack on top of the chest.

"I'll have water and suchlike sent in," Garin said. "And Mic and I will be back in a bit to dine with you. I need to do some asking and see where you'll be allowed to go and suchlike. But don't worry. We're not going to leave you here to rot all alone."

With a brief smile Garin left, leaving the door partway open behind him, a little sign, no doubt, that Rhodry was no prisoner whether or not he was welcome. Rhodry shut it, then went to the window to look out. The late-afternoon sun was beginning to creep down behind the cliffs, and the long shadow of the old watchtower lay on the grass like a spear. On the cliffs themselves he could see just how beautifully worked the triangular bays were, no doubt housing rooms like the one in which he sat, while directly in front he could look down and pick out the launderers, gathering up their wash and packing it into big baskets. Out beyond them and under a clear blue sky the green lawns spread, a good mile or more to the tongue of land forming the entrance ramp. In the golden light of an afternoon's peace it all struck him as inexpressively beautiful.

"Lin Serr," he whispered aloud, and to his surprise, his eyes filled with tears.

Then he looked down, straight down for two hundred feet to hard ground. He grabbed the windowsill with both hands and gulped for breath as the world seemed to jerk to one side and back again.

"You coward," he said aloud.

Rhodry made himself sit on the window ledge and turn to look out and down. Even though his shirt stuck to his back with cold sweat, he made himself stay until the sun had gone, leaving the basin filled with night. From outside the city he heard the huge gong, echoing in long strokes, and then, more clearly, the answer of a gong inside. He decided that it would do as a signal and released himself from his watch.

Rhodry was just rummaging in the carved wood chest for candles when Garin and Mic returned, bringing with them two servants carrying trays of food, pitchers of water, and other necessities for a guest. Once the food was laid out and the other things stowed, the servants left, shutting the door behind them.

"Sorry about the delay," Garin said. "The council was more concerned about what to do with Otho, and I had to shout to get their attention and all that. Well, let's sit down, lads, and pitch in. I'm hungry."

So were Rhodry and Mic, and for some time no one spoke. The food was mostly mushrooms, stewed in various sauces with various vegetables and scooped up with rounds of a thin herb bread. On one platter, however, lay what seemed to be disjointed birds, crisped with some sort of batter and fried. When Rhodry tried a bite it tasted of meat, not fowl.

"Bats?" he said.

"Just so," Garin said. "Er, hope you don't mind."

"Not in the least. Rather tasty, they are."

"Good. You never know how guests will take to them, like. And, speaking of guests and all, the council says it'll allow you the run of the main cavern though that's about all. My apologies, but I couldn't get them to give you a look at the high city. No one goes into the deep city, of course, who wasn't born here, not even other dwarves."

"Well, that's that, then."

"But you can go out into the basin all you want," Mic broke in. "And over to the old watchtower. It's kind of interesting. The doorkeeper's been told to let you in and out."

"Just don't go wandering too far, with that Alshandra creature lurking about. There's enough iron in the city that I think you'll be safe outside if you stick close to the cliff walls in daylight."

"Probably so," Rhodry said. "How long do you think we'll be here?"

Garin looked disgusted and raised his hands to the heavens.

"If Otho would mind his nasty tongue, I've no doubt we'd be on our way to Haen Marn in a bare two days. If."

"I see. We could be here a fortnight, then."

"Well, I hope not that long. I'll keep a watch over him, like, and his brother will, too."

"That reminds me," Mic chimed in. "He said I can go. My father, I mean. He said I could go on with you to Haen Marn, at least, and maybe beyond if Garin here thinks it safe."

"It's never going to be safe, lad," Garin said. "Hunting dragons. But I'll assess the risk, like, when we get there. It would be a good thing for you to spend some time with Enj, if it looks like you've got a chance of living through this little adventure." He glanced Rhodry's way. "I've been thinking it's time I took an apprentice, like, and Mic here seems to get along well on the outside."

"Ah. May I ask just what your craft is, then?"

"I never did explain." Garin paused for a grin. "I'm an envoy, and among us, that's not such an easy thing to be, a man who goes back and forth between different cities, to say naught of going down among your people. You have heralds and emissaries and even warleaders, and in a way, I'm a bit of all of those. Not that I could captain a troop in a battle, I mean, but when we go outside, we need someone who can make himself listened to, like, and obeyed if the situation demands it."

"It's dangerous, outside," Mic said. "We all know that. I don't know why, but it's fascinating as well."

"And the very fact you think so, Mic lad, is the reason I'm considering taking you on. Well, we'll see what Enj has to say about it, too, but if naught else, you'll travel to Haen Marn and see what you can see. And I'll see how it affects you, being outside for so long."

"It's a fair ways to Haen Marn, then?" Rhodry said.

"It is. It lies to the north and the west, and it's not so easy to find, even for a man who's been there before." Garin paused, looking away in some abstraction. "If they don't want you to find it, you never will, and even if you find it, you may or may not be welcome there. But that's a worry for another day. First we've got to get the judges to let Otho go, so he can oversee the paying of the debt we owe you before they take up the matter of his old debt."

"If they want to hold the trial first, how long?"

"Months." Garin made a sound halfway between a growl and a groan. "It'll be deep winter by then, and we'll never survive up in the high mountains." He glanced at Mic. "Your father and I are just going to have to make your uncle mind his manners, and that's that."

Garin summoned the servants by the expedient method of sticking his head out the door and shouting. Once the meal was cleared away, Garin and Mic retired for the night as well, leaving behind them a silver flask of a murky dark liquor that tasted stronger than Bardek wine and a small glass goblet to drink it out of. Rhodry poured himself a moderate amount and sat back in the window again to watch the stars over the cliffs of Lin Serr. Where was Alshandra, he wondered, and what was she up to? He hated thinking about her for more than a moment or two, so much so that he realized he was afraid, deep in his heart, that mentioning her name would summon her.

Overhead the great drift of the Snowy Road hung across the clear sky, so close in the mountain air that it seemed he could step out of the window and walk onto it, to follow it where? Evandar's country, perhaps, or the Otherlands. He looked down at the sheer drop, hundreds of feet into the night, and laughed, just softly under his breath, then raised the goblet in a toast.

"To my one true love," he said. "My lady Death."

He finished the liquor off, then swung his legs back into the safety of the room and the solidity of the stone floor, before he was tempted to let Jill's errand go hang and join his beloved instead.

On the astral border, there was peace, too much peace to be trusted—not one gashed tree, ruined tower, burnt or plundered view, not a single hoofprint, heap of offal, cracked stone, dead animal, to mark his brother's presence or passing did Evandar see on his long ride round his country. No doubt the evil fool was plotting something, then, lurking in his own territory and scheming no good. Only Evandar himself seemed to have achieved this dark insight, however. When he gave the order to turn toward the astral river and the place they all called home, the men of the Bright Court riding behind him sang aloud. Those who possessed some sort of consciousness, whether true or rudimentary, began the song and carried the melody, while the shadow creatures, the flickerings, they who might or might not someday evolve from a concatenation of energies into individuals—they hummed and rumbled and warbled in harmony and descant. Evandar was surprised to find himself pleased that they were happy. Never before had he done a thing to make them happy, the way he'd restored their part of the Lands. He was planning on telling Dallandra about this strange thing, that he'd done them a favor, and in turn it had pleased him.

When they reached the river, flowing broad and silver in the noontime light, the golden pavilion still stood, a good omen in itself. The men of the court dismounted, scattered, flickering here and there about the magical lands and taking their less than real but more than imaginary steeds with them. Left alone, Evandar dismounted, calling for his page. Nothing answered him but silence. His horse, which was as real as he was and in the same manner, tossed its head with a jingle of silver bridle rings.

"Here! Boy! Come take my mount to its stable!"

Not a sound, not a word, not a sigh of wind, broke a silence turned suddenly grim. Leading the horse, Evandar walked to the door of the pavilion and peered inside. Tables lay overturned and broken. So. His brother had gone too far, this time, encroached upon the holdings of the Bright Court and taken himself a prisoner.

His first thought was to summon the court again and ride out to war. His second, more prudent, was to discuss this matter with Dallandra. She'd promised him, after all, that she'd return to speak with him before sinking back down in the world of Time and Death to tend to Elessario's birthing, and her return was due soon. Evandar decided that he'd stable the horse himself and then summon a harper or two to entertain him while he waited. Once he'd spoken to Dalla, then would be the time for his rescue and revenge.

For some days Rhodry waited for the judgment upon Otho's request to post-
pone his trial. For the first day, walking round the main cavern turned out to be amusement enough. The area into which he was allowed stretched several hundred yards across, and every inch of the walls lining it sported intricate decorations, some stone, some steel. Some of the

panels depicted the countryside round Lin Serr; others showed scenes of farming life or hunting in the woodlands. The bas reliefs that he found the most interesting, however, told stories from the past of the Lin Serr clan. Some showed an unfamiliar landscape which, Garin confirmed, surrounded their old home in the far west, Lin Rej. There were views of those ancient caverns as well, and portraits of the folk who had lived there.

While Rhodry made his way round, studying each panel in turn, the citizens of Lin Serr came and went, hurrying across from tunnel to tunnel on their own affairs. Most ignored him, a few honored him with gruff nods not so much of greeting but acknowledgment that he existed. Mostly for something to do, Rhodry spent hours watching them and came across a puzzle that he mentioned to Garin and Mic that night at dinner.

"I don't mean to be insulting," Rhodry said. "Or pry unwanted into your ways or suchlike, but I've got to ask. Where are your womenfolk? I've not seen a one since we've been here."

"No offense taken," Garin said. "It's a natural enough question."

"Truly," Mic joined in. "I can see why you'd wonder, now that I've been to your country. Why, you see women all over the place, walking round right in the sunlight."

Rhodry waited for some minutes, but neither said a thing more. Apparently he could ask, but he wasn't going to be answered.

The next morning Rhodry walked out to the old gates. He stayed close to the cliffs and kept a good watch, as well, but whether it was the presence of Lin Serr's iron, or whether she was off on some other evil errand, Alshandra never appeared. For a while he sat in the grass in front of the gateway and studied both towers—the freestanding spire, the half-carved column still joined to the cliffs along one tall side.

This second tower sported two smaller round structures, in shape much like a Deverry broch, at its base—the old guardrooms, or so Garin had told him. When Rhodry explored them, he found them crammed with stored weapons, iron single-bitted axes, spearheads on old and split-ting wooden shafts, knives of various shapes. They'd all been thickly greased to keep the rust off, and the smell of ancient lard in hot rooms drove him out in a short while. Before he left, though, he found some iron knives of the same crude form and primitive construction as the bronze knife he carried at his belt. He could guess that someone in

Evandar's country had seen dwarven workmanship, but of an era very long gone.

Out on the freestanding spire, a ramp ran some thirty feet up the side to an open doorway. Rhodry paused there to catch his breath and look back at the lacy cliffs of the city, then went inside. He found a tiny chamber, little more than a landing round a stone spiral staircase, sculpted out of living rock. For a moment he simply marveled at it, then started climbing, round and round in one long rise inside the spire. Even though it was cool in the shadows, damp with the smell of ancient rock, still he was sweating by the time he finally gained the top.

The stairs led him out into one last chamber, some twenty feet on a square side, where huge windows dominated each wall, cut thick out of the rock and ledged some five feet wide. Rhodry walked round from one to the next, forcing himself to look down at the various views: the long rolling plateau south and west, the river and distant hills to the east, the white mountains at the northern horizon beyond the city itself. As long as he was looking at the horizon, he felt perfectly composed, but a sharp look down brought his dizziness and the cold sweat. He felt that he was taking up a battle that he should have fought long ago and forced himself to look down for as long as he could endure it. When he finally turned away his shirt was stuck to his back and chest both.

After that first visit Rhodry took to spending long hours alone up in the old tower. Since Garin and Mic could only spare him odd moments, except for their meals together, and Otho of course was under guard at the law courts, he'd often puff up the long ramp to the guard post in the spire, where he could sit and look past Lin Serr to the white mountains, just visible over the tops of the artificial cliffs. At times, when the warm sun was coming in through the window, he'd drowse off, taking every chance at sleep like the soldier he was. In his dreams the mountains assumed some enormous importance that he could never quite remember when he woke. It would seem to him that there among the snows of the high peaks he would finally find a thing for which he'd been searching all his long life, even if he couldn't remember what that thing was. Often as well in those dreams he would feel the watchers, the calm, cold gaze of the dragon eyes, the twisted malice of the human, turning his way.

In between dreams he would often wonder how Cengarn fared. What might be happening to Yraen, Carra, Prince Daralanteriel, and all the rest galled him, because he was being forced to do nothing while they might well have been in danger. Although he never worried about Jill's safety—he was quite confident that she could take good care of herself—he did often think of her. At times, when her memory rose as he watched the white mountains, he would find himself coming dangerously close to that secret he refused to uncover, that insight threatening his entire view of the world. Perhaps, just maybe, and what if, anyway, just what if a man's soul moved on when he died, rather than dying with him, to take up some new life somewhere, somewhen else? Whenever the question crept up on him, he would shove it away with a physical shake of his head.

Late on the fourth afternoon, he was sitting in the window as usual when he saw Mic, trotting across the basin and heading for the spire, most likely coming to fetch him. Rhodry got up and left, hurrying down the long ramp to meet him halfway. Mic was grinning in sheer excitement.

"We can go!" he called out. "The council of judges met today, and they gave Uncle Otho his postponement."

"Splendid!"

But Rhodry paused, looking back at the spire rising above with a certain regret. Most likely he would never sit there again, most likely he would never see Lin Serr again, once he left it.

"What's wrong?" Mic said.

"I'll miss this place, that's all."

"Why? It's not your home city."

"Well, true spoken. Where's Garin, by the by?"

"Waiting in your quarters. He's got some kind of news, too, but he wouldn't tell me what it was."

They found the envoy sitting at the table in Rhodry's chamber with a pair of wax-covered tablets in front of him. When they came in, he made a notation and laid his stylus down.

"Just figuring out what we'll need to take with us," Garin remarked. "We'll have the mule at first, but we'll have to leave him off at one of the last farms or suchlike. No doubt the farmers will board him for the use of him."

"No doubt," Rhodry said. "Mic told me you had news?"

"I do, and a very strange thing it is. Mic, go find your father and your uncle."

Mic opened his mouth to protest, thought better of it, and left the chamber. Garin waited a few moments.

"The thing is," the envoy said, "this is totally unprecedented, so I'd just as soon as few people know of it as possible. Otho's mother wants to see you."

"Otho's mother?"

"Just that. She's very, very old, Rhodry, and so sick she's bedridden, but she's been clinging to life for years in the hopes that Otho would return so that she could bid him farewell. Now thanks to you he *is* back, and she wants to meet the man who saved her eldest son's life."

"I see. I take it that your womenfolk don't allow strangers to see them very often."

"Just so." Garin hesitated for a long moment. "And here's the hard thing. Will you travel blindfolded into the deep city? Once we're down, we'll take the hood off, but for you to walk down sighted is against every law we have."

Rhodry hesitated, but he was always aware that his success in finding the dragon, to say naught of staying alive, depended on Garin's good favor.

"Well and good, then. Blind it is."

"My thanks. I would truly hate to disappoint the old woman. She's not got long left now."

"Then far be it from me to cause her anguish. When do we go?"

"Soon. One of her servants—her youngest great-grandson, in fact—will come to fetch us when she wakes from her nap."

"Ah. Very well, then. Could you answer me one thing? As long as it doesn't go against your laws, I mean. Why do your women hide themselves away? Out of modesty, like our priestesses?"

"There's some of that, but it's more that they hate the outside, and they shun the sunlight, too." Garin picked up the stylus and began fiddling with it. "Well, hum. Don't know how much I dare tell you."

"Now here, it's just curiosity on my part, so don't trouble your heart over it."

"My thanks. Now then. When we leave Lin Serr, think you'll be able to carry a pack when you have to?"

"If I've got a few days walking first to get my muscle back, I should be able to." Rhodry flashed him a grin. "I won't have any choice, will I?"

Before Garin could answer a knock came at the door. Rhodry opened it to find a boy, a scant three feet high but no infant, waiting outside. Barefooted, the lad wore only a knee-length smock, though he carried a scarf of some fine white cloth. When Garin smiled and spoke to him in Dwarvish, the boy answered in the same, his voice as clear and high as a flute.

"She's ready," Garin told Rhodry. "Her maidservant's just giving her a hot drink, like."

Rhodry took the long scarf and tossed it over one shoulder. If he was going to have to walk blind at some point, he wanted to carry his own hooding. In the pale blue light from the phosphorescent walls the three of them hurried across the main cavern, skirting the maze, and turned into an alcove. Massive stone stairs led down, plunging straight and steep, much like the flights inside Cengarn, to a narrow landing below. To either side of the marbled floor, tunnels branched off, while ahead yet another flight of stairs plummeted down. Garin waved at the side tunnels.

"These lead to the high city, and truly, if we weren't leaving so soon, I'd try to talk the council round to let you see it. It's a nice bit of work, if I do say so myself. But with luck, we'll be out of here by the morrow noon."

"I see." Rhodry glanced down the stairs to darkness. "Doesn't look like this scarf's going to be all that needful."

"Well, if you didn't have elven blood in your veins, we wouldn't bother, like, but you do." Garin considered the slope for a moment. "I think me that for safety's sake you'd best be able to see on the way down."

With careful small steps they climbed down, keeping close to the wrought-iron handrails at the side. After some fifty feet the blue light from the landing above faded away, leaving the darkness gray to Rhodry's half-elven sight. The steps just below him he could see, naught else. He had a brief wondering if dying was going to look like this, a peculiar light that would fade into a black like fur, as this light did at the bottom of the stairs.

"Here we are." Garin was whispering. "Hold where you are."

Rhodry did as he was told.

"I can't see a thing," he remarked.

"There'll be light farther on."

"Well and good, then."

When Rhodry tied the scarf round his eyes, he truly could sense little difference. Garin laid his hand on his arm to guide him.

"Just down here. There aren't any more steps, by the by."

"Good. How high's the ceiling?"

"A grand thing that you asked." Garin sounded profoundly apologetic. "You'll have to stoop a bit, I'm afraid."

When at a tunnel entrance Rhodry reached up, he found the ceiling some inches shorter than he was. For some fifty paces they walked straight ahead; then Garin guided him round a corner. Through the scarf Rhodry was aware of reddish light, and he could smell charcoal mixed with a resinous incense. As they walked on, the red light faded to be replaced with a dim ghost of the usual blue phosphorescence. He heard a door open, then shut behind them; they turned a number of times; there were other doors. The dwarves need never worry, he decided, about his ever finding his way through this maze alone. Just as his back was beginning to ache from walking crouched, Baeo piped up in Dwarvish.

"The hall of the mothers," Garin translated. "You can stand up here, Rhodry, and pull that scarf off."

"My thanks."

When Rhodry did so, his eyes adjusted fast to the pale blue light, streaked in places with fine silver fibers—some new kind of moss, he supposed. They were standing in a circular cavern of living rock under a dome of the same, festooned with blue and silver light. Behind and ahead, to his left and his right, tunnels led off into darkness. Fresh air wafted through, and he could hear water running with the whisper of a distant waterfall. Waiting in the center was a group of three women, dressed in long white smocks, belted high under their breasts. Their long jet-black hair was braided or swept up and piled on top of their heads, kept in elaborate place with combs and pins of red and purple gemstones. Although they were no taller than Deverrian girls, they moved with such authority that no one would have ever considered them immature.

When Garin spoke in Dwarvish, they nodded, answering briefly in the same while they looked Rhodry over in some curiosity. One of them walked over and reached up a small and slender hand. For a moment he thought she was going to lay it on his chest, but she merely held it in front of him, moving it in a circular pattern as if she were feeling something in the air while she studied his face. Finally she nodded with a certain satisfaction.

"You may travel on," she said in Deverrian, and her accent reminded Rhodry sharply of Jahdo's. "I think you be an honorable enough man, Rhodry son of two fathers, or so I hear be true. Bain't?"

"It is, my lady, in a manner of speaking. I was fathered by one man and raised by another."

She nodded again, considering.

"Othara do be old," she said at last. "She will ramble on, no doubt, but I would ask you be forbearing."

"I will, my lady."

With a last nod she glided back to the other women. The three of them moved aside, waving delicate hands at a side tunnel, standing in tableau as the men moved through their domain and onward. In the tunnel Rhodry had to crouch again, but mercifully they had only a few yards to travel to a small wooden door. Baeo spoke to Garin briefly, then knocked.

"You'd best go in alone," Garin said. "She tires too easily to have a lot of visitors at once."

A young dwarven woman, dressed in brown, her hair pulled simply back and tied with a thong, opened the door and ushered him inside. Although he had to stoop to enter, inside the large chamber, heavily perfumed with incense, he could stand. Here the light shone green and silver, and it took him a moment before he could see. The room swarmed with shadows because it was crammed with things: fine chests, chairs, small tables heaped with oddments of silver and steel, leather sacks, cloth sacks, all bulging and piled in corners or arranged on the chests.

On the far side from the door, in a bed made of wrought iron, an ancient, tiny woman lay propped up on pillows and covered by blankets. Her maid had apparently put some effort into this visit, because Othara wore a fringed scarf round her neck, and her thin, pure white hair was elaborately dressed, studded with at least four combs that Rhodry could see. At the sound of his entry she smiled, and her skin lay so tight and thin upon her face that she was no longer truly even wrinkled. When the maid gestured him closer, Othara turned her head his way. Her eyes were so milky and blank that he knew age had blinded her.

"Is this the man that did bring my son to me?" Her voice creaked like a door in the wind. "Come here. It's pleasing for me to know what you do look like."

"Of course, my lady."

Rhodry knelt at the bedstead and let her touch his face, her fingers moving light and sure as they felt out the shape of it.

"And a handsome lad at that," she said with a little laugh. "What be your name again?"

"Rhodry Maelwaedd, my lady."

"I shall call you Rori, because it be much like a dwarven name, and more becoming." She turned her head toward her maid, standing in a shadowed corner. "Lopa, pour the man somewhat to drink. Men always want drink when they pay visits."

The maid smiled and rummaged at a little table, gliding over in a moment with a glass goblet of the usual dark liquor.

"My thanks." Rhodry took a sip for politeness's sake. "It's very good."

"Of course. Do you think I'd be serving less than the old vintage to the man who did save my son? Ah, my eldest he is, at that, and always a wayward lad, but if a mother love not her son, then who will, I always say. Eh?"

"Indeed."

She nodded, turning her head in a gesture that reminded him of Meer, glancing round as she remembered what it was like to see.

"We do sit deep inside the earth, Rori. Is that distressing to you?"

"Only at moments, my lady. My people are creatures of the grasslands and forest, and at times, the dark here does touch my heart."

"No doubt. It aches the heart of most men, even our men, who long to wander in the light above. Never have I seen the sun, Rori. Never did I want to. What do you think of that, eh?"

"I'm surprised, truly."

She smiled, pleased with the effect.

"I have heard of the high world from my sons. Does that not be one of the things a son does for his mother, to tell her of the world above? But I be a woman and a mother, six times a mother, twenty-two times a grandmother, and now and already seven times a great-grandmother, and the earth I do know. I did earn my place, here in the heart of the earth, six times over. In the heart of the earth women be born, and we do rest in her heart, our mother's heart, and we do hear her tales, long tales of fire and rock, and in the end, we do die upon her breast." She smiled again, nodding a little as if she heard distant music.

Lopa came forward with a cup of steaming water that smelled of herbs and helped the ancient dwarf take a sip.

"Ah, well brewed, my dear," Othara said. "Very well brewed. Does our guest need more drink?"

"I don't, but my thanks," Rhodry said hastily. This "old vintage" was turning out to be quite strong, and he did have the long stairs to climb back to the upper world. "It's truly good."

She smiled, nodded, glanced round the room with milky eyes.

"They tell me, Rori, that you do travel north, hunting an ancient wyrm among the fire mountains."

"I do, my lady."

"Ah, the north, the dragon north, the country of the Great Rift. We women call it the land of blood and fire, the earth's blood, that do be, that do run red and gold through all the black veins round the rift. A land of splendor in the way we women think, but the men, they do fear it, the blood of fire. Do you know, Rori, why the earth does bleed so, there in the northland?"

"I don't. Will you tell me, my lady?"

"I will, for be it not a woman's work to tell the men tales of the deep earth? We live and we listen in the deep earth, and we do hear her tales, and we pass those tales on, mother to daughter to granddaughter, so the sons may know." She paused, motioning for another sip of herbed brew. "The northland and the southland, they do be joined along the high mountains, the Roof of the World, or so the sons call it, but I tell you that it be no roof, no sheltering there, but the Great Rift." For a long moment she rested, her mouth working. "The northland and the southland, they do go their own ways, Rori, like a wife who grows to hate her husband and does send him back to the high city. The earth splits and tears along the high mountains, and she bleeds, she bleeds. Some fine day the tear will run so deep that it will reach the sea, and in will rush the water, cold and salt, to soothe that burning."

Rhodry caught his breath. Othara laughed, a low mutter like gravel sliding downhill.

"Be you frightened at this thought, the earth rifting and splitting?"

"I see no shame in admitting it, my lady. I am. What of the folk who live there?"

She laughed, then coughed. Lopa slipped an arm under her, helped her sit upright, and held the cup. Othara drank more of her medicinal, then lay back, resting before she spoke again.

"Oh, they have a few more years before they'll feel the danger, thousands upon thousands of years, Rori, a thousand thousand times a thousand thousand, no doubt. The earth runs deep, but she runs slow."

"Well and good, then."

"The men think the earth is steady, but we women know that rock moves, floating on a sea of fire. It be our life, the earth, the deep, deep earth. Did you know that the very rocks do float upon fire?"

"I didn't, my lady, and I give you a thousand thanks for the telling of it."

She smiled and yawned. One hand plucked at the edge of the blankets, her fingers as long and thin as twigs, and as gnarled. Lopa stepped forward, alarmed, turning to Rhodry and framing a few silent words, "Leave soon." He nodded to show that he understood, but Othara recovered herself.

"I'll give you a present, Rori, for all that you're both a man and an elf, because you've brought my son back to me." The old woman turned her head Lopa's way. "Open the chest in the corner. Find the lead casket and do open that. You shall find a bit of blue silk. Well, it were blue once. Unwind it and you shall find a blue stone upon a chain."

The young woman scuttled off to do as she was bid. Out of a developing sense of what dwarven courtesy would include, Rhodry pointedly refrained from looking her way as she rootled through the ancient woman's treasures. While they waited Othara closed her eyes, and her breathing rasped so loudly that Rhodry feared she'd drifted off. When the girl returned, though, clutching a gold chain, Othara held out her hand. She took the stone from Lopa, felt it carefully, then passed it back.

"That be the one. Give it to him."

With a low whistle of awe, Rhodry took a chunk of lapis lazuli the size of a crabapple, fine-shaped and polished into an egg. At the narrow end the fine gold chain ran through a drilled hole lined with silver, to prevent wear, he supposed. Instinctively he closed his hand over it.

"It feels like a presence," he burst out. "A live thing, not a stone."

He opened his hand and looked again: it seemed an ordinary gem, if indeed so big a piece of such a rare thing could be called ordinary. Othara smiled, a draw of blue lips.

"You feel it, do you?" she rasped. "Good, good. Then you be fit to own it. There be great dweomer on that stone. Wear it, and I think me your enemies shall find it a great travail to scry you out."

Rhodry slipped the chain over his head and settled the gem under his shirt.

"I don't know how to thank you enough," he began. "You're most generous—"

The old woman had fallen asleep, her head turned into her pillow. With a waggle of her finger and a flick of her apron, Lopa shooed him out of the chamber to the corridor, where Garin waited.

"Well, that was kind of you to indulge the old dear," Garin said.

"Ye gods! 'Old dear' indeed! She's one of the most powerful women I've ever met, and that includes Jill. Truly, my only regret is that Jill's not here to sit with Othara awhile and hear her lore."

Lopa shot him a glance brimming with approval, but Garin seemed, really, to have heard not a word.

"Very kind," he said again. "Well, we'd best be getting back up. We've a lot of planning to do before we leave."

Over the weeks that Rhodry had been gone, Jill had fallen into the habit of scrying for him several times a day. Since she knew him so well, all she had to do was focus her attention on some mottled natural thing—a fire, a bank of clouds, wind moving over trees, and suchlike—and think of him to see his whereabouts. She'd traced his way through the hills and into Lin Serr, seen the old gatehouse through his eyes as well, and stored in her memory a hundred questions to ask him about these strange places in the hope, at least, that he'd live to tell her.

It was just after Rhodry had been given his audience with Othara that Jill was sitting in her tower room, looking out the window at a summer storm piling dark on the horizon. When she thought of Rhodry she saw nothing, not the barest trace or flicker of an image, not the slightest feeling of his presence.

"Odd," she said aloud.

On her table stood a cup of water. She picked it up, swirled the liquid round, and scried into that. Not a thing. She set it down and returned to the window, but no matter how carefully she focused her mind, she simply could not scry Rhodry out. More annoyed than frightened, she turned her thoughts to Otho instead and saw him immediately. With Mic trotting beside him, the elderly dwarf was hurrying down a corridor that shimmered with phosphorescence.

As Jill watched, he crossed the main entry cavern of the city, turned down a short tunnel, and knocked on a door. She recognized it as opening onto the room in which she'd previously scried Rhodry out, but the moment the door opened the vision vanished into a blur of gray like smoke. Even though she called upon the various elemental lords that presided over scrying, her vision simply refused to penetrate the smudge.

Muttering several truly foul oaths, Jill turned from the window and began pacing back and forth across the room. Someone had thrown a dweomer shield over Rhodry, then, but whether that someone was friend or foe, she had no way of knowing. Yet she felt no fear, sensed no danger, either, and knew that she would if Rhodry were in some mortal jeopardy. There was nothing left for her but to hope that at various times Garin or Otho would move far enough away from Rhodry for her to trace their party as they traveled.

She wandered to the window, stood looking out at the scudding clouds while she debated flying one last patrol round the dun. Scrying in the etheric double during a storm would be impossible.

"Jill?" The voice rang outside her door. "Wise One, may I disturb you?"

"Of course, my prince. Come in."

Daralanteriel flung the door back and strode in, one hand clutched on his sword hilt.

"What's so wrong, Your Highness?" Jill said.

The prince seemed to catch himself on the edge of some fault. He took a deep breath, letting his hand drop from the weapon.

"My apologies, but it's about that huge lout of a Round-ear."

"I beg your pardon?"

"Yraen. Every time I turn round he's right there."

"Well, Your Highness, I asked him to stand guard—"

"Oh, I know, but I've got twenty men of my own, don't I?"

"When you ride out to hunt, they ride with you."

"I could leave some of them behind to guard my own wife, if that's what you mean."

Jill thought she understood—his pride was wounded.

"Your Highness, never would I impugn your ability to keep Carra safe. It's just that human treachery is best spotted by human eyes. Yraen's a shrewd and suspicious man who's been in some rather ugly situations in his day. He knows the worst side of his own kind quite well."

Dar considered, chewing on his lower lip. By elven standards he was little more than a boy, much as Carra by human ones was still in many ways a girl, and he looked it that evening, with his hands shoved in his pockets and his dark hair uncombed and tousled.

"It's because of Lord Matyc," Jill went on. "Consider how close he was to the gwerbret, how well entrenched here at the dun. If Rhodry hadn't spotted him, he could have worked untold harm."

"Ah." Dar looked up with a brief smile. "Well, that's true spoken. Wise One, my apologies. I hate to argue with such as you, but it griped my soul, always seeing the man there. But you're right." His voice colored with learned contempt. "He *is* a silver dagger."

"Just so, but a decent man and a fine watchdog withal."

"If the Wise One says so. My thanks for hearing me out."

"You're most welcome."

Dar lingered, studying the floor.

"Is there somewhat else, Your Highness?"

"Oh, not truly. I was just wondering, we were all wondering, truly, if you'd seen anything yet. Enemies, I mean. The waiting's starting to stretch everyone's nerves like bowstrings."

"I'm afraid I haven't. I assure you that you'll know as soon as I do."

Prince or not, Dar had to be content with that. Over the next few days, whenever she walked about the dun, Jill could see the truth of his words. Servants squabbled and swore, while the men in the warbands shoved each other and got into fistfights; Carra and the serving women seemed always on the edge of tears, while Lady Labanna was very, very cheerful, except in repose, when she looked deathly ill.

Once, even, late on an afternoon when everyone was hungry for their dinner, Jill rounded a shed out by the stables and saw pages brawling, screaming and punching each other while they rolled back and forth on the filthy cobbles.

"Stop it!" Jill yelled, darting forward. "Stop it right now, or I'll turn you all into frogs!"

The threat brought instant peace. The boys broke apart and rolled free of each other, young Lord Allonry to one side, Jahdo and Cae to the other. Although Jahdo and Cae seemed mostly bruised and filthy, Alli's nose bled and his lip was split.

"He was hitting Cae," Jahdo burst out. "I was trying to make him stop."

Cae nodded fast agreement. Alli merely sniveled.

"I see," Jill said. "My lord Allonry, I should have thought you'd have tasted enough trouble over that matter of the root cellar without wanting another meal of it."

"They all hate me because of that," Alli whined. "They mock me all the time and they won't let me forget the whipping I got."

Jill fixed Cae with a sorcerous-seeming eye. He turned white and began to stammer.

"A bargain," she said. "Jahdo and Cae, neither of you mention the root cellar again. Alli, in return, no more mocking Jahdo for a bondman. The first one to break the bargain—into the marsh with him!"

Never had Jill had anyone agree with her so fast as the three lads did. She sent Cae off to the cook and Alli to the chamberlain, but she took a look at Jahdo's bruises herself.

"Naught too bad," she announced. "But you'll need a bath before dinner."

"I do know that, my lady, and bathe I shall, though it be likely it be in the horse trough there, all cold as it be. I do miss the hot springs of home, I truly do."

"No doubt. Well, with luck we'll get you back home one of these days soon."

"Do you truly believe this thing, my lady? I daren't hope, from the wanting of it so bad."

Jill considered the question seriously, but the only dweomer feeling she received was a small surety.

"I do believe it, Jahdo, though I'll wager the way home won't be all that easy to walk. I'll do my best to make it so."

Jahdo grinned, a lopsided gesture what with the swelling on his right cheek.

"If you do say it, then it be so," he pronounced. "Yraen do say that sorcerers, they do know what be so and what be not. He says you'll find these enemies as soon as soon."

"Let's hope Yraen's right, then. Now go wash that muck off you."

The boy's blind faith in her power wrung Jill's heart, because there was nothing she could do but watch and patrol, whether in the hawk form or her etheric double. Although at moments she was tempted to hope that Alshandra had given up her mad plan, deep in her heart, deep in her very soul where all dweomer warnings spring, Jill knew that there was no hope, only waiting.

When Rhodry and the dwarves left Lin Serr, at first they had easy walking, with a pack animal to carry their gear down a proper dwarven road and farms close at hand to sell them fresh food. At every farm where they stopped, Rhodry saw only men, most of them young, some little better than boys, who lived a life as communal as any warband's. As far as he could tell, anyway, from his brief looks round, and he certainly didn't want to be caught prying, they slept in barracks and ate in communal cook houses as well.

After three days of this comfortable travel, they reached the edge of the plateau, where the farmland petered out among the rising hills and the white mountains towered close. Like clouds the snowy peaks seemed to float above pine forests so dark a green they seemed almost black, streaked here and there with outcrops of gray basalt. At the last farm Otho traded the mule for the privilege of cramming their packs with all the dried food and cheese they could hold.

"And it looks scant enough," Otho remarked with a sigh. "No doubt the gods will starve us before they throw us into the dragon's maw, just to make us suffer, like."

"Otho old lad," Rhodry said. "If you'd stayed behind you'd be handing over your life's fortune in jewels to your debtors right now."

Otho snarled and swung a weak fist in his direction.

"We may be able to snare a rabbit or two," Garin put in. "Gather a few wild herbs, certainly, and spear some trout along the way."

Rhodry found that a heavy pack sits lighter on a man who's used to walking. Although his back burned by the end of the first day's march, bit by bit he grew accustomed to the weight until he could almost keep up with the dwarves, not that he would ever match their stamina fully. Even once he hit his stride, they were still forced to stop for rests they didn't need and to make camp a little earlier than they would have chosen on their own.

The terrain was hard traveling, anyway—steep, rocky hills, thickly forested valleys, some narrow enough to be called ravines and little more— treacherous enough to make them decide to march during the day. Although Garin seemed sure of the route, Rhodry never was aware of their following anything that could be called a path, merely places where the scrub and brambles grew less thickly. At times, only some hard work with a dwarven ax got them clear of underbrush without doubling back. The traveling might have been easier, of course, if it weren't for Otho's constant grumbling, whether he was snarling in rage or merely muttering under his breath. At least once a day Garin would threaten to drown the old man and leave his bones for the ravens.

Every night they camped as high as possible and preferably among rocks, not trees, where they could take turns standing watches and keep an eye out, as Garin said, just in case something was following them. Yet they never saw an enemy, not in the night or even during the day. For the first time all summer, Rhodry slept without dreams of watching eyes. From these high camps he could see for miles, looking back down toward Lin Serr and Deverry itself, lost beyond the horizon, as if it had fallen away from this vertical world of rock and ravine. When he turned north he would see the white peaks, so close in the morning air that it seemed he could jump, stretch, and touch them.

After some six days in wild country, when they were beginning to run low on supplies, the weather began to change. Toward sunset cirrus clouds wisped across the sky from the west, and by the time the moon rose, about halfway between its first quarter and its full, a mackerel sky webbed its silver light. Morning brought a gray roil of cloud. In a whipping wind they broke camp and headed north in silence, looking up as often as they looked forward.

"How far to Haen Marn?" Mic asked.

"I don't know," Garin said, chewing on his lower lip. "But we should find the first road stone today."

"What do you mean you don't know?" Otho snapped. "You've been there thrice."

"And each time it appeared at a different twist in the road."

Otho goggled.

"It did, and there's naught more I can say about it." Garin shrugged mightily. "Disbelieve me all you want, but I know what I saw. And the third time no one let me in, either."

"What is this place?" Rhodry said. "A dun? And what kind of people would turn a stranger from their gates, anyway?"

"People who live by different laws than yours, but they made sure I had the food to get myself home again. I'm not saying a thing more, because you won't be believing me, anyway. You'll all see for yourselves, you will, and with luck it'll be soon now."

Round midday they panted up a particularly steep hill, crested a lifeless rise of black basalt, and looked down into a thickly forested valley, some two hundred yards across at the widest point and about five hundred long. Down this length a stream ran, crossing the middle of a clearing about fifty yards wide and too precisely circular to be a natural formation.

"Oho!" Garin said. "Now that looks promising, lads."

They fought their way downhill through grasping brambles and thick shrubs to the valley floor, hit the stream, and followed it back and forth along what seemed to be its entire length. They never found the clearing.

"Ye gods," Garin whispered. "It's starting already. Well, we might as well get out of this cursed gulch."

"Now wait," Rhodry said. "I for one need a meal, and a clearing like that just doesn't up and take itself away."

"It doesn't, eh? Well and good, then. You lead and we'll look for it."

"Done, then. Even a wretched elf like me can follow a running stream."

Back they went, and this time they'd gone not more than twenty yards when the trees began thinning ahead of them. Grinning in triumph Rhodry led them straight out into open ground.

"There we are! I knew it—" All at once he felt his grin disappearing. "But where was it before?"

"Just so," Garin said. "Just so."

Mic and Otho were looking round openmouthed.

"What's that over there?" Mic pointed. "Looks like stone."

Stone it turned out to be, a huge pointed slab of black basalt, tipped on end and graved with writing in the dwarven language. Garin ran one finger down it, as if to assure himself of its reality.

"This is the first marker on the road," he said. "The one I was talking about. I doubt me if I would have found it, but Rhodry did, and that tells us somewhat, lads."

Everyone looked at him expectantly.

"Ye gods, think!" Garin snapped. "It means he's been foreseen or foretold or suchlike. From now on, Rhodry lad, you lead."

"What?" Rhodry said. "I've never been here before, and you've been thrice."

"So? I'll act as guide, like. You're the leader."

Otho moaned and rolled his eyes heavenward.

"To think a cousin of mine and him an envoy at that would have gone daft! And us in mortal danger, too!"

"We're not in any danger at all," Garin sighed. "And I know what I'm doing."

"Well and good, then," Rhodry said. "Far be it from me to argue with dweomer, and this place stinks of it. Here, O Guide." He paused for a grin. "What sayeth this most ancient stone?"

"If you're going to talk like an apprentice bard," Garin said with some asperity, "I'm going to tip you over the next cliff. It says, and in good plain language, too, 'This is the first writing stone on the road to Haen Marn.' As I remember, the first two times I came this way, I found two more, and the last time I found four."

"And I'll wager that they were always in different places, too," Otho put in.

"Just that." Garin glanced up at the threatening sky. "At the moment, lads, I'd say we need to find shelter more than another trail marker."

As if in agreement a few fat drops fell, splashing on the black stone. Distant thunder cracked.

"I knew our luck with the weather wasn't going to hold, not this time of year," Garin went on. "Over there, O Leader, your guide see-eth a clump of trees that look a fair bit lower than the rest. I say we get under them and let the tall trees draw the lightning."

In a patter of drops on branches above them they finished their meal, but as soon as they took to the trail again, the rain began in earnest. Although the greased canvas lashed over their packs kept the food dry, the men were soaked in minutes. They sloshed on, keeping to the lower ground and letting the lightning seek the high. Even though he was wet, chafed, and tired, Rhodry found himself singing whenever he had the breath, just odd snatches of elven songs that he'd learned from his natural father. He found himself laughing at every crack of lightning. Above them the white peaks hung invisible, shrouded in cloud.

They camped wet that night and traveled the next day in weather that alternately threatened and made good its threat of rain, until finally, at midafternoon, on a race of wind the storm blew over. By sunset, the sky was clearing to the north and east. When they began looking for a campsite, Rhodry was expecting that he'd find another marker stone as well, just because it seemed fitting and no reason more. They clambered out of one last valley and climbed to the top of a hill, where boulders among high grass offered some kind of shelter. While the dwarves squabbled about it, Rhodry stood on the crest and looked back to the south, down the long slope up which they'd climbed, where dark clouds lingered over the forests, wreathed with mist as blue as smoke in the far distance. His old world lay under that mist, and he wondered why he was so sure he'd come into a new one.

"Oy, Rhodry!" Garin called. "Are we camping here or not?"

"We're not. I don't know why, but we're not."

The answer lay not a half mile beyond. They scrambled down the hill on the north face, made a little turn between two slopes, and came out facing west to see ahead and some hundred yards down into a long valley, bisected by a deep river, flowing north to south. To the south, their left, grassland scattered with oak trees lay between steep hills all brushy and forested. To the north rose a high wall of cliff, blocking a view of hills beyond—they could just see peaks, black with trees, over the rise of sheer rock.

"Oh, ye gods!" Garin whispered. "Haen Marn."

Rhodry laughed, one of his berserk peals as wild as a thunderclap.

"This is it?" Otho snapped. "I don't see a cursed thing but trees, neither dun nor hovel, naught. Wait! Those trees! Oaks don't grow this high up."

"Worms and slimes!" Mic sputtered. "What's wrong with this view? Is it my eyes?"

As long as they looked down into the valley, "this view" made perfect sense, but when Rhodry looked round, he couldn't see how the crest where he stood, on the east slope above the valley, connected up to the cliffs at the valley's north end. They saw no dweomer-induced cloud or magical blackness swimming in the air; it was simply impossible to look at the place where the geographies must have sorted themselves out. The crest trotted right along, and the cliffs picked up—except they couldn't have, but they did. The valley lay self-contained in one landscape; they all stood in another. The other dwarves were fuming, looking down, looking up again, staring all round them, but Garin merely sighed.

"Haen Marn," he said again, as if that explained everything. He pointed north, where the river flowed out through a crack in the cliff face. "That's the entrance. Haen Marn itself lies beyond the cliffs."

"And what do we do, swim?" Otho snapped. "It's a cold dark day for that."

Garin ignored him. Automatically Rhodry looked at the sky. The sun was already sinking off to the west, turning the scudding clouds deceptively bright.

"Well, at least we won't camp wet," Rhodry said. "Better get on down, lads. Night's falling."

Otho snorted profoundly. Settling their packs, they headed downhill, picking their way through the underbrush and boulders to come out into a valley brimming with shadows. When Garin turned north and began marching purposefully toward the cliff, the rest trailed after, looking up and around them. While the valley itself matched the view they were remembering from the crest, some other thing fit wrong, so subtlely skewed that none of them could specify it. Off to the north, above the rise of cliff, Rhodry could still see the white peaks, about where they should have been and as high, too.

"It's the wind!" Rhodry said abruptly. "It was quiet up above, but it's blowing here. Should be the other way round."

"Just so," Otho snarled. "It's eerie and dweomer-soaked and un-canny, and I hate it."

Mic nodded; there was not much more to add, truly.

Eventually they caught up with Garin, who was rootling about between a trio of enormous gray boulders that lay at the foot of the cliff. Just as they reached him he grinned in triumph and pulled free a silver horn, all nicked and tarnished, at the end of a long chain.

"There," he said. "I'll call, and let's hope someone answers."

"Before we grow much older," Otho muttered.

"Don't get your hopes up about that."

Even though the horn looked as if someone had been kicking it back and forth on the rocky ground, when Garin blew, the sound rang piercingly sweet, three long notes that brought tears to Rhodry's eyes, although he could never say why, not then nor later. When he glanced at the dwarves, he caught Mic wiping his eyes on the back of his hand, and even Otho seemed moved. Garin blew the three notes three times, then returned the horn to its hiding place in a hollow among the rocks.

"Now we wait. Naught else for it."

In the event they waited till the next afternoon. Some hundred yards from the river they found a sheltered spot among rocks where they could peg and weight their canvas lean-to. In between their watches the dwarves drowsed, sitting upright, heads on knees, and Rhodry slept, wedged tight between the packs and a boulder. He woke once in the middle of the night to hear rain drumming overhead, and a second time, some hours before dawn, when Mic shook him awake to go stand a watch.

Stretching and yawning Rhodry eased himself free of the shelter. Outside the rain had stopped and the wind risen. When he looked up he could see the clouds rolling and scudding before the nearly-full moon. The stars winked through the drifting gray, then disappeared again, only to return in sheets of sky. He paced back and forth, cold and aching from one night too many spent sleeping on hard ground. He yawned, rubbing his face with both hands, frowning a little at the growth of beard. All his life, Rhodry had hated being bearded. When he thought back to some of the trouble he'd gone through to keep himself clean-shaven on the long road or out in the Westlands, he had to laugh at himself, in fact, but he was definitely hoping that this mysterious Haen Marn would offer a traveler soap and hot water.

Still smiling he glanced at the river, swore, and rose to his feet. Walking on the river as if it were a silver road came a procession of tall, slender women, all dressed in white, with silver kirtles at their waists and silver torcs round their necks. They walked in pairs except for their leader, who carried a spear with a silver point. As they walked, they wept, tossing their heads and whipping their disheveled hair round, sobbing and covering their faces with slender hands. Without thinking Rhodry ran to the bank and called out.

"My ladies, what's so wrong? Can I be of help to you?"

At the sound of his voice, the woman with the spear turned her head and smiled at him, just briefly, before they vanished, leaving only a faint mist blowing over the silver ripples of the river. Rhodry tried to tell himself that he'd been asleep and dreaming, but no man spends his dreams thinking about shaving. He turned cold, shuddering. He stayed on his feet, walking by the river, until the dawn brightened gray with the first sun.

As he was debating whether or not to wake the others, Rhodry heard a sound so distant that at first he thought it might only be some echo of water over rock. He paused, listening hard, heard it again—a definite ring or clang of metal on metal. He trotted back to their improvised camp just as Garin hauled himself out from under the lean-to.

"Did you hear that?" the dwarf said.

"I did. Like a sword striking a metal boss, in a way."

They stood together and listened, straining into the wind. Around them the sunlight brightened, and Otho joined them, muttering to himself until Garin cursed him silent. They heard nothing.

"Well, worms and slimes," Garin said at last. "We were probably just imagining things. The high mountains do that, sometimes, to a man. Go wake your nephew, will you? I'll start taking down the shelter and suchlike."

For a few moments more Rhodry stayed by the riverbank and watched the river swirling out of the crack in the cliffs. In the morning light he could see the break more clearly. At the surface it gaped some twenty feet wide, fringed with white water though the river ran reasonably steady in the middle. As it rose it narrowed, closing completely just before the top of the cliff.

All day they waited, while the wind sighed through the valley and sniffed round their camp. The dwarves mostly slept or diced with each other while Rhodry paced back and forth, unable to sit and rest no matter how tired he'd been the day before. Although Garin invited Rhodry to join the game, he preferred to watch rather than get into one of the heated squabbles that seemed part of the amusement. Toward evening, when the sun was sending long shadows through a blue haze, Rhodry walked down to the river and stood studying the white water. Directly inside the tunnel mouth, it seemed, he could see some huge thing clinging to the wall, but because of the boulders piled on the bank at that point, he couldn't get close enough to see it clearly. Since it never moved, he could assume that it wasn't dangerous. Just as he gave it up and turned to go, he heard the clang again.

This time he could identify the sound as one of the brass gongs he'd heard in Lin Serr. Echoing and bouncing it seemed to come from deep within the cliff, as if someone were striking in an interrupted attempt at rhythm. Before he could hail the others, a boat shot out of the crack, riding high on the current. All painted green and carved it was, long and narrow, with a tall prow in the shape of a dragon, or so he assumed, a long neck with a small snakelike head, the mouth open to reveal gilded teeth. As it glided past he could pick out a helmsman at the stern, two oarsmen amidships, and in the prow a man holding a rope with a huge flower of iron hooks at one end. Near this anchorman hung a brass gong on a wooden frame, bolted right into the boat.

"Oy!" Garin yelled, waving madly. "Here!"

All the dwarves ran toward the bank, but the ship had passed in an instant, gliding on downstream toward the bend in the river. The dwarves barely had time to start swearing, though, before it began to turn about, oars flailing, the helmsman leaning and hauling madly to use the shifts in the current to his advantage. Since he'd been raised round boats and water, Rhodry took off running downstream. The prow came round, and the oarsmen began rowing for the bank.

"Hila!" the anchorman called, then threw.

The iron hook gleamed and spun through the air. Rhodry grabbed the rope just behind it, whipped it round, and sank it hard into the damp turf. The anchorman leapt ashore to jump with his full weight on the hook cluster's flat head, sinking it deep and tethering the boat to the earth. The oarsmen followed, and with Rhodry's help they ran her up into the shallows. When the anchorman panted out a few Dwarvish words and smiled, Rhodry smiled in return, knowing a thanks when he heard it no matter what the language. The other dwarves came running up, or rather, Mic and Garin ran, with Otho stalking behind.

"Very impressive, silver dagger," Garin said, then turned to the anchorman and spoke rapidly in Dwarvish.

The anchorman said nothing, merely pointed at the helmsman, who was just leaping ashore. The helmsman was tall for a dwarf, and slender, too, though at just over five feet he was short for a human being and decidedly stocky. Although the boat crew were all dressed more or less alike, in rough brown trousers and floppy brown shirts that gave their arms plenty of room to move, the helmsman sported a silver brooch pinned to one shoulder, a free-form dragon shape, neck and tail all twined and knotted round each other. With a nod Rhodry's way, Garin switched to Deverrian of a sort, laden with Dwarvish words.

Rhodry had a good deal of trouble understanding the conversation. It seemed that Garin was trying to get them all passage into Haen Marn, while the helmsman suffered from grave doubts about the wisdom of such a thing. Finally the helmsman turned to him and spoke a few words that Rhodry could pick out.

"What be your name?"

"Rhodry from Aberwyn."

Shrewd dark eyes considered him for a long moment.

"And it be needful that you talk with Enj? Why?"

Rhodry saw no reason to waste time in courtesy or fencing.

"I need his help to hunt a dragon."

The helmsman blinked rapidly several times.

"Ah," he said at last. "I think me you be expected. Get your accoutrements into the boat."

Rhodry exchanged a startled look with Garin. The dwarf shrugged, then trotted off back to the camp. Once they had their packs and suchlike stowed, the oarsmen helped each in turn clamber aboard, but Rhodry swung himself up with a laugh. The anchorman pulled the hooks free, then ran, leaping aboard just as the boat floated clear, nosing round into the current.

Rowing upstream was hard work, and the closer they came to the crack in the cliff face the harder and slower it became, because the river narrowed. Rhodry began to wonder how they could possibly get through, even if every passenger found oars and set to. The anchorman, hooks in hand, stood at the prow, peering forward, tongue sticking out the side of his mouth in concentration. When the prow inched its way under the shadow of the cliff, Rhodry saw a riband of braided ropes, a sort of flat strip of web work, hung along one side of the tunnel and threaded through a huge iron wheel.

"Hila!" the anchorman whirled the hooks round his head and threw.

The cluster hit the braid, grabbed and stuck fast in the web. The anchorman flung his whole weight back, tightening the throw rope.

"Gong!" he yelled.

Rhodry grabbed a padded stick he found dangling from a chain and swung hard. The boom echoed and quivered over the sound of the white water. With a creak and almost human groan the wheel began to turn, and the webbed strip began to move, hauling them upstream against the current while the rowers bent and sweated. It was no wonder Haen Maen had the reputation of being so inhospitable, Rhodry thought, if it took all of this to bring strangers in. With the anchorman clinging and leaning to the rope like a groom, the boat bucked like an angry horse, but they moved forward, creeping past the rough stone walls toward a small and distant patch of light. Rhodry heard the helmsman yell something in Dwarvish.

"Keep striking the gong," Garin yelled, translating. "He says our lives might well depend on it."

Rhodry struck, grabbed the stick in both hands, and swung again, finding and keeping a regular rhythm as the boat inched along, its slender figurehead bowing and rising, the helmsman cursing a steady stream as he fought with the current. If the prow should dash against the stone wall, they were all lost. When he glanced up between strokes, next to the widening square of light Rhodry saw another wheel. Just beyond, on a sandy strip of beach, two dwarves bent over a crank such as turns meat on a spit.

"Hila!" the anchorman called.

"Hola!" they called in return.

The boat inched past the wheel, then broke free of the dark, scooting with a sudden lunge to the rope's length out to gray light from an open sky and Haen Marn. While the anchorman struggled to free his hooks from the web of ropes, and the two dwarves who'd been cranking the pulley scrambled aboard, Rhodry stared across the lake, wide miles of dark water, surrounded by hills that plunged down steeply without a sign of level shore. He could just make out forests marching down, deeply shadowed in the last of the sunlight. Directly across from the entrance flashed a silver glint that seemed to be a waterfall pouring into the lake from some great height.

Out in the center rose a small island shaped like the crest of a rocky hill and topped by a strange tower, all right angles and built square, with other rectangular buildings huddled beneath it. Off behind this main island rose islets, some no more than huge boulders poking their heads above water. He found himself remembering Jahdo's description of Cerr Cawnen and Citadel, because mist rose heavily in the far reaches, hinting at warm water bubbling up from springs.

"Gong!" the helmsman screamed. "Gong now!"

Rhodry realized that he'd been so taken with the sight that he'd slacked off. He swung two-handed, found his rhythm again, and kept it up while the new dwarves bent to the oars. With fresh oarsmen the boat darted across the lake. Echoing off the distant hills, the sound of the gong fled before them, then turned to greet them again as the island came closer and closer. Garin scrambled to his feet and moved up next to Rhodry.

"They say the noise drives beasts away," Garin yelled. "I'll take a turn."

Rhodry surrendered the stick gladly and moved away from the boom, which was beginning to throb in his temples with a tangible ache. He found a spot on the other side of the figurehead where he could lean on the prow and have a good look round. When he looked behind, the flat cliff rose high about the water level, then leveled at the top in a suspiciously regular manner. So, then, the entrance ran through some sort of dam, and Haen Marn was not entirely a natural creation, no matter which world it belonged in. When he looked ahead, he could see the main island clearly, with its tall watchtower rising from a grove of windbent trees, and what seemed to be a long manse at its base, a cluster of small sheds round that, and then a boat dock jutting from a covered boathouse. Off to his left a trail of tiny islets led back toward a cove among the hills.

In the cove something was moving, gliding through the gathering mists, not very large or visible from its distance. At first Rhodry assumed it was another longboat, because he could see the same curved neck, the same tiny head arching above the rippling water, but this head suddenly turned, swiveling on a neck as glossy as snake skin. A massive wave formed and buckled as a body like an overturned boat rose out of the lake. Rhodry yelped and swore. The dwarves all screamed.

"Gong!"

Garin pounded harder, faster. The other dwarves began screaming and swearing at the top of their lungs. The creature hesitated, staring their way, waves rippling round it as, or so it seemed, it kept its place with some subaqueous paddling motion. It swung its head away, swung its body majestically after, then arched its neck and dove, heading back toward the distant inlet and cove. As it disappeared under mist and water, Rhodry was for a moment unsure that he'd really seen it, simply because it moved so smoothly, so silently. The others seemed to have no such doubts. They kept up their deliberate cacophony until at last the boat pulled in beside the wooden jetty.

"They hate noise," Garin yelled at him over the general din. "Or so I've been told. The beasts, I mean."

"I see," Rhodry yelled back. "Are they common?"

Garin merely shrugged to show his ignorance.

On the jetty someone stood waiting, dressed in a pair of bright blue trousers of fine wool, a Deverry style pullover shirt, belted in at the waist, and a gray cloak, fastened at one shoulder with a dragon-form brooch as big as a man's hand. Judging his distance the anchorman crouched, then leapt onto the jetty, wrapping his rope round a bollard while the oarsmen backed water. Hawser in hand, the helmsman leapt out as well. The waiting figure strolled over just as they got the boat secure.

It was a woman, standing a bit over five feet tall with the dark narrow eyes and thin slit of lips of the dwarven race, but her mane of pale hair, pulled back into a loose braid, indicated Deverry blood in her veins. In the fading light it was impossible to tell her stage of life, but she stood and looked about with far too much authority to be a lass.

"Angmar!" the helmsman cried. "Guests!"

She nodded, looking his passengers over one at a time, slowly, carefully, while they scrambled out of the boat and got their gear safe on the jetty. Rhodry she saved for last, looking him over coldly even though he bowed to her. Her eyes carried such authority that he wondered if she had dweomer.

"Welcome to Haen Marn." Angmar spoke in Deverrian of a sort. "You be the man who covets a dragon, bain't you?"

"I am," Rhodry said. "I was told that a man named Enj could help me."

"Enj be my son, not but what I have rule over him no more, not this long score of year or mayhap it be more now. But over Haen Marn I do have rule, and of more import I have knowledge of its ways, and it were a wise thing that you all do remember such."

"My lady." Rhodry bowed again.

Garin had already followed his lead several times. Otho and Mic looked back and forth, one to the other, then bowed as well.

"And what do it become me to call you, then?" Angmar said.

"My mother named me Rhodry, but a woman who lived deep in the heart of the earth called me Rori once, saying it was a better sounding name. Which do you prefer?"

She looked him over, smiling a little.

"Then welcome to Haen Marn, Rori, you and your friends both." She nodded their way. "Envoy Garin, welcome."

"My lady. It gladdens my heart to see you again."

Angmar acknowledged his bow with a small nod, then turned and began snapping orders in Dwarvish. The helmsmen picked up the gear and carried it as they all trooped down the jetty and onto the island, heading for the manse with Angmar in the lead, clumping along like a boy in her sheepskin boots. A little path led away from the lakefront through trees all bent and twisted from the wind, then came out into a vast kitchen garden, passing through row after row of cabbages and turnips, winding round a henhouse, too, before it brought them to the manse, where windows glowed with firelight, and the massive oak door stood ajar.

Dwarven servants, all young men, waited to take the baggage and lead them inside to a great hall where fires crackled in two hearths of slabbed stone, one on either side of the square room. The walls were made of massive oak planks, scrubbed down and polished smooth, then carved in one vast pattern of graved lines rubbed with red earth. Looping vines, spirals, animals, interlace—they all tangled together across each wall, then swooped up at each corner to the rafters, before plunging down again in a riot of carving. At one hearth a small boy turned a spit where an entire side of beef was roasting; at the other stood tables and benches, scattered hospitably over the water-polished plank floor. At the far end a wooden staircase swept up into shadows.

"Show them chambers," Angmar said to the servants. "And bring them what they need as to water for wash and suchlike." She glanced at her guests. "When you do assemble here again we will begin our eating."

"My thanks, my lady," Garin said. "Is Enj in residence here?"

"Not this day, no, though I do think he will appear as soon as soon. All his life has he dreamt of the searching of high mountains for a great wyrm and of the seeing of such fly. If he do not know that his hour has come, then he be no son of mine."

Rhodry's chamber turned out to be square and spare, a mattress upon a wooden floor and naught else, though when Rhodry begged water for shaving a servant did bring him a stool to put the basin upon and a silvered bronze mirror as well as a chunk of soap, herbed with bergamot. The water itself came in a big iron pan, so hot that the servant wrapped his hands in rags to carry it, and the water stayed warm enough for all the time it took Rhodry to rid himself of ten days beard. He was just finishing when the dwarves knocked on his door and let themselves in.

"Just like an elf," Otho said. "Shaving a perfectly good beard away. You people have no sense, you know."

"Hum." Garin looked round. "More than a bit plain, this room. We've fared a good bit better in ours, I must say, with proper beds and shutters at the windows and suchlike."

"It'll do," Rhodry said. "Silver daggers are used to taking what they get."

"I should hope it's dawned on you by now that the silver dagger doesn't mean one cursed thing up here." Garin gave him a grin. "Our people think you carry it because it's a nice piece of work and naught more."

Rhodry laughed.

"It hadn't occurred to me, truly. But of course you're right, and it's a relief as well, knowing that."

They went downstairs to the great hall and a meal set for them and

Angmar alone, strong ale and beef, mostly, though an elderly servant brought in a scant ration of bread apiece before retreating as if he were afraid they'd ask for more. Rhodry and Garin shared a trencher at one side of the table, the other two dwarves at the other, while Angmar ate alone and sparingly in her chair at the table's head. Outside the wind rustled and whistled. Shutters banged in distant windows, the front door creaked, candles guttered on the table and in the sconces, while from outside came the slap and murmur of waves on the shore.

Rhodry thought on occasion of making conversation, but whenever he glanced Angmar's way, she seemed so distant, so wrapped in brooding, that he found nothing to say. In the shadowed light she seemed too young to have a grown son, though no doubt as a dwarven half-breed she had a life span as uncertain as his own. While he never would have considered her beautiful—and he suspected that such a soft compliment would have offended her—she was an attractive woman, slender and muscled all at once, reminding him in some ways of Jill when she'd been young. Loosed, her mane of blond hair would set off her high cheekbones and clean features, he supposed. Every now and then she would glance his way, but her dark eyes revealed nothing of her possible opinion of him.

All at once Mic swore and slewed round on the bench. When Rhodry looked toward the door, he saw the woman in white, her silver torc gleaming in the candlelight, leaning on her spear and watching them while tears ran down her cheeks. Although the dwarves sat stunned, Rhodry swung himself free of the bench.

"My lady," he said. "We meet again. My sword is at your service if you have need of it."

She smiled and, smiling, disappeared.

Openmouthed and gaping the dwarves exchanged troubled glances on the edge of words, but Angmar merely picked up her tankard and had a sip of ale in such an ordinary way that Rhodry felt abruptly foolish. He sat down again, looking her way. She merely smiled vaguely, then attended to her meal. Rhodry decided that following her lead was the best idea. The dwarves seemed to agree as well, and for a while they all ate in silence.

"Be there enough food on my table for you?" Angmar said at last.

"There is, my lady," Garin said. "And you have our humble thanks indeed for so splendid a meal."

She rose and walked out of the room without another word. The servant bustled in with a bowl of apples, then withdrew. For a few moments they all waited, but when there was no sign of Angmar, Mic could stand it no longer.

"What was that woman with the spear?" he burst out. "A ghost?"

"I've no idea," Garin said. "I didn't see any apparitions before, when I was here the other two times, I mean."

"I was going to ask you that," Rhodry said. "You saw naught so weird?"

"Naught, except, well, for Haen Marn itself, and the road to it. I came on strict business from our merchant guilds, of course, on some mundane affairs, not hunting dragons in the midst of a dweomer war."

"Bound to be a bit of a difference," Otho sighed. "These cursed bizarre things seem to hover round our Rori here like flies round horseshit."

"Otho!" everyone snapped at once.

Otho mugged dignity and poured himself more ale. Though they lingered by the fire a long time that evening, drinking and wondering about the woman in white, Angmar never returned.

Although the servants brought her guests everything they needed, the lady kept herself hidden all the next day as well. It was sunny, too humid for sitting in the great hall, and Rhodry and the dwarves walked round the island, though none of them went too close to the waterline for fear of the long-necked beasts. The wind lapped at the water and drove waves on the pale sand of the island's shore, rustled in the trees, whined and sighed through the warren of buildings clustering round the stone tower. Every now and then Rhodry thought he heard a woman weeping, but most likely, or so he told himself, it was only the wind.

"Tell me somewhat, Garin," Rhodry said. "Well, if you can, anyway. What does the name Haen Marn mean? Old what?"

Garin laughed.

"Haen may sound like the *hen* in your tongue, but in ours it means black. Haen Marn. Black stone."

"Ah. My apologies."

Their circuit brought them back round to the boathouse and the jetty, where the oarsmen of the day before were sitting, legs dangling over the edge, and fishing. When Garin hailed them, they spoke up in

Dwarvish, beckoning for the guests to join them. Rather than listen to talk he couldn't understand, Rhodry decided to head back to the manse. He wouldn't mind a tankard of ale, he decided, and the servants had made it clear that it was theirs for the asking.

He began following the path that had led, the night before, through the kitchen garden and to the door. Ahead, through the trees, he could see the peaked roof of the manse and beyond that the stone tower. He walked along, thinking that the path was a bit longer than he'd been remembering, rounded a little bend, and found himself at the lakeshore. He'd taken a wrong fork, no doubt, and he turned to retrace his steps. Ahead rose the manse, on the other side of a stone wall and some hedges. He headed toward it, found himself among trees, could still see the manse, walked a few yards more, and saw the boathouse directly ahead of him.

"Oh. Well, more fool me!"

Still, he decided to try one more time. This time he sighted on a shed near the manse in the hopes that perhaps he could trick whatever road dweomer lay upon the place. The path led him right along to the lakeshore on the opposite side of the island. He turned to find the tower directly in his way.

"Rori!"

Angmar came striding along the lakeshore. He waited, afraid that if he went toward her, he'd lose her.

"My apologies," she called out. "You've no dwarven blood, and by your onliness it be not allowed for you to come near the manse."

"I see. This place has some powerful dweomers upon it."

"You might say that."

She strode up and joined him, her golden hair shining thick in the sun.

"No doubt you be a-wondering when my son will get himself home. From what the envoy has said, this task be needful for you to complete soon."

"It is, truly. And sadly, as well. Haen Marn seems a pleasant place for a man to linger."

She smiled, just faintly.

Rhodry caught movement out of the corner of his eye, glanced at the lake, and saw the woman with the spear, standing upon the water and watching him. When he caught his breath, Angmar turned and saw her as well. As before, the woman wept until he spoke to her.

"My lady, please, what aches your heart so badly?"

She vanished without a word. Angmar was considering him with a peculiar lack of expression, as if it were important for her to show not a shred of feeling.

"Well, here," Rhodry said. "I don't know how much it's lawful for me to ask."

"Ask all you want. The answering is mine to judge."

"Fair enough, then. Whose spirit is that?"

"It be good you do ask, but that I mayn't answer."

"Ah. I rather thought not. Did you lay the dweomers here, my lady?"

"I did not, though I may maintain them, for I were not born here on Haen Marn."

"And it's needful that the lady of this place be born here?"

"It is. The last true lady had only sons, and I was brought here for the marrying of her eldest." She seemed amused about something. "I think me you do understand the unwinding of dweomer ways more than another man might, Rori."

"Whether I wanted it or no, the dweomer has ruled my life, my lady. I feel like one of those wild horses out on the grasslands, caught in elven ropes and dragged off where I've no stomach to go."

"A bitter man you sound."

"Do I? I suppose so. My Wyrd's been a bitter one, you see, and it's ruled me ever since I was a lad. I've given up kicking and let them saddle me."

He strode to the edge of the lake, stooped and picked up a stone, rubbing it between his fingers. In a moment she joined him. When Rhodry sailed the stone flat over the lake, it skipped seven times before it finally sank, far out from shore.

"A good toss," Angmar said, grinning.

"In Aberwyn, where I was born, they say that seven skips like that mean a good omen."

"Do they now? Let us hope they be right."

For a few moments they stood together looking across to the far

shore. In the hot sun the forest exhaled a fine blue mist, beyond the
power, apparently, of the endless wind to blow away.

"Well now," Angmar said abruptly. "I do think my daughter may
know when her brother will come back to Haen Marn."

"I didn't know you had a daughter."

Angmar glanced up at the stone tower.

"I do, though a pitiful creature she be, a mooncalf, truly."

"That aches my heart to hear."

"Tell me, would you let her look upon you? I do have a reason for
the asking."

"Well, then, of course."

"My thanks. Come with me."

Angmar strode off, heading away from the lake toward the tower.
Rhodry followed as she pushed open a heavy oak door in its base and led
him inside to a tiny room smelling of damp and stone. An iron staircase
spiraled up past landings and into shadow.

"You wear some talisman of hiding power, don't you?" Angmar said.

"I do." Automatically he laid his hand on his shirt over the lapis
lazuli. "Why do you ask?"

"Curiosity and naught more. I did think so, when she lost the sight
of you. Come up."

They climbed up to the first landing, all piled up with full sacks and
shabby chests, a broken chair, a heap of firewood. Inside the tower the
wind moaned and hummed. Angmar pitched her voice louder to carry
over it.

"I would not wish you to think she be prisoned here. She herself
does cling to the heights and refuse the ground."

As they were climbing to the next landing, Angmar suddenly paused
and called out.

"Avain, Avain!"

Although no one answered they resumed their climb, coming out
on the next landing into a proper room (though the stairs continued
through it), sunny and bright from big windows, even though the walls
were dark, undressed stone. To one side stood a table and a half-round
chair. Sitting next to the chair on the floor among clean straw was a lass,
no more than fifteen summers, Rhodry supposed, as yellow-haired as her

mother, but plump in a soft and puffy way, with a big round face nodding over a round body. In her lap she held a broad but shallow silver basin, filled with water, and she was staring into it and singing to herself, a high tuneless song without words.

"Avain?" Angmar whispered. "We do have a guest, my sweet."

She looked up at Rhodry with the dragon eyes of his dreams. They were round, nearly lidless, and green, slit vertically like a cat's or elven eyes, with the yellow iris showing. When she smiled, he was expecting fangs, but all else about her was human enough. She spoke a few words in Dwarvish.

"She says that she did see you in the town where men live," Angmar said. "Do be forgiving of her. It were a struggle to teach her what little of her own tongue she knows, and any else were beyond her."

"Of course, my lady. Tell her that when I slept, I saw her watching me."

"Did you now?"

When Angmar spoke to the lass, she laughed and clapped her hands, joggling the basin. Sunlight flashed on moving water, and the glints speared her attention. With a little contented sigh, she nestled into her straw and stared at the moving patterns. Every now and then she dipped a finger in the basin and touched a drop to her forehead, just above the bridge of her nose.

"I'll ask her about Enj."

Angmar knelt beside her in the straw and spoke a few words. For a long moment the lass frowned into her basin, then replied in a singsong of Dwarvish.

"She does see him far away, though he be a-heading in a homewards direction," Angmar translated. "He does love to wander, our Enj, and all his father's people do think him dafter than his sister for it, his walking here and there in the light of the sun, just for the seeing of what may lie upon the ground. But what she sees she sees in this water, and if ever the basin spill, then she do weep and carry on until someone brings the filling of it again."

"Why did you watch me, Avain?"

Angmar laughed and didn't repeat the question.

"A word such as *why* will have no meaning for the likes of her, Rori. She sees all that does concern Haen Marn, and so your approaching did appear to her, just as the approaching of a storm or some doings of the beasts in the lake would appear."

"Oh. Well and good, then."

So this was why he'd been expected. He could remember how neutral the dragon eyes had felt in his dreams, a simple noting of his presence and naught else, unlike the malice of the other pair. She must have been telling her mother of his progress all along their way, until of course Othara had given him the talisman.

"But the boatmen knew I was hunting a dragon."

"Avain did say this thing, many times over. I did wonder how she knew, but the poor child could not tell me, though I did ask the question in as many simple ways as I could invent. It distressed her so that I did stop, for she would weep at the mention of you after that."

"Then my apologies. Here, tell her that I mean this dragon no harm, that I only wish its aid in a grave matter."

"Be that true? She will know the truth of it, you see."

"I swear it on my silver dagger."

When Angmar passed the information on, Avain looked up with the most beautiful smile that Rhodry had ever seen on a child's face, joyful, relieved, and loving all at once, though her dragon's eyes never blinked the whole long while she looked at him. Angmar ran her hand through her daughter's hair, smiling herself while she straightened out the tangles. Avain leaned into the touch of her hand like a dog. When Angmar spoke to her briefly, the lass nodded and returned to her basin of water, perfectly happy, apparently, even when her mother rose to go.

"Again we will ask her for some news of Enj," Angmar said. "Let us be going down now."

Angmar escorted him to the manse by a path that stayed put and ordinary, but she stopped outside the door.

"I won't come in," she said. "I'll be seeing about my daughter's food, and I'll go up and help her with the eating of it. Cutting meat she cannot do. But one last thing. Before I did find you upon the lakeshore, I met Envoy Garin, and he did complain to me about the chamber in which you sleep."

"Oh, here, no need to worry about that! It's perfectly fine for a man like me."

"Some of my servants care not for those with elven blood. I'll have it tended to and a better chamber given."

Without another word she walked off, heading for one of the side buildings. Rhodry went inside the manse and found Garin, Mic, and Otho sitting in the great hall at a table by the main door to catch the air and sunlight. When he joined them, the elderly servant brought him a tankard of ale, then glided away again. All the other tables in the vast room stayed empty.

"The silence here is beginning to gripe my soul," Rhodry said. "I'm used to a bit of life in a hall, I am."

"Me, too," Garin said. "It was different last time I was here. The boatmen ate with us, and there were always people coming and going. I seem to remember a bard, too, or at least a singer with a harp, if he wasn't a proper bard."

"Was Angmar lady here then?"

"She was, but her husband was still alive, of course. Hum." Garin considered for a moment. "Most likely being a widow has broken the poor woman's little heart. A sad thing it was. He was drowned in a storm, and here her daughter was just born by a fortnight."

"Living in this cursed wind would drive me draft," Otho said. "Worse for a woman, I should think, all this whining and wailing air."

"Er, about her husband?" Mic put in. "You say he was drowned? Did they recover his body?"

"They did, and he's buried over in the hills with his ancestors," Garin answered. "Why?"

"I was just thinking about that beast we saw."

"Ych!" Otho snapped. "Don't be disgusting!"

"For a change, your uncle and I agree about somewhat," Rhodry said, softening the remark with a grin. "Her husband was one of the Mountain People, then?"

"Well, he looked like one of us. A tall man, for us, but not unduly so." Garin paused, stroking his beard. "He said he was of dwarven blood, and truly, I never saw a thing to counter him."

"You sound doubtful anyway."

"True, true." Garin glanced round. "This isn't the place to be discussing it, though."

"Of course. My apologies."

All that day, and on into the evening, Rhodry stayed on guard, watching and listening for the woman in white, but he never saw her. At the evening meal Angmar ate as silently and as sparingly as before, then left before the men were done—to tend her daughter, Rhodry supposed. After the meal was cleared away, Garin brought out dice, and the three dwarves settled in to one of their tournaments. Wondering whether the prize would go for squabbling or dicing, Rhodry watched for a while, then made his good nights, took a candle end, and went upstairs.

He found his old chamber empty, remembered that Angmar had promised him a better one, and stood in the corridor, wondering whom to ask where his gear and bedroll might be. Drawn, perhaps, by the candlelight, an elderly dwarven woman, her gray hair tied back in a thong, came shuffling along, carrying a punched tin candle-lantern that threw dots and slashes of light over the deep carved walls.

"Follow me," was all she said.

Rhodry did so, down the long corridor, round a corner, up a narrow flight of stairs and out onto a landing. Opposite them stood an oak door, bound in iron and carved with birds and twining bands of interlace in a loose and wandering style that Rhodry had never seen before.

"In there," the woman said.

She turned and shuffled off down the stairs, leaving him alone with his guttering candle end for light. Hospitable lot, Rhodry thought to himself. He pushed the door open and found himself in a chamber some twenty feet on a side, with its own hearth at one end and a big window, overlooking the lake, on the other. He set the candle holder down on a little table and looked round—luxury indeed, a bed with embroidered hangings, big carved chests, a round table with two cushioned chairs. His pack and bedroll lay by the hearth. All at once he realized that he wasn't alone. Angmar was sitting in the window seat, so quietly that he'd never noticed her at first.

"This chamber," she said. "Does it suit you better?"

"It's yours, isn't it?"

"It is."

"Then it suits me better than any chamber I've seen in years and years."

She smiled but sat unmoving, watching him as he crossed the room and sat beside her. When he glanced out, he could see far across the lake to the hills, black against a starry sky.

"I'll have to leave here as soon as ever I can," Rhodry said. "Whether I want to go or no."

"I do know that."

"Well and good, then."

When he put his arms round her, she turned toward him and reached up, kissing him openmouthed before he could kiss her. With one hand he untied the thong, and her hair spilled round her shoulders and over his fingers, soft as silk thread.

5

CARCER

An evil figure to the extreme, unless it fall into the House of Salt. Under that crystal presidency it does bode most well for the burying of treasures gained by some unseemly means and the concealing of secrets best left hidden from the light of day.

The Omenbook of Gwarn, Loremaster

ONE OF THE SEVEN WORST SETBACKS in war, Meer would later call it: a surprise attack. When the siege began, it came faster than Jill had ever imagined. On a sunny morning she'd just returned from flying and settled into her tower room when she saw a messenger come riding in the gates. Hurriedly she dressed and rushed down to the great hall, coming in to find the gwerbret conferring at the table of honor with all of his servitors, who clustered grim-faced over a letter spread out on the table. Next to the chamberlain the scribe hovered, looking pale, as if he'd just read some hateful thing—which in fact he had. Lord Tren had replied at last, a message that came perilously close to demanding rather than asking that Cadmar turn his dead brother's holdings over to him.

"I shall ride to Cengarn soon but on my own terms," Jill read out the ending. "Let us hope this matter has a quick settlement."

"No courtesies, no title, naught," the equerry sputtered. "The gall of the man!"

"Worse than gall," the chamberlain said. "I think me that this sounds dangerous."

"I agree," Jill said. "Your Grace, do you think that the time's come for alerting the countryside and your lords and suchlike?"

"I do indeed." He turned to the equerry. "My lord, see to it." And to the chamberlain. "How well provisioned is the dun?"

"It could be better, Your Grace. The harvest's still coming in."

"But here, Your Grace," the equerry broke in. "Even with his brother's men joined to his own, Lord Tren could never siege Cengarn."

"I'm well mindful of that, my lord. But what if he joined up with these other enemies of ours? Some new thing's made him arrogant, hasn't it?"

The equerry swore under his breath in agreement. All at once Jill saw what she should have seen weeks ago, or so she remonstrated with herself, a thing that seemed blindingly obvious now that, at last, she had seen it.

"I've been a dolt and a lackwit," she said, surprised at how quiet her voice sounded. "Your Grace, how long ago was this letter written? How far away is Tren's dun?"

"Close to two days ride, straight north." The gwerbret had swiveled round to stare at her in something like fear. "Jill, what—"

"The situation's grave, Your Grace. Our enemies could be upon us at any moment. They could fall upon us like dweomer, because dweomer is exactly what they've been using."

"What? Are they invisible? It's going to be a task straight from the Third Hell, fighting invisible enemies."

"Nah nah nah—naught so bad as that! You'll see them plain enough when they ride off the end of their dweomer road and appear under your walls. Your Grace, there's not a moment to lose. Alert the countryside, send for your lords, I beg you—do whatever needs to be done!"

Jill turned and ran for the door of the great hall. Although she feared a direct outpouring of the army near the town itself, the letter had implied that Lord Tren would be joining the force before it struck. Thus there was a chance that Alshandra's minions had brought their army out of Evandar's country at Tren's dun and were planning on riding an ordinary road down to Cengarn. If so, she'd be able to scout them out in the falcon shape and bring back some solid information. She ducked into the side broch, climbed the staircase as fast as she could, then rushed into her chamber and barred the door. Panting for breath, and stripping off her clothes as she moved, she walked over to the window. Already, down in the ward, men of the warband were hurrying toward the stables—messengers, no doubt, to rouse the countryside.

As soon as she'd quieted her racing heart, Jill transformed herself into the falcon. As she leapt from the window and flew, she heard a strange noise jangling and booming over Cengarn. Since her senses were bound to the perceptions of the etheric plane, it took her a moment to recognize the sound of temple bells, ringing out an alarum for the town and for all the farmers round about. Down below, the streets and houses, seen from the etheric in full morning light, looked grotesquely dead, all black and gray as if they were carved from shadow made palpable. Among them she saw the auras of the townsfolk swarming about, rushing here and there, some to man the gates, some toward the dun itself. Others milled and bobbed about the streets or clumped in the open spaces, moving aimlessly like particles of flour move, sprinkled on a bowl of water.

Before she headed north she swung out wide, taking a turn south and east over the settled farmlands, where she saw, among the reddish auras of field and forest, the same orderly panic. Already a few farmers were driving herds of cows, judging from the size of the yellow horizontal auras, toward the city. Behind them trudged women, leading children and pushing handcarts. Warned for weeks now, the people were ready to move. In that she could take what comfort she could, and truly, there was little else she could have done to improve their lot. Even if she'd thought of the mothers of all roads that ran through Evandar's country and had remembered earlier that Alshandra had the same access to them as Evandar himself, the town never could have sheltered the surrounding farmers, with all their families and livestock, for these last weeks of waiting. Things would soon be bad enough inside the walls as it was.

North of Cengarn lay very little but wild hills. As she flew steadily over the dirt track that did for a road north, Jill saw only a pair of shepherds and their dogs, driving a small flock toward the town. Beyond that lay wilderness, forest and stream, boulders and hill, unrolling under the unnatural speed of the falcon's huge wings. Even though the wind blew in her favor, Jill wondered if she could fly the entire thirty miles or so to Tren's dun and still return safely in a single day. Fortunately her long weeks of scouting had built up her physical strength to some extent, but she was still, underneath, an old woman trusting in the unnatural vitality of the dweomer rather than to sound muscle and bone.

The sun was just past its zenith when she saw, far ahead at the edge of her view, the clearings in the forest marking the first fields of the late Matyc's demesne. His brother's lands lay to the east, the chamberlain had told her. She let her right wing dip, began to turn, beating a little in a gust of wind, and saw far below her the raven. Even from her height she could tell that it was much too big to be an ordinary bird. Like a real raven it flew low, swooping over the cleared fields as if it were feeding on gleaned grain, while, like a real falcon, Jill could fly high enough to be virtually invisible.

For a moment she hesitated, riding the wind while she debated. Even though her human instincts counseled mercy, here was a splendid chance to rid herself of a powerful enemy. On the other hand, attack would reveal her own existence, another mazrak on Cengarn's side. Yet, once the siege began, she'd be forced to reveal herself, anyway, if, for instance, this enemy dweomermaster should think it could fly over the dun with impunity. The feathers on the back of her neck lifted in rage at the thought that some threat might fly over a place that the falcon instincts saw as her nest and endanger those that the falcon considered fledglings. Jill took her mark, stooped, and plunged.

Down the falcon plummeted, talons extended for a deadly thrust, with the rush of air singing round her like a war cry. All at once some avian instinct must have warned the mazrak below. The raven shrieked in sheer terror, flew and dodged barely in time, and began flapping madly north. Jill sheared off, turned, and rose again for another strike as the clumsy raven flew for its life, shrieking and cawing all the while. If some huntsman had watched, he would have seen an ordinary-seeming pair of birds, except for the size, and an ordinary enough pattern, one he'd seen a hundred times, of a determined falcon marking its panicked kill, stooping and plunging, barely missing while the exhausted raven dodged frantically and flapped northward.

When Jill rose again she knew that this time, she'd have the raven, just as a falcon will, in the end, wear down the wiliest of birds. Yet the raven suddenly steadied itself, collecting its human wits, most likely. Just as Jill plunged, it flew straight ahead—and disappeared. One moment it was there, flying in full sun over a field of ripe barley; the next it was gone, simply and completely gone. With a shriek of her own Jill broke off the stoop, flapped wildly for a moment, then turned and headed back south. She'd seen what she needed to, another mazrak, sure enough, and one that could fly into Evandar's country and travel the mothers of all roads. Now she needed to make her own retreat. She had no illusions that she could best an enraged Alshandra, if the raven should bring her "goddess" back with her from the astral plane.

Jill flew off south, but just as she reached the forest edge, she circled back for a look behind her. Sure enough, the black flapping shape of the raven had reappeared, and this time, it flew east. Not quite wily enough, were you? Jill thought. She flew up, stayed as high as she could and still keep the raven in sight, and followed her unknowing guide. In just a few more miles, the raven led her to a camp, a vast spread of soldiers and mounts, wagons and servants, apparently stopped for a noon rest, the auras like a bed of glowing coals scattered across the dull bare ground. Without flying lower Jill simply couldn't see whether inside those auras stood humans or Horsekin, but there was no doubt that the enemy was marching. She circled south and flew off for home, beating strong and steadily against the wind.

It was sundown when she reached Cengarn. Already the town was crammed full of people and animals; with her etheric sight it seemed that in the gathering shadows Cengarn lay burning, all gold and flickering yellow with here and there the red of a warrior's aura to mimic flames. As she swooped over the dun, she circled to lose speed and height, heading over the ward toward her tower window. Since she knew him well, she could pick out Yraen's aura in the general confusion. He looked up, saw her, shouted, and began trotting toward the side broch that housed her chamber.

By the time that Jill had landed and returned to her own proper shape, Yraen was pounding on her chamber door. Yelling at him to be patient, she clambered into a pair of brigga, pulled on a shirt, and ran barefooted to unbar the door and let him in.

"Have you seen Dar?" he blurted. "Do you know which way he rode?"

"Which way he what?"

"This morning, before you raised the alarum, he rode out. I mean, him and his men. They rode out to hunt."

"Well, ye gods, man, they'll probably ride back before night, like they usually do. The enemy won't reach us before tomorrow."

Yet even as she spoke she felt a stab of danger. At times, sick of being penned up in what they called "stone tents," Dar and his men stayed overnight in the wild forest.

"I can't fly anymore today, Yraen. I'm exhausted. All I can do is scry him out and try to tell you where he is, and you can send a couple of men out to meet him."

At this blunt mention of magic, Yraen rolled his eyes like a spooked horse.

"My apologies, my lady, for forgetting how tired you must be. I'll go fetch you meat and drink."

Yraen bolted like the spooked horse, as well, rushing out of the chamber and clattering down the stairs.

Jill walked to the window, leaned upon the sill on folded arms, and looked up at the trail of clouds gleaming gold against the velvet sky of twilight. When she focused her Sight and thought of Dar, she saw him standing in an utterly undistinguished clearing by an utterly undistinguished river, and then, slowly, like figures walking toward her out of a sea fog, his men came into her vision as well, all of them dismounted, standing round their prince and arguing furiously. As far as she could tell they were miles from the town and squabbling, perhaps, about whether to try to ride back in the darkness. When she felt a stab of rage, that today of all days they'd ride so far, she was tired enough that she lost the vision.

All at once she had to sit down. She staggered over to her chair and slumped into it, leaning forward and bracing herself against the table. Dimly, as if she sat at the bottom of a deep well, she heard the clatter of Yraen coming back up the stairs. In a few moments he appeared with half a loaf of bread and a plate of pork and cabbage.

"Ye gods," he snapped. "You look as pale as Death! Tell me what to do for you."

"Pour me water from that pitcher on the chest."

Jill forced herself to eat a few bites of bread and wash them down with the water while Yraen hovered helplessly nearby.

"Are you sure the prince rode south?" she said at last.

"I am, though later he could have gone in any direction, depending on the deer and suchlike."

Jill swore, mustering oaths that would have shocked her silver dagger of a father. Unconsciously Yraen stepped back, as if out of reach.

"Carra must be frantic," Jill said, once her feelings were sufficiently relieved. "Is she in the women's hall?"

"She's not, but in her chambers."

"Then go get her and escort her to the hall. Tell her to stay there, too, until her husband returns. There must be an extra bed or suchlike, near where the serving women sleep. Tell her it's my order, and if she breaks it, I'll turn her into a frog!"

"I will then."

Yraen fled her ill temper, banging the door shut behind him. With a massive sigh Jill leaned back in her chair. The lard-glazed food looked hideous to her, but she forced herself to pick at it while she considered what to do. In a few moments she would have to summon her energy to bring the news to the gwerbret. Her physical loathing at the thought of climbing down the stairs and back up again made her realize that no matter what danger Dar might be in, it was truly impossible for her to fly to warn him. Since she couldn't identify where he was, sending ordinary messengers after him would only mean losing them as well. If only he'd been another dweomermaster, trained to hear her thoughts!

All at once she laughed aloud. Dweomermaster, no, but he was not only a full-blooded elf but a prince, only two generations removed from an extremely inbred line of royalty that had been, if she remembered her history rightly, known for its innate dweomer talent. She smiled to herself, rather grimly, and finished the water in her cup. Trying to reach him on the etheric was at least worth a try. Since all elves can see the Wildfolk and other etheric forms, he would be able to see her etheric double whether he could hear her thoughts or no. If she waved her arms and made all sorts of dramatic gestures, he would at least know that some sort of danger was pending.

Someone knocked—pounded, really—on the door.

"My lady, my lady? Be you there?"

"I am, Jahdo. Come in."

All tousled hair and huge eyes the boy burst into the room.

"Oh, my lady, I do be sorry for the disturbing of you, but his grace did send me to fetch you. All the pages, they be busy as busy, rushing here and there on messages and suchlike."

"No doubt." Jill got up, grimacing a little at her exhaustion. "Excited, are you?"

"I am, my lady, but oh, I be scared. Meer does keep telling me about how horrid sieges be, one of the seven great disasters for a city, he did say."

"What are the other six?"

"Well, now, I don't truly know them all. He didn't say, like, though I do think that one other be plague. My apologies."

"It doesn't matter. I don't even really know why I asked. I think I'm scared, too."

At that Jahdo turned more than a little pale. Jill caught his hand and let him lead her to the stairs.

Down in the great hall the gwerbret was pacing, leaning hard on his stick, back and forth by the dragon hearth. Behind him trailed his worried servitors. Jill was glad to see that Lord Gwinardd stood among them in the company of several lords that she didn't know by name. Apparently Cadmar's loyal vassals were riding in to join their lord. When she glanced at the far side of the hall, she found it crammed with men, eating and drinking in a grim silence.

"Your grace summoned me?" Jill made Cadmar a bow.

"I hear from Yraen that you have news for us."

"I do, Your Grace. May I sit?"

"Of course." Cadmar looked round him, startled as a man coming out of a faint. "We'll all sit. Ye gods. Don't know what's wrong with me, trotting back and forth like an old ram who sees a young one in his pasture."

When Jahdo pulled out a chair for her, Jill sat gratefully. She could only hope that the noble-born would let her tell her news and leave fast. But as the plans and the arguing dragged on, so did the evening, hot and seemingly endless.

Daralanteriel and his men had indeed traveled a good score of miles through rough country that day, hunting the gray deer. Although he'd wanted to push hard and return to Cengarn, their horses were exhausted from the chase, and unlike their elven masters, they couldn't see with only starlight to guide them. He may have been a prince, but he was always mindful that in the current situation of the Westlands, his men were his equals in everything but name. When they shouted him down, he listened and eventually agreed to make camp, especially once they'd found a perfect spot, a sizable clearing with grazing for the stock and a nearby stream. Since the night was so hot, and light a luxury to those with elven sight, they dispensed with lighting a fire.

Although the rest of the men jested and laughed, pleased with the chance to spend a night in open country, Dar felt his bad mood settle round him like a wet wool cloak. He kept to himself, brooding at the edge of the clearing. The wheel of stars was turning toward midnight when, a few at a time, the men stretched out on the grass to sleep. Dar's lieutenant, Jennantar, came and found him where he'd been sitting, on a dead log off among the trees.

"We'd best post a guard," Dar said.

"Why? Jill's been scrying and suchlike for weeks now and never seen a trace of an enemy."

"Oh, I know, but I've got the strangest feeling round my heart. I don't like this. We should have gone back."

"My prince, we couldn't get back."

"Well, then, we never should have ridden so far." Dar got up, suddenly furious. For the first time in his life he wished that he had the power of one of his fabled royal ancestors, to speak once and be obeyed. "I told you this afternoon! We needed to get back."

"But that stag! I've never seen a stag like that, all white, and with horns that big."

"Well, neither have I, but he gave us the slip in the end, anyway, didn't he? So here we are, way out in the middle of nothing and no stag to show for it."

Jennantar merely shrugged at the luck of the hunt. Dar had the brief thought of slapping him, caught himself, and let out his breath in a long sigh.

"Something's truly gnawing at you, isn't it?" Jennantar said.

"Yes, and I don't know what."

Just as he spoke Dar felt a cold ripple down his back, as if an icy hand had stroked him. He threw up his head like the stag, listening. Something was moving in the woods nearby. He never thought, merely yelled.

"Wake up! Arm!"

And that was the only reason that any of them lived. Dar drew his sword and rushed among his men, kicking them awake, while a cursing Jennantar grabbed his hunting bow and slung his quiver. All at once torches flared, war cries shrieked, and a party of armed warriors came rushing toward the clearing. The elven hunters had barely enough time to get to their feet, grabbing for bows and swords, before the enemy was upon them, huge hairy beings, reeking of horse sweat. Later Dar would realize that there'd been easily fifty of them, but at the moment, there was no time for thinking.

"Meradan!" Jennantar howled. "The Hordes!"

When he shot with a hiss of a hunting shaft, and the lead warrior screamed and crumpled, clawing at his abdomen, the others hesitated, giving the elves the briefest of moments to fall back round their prince. Jezryaladar had a bow as well, and he and Jennantar loosed another round, then another, as the Gel da'Thae warriors re-formed and charged again. The two elves in front went down, hacked and bleeding, but the line held. At the rear of the charge someone threw a torch into the pile of saddle blankets and other gear; greasy flames shot up and crackled with a foul blast of smoke. Dimly Dar heard horses neighing in terror, and the sound of hooves pounding and dancing.

"Ranadar avenge us!" Dar shouted out the ancient war cry of his house. "To the hells if need be!"

The enemies screeched a babble of foreign words. Dar could put together a bare impression of their huge size and of manes of hair, long and braided, glittering with little charms and beads, before they charged again.

At close distance the bows were useless. Jennantar and Jezryaladar had no choice but to fall back and circle round the pack, hoping for a clear shot in the ghastly light of the fire creeping through the grass, as the rest of the men, unarmored and outnumbered, fought to the death. Dar was barely conscious of where he was and what he was doing; he was all instinct, slashing, parrying, dancing in for a stab and whirling back, his innate grace his only shield as the clumsier Gel da'Thae hacked and swore. When something rolled against the back of his legs, Dar jumped and twisted round, found Farendar lying dead in a pool of blood, and killed the warrior who'd stabbed him with one thrust to the throat.

As that Gel da'Thae went down, Dar jumped over his corpse and charged the grunting warrior behind. The fire caught the dry shrubbery at the edge of the clearing and flared up high, sending a wave of yellow light over the clearing. The Gel da'Thae facing Dar screamed in terror, threw his sword onto the ground, and began howling out a trio of incomprehensible words over and over. All Dar could assume was that he was terrified of fire, that they all were, because suddenly the enemy was breaking, running, throwing down their weapons, and howling in panic as they raced away through the woodlands. Panting and sobbing for breath Dar spun round. Jennantar still lived, pulling a wounded man away from the spreading fire. Jezryaladar came running, grabbing the fellow's feet.

"Let's get out of here!" Dar yelled. "Is there anyone else? Get across the river!"

The only other man alive was Devalanteriel, and he was bleeding all down his side, and coughing up blood, too, as he stood weaving, trying to keep his feet. Dar threw an arm round him just as he died, crumpling forward onto the grass. The fire was roaring in a circle half round them.

"Dar!" Jennantar screamed. "Get out of there!"

Dar sheathed his sword and ran, splashing into the shallow river, stumbling across in water up to his armpits, letting it wash his friend's blood away. It was so hard to breathe that he thought for a moment that he'd been wounded; then he realized that he was sobbing aloud. At the far bank Jennantar grabbed his arms and hauled him ashore. He too was weeping.

"Forgive me," he kept saying, over and over, "I should have listened to you. Forgive me."

"No time for that now."

He knelt down by the wounded man—young Landaren—and found blood soaking his tunic. When he pulled the gory cloth back, the wound proved superficial, a sideways slash across ribs and skin.

"He's been smacked across the head, too," Jezryaladar said. "But I don't think his skull's broken. He'd have died if it was, when we were hauling him through the water."

Dar nodded, drawing his dagger, and began cutting a reasonably clean strip of cloth from his own tunic to stanch the wound.

"We've got to get out of here," he said while he worked. "I don't know where they came from, but there's bound to be more. Oh, by the Dark Sun herself! Carra!"

For a moment he could neither move nor speak, just from his sheer terror on her behalf. With a sob he caught his breath.

"I've got to get back to Cengarn."

"Don't be a fool."

The voice sounded so hollow, so strange, so much inside his own mind that he shrieked, twisting round to look. A little ways away from their group and as far as possible from the river hovered a pale blue shape, mostly human, though strangely smooth and transparent. It was slight and frail, probably feminine, though the shape of its head indicated cropped hair. The others had seen it, too. Jennantar tried to speak but could only make a strangled sound.

"Jill!" Dar whispered. "Ye gods, are you dead then?"

"I'm not." Her words echoed in his mind again. "I came in the dweomer body to warn you, and I see that I'm much too late. Dar, the enemy's marching for Cengarn. Can you reach Calonderiel? Your horses have stopped bolting and are herding, well, some of them, anyway, just beyond the river to the south."

"We'll have to try, then, won't we?"

When he glanced at Jezryaladar he realized that the others had heard nothing.

"It's Jill," he said. "I can hear her speaking."

They merely stared, glazed and trembling.

"Jill, those Meradan, they're afraid of fire. Can't you use that against them?"

He could feel her amusement, rather than hear her laugh, though a bitter feeling it was.

"It wasn't the fire. I saw the whole fight, and I only wish things were so simple. It's you they're afraid of, Dar. Once they could see you clearly, they thought you were the children of their gods, and that they'd just committed a horrifying sacrilege by killing sacred beings. But their leaders will disabuse them of the notion soon enough."

"What? I don't understand! No one can kill a god."

"No time to explain. I'm exhausted, and I can't keep this up. Get to Calonderiel. Bring as many elven warriors as you can, but don't go rushing right into the sieging army. Send scouts."

For a moment longer he could see her, speaking and gesturing, but he could not hear. She grew thin, transparent, wisping away like smoke in the fire, then gone.

"If Jill's dead," Jezryaladar whispered, "then everything's lost."

"She's not and it isn't! That was dweomer, you dolt, not her ghost."

For a long moment none of them spoke. Across the stream the fire was dying down as it reached damp forest and green summer wood. Landaren groaned and stirred.

"Lie still!" Jennantar snapped. "Don't even try to sit up."

"We can't move him far, can we?" Dar said. "Not right away. Listen. Jill said that there's some of the horses not far from us. Hide Lan somewhere, see if you can get some of the Wildfolk to guard him, and then go fetch the stock. Start moving south, but very slowly, a few miles at a time."

"Now just wait. What are you—"

"I've got to try to see if I can make it to Cengarn and Carra before the siege closes round."

"You idiot! You royal dolt!"

"*I'm* a dolt? If you'd only listened to me we wouldn't—"

The moment he spoke Dar regretted it. Jennantar reeled back, turning his head as fast as if he'd been slapped with the flat of a sword.

"Jenno, I'm sorry. That was uncalled for."

"Wasn't." Jennantar's voice was barely audible. "You're right. I wish I'd died instead of the others."

Dar tried to speak, found no words, tried again, and then got to his feet, shuddering as if he could physically throw his botched words off and away.

"I'm heading out now," he said. "If I don't catch up with you in three days, ride for the south with all the speed you can."

Jennantar nodded, staring at the ground. Jezryaladar rose.

"Don't you want a horse?"

"I'll be harder to find, slipping through the woods on foot."

Jezryaladar nodded, considering something.

"You should have one of the bows," he said at last.

"I'll take it, truly, but only a few arrows. You'll need them more."

He waited, desperately searching for something to say to Jennantar, while Jezryaladar counted out their meager stock of arrows and gave him ten, a full quarter of their hoard, to take along with one of the bows. All at once one of the old stories of days of the Seven Kings came back to him, and the wise words of some councillor or other in the long-dead Vale of Roses.

"Jenno," he said. "No man can turn aside another's fate, not even me, and I'm a prince of the last of all the royal houses. We were all instruments of Fate today and nothing more. If you forgive me my fault, I'll forgive you yours."

Jennantar looked up with tear-filled eyes.

"Done," he whispered. "And my thanks."

"And you have mine."

That said, Dar could turn and leave, heading upstream by the last light of the dying fire.

For two hours Dar kept moving fast, driven by sheer rage for his dead men and terror for the safety of his wife. He kept to the trees, moving from shadow to shadow in the moonless night, concentrating on making no noise, pausing often to listen. Eventually his exhaustion caught up with him. He began stumbling, kicking dead wood, cracking branches like shouts in the night. He found a thick tangle of shrubs and young growth where he could work his way inside to a profoundly uncomfortable but relatively hidden gap, too small to be called a clearing. By sitting just right and curling himself round his drawn-up knees he could drowse in relative safety, though he woke often from dreams of blood running through creeping flames and the sound of Meradan, the demons of the days of old, shrieking as they charged.

Dar woke to a cry in the real world, but one far distant in the graying dawn. For a long while he sat dead-still, listening, but no other cries reached him. Slowly he began to move, working each cramped muscle in turn, letting his circulation return, until he could get up without making noise and work his way free of his shelter. All round him the oak forest was coming to life in the dawn, the leaves shivering in a rising wind, the birds singing and flying. Here and there he could sense animals rustling through the underbrush. They would warn him by falling silent if the clumsy Gel da'Thae came trampling through the woods.

All that morning he worked his way north, keeping to the wild country and angling round to the east, where a rise of hills and forest would shelter him. Every time he felt hungry or tired, he would think of Carra, and her danger drove him worse than any spur or whip. Yet in the end, he found her beyond his reach and protection. Late in the day he came free of the forest, just at the crest of a rise. Down below him a rocky hill fell away to a little valley and a stream, then rose again to a grassy crest, bare except for one scraggly copse of second-growth saplings. By his reckoning Cengarn would lie not far beyond. Although he debated crossing the open country, he knew that time was slipping away.

He gathered his strength and ran, leaping downhill, letting his momentum carry him through the shallow water, racing uphill with his heart pounding and his breath coming in big gulps to plunge at last into the relative safety of the copse. There he could pause to catch his breath and look ahead. Sure enough, Cengarn's familiar hills rose about a mile away, topped with their walls and towers. Yet, far off in the distance across the plain he saw what seemed to be a cloud of dust or smoke ringing the city round in one vast swirl, moving and pulsing, glittering with points of light reflected from metal. For a long time he stared, bewildered, until he realized that he was seeing an army. The siege of Cengarn had begun.

"Carra!" He forced himself to whisper, though he would rather have howled like a madman. "Carra!"

He turned on his heel and trotted off downhill, heading south to rejoin his men. Though he had only his rage alone to guide him and his men and keep them safe during their long hard ride to Calonderiel's camp, he knew it would be enough. If the gods had any heart for justice, soon he would ride back at the head of an army. He vowed it deep in his very soul, that his dead men would be avenged—a hundred deaths for each of theirs.

"There's one thing I simply don't understand," the chamberlain said. *"How do these creatures think they can possibly win this siege? My lord Cadmar's called in his alliances—two other gwerbrets in Arcodd alone, and another in northern Pyrdon, and in this grave need, they'll be gathering all their vassals. And if they can't lift the siege, then the High King himself will march. It's not just a question of his highness honoring obligations, though we know he will. His interests demand a secure northern border."*

"We know it," Jill said. "They don't."

"But Lord Tren—"

"Is probably being ignored. I wouldn't be at all surprised if he's good and sorry that he betrayed Gwerbret Cadmar, now that he's seen who his new allies are."

The old man turned to give her a look of pure surprise. In the hot summer sun Jill and Lord Gavry were standing on the catwalks of Dun Cengarn, looking over the town and out to the besiegers beyond. The army spread out round the walls in a vast flood of men and horses. Red banners fluttered; armor and swords winked and glinted in the noontide.

Jill estimated that there were at least three thousand men, though many of those at the rear would be servants and horse handlers. For all that she'd survived many a war, every one of them had taken place on the kingdom's borders in poor provinces, and she'd never seen such a large army in her life.

"I doubt me if Tren knew before," Jill went on, "about his fellow devotees of this new goddess not being ordinary men like him. Weren't we all taken by surprise when we found out that the Hordes were real enough and still a threat?"

He nodded, sighing a little in agreement. Jill shaded her eyes with her hand and peered into the enemy camp. So far, at least, no one had seen one single piece of siege equipment, not one ballista or catapult, not so much as a ram. Whether this was a good omen or an ill one, she didn't know.

"How fares the Princess Carra?" Lord Gavry said.

"Better. She steadied down somewhat when I told her that her husband still lived, and breakfast seems to have done her some good after all those hysterics."

"My good sorcerer, please! Don't be so harsh with the lass, because, truly, a lass she still is, and carrying her first child, too."

"Well, that's true spoken. Tell me, how long do you think the town can hold out?"

"Months if we have to. The trouble will come later, if the farmers never get to plant the year's second crop." All at once his voice cracked. "It's going to be a hard winter for Cengarn, a hard, hard winter indeed."

"How long before—"

"A turning of the moon, no more, or so the yeomen tell me, if we're going to get a full yield at harvest. We have a few weeks more if we bring in a scant one, and then beyond that—" He shrugged, holding empty hands palm upward.

"Well, if the winter comes late this year, the growing season will be a few weeks longer."

"If. How can we know that it will be?"

Jill merely looked at him and smiled.

"Well, then." Gavry swallowed heavily. He seemed a bit pale. "We might have two turnings of the moon, then. But I hope that my lord

Cadmar's allies will have ridden before then to lift the siege. I worry about keeping up people's spirits, and panic in the streets, if it seems our enemies work magic against us."

"Just so, but I don't intend to let things come to that."

Although she spoke confidently for the sake of his morale and the dun's, Jill was suffering her own doubts. While she might well have bested the raven mazrak in some sort of battle, there remained Alshandra. Jill had never seen this strange and powerful being, merely heard reports of her, garbled ones from Rhodry, careful and technical ones from Dallandra, but secondhand information, all of it. Jill did know for a certainty that her ignorance of the dweomer of the roads put her at a decided disadvantage when it came to dealing with Alshandra and her followers. Could her army establish some line of supply with a territory far away, thus allowing them to outlast the town's provisions? What if it was possible for Alshandra to lead part of her army to Evandar's country and then march them back to dump them into the middle of town? Jill simply didn't know what her enemy had the power to do or not.

Lord Gavry spent the rest of that first day of the siege in drawing up a plan for allotting food and water. Jill spent it constructing magical defenses. The first thing she did was find the arms master and get a couple of old iron pot helms that were too dented and rusty to be much good in a battle. The blacksmith supplied a small puddle ingot, once a knife blade that had got snapped; he'd melted it down but never got round to using it again. These Jill took up to the women's hall.

She found Carra alone, sitting in a chair by the window with sewing lying unfinished in her lap. Since the lass's dress hung loose and unkirtled, Jill noticed that her pregnancy was beginning to show. Although Carra looked pale, she greeted Jill calmly, even steadily.

"What have you got there, Jill?" she said, managing a smile. "Am I to arm and ride to battle? I wish I could, frankly. It'd be better than sitting round here."

"I can sympathize with that, but I'm afraid you've got the harder task of just waiting. I've brought these old helms because they're iron and no reason more. You see, the being that's trying to harm you can't stand its presence. I want you to keep these two helms on either side of your bed, and here, take this little lump. Keep it tucked into your kirtle at all times. I see you've got a table dagger, too. Good. Carry that with you always, whether it's time for a meal or not. Sleep with it, too."

"Very well." Carra took the ingot, which just fit into the palm of her hand. "If somewhat happens, should I throw this or suchlike?"

"Never that. Keep it with you always. Just hold it up, just like you're showing it to me. That should do the trick."

Although Carra looked profoundly puzzled, Jill had no time to explain, and indeed, she understood little of the theory behind the iron herself, except for a few vague remarks that Nevyn had once made about lodestones. In fact, beings who exist on the etheric plane but can take on physical form, thanks to the weaving of astral substance, exist in a magnetic field and in a state of magnetic flux, which iron will first absorb, becoming magnetized itself, then disrupt to painful effect. Jill only knew, at that historical point in the development of dweomer knowledge, that beings such as Alshandra and Evandar couldn't abide the touch or close presence of iron. The effect, she hoped, would work without Carra having to know the cause. It occurred to Jill as well that with all the armor and weaponry the Horde outside the gates was carrying, Alshandra couldn't possibly be there upon the physical plane with them. Even though she could work harm just as easily from the etheric, the thought was somehow cheering.

After she left the princess, Jill was crossing the ward on her way to her own side broch when she saw a small party forming at the gates, a herald, carrying a staff wound with ribands, and an escort of warriors to take him through the town. The equerry and Gwerbret Cadmar himself, leaning on his stick, were standing talking with the young herald. At his right hand, and all dressed in clean clothes for the occasion, stood Meer with Jahdo to lead him. When Jill joined them, the bard stepped forward, swinging his massive head from side to side.

"Is that the mazrak?" he bellowed.

"It is, indeed," Jill said. "What are you doing here?"

"I have offered my services to the gwerbret in thanks for his generous treatment of me and my lad. Among our people one of the twelve essential conditions for a parley is the presence of a bard. Besides, if these savage swine don't speak your language, the herald will need a man along who speaks theirs."

"Just so, and my thanks. Savage swine, is it? They're Horsekin from the north, then."

"They are, and I don't like the smell of them. Somewhat evil's afoot here, but you don't need me to tell you that."

"I'm afraid not, good bard, I'm afraid not." Jill turned to the gwerbret. "Who's called for the parley, Your Grace?"

"They have. They want to deliver a demand and terms." Cadmar's face flushed red with rage. "The filthy gall, thinking they can make demands upon me!"

"I'm willing to wager what they'll be, too," Jill said. "Hand over Princess Carramaena and thus the unborn child."

Although the herald looked profoundly skeptical, in the end Jill was proved right. Those sent to the parley rode back soon and fast. Though the herald himself was white and shaking, Meer raged, bellowing and stomping his way into the great hall. Jill hovered by the dragon hearth while the herald delivered his news. Everyone in the hall, whether noble- or common-born, went dead-silent to listen.

"They demand we hand over the princess, sure enough," the herald said. "The only terms they offer are these, that we may kill her ourselves, to assure ourselves that her death is a merciful one, and hand over her dead body instead."

The hall broke out in rage—curses, shouts, inarticulate howls of sheer horror. Meer turned to Jill and hissed a single word, "blasphemy." Cadmar rose, pounding on the honor table with his stick until he got silence.

"It gladdens my heart to hear you as furious as I." The gwerbret's voice rang loud but steady. "Never fear. Never would I turn over any woman to this swarm of filthy maggots, whether she were princess or tavern wench."

A roar of approval answered him. Jill could only hope that they'd feel the same if the siege dragged on into long months of starvation and disease. With Jahdo at his elbow, Meer strode forward and made a bow in the gwerbret's direction. The hall silenced itself again, straining forward in curiosity.

"Your Grace, I have a thing that I must say, for it burns in my mouth. These people are not my people. They may be Horsekin, but they are not Gel da'Thae. They would kill a woman who carries a child, and such is one of the four greatest offenses to our gods. They are blasphemers, idolaters, followers of perverted magicks, filth clotting the pure face of the earth and a stinking dung heap under the sky. I abjure them, I abhor them, I turn my back upon them forever and utterly."

The crowd in the hall muttered to one another, but quietly, waiting for his grace's answer.

"For that you have my thanks, good bard," Cadmar said. "And from now on, I shall consider you one of my own men. Even if you choose to leave us, you will always have a place here in my dun and at my table, anytime you see fit to return."

The crowd sighed, nodding approval.

"My lord has my humble thanks. He has shown the greatness of his heart and soul this day." Meer bowed again, then whispered something to Jahdo, who turned him in Jill's direction. "Mazrak, everything I know, all my twelve levels of lore, is at your disposal. Ask, and I shall answer everything, with naught locked behind walls."

The delighted crowd applauded, even though they doubtless had no idea of the enormous scope of the gift he was offering. Jill was so pleased that she found it hard to speak. Here was a weapon she'd never hoped to earn: Meer's aid.

"My thanks, good bard. Tonight, if it pleases you, we shall dine together in my chamber."

"It pleases me indeed, mazrak." Meer hesitated. "Wait. Such address is not correct. It pleases me—Jill."

With one last bow the enormous bard gestured to Jahdo and strode off, swinging his head from side to side with a rustle of his braided mane, tapping his way with his long staff through the crowd, which parted to let him pass. No doubt he needed to be alone with his grief, that a tribe of his own kind, even if it weren't his own tribe, would betray their gods and all that such stood for.

"We shall have mead," Cadmar called out. "I need to wash the taste of these impious demands out of my mouth. Let the swine wait for their answer."

The crowd roared again. As the serving lasses and pages scurried off, Jill glanced round, but there was no sign of Carra. Yraen, however, was standing by the foot of the spiral staircase. He seemed carved of granite, he'd gone so gray and still. When Jill hurried over, he bowed to her, but he said not a word.

"Where's Carra?" Jill snapped.

"In the women's hall, where I can't go." His voice shook badly.

"Well, there's Lady Ocradda, over there by the window with the bards. Get her to take you up. Carra's going to hear the news sooner or later, and I'd rather she heard from you and Occa, not from her maid's gossip or suchlike."

Yraen nodded and trotted off to follow orders.

Jill had a peculiar sort of battlement to build round the dun and the town. Even though it was broad daylight, and the ward and the walls were filled with people, she decided that she had no time to waste in waiting for darkness, and that the dun had seen enough dweomer by now to put up with her standing on the tops of towers and doing odd things. She puffed up the spiral staircase to the roof of the main broch, where she'd taught Rhodry how to intone a magical formula, and found tidy little pyramids of round stones, stacked at the edge at regular intervals, ready for some desperate defense of the dun. Jill walked into the center of this circle and stood for a moment, catching her breath.

When she was ready, she focused her mind on the blue light of the etheric. Slowly it seemed that the bright sunlight round her faded and a different light rose, dim and silvery, though through it she could clearly see the physical world around her. In this bluish flux she raised her arms high and called upon the power of the Holy Light that stands behind all the shadowy figures and personified forces that men call gods. Its visible symbol came to her in a glowing spear that pierced her from head to foot. For a moment she stood motionless, paying it homage, then stretched her arms out shoulder-high, bringing the light with them to form a shaft across her chest. As she stood within the cross, the light swelled, strengthening her, then slowly faded of its own will. When it was gone, she lowered her arms, then visualized a sword of glowing light in her right hand. Once the image lived apart from her will, she circled the roof, walking deosil, and used the sword to draw a huge ring of golden light in the sky.

As the ring settled to earth, it sheeted out, forming a burning wall round the entire town of Cengarn. Three times round she went, until the wall lived on the etheric of its own will. At each ordinal point, she put a seal in the shape of a five-pointed star made of blue fire. Once the sigils of the kings of the elements blazed at the four directions, she spread the light until it was not a ring but an enormous sphere of gold, roofing over the dun and the town both and extending down under them as well. Two last seals at zenith and nadir, and Cengarn hung in the many-layered worlds like a bubble in glass.

At the end of the working, she withdrew the force from the image of the sword, dissolving it, then stamped three times on the roof. Sunlight brightened round her, and she could hear the sounds of the dun, shut out earlier by sheer concentration. The portion of the sphere above the earth, however, remained visible—that is, visible to someone with dweomer sight. Although she would have to renew the seals five times a day at the changing of the astral tides, everyone inside the sphere would be safe from prying eyes as well as spirits sent by their enemies.

"And we'll see," she said aloud. "How our fine Alshandra likes that."

Yet she knew that she was as guilty as any green warrior of sheer braggadocio. For all she knew, Alshandra would be able to brush the seals away like so many cobwebs. If only Dalla would return! Jill had that thought a hundred times a day. But a useless sort of thought it was, she reminded herself just as often. Rather than stand round wishing, she hurried down to try to convince the arms master to help her salt the entire dun with whatever bits of old iron they could find.

After Meer pledged himself to sorcerer and gwerbret both, Jahdo led him over to the servitors' table where the young bard and his lady were sitting together. Meer sat himself down across from them and bellowed for ale.

"Be it so that you have need of me?" Jahdo said.

"Not for some while, lad. Run off and find your friends if you'd like."

Instead, Jahdo hurried up the spiral staircase after Yraen and Ocradda. On the landing, by the door into the women's hall, Ocradda told Yraen to wait while she broke the evil news to Carramaena as gently as could ever be possible. Jahdo lingered, half-hidden on the stairs, till the lady was well inside, but Yraen's sharp eyes spotted him.

"What do you want, lad?"

"Oh, naught, truly. I did, but, er, well . . ."

"Out with it!"

"I be so scared, Yraen, that they'll harm the princess."

Yraen made an attempt at a smile that failed.

"You know somewhat, Jahdo? So am I, but by every god in the sky, before they can get at her, they'll have to kill me, and that's not such an easy thing to do."

"Truly, that be so." Jahdo climbed the last few stairs up to stand beside him. "But I did think, well, there be dweomer here, and what may we do 'gainst that? So I did come up with a plan. I do have these talismans that Meer did give me, long ago now, and I want the princess to wear them. Great sorcerers aren't going to come a-bothering the likes of me."

"Now, that's a noble thought you've had, truly, and I'm proud of you." Yraen paused to listen at the closed door. "Whist, here they come! You kneel and get ready to ask her, like."

Jahdo got down on one knee and hurriedly ran his hands through his hair, lifted off the charms, rumpling his hair in the process, and was just smoothing it again when the door opened. Flanked by Lady Ocradda, Princess Carramaena stepped out, her head held high, her mouth set hard in a tight line like a warrior's. Jahdo thought that he'd never seen her so beautiful, but still fierce and defiant, like a white eagle, dressed as she was all in white linen, broidered with rich color at neck and sleeves.

"What's all this?" Ocradda said, waving vaguely at Jahdo.

"He has a gift to offer her highness, Your Grace," Yraen said. "Jahdo, go ahead."

For a moment, though, Jahdo's heart pounded so hard that he simply couldn't speak. Carra encouraged him with a little nod.

"Your Highness," he managed the words at last. "My master did give me these talismans that the high priestess made. The high priestess in Meer's own city, I mean, and she does know Gel da'Thae dweomer better than anyone. So I did think that you should have the wearing of them, because the Horsekin sorcerers, they be trying to work you harm, but never would they care about a lad like me."

"Jahdo, how kind of you." For a moment Carra's voice wavered, but only a moment. "But never could I take your safety away."

"Your Highness?" Yraen spoke rather bluntly, Jahdo thought, considering he was speaking to royalty. "You need them. He doesn't."

"Just so, Your Highness," Jahdo said. "Oh, please, if it were that you were wearing them, I would be sleeping so much better."

Carra smiled, a sudden burst of gratitude like sun through clouds, and took the thongful of charms. When she slipped them over her head, when he saw them lying against the pale skin of her neck, Jahdo felt abruptly warm all over. He simply couldn't understand why he'd turned so giddy and shy all of a sudden, though his heart pounded harder than ever.

"You have my undying thanks, Jahdo," Carra said. "I'll wear them always and think of you."

Although Jahdo felt himself grinning and gaping like a fool, he couldn't force out another word. When, guarded between Ocradda and Yraen, Carra went downstairs, Jahdo stayed kneeling on the landing for a long time, wondering if he'd ever been so happy in his life, siege or no siege. In his mind he could still see the memory picture of the thongs nestling at the hollow of her throat, the bound feathers, the silver disk—

"Oh! That other disk!"

He leapt to his feet just as a memory leapt into his mind, the peculiar sigil on the pewter disk that Jill had shown him out in the stableyard. He rushed downstairs dangerously fast, tore through the great hall, and burst out into the ward just in time to see Jill climbing down from her warding ritual.

"Jill, Jill," he shouted. "I remember, I remember!"

Laughing, she took his arm and led him away from the puzzled crowd of warriors standing round the ward.

"Remember what, lad?"

"The squiggly thing on Thavrae's amulets. Remember you it? You did show me when you'd taken them from the old jailor, and there were this squiggly thing on the pewter disk."

"I do remember, indeed. You said you'd seen it before?"

"And I know where. I did find one just like it, lying in the grass outside the gates of Cerr Cawnen."

"Ah." Jill let out her breath in a burst. "Did you now? And what did you do with the thing?"

"I did give it to Tek-tek for her hoard. She be one of our ferrets, you see, and they do love to magpie away shiny bits and other such that catch their fancy. She took it thong and all into her treasure ball among the straw, though truly, Ambo, our big hob I mean, it may be that Ambo did steal it from her later."

"But it's among the weasels still?"

"It be so, for truly, I see no reason why Mam or Da would have taken it. It be a fair bit mucky by now, I wager."

Jill laughed, a quick peal quickly over.

"Well and good, lad, well and good. Then I doubt me if our enemies will go a-hunting for it, and if we ever get you home again, there it'll be, waiting for us to have a look at it."

During those long days passing in the world of men, for Dallandra, Time's wheel had turned little more than an afternoon's hour. She'd occupied herself in alternately fuming at her captor and laying plans. If only she could get out of her prison and reach the page before he or his men could, grab him somehow and put him behind her, then they could both take their chances together in a fight. The question was how. Often in Evandar's country things that seemed solid were nothing but illusion, and in the spirit of experiment she focused her mind on one of the cage bars nearby. If it didn't exist, her mere skeptical attempt to put her hand through that bar would dissolve it, but when she tried, she got a solid bump for her trouble. It had proved hard-woven astral substance, perhaps even of Evandar's making, if he'd created the trees her captors had destroyed to imprison her.

Although any piece of physical matter, if it had been possible to transport such to this plane of existence, would have gone right through the cage, her own illusion of a body was woven of the same stuff. Thus it behaved in relation to the "things" of Evandar's country the same way as real flesh would behave in the physical world. Her body was also real enough to ache or, rather, to register the sense impressions of her etheric double as pain, modeling that feeling, most likely, on her memories of actual physical pain. From her rough capture she still hurt, a constant, distracting gnaw. She found herself rubbing the amethyst figurine round her neck to ease her bruises, just as she might rub a sore shoulder back on the physical plane.

She lay down on her stomach on the cage floor and pretended to sleep, but she was actually studying the layout of the camp. The herald had wandered off into the forest, perhaps to nurse his sense of dishonor at his lord's conduct. The ursine fellows had fallen asleep and snoring from their lord's—Dalla had taken to calling him Lord Vulpine for want of a better name—from Lord Vulpine's magically created mead, but the wolf warrior, the other foxlike creature, the distorted human, and the lord himself all sat alert and chatting by their fire.

If only she could get out of the cage, she could use that fire against them, make it flare and explode with salamanders, tossing flames all over the clearing. Nothing would truly burn, but she doubted if they'd realize that in time, and their astral bodies would register the raw energies of elemental fire as pain. In the panic she perhaps could get the boy out of his prison. Making a great show of yawning, she rolled over on her back and flung one arm over her face, peering out from under it to study the lashed branches. If it were dark, she could probably unpick knots, but when or even if night would fall in this magical country was problematic. She rolled over again, carefully and slowly, so as not to attract their attention, and considered what weapons might lay to hand if she could gain the ground.

All of a sudden, from the forest edge, the herald shrieked and howled. Dallandra sat bolt upright as down below the bear warriors woke with a grunt, and Lord Vulpine and his other men sprang to their feet. Waving his staff and moaning the herald waddled out of the forest with a black-mailed warrior striding behind. Like his lord he was mostly human, with only his red roach of hair and clawed hands to betray him.

"Our borders!" the herald called out. "A breach, a breach."

Dallandra nearly laughed aloud, thinking they meant Evandar. In his cage on the ground the pageboy leapt up, too, and leaned against the bars to listen. While the herald moaned and dithered, the armored fox warrior knelt at Lord Vulpine's feet.

"My lord! The rebels have marched across our land, hundreds and hundreds of them, and they had an army with them, strange horrible beasts with horses and manes like horses on their own heads."

Lord Vulpine swore and raised his hand. A silver sword manifested within his grasp.

"That bitch Alshandra!" the kneeling warrior said. "She was at their head in the form of a huge raven. They traveled into Evandar's country, where we dared not follow, so I know not where they went."

Dalla clutched the bars of her cage so hard the structure swayed on its ropes. She could guess the ultimate destination of that army. They were marching on Jill, Cengarn, and the child and her mother. Images of slaughter and terror flashed into her mind beyond her power to stop them.

"Where were our guards?" Lord Vulpine snapped.

"Overrun. These creatures—they carried iron."

His lord threw back his head and howled, a long wail of rage and frustration. All at once Dallandra realized that he could be a weapon in her hand, if she could seize it without cutting herself.

"Oho!" she called out. "You! Dog Nose! Some fine lord you are."

He spun round, peering up, flicking the sword point in her direction.

"Hold your tongue, elven bitch, or I'll cut it out."

"Huh, no doubt you would. That's an easy thing, torturing a helpless woman and a child." She gestured at the page. "A good way to forget your defeat, I suppose."

"Hold your tongue!"

Behind his lord's back the herald lifted wrung hands, as if imploring her to stop. She ignored him.

"You forgot one thing, didn't you now? That raven your man saw, that can't be Alshandra, not so close to all that iron. How could she travel with that army?"

He opened his mouth, then hesitated, thinking.

"Well, that's true," he said at last. "So?"

"Then where is she? She's lurking round the Lands still, no doubt on your side of the border, because she's terrified of Evandar, as well she might be."

He snarled, then kicked the warrior kneeling at his feet. The man whined but stayed where he was.

"You can't keep Alshandra out of your territory, can you?" Dallandra pitched her voice to an insolent lilt. "Oh, a fine border you keep! Even Evandar's cast-off woman can go strolling past your guards anytime she has the fancy to."

Lord Vulpine growled, clutching the sword in a hand suddenly become furred. She could see fangs, too, biting into his lower lip, as if he would transform into an animal in front of her.

"My lord!" the herald shrieked.

With a toss of his head the lord collected himself and became, again, mostly elven.

"You forget, slut," he snarled, "that her warriors carried iron."

"They did, certainly, but how could she do the same?"

He hesitated, caught. She laughed.

"You, herald!" she called out. "How does it feel to serve a coward, one who can threaten a caged woman but not guard his own borders?"

The herald gaped his long slit of a toad's mouth and made a gurgling noise in his throat, as if he were swallowing prayers. With paws cocked to noses the bear warriors looked back and forth between their lord and the others. Lord Vulpine swung backhanded and smacked the herald so hard he fell.

"Summon my men!" he snarled. "We ride for the borders!"

His band cheered him.

"You!" Lord Vulpine spun round, pointing at each warrior in turn. "Guard them well, the lad and the elven shrew. Once the army's on the way, the herald here will be keeping an eye on you. There will be no parley, old man, so I don't need you. You stay here, and if I return to find these prisoners gone, I'll slice those folds of flesh away from your neck while you beg me to let you die."

The herald squawked wordlessly. Lord Vulpine grabbed his arm and hauled him up.

"Summon my men, I said."

He dragged the herald off into the forest while the warriors argued and swore, bewailing their guard duty and a lost chance to ride with the army. So far so good, Dallandra thought. She reminded herself that even if night lay close at hand for her, weeks might pass in the lands of men before the sky above her turned dark. She was going to have to scheme out some fast escape.

On the third day of the siege of Cengarn, Jill rose at dawn and climbed to the top of the main tower to renew the astral seals. After she finished her working, she stood for a moment looking out over the enemy army, ensconced now some hundred yards back, well out of a bow's range, from the city walls. Beyond this neutral ground rode a few guards, ambling on their enormous horses in a lazy circle. Beyond them lay ground kept clear for possible fighting, and farther still the tents. As the sun brightened, it glittered on armor and weapons as the soldiers strolled through the camp, getting their rations, probably, since just past the tents stood the wagons, extra horses, and supplies.

At the outermost ring, the enemy had begun to dig trenches behind them and pile up earthworks to defend themselves from an army riding to relieve the town. Thanks to Cengarn's position, straddling hills on the edge of more hills, the Horsekin had a difficult emplacement to defend, broken in places by rising land, in others by valleys. It would take them a good long while to dig themselves in properly, Jill supposed, or so she could hope. Whether or not they had magical defenses was the question that was truly vexing her. From her position in the dun, she could spot nothing but clouds of faint purplish glow, here and there, that indicated personal talismans of one sort or another—Horsekin magic, such as Meer and now Carra wore round their necks.

Even though the dun stood on the highest inner hill, thanks to the broken landscape not all of the enemy camp stood visible. Since Meer had told her that the Horsekin not only carried hunting bows but prided themselves on their skill, she had no desire to go flying over the camp in falcon form to scout. Later that morning, in the company of Lord Gavry, she went down to the town walls, which of course lay farther out than those of the dun. With a yeoman captain, Mallo, to guide them, they climbed a ladder up to the wood catwalks. Although Mallo wore a stout iron pot helm, the rest of his accoutrements were made of boiled leather, studded here and there with brass. Jill could guess that most of the town defenders had no better.

As they walked their slow circuit of the walls, stopping now and then to peer out between the merlons, Jill let the two men fall a little ways behind. She opened up her etheric sight, turning the stone walls round her so black and dead that she felt as if they'd crawled into a cavern, and began a careful study of the enemy camp. Round the western side, right under the dun itself, she of course saw nothing new, and nor did she find any traces of magic up to the north, where the town looked out into the rising hills about a half mile beyond the enemy camp.

The eastern quarter brought her better hunting. Here the northern hills circled round, coming closer to the town in a couple of low fingers of land, and here stood the east gate, where Carra had tried to slip inside unobserved after her brief jaunt some weeks earlier. Out on one of those fingers of land, about some five hundred yards from the town, Jill saw a bubble of pale gold light, dotted at the cardinal points with glowing specks that, at some closer distance, would probably prove themselves magical seals. She refocused her sight to the physical and saw white shapes much like distant tents, and the occasional flutter of a red banner.

"There we are!" she called out, pointing. "Some rather eminent persons are camped in those tents, I'll wager. Their cadvridoc, perhaps, and their mazrak."

Gavry and Mallo hurried to a space between merlons and peered out, shading their eyes.

"Lord Gavry, when we get back, you'd best report this to his grace," Jill went on. "Mallo, how well defended is this gate?"

" 'Tisn't a gate no longer, good sorcerer. We've sealed her up and good. This was always the weak point of the whole town, and some of the dwarven gentlemen, what are sieged here with us, I mean, they supplied these sacks of grayish stuff. Magic, I suppose it be, but when you mix it with water to a porridge, like, and ladle it round your gates, then it dries as hard as stone. We did seal the gates, and pile up loose gravel and bits of rock behind it, and slop a fair bit of that magic stone round and over the pile, and I doubt me if a god could break his way through the east gate now."

"Splendid!" Jill said. "Now that's the kind of magic we could use more of."

The men laughed, but uneasily. Jill refocused her sight to the etheric and walked on, pausing every few steps to peer out at the enemy camp. In the quadrant that ran from the domed and sealed tents down to the south gate, she found more and more magical traces, glimmers of purplish light, streaks of pale red from some different sort of talisman. They were nearly to the south gate when Jill saw what seemed to be three shafts or slender towers of black light, unimaginable as that sounds, huge beams of light turned to perceptible darkness, glittering like obsidian from the fire mountains of the north and rising some thirty feet into the air. Down her back ran the ice touch of dweomer warning.

"I don't like this," she burst out. "Mallo, are the men on alert?"

"They are, my lady." He patted a silver horn hanging at his belt. "All I have to do is signal, like."

Jill walked on, a little faster. The dweomer traces out in the massed enemy camp grew brighter, more clustered. At the towers over the main gates, the southern pair, she found four of the gwerbret's men, mailed and armed with hunting bows, leaning over the merlons and arguing among themselves about something they saw outside. Jill brought her sight down and stared with them. In the Horsekin camp some sort of activity was stirring up dust.

"Mallo!" Jill yelled. "Sound the alarum!"

Like birds the silver notes swooped over Cengarn. Down in the streets men shouted, town guards came rushing to scale ladders, women shrieked and ran, grabbing children and dragging them back from the walls into the relative safety of the center of town. Up in the dun another horn called in answer. As soon as they could grab weapons, the gwerbret's men would be reinforcing the guard on the outer walls.

"Gavry, get down!" Jill shouted. "You'll only be in the way."

The elderly lord was more than glad to follow her order, scrabbling down a ladder to hurry back to the dun. Jill found a spot where she could wedge herself next to a tower and out of everyone's way, then brought her sight back to the etheric. The pillars of black light were moving closer.

"Siege towers," she yelled. "Hidden by dweomer, but they have them."

She heard Mallo yelling orders about fire, and in a few moments she could smell wood smoke and the sickening odor of melting pitch. For a moment she debated trying a banishing against those towers of blackness, but if she could simply guide the archers? Better yet! Let their enemies wonder how their dweomer defense had been pierced! She switched her sight down and noted the lay of the land, then returned it up to mark the towers of black light. From auras and the traces of talismatic magic she could easily keep track of the various squads of men.

"Directly behind the five mounted lords," she called out. "Sight over those ranked foot soldiers in front, sight some five feet behind the horses, now lift your aim to about ten feet above the ground."

With a whoosh and a stink of smoke the first course of flaming arrows flew. Jill could hear the Horsekin screaming in rage, but she kept her sight focused on the etheric plane—the higher ground in this peculiar battle.

"Just a little to the left!" she screamed.

The second flight whistled out. One of the black shafts of light exploded and vanished in a rush of pure elemental energy, the red and gold of natural fire. As the rest of the arrows fell into the army, shrieks of pain howled up with the battle cries. Taken off-guard the enemy squads were milling round, trying to form into some kind of order for a charge.

"A strike! A strike!" the guards cried.

"There's two more," Jill called. "Swing to your right. Over the men holding that—ye gods, they've got a ram! Behind the ram, then, and just five feet behind and the same height as your last volley."

This time the first flight struck home, and another black shaft vanished into fire. Down below the enemy charged; from the walls a single flurry of stones greeted them. This early in the siege the defenders would have to trust in their walls and gates rather than depleting their supply of weapons. Jill sighted on the third siege tower, called down the flaming arrows again, and again, they struck home, setting the engine alight. Cengarn's walls rang with jeers and catcalls as the soldiers carrying the ram tried one feeble bounce, then retreated fast under a covering fire of arrows that stilled the defenders' laughter. Jill dropped below a merlon just in time, and a curse next to her told her that one of the guards had lingered too long.

She brought her physical sight back fast, and kneeling, she crawled over to him, but he was already dead, pierced through the neck by sheer luck and little else. All Jill could do for him was close his eyes. Mallo came crawling to join her and swore when he saw the corpse.

"We've driven the bastards off," he said to the dead man. "You didn't die in vain, lad." He glanced at Jill. "He's our first, is he? I'm not fool enough to think he'll be our last."

Nodding agreement Jill rose, risking a look through two merlons. The enemy had withdrawn, leaving their siege towers burning like huge torches in the neutral ground while they dragged their dead and wounded away. Black smoke rose to defile the sky.

"Well and good," Jill said. "We got a claw into them, did we? And now they'll have to think for a while before they risk feeling the whole paw."

•　•　•

At the same time as the Horsekin were mounting their abortive attack, up in his own country Evandar was listening to the harpers sing a pair of songs and not particularly long ones at that. Sweet though the music was he grew distracted, suddenly leaping to his feet with an oath.

"Leave me! Take those squalling strings and go!"

With little shrieks of fear they clutched their harps to their chests and fled, rushing out of the pavilion. Evandar began to pace back and forth. What was taking Dallandra so much time? Normally she felt his moods and rushed to his side whenever he wanted her. Why was she dallying in the world of men? She had promised him a quick return, and he wanted a quick return.

Evandar strode outside to the long green lawns. These normally soothed him; he'd modeled them upon the royal taste in gardens from the long-dead elven city of Rinbaladelan, and they reminded him of happier times. Even there, however, he was distracted, in this case by a sudden rush of wings and the shrieking of birds. He looked up to see a brilliantly colored flock wheeling toward the pavilion, cockatoos, macaws, parrots with emerald wings. As they settled in the grass they transformed themselves into women, dressed in flowing silk. Shrieking and calling out, the night princess and her ladies rushed across the grass.

"Here, here, what's all this?" Evandar snapped. "What's so wrong?"

"We saw her, we saw her," they all cried at once. "And then the men came, all hairy and cruel, with iron strapped to their bodies, and they led horses, horses, stinking of iron."

"Saw whom?"

"Alshandra, Alshandra."

They shrieked, dancing round and gabbling until Evandar yelled them into silence. The night princess composed herself and curtsied.

"My lord," she said, calm at last. "As we danced among the lilacs we heard a great rumbling, as if the earth would split open. We turned ourselves feathered and flew up into the sky just as an army began to ride out of the mist. At their head flew a huge raven. When it saw us, it screeched and attacked, pecking and striking, till we flew away. But we circled back, because the army was like a river, flowing and flowing, marching and marching, and they marched and led their horses for ever so long a time, and so we saw them after the raven had flown away."

"These were not my brother's men?"

"No, my lord, because they carried iron. Nor were they men or elves, but ugly and hairy and huge, with strange designs bitten into the skin on their faces. Never have we seen the like. Their horses too were huge and ponderous, with fringed hooves."

"Are they still here, violating our borders, raping my lands with their very passing?"

"They are not, my lord, for they marched into another mist and were gone."

Evandar stood stunned for a long moment. He had absolutely no idea what all this might mean.

"Ye gods," he snapped. "Just when I need her more than ever, she's gone! Dalla, I mean, off frivoling her time away in the lands of men!"

"She's not there, my lord. We saw her, just before the army marched."

"What? Where?"

"Here, my lord." The night princess waved a slender dark arm in the vague direction of the hill and Dalla's garden. "She said she was waiting for you."

For a second time Evandar found himself speechless. A few at a time the women wandered away, flickering and re-forming, melding and separating out again, as they drifted into the pavilion nearby. Only the night princess remained whole and steady, waiting for his answer. Evandar raised his hand and summoned his silver horn.

"One more thing before we ride," he said to the night princess. "This raven. Are you sure it hid Alshandra? Never has she taken that form before."

"Then I know not who it was. And another strange thing, my lord. So much iron did these monsters carry that the Lands turned all strange and glassy round them, and the trees did seem to burn and the grass to melt away, but the raven flew with them and above them, and never a cry of pain did it give."

"Not Alshandra, then. By those hells men speak of! I wonder if my hag of a wife has gone and worked Dallandra harm? I think me I'd best look into this. At the lilacs, you say? Well and good, then."

He plucked the horn from the air and blew. In answer his court came flooding round him, swordsmen and archers, leading horses, donning armor, shouting their war cries, in a flood of rage like a winter river, cold and killing both.

"To the border!" Evandar cried. "And if my bastard-born brother tries to forbid me passage, then this day I'll have his head on a pike."

In a howl of laughter the Bright Court rode out. Their silver weapons and armor flashed and jingled as they sang of vengeance for old wrongs. As they passed through the green grassy lands, Evandar visualized a huge and towering silver drinking horn that rose from him and above him. Through this channel, light and life-stuff poured down, and through him as well it spread out to the Lands, turning them solid, filling their forms with energy and the illusion of life—the trees, the flowers, the rivers, even the images of distant towns, all sprang from his mind and vivified by his effort alone. Yet when he saw the dark forest that straddled the border, he stopped working dweomer and concentrated only on the task ahead.

With one long note of his silver horn, he halted his army in the midst of a grassy plain. As they milled round him, those with true minds crowded close to listen and advise, urging their own horses up next to his golden stallion.

"And where do you think Alshandra will be?" Evandar called out.

"Always did she hate the deep woods, my lord."

"And she scorned the cities as well."

"She loved the streams and rivers, and the silver lakes."

"And the flowers and thickets, where the lilacs blow."

"None of these, my lord, but sheltering in your brother's country out of fear of you."

This last was spoken by a warrior with yellow hair as bright as Evandar's own, though his eyes shone deep blue, and the shape of him was more human than elven.

"Have you a name?" Evandar said to him.

"I do not, my lord."

"Then take one, for you've earned it this day. I think the same, my lords and vassals. We ride to the battle plain."

•　　•　　•

While the news of Alshandra's army was spreading across what had once been her homeland, Cengarn reached the seventh night of the siege. Long days of scattered rain and wind turned the town damp and miserable, though those caught camped in it could take some pleasure in knowing that their besiegers were a fair bit wetter still. From the safety of her alcove in the women's hall, Carra spent sleepless nights watching the rain pour down, or catching in those odd moments when the sky cleared glimpses of the new moon, swelling into its first quarter. Several times a day Jill would find her and tell her that she'd scried out Dar, riding south with his remaining men in safety, but glad as Carra was of the news, it always reminded her of the men who had died, Dar's own men, those handsome, laughing young archers of his escort. Although she hadn't know them well, the simple fact that they'd died because of her made her mourn them as bitterly as she would have a brother.

"Well, more bitterly than I would have mourned my brother," she remarked to Yraen. "I really did rather hate him. I meant less to him than one of his dogs."

He merely nodded, which was often the only answer she got from him in these talks. They were sitting that morning in the herb garden behind the kitchen hut, simply because she'd felt that she had to get out in the sun or die, and it was the only reasonably private place they could find. Yraen had fetched her a wobbly bench and placed it up against the dun wall, so she could sit with her back against the stone, while he sat in the dirt at her feet, leaning back against the bench with his long arms clasped round his knees.

In the hot sun the rain-washed herbs smelled sharp and spicy and sweet all at once, and the drowsy air hummed with bees. She thought at moments that Yraen had fallen asleep, but whenever she looked his way, he would turn his head and look at her in return, as if waiting for some request or order. Often she'd considered asking Jill for another guard, but if she did, Jill would want to know why, and Yraen would end up humiliated. If Carra had truly been a princess from one of the great clans down in Deverry proper, the comfort and the feelings of her guard would have been of absolutely no moment to her, but as it was, she was always aware that she'd married a prince by accident and him without a throne at that. Besides, if Otho's gossip was true, Yraen would be her equal in rank. Eventually, when she went to look at him, she found him studying her face, and before she could control herself, she blushed.

"You should get more sleep," Yraen said abruptly. "You're getting dark circles under your eyes."

"Oh, and how can I sleep? Worrying about Dar, worrying about the whole town, really. Sometimes at night I walk round and round the women's hall, and if you look out this one window you can just see over the wall. I look at the little fires the army has going, and I think that, well, I really do think sometimes that I should just go hand myself over to those creatures and let them kill me. Then they'd ride away and everyone would be safe."

Yraen swung round and grabbed her wrist in one huge hand so hard that she yelped.

"Don't even think of it. Don't. Oh, ye gods, I'd tell Jill and have them lock you in your chamber if I thought you would."

With a wrench she pulled her hand free.

"Do you think I've got no honor or shame of my own? Have you ever seen a town starve, Yraen? Have you? Well, I have, and I'd rather die than have that on my head."

He was staring openmouthed. She choked back tears, surprised at how strongly the memories flooded back, beyond her power to wipe them away.

"It was a long time ago now, and I was but a child, but the winter came early that year and ruined the harvest. I mean, it wasn't even a siege or suchlike, just the will of the gods, but by snow melt there was barely a stored handful of rotten barley left, not for lord nor peasant, not for the High King himself if he'd ridden our way. I remember being hungry, we were all so hungry that all you could think of was food, every day, waiting for the wheat to grow and turn milk-ripe, at least, so we could make a porridge of it. My father and my brother caught fish, and what little birds they could snare, and I wept to eat little swallows and sparrows, but I ate them. And in our village there was an old woman who starved herself to give what she had to her little grandson. Not a week after she died he got a fever and died, too, so she'd starved herself all for naught."

All at once she was sobbing, remembering. "And now there's this whole dun, and a town, and all the folk roundabout facing that or worse, and ye gods, don't you see? It would be better to hand me over than that. I'd rather die than have it on my head."

She felt arms round her, drawing her close, holding her close to his chest while she sobbed. Yraen smelled so familiar, so like all the other men she'd ever known, of horses mostly and sweat and wood smoke, that she could pretend for a moment that he was Dar. She found herself wishing and praying that when she opened her eyes, some dweomer would have changed him for Dar, even as she forced herself to push him away, to shove away the comfort she so badly wanted.

"Yraen, I'm sorry," she said, stammering. "I shouldn't burden you with such black thoughts."

She was shocked to find tears in his eyes. She fumbled in the folds of her kerchief, found a bit of rag, and blew her nose while he merely watched, unmoving on the bench, unspeaking.

"Well, don't you see?" she said for want of anything better.

"I do." His voice cracked. "I'm just—well, it—I've never known a woman more fit to be a princess than you."

For a moment she was angry that he would fish a compliment out of what she saw as merely her duty; then she realized that he meant it. She blushed and looked away.

"My thanks." She rubbed her damp face on her sleeve. "And I'm sorry I bawled like a calf."

He smiled, again that bare twitch of his mouth, then rose to sit on the ground at her feet. Neither of them spoke until she decided that it was time to go in.

Late on the morrow, Jill was sitting in the great hall with Gwerbret Cadmar and Lord Gwinardd when Draudd came clattering in, wearing mail and carrying his helm from guard duty. He knelt so fast that he slid on the rushes almost into Cadmar's feet.

"Your Grace!" he stammered. "We've spotted riders that looked like they might be from your allies."

"Splendid, lad. Now suppose you start at the beginning of the tale, eh?"

"My apologies, Your Grace. I was on watch up on top of the main tower with two other men, and we saw two riders coming way off from the south. From the way the sun glittered on them we could guess they were wearing mail. And they crested a hill, paused for a moment, and then turned and rode back south like the hells were opening under them."

"Did any of our enemies ride out after them?"

"They didn't, Your Grace. We waited to make sure before I came down, like, to tell you."

"Good." Cadmar glanced at Gwinardd. "Sounds like messengers from Gwerbret Pedrys. The time's about right."

"So it is, Your Grace." Gwinardd allowed himself a brief smile. "If it is, then our allies know what's facing them."

"Just so, just so, and it gladdens my heart to think so." The gwerbret turned to Jill. "When I sent out the messages, you see, I had no idea how big an army this was going to be. Things are more than half-wild, here on the border, and there's not a lot of men to spare for warbands and suchlike. It's going to take a long while, alas, for Pedrys and Madoc to raise an army to take this lot on."

"I see, Your Grace. You have my apologies for not giving you better warning sooner."

"Ye gods, will you stop feeling shamed?" Cadmar smiled to take the sting from his words. "There's no fault to be laid at your door, Jill. It's thanks to you that our position's as strong as it is."

Although Jill rationally knew that he was right, still she berated herself for not seeing the truth earlier and doing something, anything—though what it might have been she couldn't say—to stop Alshandra's army. That evening, she stood in the window of her tower room, looking out over the dark ward and the town beyond. She was considering ways to take the dweomer battle to the enemy, but it seemed that every maneuver she thought of was countermanded by prudence. She might set the enemy tents burning, for instance, but if the enemy dweomer-worker should douse them, then the Horsekin morale would rise while Cengarn's would fall. What she truly wanted was to challenge the raven mazrak to combat, but again, if she should lose, then the town would have no magical defense at all. She was, she supposed, going to have to take her own advice to Carra and simply wait.

That idea pleased her so much that when someone knocked on her door, she whipped round and yelled, "Who by all the hells is that?"

Looking round as if he feared flying daggers Yraen stepped in, staying near the door.

"My apologies. I was just wondering if you had any—er, well—news of Rhodry. If he was safe and suchlike."

"I haven't the slightest idea."

Yraen stared.

"My apologies, lad, but I don't. I can't work miracles, I can only follow the laws of the cursed dweomer, and I've got no idea of where Rhodry may or may not be, so why don't you get out of here and leave me alone?"

Yraen fled, slamming the door behind him. Jill kicked the table leg so hard the table rattled. Wildfolk scattered like terrified chickens. With a growl for them as well, Jill went back to her brooding at the window.

In Haen Marn's great hall Garin, Mic, and Otho lounged round a table at one of their perennial dice games, but the joy of it seemed to have run thin. Mic propped himself up on one elbow and drew little patterns on the table with a bit of charcoal, while Otho and Garin rolled the dice this way and that between them with not one snarl or insult. Rhodry leaned in the sunny doorway, yawning and watching them.

"Would you either sit down or leave?" Otho snapped. "It drives me daft, having you hover there for hours like that."

"Oh, hold your tongue!" Garin said. "Look, we're all on edge, waiting like this, but there's no need to be making things worse."

Otho merely growled. In the spirit of compromise Rhodry dipped himself a tankard of ale from the open barrel by the hearth and sat down next to the envoy.

"Care for a turn at this game?" Garin said.

"I don't, but my thanks."

"Hah!" Otho said. "He's found other ways of amusing himself. Leave it to the elf among us to seduce our hostess."

Rhodry threw the ale in his tankard full into Otho's face. With a yelp the old man scrambled up.

"Say what you want about me." Rhodry slammed the tankard down. "But leave her name out of it."

Before Garin could stop him, Rhodry swung himself free of the bench and stalked round the table. With a little shriek Otho stepped back and back till he fetched up against the wall and could step no farther. Rhodry grabbed him by the shirt and lifted him off his feet.

"My apologies!" Otho wailed. "I meant no insult to the lady."

"Just to me, eh?"

Rhodry laughed and let him go, setting him down gently and brushing drops of ale from the old man's face with the side of his hand.

"Well and good, then. Better go wash your beard, Otho my friend. It stinks of strong drink."

When Otho ran out of the great hall, Mic got up and followed him. Rhodry sat down across the table from Garin and gave him a sunny smile.

"You're daft, Rori. Do you know that?"

"All berserkers are daft. It comes in handy, like."

"Well, I wouldn't know about that, but I'll admit that the old man had it coming. He's been riding you for weeks."

"For years, if truth be told, ever since the first day we met. I don't truly remember, of course, but I think that he may have handed me my first insult before he even knew my name."

Garin sighed, rose, and took their tankards to the barrel to refill them. For a few minutes they drank in a companionable silence.

"It's that nasty tongue that actually got our Otho exiled," Garin remarked. "Not paying his debt was the formal charge, but he showed the judges—well, shall we say less than full respect?"

"I can believe it of him. Tell me somewhat. Will things go badly for my lady because of me?"

"Why would they? She's a widow and the mistress of Haen Marn as well. If she chooses to keep her bed warm at night, who's to say her nay?"

"Well, things are a fair bit different in my country."

"True, true, but we're not in it, are we?" Garin smiled, just briefly.

"Well, so we're not."

They drank for a few moments more.

"I do wonder about Enj," Garin said. "I get the odd feeling that he's staying away on purpose, odd because the servants here have all confirmed what I've been thinking all along. He's going to covet the joining of this hunt."

"Splendid, but if he doesn't even know we're here—"

Garin looked at him and lifted one eyebrow.

"You think he does know?"

"Rori, we're in Haen Marn. The lady and her brood are not what you'd call ordinary souls, are they now?"

"Um, well, true spoken. Let me see, we got here just before the moon turned full, she went to her dark time, and now she's what?"

"She reached the waxing quarter last night." All at once Garin looked into his tankard and struggled to suppress a grin. "No doubt you've been a bit too busy, like, to notice."

Rhodry swung one hand toward him in a mock blow.

"Be that as it may," Garin went on with some dignity. "The summer's not getting any younger. You're going to have a fine time of it up on the Roof of the World if you don't get yourself there soon, and it's not what you'd call a short journey."

"True. Well, I'll go see if I can find Angmar. She's often in the tower this time of day."

In the tower was indeed where he found her. Angmar had persuaded Avain to set her basin upon the table and sit in a proper chair; she herself sat opposite, while Rhodry leaned against the wall and watched them, two golden heads together in the sunlight, the one so strong, the other so vulnerable to every ill whim of a world she'd never be able to understand. Safe under her mother's protection Avain was so sunny, so loving, that it was hard not to like the child. Even the dourest servant, Angmar's maid, always had a smile for her when she came up to help with some task or other.

"She will get round to Enj some while soon," Angmar said. "There be no hurrying the child. I doubt me if she may choose what she do see or not."

"Probably not, truly."

Not that he would have blamed her, but Rhodry did have a brief wondering if Angmar was postponing his leaving for her own reasons. He wondered about himself, as well, and his own lost appetite for taking up the burden of his Wyrd. When Avain started talking in broken fragments of words and sentences, Angmar frowned, trying to decipher.

"An odd thing, this. She do tell that back in the city of men, the many-towered city where first she did see you, a woman be looking for you, and that she does vex herself over your being gone. A woman with white hair, and very frail and slender. Be it your mother, Rori?"

Rhodry laughed.

"It's not, but the dweomermaster who laid the geas upon me to find the dragon."

Told this news, Avain giggled, cocking her head first one way, then the other, several times running in a sort of dance before her mother stopped her with a gentle hand on the cheek. She looked down again, frowning into her basin, shaking it every now and then to dance the ripples round, then all at once cried out. She began babbling in a flood of words that even Angmar had trouble understanding. At last, however, something came clear. Angmar looked up, pale and trembling.

"Rori, the town where that geas master does live? It be sieged. A huge army camps all round it, and they be neither human nor Mountain People, but some strange folk the like of which she can barely tell. Hairy, she says, and that's all she does say, hairy and big, Mam, hairy and big."

Rhodry grunted. The news hit him as a physical pain, a run of rage down his back that wrenched him away from the wall and made him arch like Dar's bow. When Avain cried out, he forced himself calm, unclenched his fists, and let out his breath in a gasp. He knelt by her chair and smiled.

"My thanks," he said. "Don't worry."

His tone, his smile, made her smile in return. Angmar spoke for a moment or two in a soothing way. In a few moments the lass returned to her scrying, murmuring Enj's name.

"We'd best be gone," Angmar said. "With you here she'll be returning to that siege, and I want that not."

"Nor do I, my lady."

Rhodry clattered down the staircase, waited for her just outside the tower while he stared across the lake without truly seeing either water or hill. Together they walked down to the shore without saying a word and stood, a little ways apart, watching the waves run up onto pale sand. The wind whistled round Haen Marn like a dirge.

"Will you be leaving us straightaway?" Angmar said at last.

"To go back to Cengarn, you mean? What good would that do, one more swordsman against an army? The lord of that city has powerful allies. No doubt they'll be riding to relieve him with all the men they can scrape together. I can't know, but I think me that the best thing I can do is carry out my geas." All at once he laughed, a brief echo of his berserker's howl. "I doubt me if the dweomer will give me much choice."

"I did wonder. You have spoke to me many times about your friends in that city."

"And my heart aches for all of them caught there. It's a terrible thing, being besieged."

"So I've heard. My mother was taken in a siege, and she did often tell me of it, when she were in one of her black moods and crying for her homeland."

"Your mother was one of the Mountain People, then?"

"Nah nah nah. It were them what took her, as tribute like when her town fell."

Rhodry spun round to stare. She smiled, a wry twist of her mouth.

"Envoy Garin be a good man, and many of his people, they too be good folk, but they do like to nurse their injuries and claim how they were put upon by my mother's folk, by our folk, Rori. But it do take two to twist a rope, I always say, and not all the injustice does get birthed south of the Deverry border."

"Just so. And so you were raised in a dwarf hold?"

"I was, and brought here when the lord of Haen Marn did need a wife. They did rightly think that I would flourish more in the sun and air, where a Mountain woman would have sickened and pined."

"You weren't given much choice in the matter, were you?"

"None." Her mouth twisted in the same smile. "But I were well pleased, all the same, to walk in the light, and he were in his way a good man. When he did drown, I wept."

He could hear old pain in her voice. He glanced round—no one in sight—and took her hand to pull her close beside him. She sighed, letting her head rest against his shoulder, just briefly before she pulled away.

"Where Enj be I know not," she said. "I would worry about those enemies who did try to prevent you here, but Avain has seen him many times, safe and on his way."

Rhodry heard then what she must have heard, the crunch of footsteps on gravel. With a face as sour as old vinegar and the smell of it hanging about her as well, the maidservant walked out from among the trees. When she said something in Dwarvish, Angmar nodded agreement.

"It be needful for me to go, Rori. They be pickling beef, and I must be unlocking the salt chest."

"I'd best go back with you if I want to reach the manse."

The maidservant shot him a glance of pure venom, as if she'd been hoping he'd stay by the lake and end up feeding one of the beasts.

Otho and Mic had rejoined Garin in the great hall. When Rhodry came trotting in, they all slewed round and looked at him.

"What's so wrong?" Garin said.

"Cengarn's under siege. Avain saw it in her basin."

Garin went dead-still, sat for a long time with his hand frozen round his tankard's handle. Otho and Mic said nothing, either, merely watched the envoy as if waiting for orders. At last he muttered a few words in Dwarvish.

"Ye gods," he whispered in Deverrian. "Grim news, Rori. Grim, grim news indeed. I've got to get back to Lin Serr as soon as ever I can. We have alliances with Cadmar, after all, and kin in that town as well." He rose, setting the tankard down. "I must find Angmar. Otho, I hate to let you negotiate on your own over your debt, but—"

"Oh, don't vex yourself about that." A note of cheer crept into Otho's voice. "I'll manage, I'll manage."

"If I find out later you've been miserly, you'll pay double in fines." Garin hesitated, considering something. "Well, I'll speak with Angmar. It's too late in the day to leave right now, anyway."

He ran out, leaving the rest of them looking round at each other with not a word more to say.

That night Rhodry retired to their chamber early, undressed and got into bed, lying awake with his hands tucked under his head to wait for Angmar while she settled Avain down out in the tower. Moonlight poured through the unshuttered windows, and the damp summer breeze ruffled his hair. He had lived through a number of sieges in his life, on both sides of the town walls. No matter how hard he tried to banish them, memories crowded round him of the horrors a long siege would bring. Worse yet were his memories of a town falling to the besiegers, himself among them. He knew all too well how brutally a man could act after long months of frustration under some stubborn enemy's walls. He sat up, shaking his head hard as if he could spit out the taste of shame. He got up and went to sit in the window seat until Angmar came in to distract him from his remembering.

She barred the door behind her, then set her candle-lantern down on the little table. He got up and kissed her, then lay down on the bed to watch while she undressed, taking her time, primly folding each piece of clothing and laying it down on top of a wooden chest.

"You're truly beautiful," he said.

"Do you be thinking so? Always I did feel so strange and ugly, in the dwarf hold and to my husband as well, too tall and spindly, like, and with this yellow hair."

"I'm not one of the Mountain People."

She smiled and lay down, turning into his arms for a kiss. Before he could take another one, she laid her fingertips on his mouth.

"Tell me one thing first, Rori. Is it that you've seen the woman in white these past few days?"

"I haven't."

"When did you see her last?"

She sounded so urgent that he considered with some care.

"I do remember," he said finally. "It was some days ago, and we were lying here, and just before I took you into my arms, I thought I saw her, standing by the window. For a moment it gave me pause, but then she vanished."

"And you've not seen her since?"

"I haven't."

"Truly? Now that does gladden my heart."

There was such an odd note in her voice, a thrill of hope like a songbird flying free into sunlight, that he raised himself up on one elbow to look at her. In the guttering light of the candle, her face revealed nothing.

"Be there somewhat wrong?" she said.

"Naught. I just wondered why you asked."

"Now that be a thing I may never answer."

She threw her arms round his neck and pulled him down, guiding his hand to her breast. He found it easy to forget memories and questions both.

On the morrow morning Enj came home. Rhodry was walking down

by the lake when he heard, far away and to the north, the sound of a
gong, echoing like a call over the water. In a few minutes he heard the
boatmen shouting back and forth up at the manse. He ran round the
shore and arrived at the boathouse in time to see them untying the beast-
headed boat from the jetty. With a grin, the helmsman gestured him
aboard.

"Gong?" he said.

Rhodry laughed and swung himself on board, working his way to
the bow and the gong. The anchorman waited there, too, but instead of
his flower of hooks, he carried a simple hawser. When they pushed off,
rowing in long smooth pulls, Rhodry began striking two-handed in a
regular rhythm while the helmsman and anchorman both screamed and
yelled and made every ungodly noise they could think of to drive the
beasts away. Between strokes he watched the dark hills on the northern
shore come closer and the waterfall resolve itself from a silver line into
a roar and plunge of river. As the boat veered off from the white water,
the mists caught the sun and turned into a veil of rainbows.

With the helmsman barking orders they headed into a tiny cove and
a rickety wood jetty. Waiting for them, his pack sitting beside him on
the bleached and gaping boards, stood a young man of the Mountain
People, though he was tall for one of them at a good five and a half feet.

"Enj?" Rhodry said.

The anchorman nodded yes, judging distance with narrow eyes as
the oarsmen maneuvered the boat nearer and nearer the end of the jetty.
They swung her round, backing water frantically, and let the currents
and tides bob her closer and closer. Enj called something out in Dwarvish,
slung his pack on board, and jumped down after it before the anchorman
could throw him the rope. When the boat shuddered, the anchorman
rolled his eyes Rhodry's way, as if inviting him to share his scorn for such
a show. As the oarsmen moved her out again, Enj came forward, speaking
to everyone in turn in Dwarvish, then stopped cold at the sight of Rhodry.

"Good morrow," Rhodry said. "My name's Rori."

"And I be Enj. A Deverry man, are you? I do apologize for my
surprise, but we don't see many guests here. Do let me relieve you of that
gong work."

"My thanks."

As the boat turned into open water, Rhodry got out of the way on the other side of the bow. Where Avain had taken after her mother, Enj must have favored his father, Rhodry supposed. He had the high dwarven cheekbones and flat nose, and his hair was a brown close to black, as was his close-cropped beard. Even though his eyes were green like his sister's, they were narrow, shadowed under heavy dwarven brows. As they rowed back across, Rhodry was wondering just how the son was going to react to the news that a stranger was bedding his mother. It was a complication that, he supposed, he might have thought of earlier.

On the landing the entire household waited to greet them. Enj waved to them from the boat, but as soon as he was ashore he hurried to his mother, threw one arm round her, and kissed her on the forehead. Talking urgently together they headed off toward the tower, no doubt to let Avain see him home and safe. Garin and Rhodry walked back up to the manse together and some ways behind everyone else.

"So that's Enj, is it?" Rhodry said. "He doesn't look in the least daft, not to me, anyway."

Garin seemed to be biting his tongue.

"Imph," he said at last. "I'm cursed glad to see him, I don't mind telling you. I'll spend the day negotiating with him to take up Otho's clan debt and making arrangements for the provisioning and all, and then I've got to be heading back to Lin Serr. I hope you understand, Rori. If things were different, I'd go with you, just to keep Otho civil if naught else, but as it is, with the siege and all—"

"Of course I understand. And with Mic along, the old man will behave himself somewhat."

"So we can hope."

Since it was several hours before Angmar and Enj returned to the great hall, Rhodry had a good long wonder what mother and son might be discussing. Round noon, when they walked into the great hall, servants appeared as well, to lay a meal. For a few moments everyone exchanged strained pleasantries in Dwarvish while Angmar took her usual place at the head of the table and Enj hovered near her chair. Rhodry waited near the hearth to let him have the family seat at his mother's right hand if he chose. The hall fell silent; everyone, servants and all, turned to watch the pair of them.

Enj glanced round and pointed to another chair that was standing against the wall, half-round and heavily carved. When he snapped out an order to a servant, everyone in the room who knew Dwarvish gasped in surprise. The servant picked it up and put it at the end of the table opposite Angmar. Once it was settled, Enj sat down on the bench by his mother's right hand, leaving only one place for Rhodry to sit, and glanced his way with a brief smile.

"My thanks," Rhodry said.

As he sat down in the chair that had once belonged to her husband, Angmar looked down the length of the table between them with eyes that showed no feeling at all. She remembers that I'm leaving, he thought. For a moment he nearly howled aloud in rage at the Wyrd that kept tearing his life into pieces and then shredding what few scraps of happiness he redeemed from the ruin. He wanted to jump up and run outside, screaming like a madman. Instead he picked up his tankard and had a long swallow of ale. At the signal the servants came forward and began serving food.

With the meal Garin broached the job ahead to Enj, and once everyone had finished eating, the negotiations began in earnest. Even though for courtesy's sake Garin kept the talk in Deverrian, Rhodry said little. As long as he was eventually satisfied with the settlement, the details were none of his affair, not under either of their systems of laws. Angmar, however, listened closely, murmuring a word of advice to her son every now and again—shrewd advice, too, from the way it made Otho wince. He needed it, too, since everyone there could see that he'd have gone off tracking a dragon for no repayment at all.

As the afternoon heat dragged on through this mire of haggling, Rhodry muttered a few excuses and fled. Down by the lakeshore the wind growled through the rocks and whined in the trees. Rhodry found himself a spot under a bent and twisted pine where he could sit in the cool. For a long time he stared out across the lake at the silver riband of water falling over the cliffs on the far shore. He was tired, he supposed, merely tired to the bone of all his wandering, tired of fighting in one battle after another, whether he fought with a sword or with dweomer that he didn't even really understand. Why else would he be hating the idea of leaving Haen Marn?

"Rori?" Angmar's voice, coming toward him. "Rori, be you there?"

His eyes filled with tears. He wiped them away on the back of his hand.

"I am," he called out. "Do they need me in the great hall?"

"They do. To agree to the settling of the debt."

When Rhodry picked his way through the rocks and joined her, she smiled at him, but so blandly that he knew she wished nothing of any import said aloud. He caught her hand and squeezed it.

"We'd best go back then, my lady."

"So we should, my lord."

Hand in hand openly they returned to the great hall, where a smiling Garin was standing by the hearth while Otho, Mic, and Enj sat drinking at the table. From the way Otho was belting the ale back, Rhodry assumed that the settlement had turned out high. With one last clasp of his hand, Angmar left him and went to her usual chair.

"Well, envoy," Rhodry said. "And does the settlement strike you as fair?"

"It does, though Otho may have other feelings." Garin paused for a grin. "There's the quittance fee, of course, for the assumption of clan debt by the heir of Haen Marn, and then the indemnity we pay his mother, in case some evil thing befalls him, and the replenishment of Haen Marn's stores for the provisioning of this expedition. All in all, it'll amount to a nice pair of matched gemstones for the lady of Haen Marn to tuck away safelike. However, since Enj here insists that it's best if you and he go alone, then Otho's free of the indemnity for young Mic, so he'll save a fair bit there."

When Rhodry glanced at Mic, he found the lad on the edge of tears.

"Ah now, here, Mic, if you go and 'prentice yourself to Garin, there'll be more excitements coming your way."

"So the envoy and Uncle Otho *say*."

"It truly be for the best," Enj broke in. "Where we'll be going, Rori, it's too long a road to carry even half of what we'll be needing upon it. Otho did tell me that you've got a good hand with a bow, and I've one with the fishing, but if the game be scant, feeding four or even three—" He shrugged to show the uncertainty of it.

Mic got up and stomped out of the hall.

"Lin Serr owes Gwerbret Cadmar a contingent of axmen," Garin said and very softly. "I think me our Mic's going to have more excitement than he'll like, and soon."

"No doubt we all will." Rhodry felt suddenly profoundly weary.

"Well, Otho, on the contingency that these fees be paid over promptly to Haen Marn, I hereby release you from your life's debt to me in front of these witnesses."

"Done then." With a sigh Otho stood up to shake hands. "And I agree. When we return with the provisions, and that'll be as fast as we can walk back and walk here again, the lady shall have her pick of the best gems I own."

"And I'll make sure he brings the best, too," Garin remarked to Angmar. "I can't return myself, but a man I trust will."

"I do have faith in that, envoy, for always have you dealt fairly with me and mine." She glanced at Enj. "You've done well."

After the evening meal, while Angmar tended her daughter and the envoy and his party gathered provisions for their trek home, Rhodry and Enj walked by the lake. The last light, glancing between hills, sent shades of pale gold and faint color onto the quiet water of the shallows, while across by the farther shore, the mists were rising and gathering in the coves.

"One thing worries me," Rhodry said. "Your mother's safety while we're gone. I've got enemies who might track me here, and if they do, they're dangerous. Does Haen Marn have vassals or allies round here that might owe you men?"

Enj laughed.

"There be no other dun or settlement round here for miles and miles. But Haen Marn won't be in any danger."

"Are you sure? These enemies are utterly ruthless, not human nor dwarven, either."

"Any enemy has to find a dun before they can be taking it, human or not."

"Well, true spoken, but they'll have powerful dweomer of their own on their side, powerful beyond anything I've ever seen before, certainly."

Enj considered. Rhodry could just see him frowning down at the sand.

"I'll just be going to say a good night to my sister," he said at last. "And I'll tell my mam what you've just told me."

Sometime later, Rhodry was sitting drinking with the dwarves when Angmar appeared at the door of the great hall. At her beckon he left them and joined her outside in the flickering spill of candlelight. By then the night wind had come up, sighing and snuffling round like some gigantic hound between the crooked trees.

"Rori, I would not have you worry about me and mine."

"How can I not? I'd rather turn myself over to my enemies and be done with it than bring the slightest harm to you."

"And would I not do the same for you?"

For a moment they stared at each other on the edge of anger. It was the closest they had ever come to admitting that their mutual comfort had turned to love. All at once she shook her head and smiled with a wry twist of her mouth.

"Haen Marn protects its own," she said. "I mayn't say how, because in part I know not how, but have no fear of it."

"Well, then, that gladdens my heart."

"I suppose it gladdens mine, but—"

"But what? These are evil times, my lady, and you need a shield over you."

"No doubt." Her voice shook. "But it be a baleful thing, the hefting of this shield. Pray, Rori, pray that never it be needful."

Angmar turned and strode off, heading back to the tower. Later, when they were together in their bedchamber, neither mentioned his leaving at all.

At the morrow dawn Garin, Mic, and Otho carried their gear down to the boathouse. While the boatmen fussed round, preparing for the effort of not so much getting them out as getting back in again themselves, Rhodry stood on the jetty with the three dwarves from Lin Serr. Although a feeble wind blew, the day promised suffocating heat.

"You won't be able to travel far today," Rhodry remarked.

"Not if it's like this outside," Garin said drily. "Who knows if it will be or not?"

"Well, truly. At least most of your way will be downhill."

"Just so, just so."

Leaving Mic and Otho to load their gear into the boat, Garin led Rhodry out to the end of the jetty. For a moment they stood watching the waves lapping round the pilings.

"I'll wish you the best luck in the world, Rori," Garin said at last. "I wish I could believe that you won't need it."

"My thanks. And I'll wish you a goodly share of the same, my friend. In fact, I've been thinking. I should do more for you than wish luck."

"If the Horsekin are on the move, we'll all need a fair bit more than luck." Garin glanced at the sky. "I wouldn't mind having more faith in those gods you people are always swearing by."

"Neither would I." Rhodry reached into his shirt and pulled Othara's talisman free. "Take this, will you?"

"What? And leave you exposed to enemy eyes? We don't even need the thing!"

"You do, at that. Weren't you the one who passed an ax through Alshandra's back on the road to Lin Serr?"

Garin whistled sharply under his breath.

"I'd put that out of my mind, like," Garin said. "Stupid of me."

"For Othara's sake alone, I'd have you take this stone."

Garin hesitated, and it seemed for a moment that he was about to reach for the chunk of blue; then he shook his head no.

"From everything that Jill said back in Cengarn, and the loremasters said in Lin Serr, it's on the important side, for all of us, like, to get this dragon found. There are other envoys, if worse comes to worst."

"But I—"

"Noble gestures are all very well, but it's the winning of this war that's important." Garin paused for a grin. "Silver dagger."

Rhodry smiled, more than a little ruefully, and settled the talisman back inside his shirt again.

"Besides," Garin went on. "Without you along, we dwarves can travel fast, and we can travel sneaky, like, too. I've been warned, and for that I thank you, so fear not. This hag of an Alshandra will have a good job of it, finding us, dweomer or no. Even Otho would wager a nice bit of coin on her failing."

"Well and good, then."

"Now as for you, will you be leaving today?"

"We won't, though as soon as we can. We need to ask Avain's help, and there's no rushing the lass."

Behind them the helmsman sang out in Dwarvish. When Garin held out his hand, Rhodry clasped it.

"May we meet again," Rhodry said. "But don't wager coin on that."

Garin merely nodded in a grim sort of way and strode off down the jetty to board. Rhodry waved as the boat pulled away, then turned and walked back to the island rather than watch them go.

Over the next few days Rhodry and Enj spent much time working over their gear, testing ropes, greasing canvas, drying beef and suchlike, and even more sitting with Avain in her tower room. She would fold Rhodry's ring in one hand as she peered into her basin, and judging from her flood of words, she found the dragon easily so long as she was clutching its name. As she talked, Enj would write the occasional word on a waxed tablet—landmarks, he told Rhodry, some he knew, some he didn't.

"You can't expect her to judge the directions things lie, nor the distances between them, but when she speaks of a rock face that looks like grains of wheat, I do know that place. There be others, like this valley she calls the 'Gods' Soup Bowl,' that never have I seen in my born days. But at least I know which way to head, and bit by bit we'll piece out our route in our going."

"With more than a little luck?"

"Just so."

"It's a cursed useful thing you can read and write."

"My mam saw to it that I was taught letters, both in Dwarvish and in the language of men. They did send me to Lin Serr, when I were but a lad, to learn where there be priests and books. I lodged with Envoy Garin, you see, which is why I can speak your tongue a fair bit, or better than my mother, at least, for all that she learned what she knows of it from her own mother, down in the women's quarters."

During these last few days Rhodry and Angmar both worked hardest at pretending that their time together would last an eternity. When they were together during the day, they spoke mostly of the small doings of the island, as if nothing of more import than a caught fish or a servant's twisted ankle existed in the world. Yet at night, they made love with a desperate greed, and despite the hot weather, they slept clasped in each other's arms.

In the end, of course, the last morning came, a hot, dry dawn, good traveling weather and a betrayal. Rhodry woke and slipped out of bed without waking her to sit in the window seat and watch the brightening sky while he cursed his Wyrd. In a few moments, though, she felt him gone and woke, sitting up, yawning and smiling, glancing his way, letting the smile fade when she saw the sun outside. She got up and joined him, sitting down at an angle so they could see each other's faces.

"Think you that the pair of you will find this beast?"

"Enj swears he will, now that he knows where to look, and I'll take his word for it. Your son knows more about such things than your man does."

"It be lairing north, he did tell me."

"It does, and so if we succeed, we'll be coming back this way."

She smiled a little at that, hesitating, speaking again finally in a small voice.

"And after that? I know it be needful for you to leave again, as soon as ever you can."

"It is, but I don't want to go."

"Ah. That were what I did wonder."

They shared a brief smile that made her look as weary as he felt. The wind sighed through the open window with a damp scent of pine.

"It be not too likely that ever you'll return that second time," she said at length.

"It's not likely that I'll live to return."

She swung her head round to stare at him, her lips half-parted.

"Forgive me. I should just hold my tongue."

"Nah nah nah, Rori, what think you I be, some lass to live on false hope and dreams? This thing you speak of, the dweomer war, be it as bad as all that?"

"It is, and it's only beginning. Angmar, please, believe me. If I thought there was any sound chance at all that I could return to you and Haen Marn, then I'd promise you I would."

"It means much, knowing that. I'll remember you saying this thing, when I think of you."

"Ah, ye gods, don't think of me! I'll beg you: forget me the moment I'm gone. Find yourself another man, and don't trouble your heart over me for one moment more."

"In this we be alike, Rori. I will not promise a thing I cannot fulfill."

When he held out his hand, she took it. He clasped her fingers tight in his, and for a long time they sat together, looking out over the lake without speaking, until they heard Enj calling to them from what seemed like an infinity away.

All through their last meal together her calm held, and seeing her strong he could be so as well. Even when he kissed her farewell, they smiled at each other and spoke of little things. But when the boat carrying him pulled away, turning toward the north shore of the lake, he looked back and saw her standing at the very end of the pier, doubled over with grief. He tossed back his head and keened, an animal howl of heartache that echoed round the lake louder than the thrumming of the brass gong.

At about the time Rhodry and Enj were taking ship to leave Haen Marn, Dallandra looked up through the bars of her cage in the Lands and saw that the tedious afternoon of her capture was still refusing to drag itself toward evening. She realized another thing as well, however, that she was finally beginning to recover her full complement of wits after the morning's ordeal. She sat up cross-legged in the middle of her cage, sipped the water her captors had given her, and watched the camp below. In his cage, flat on the ground, the page was pacing back and forth for the few steps allowed him either way.

Round the fire Lord Vulpine's men had spent the past hour or so drinking, passing round big skins of whatever liquor it was that their leader had left them and guzzling the stuff so fast that it darkened their green tunics. By now the ursine fellows were stretched out snoring again, the human and the wolf warriors were singing together, and the vulpine contingent stared into the flames and smiled to themselves. In a little while they'd all be drunk.

Or they would have been if it weren't for the herald, who was cold sober and sitting on the edge of the group, keeping a sharp eye on the guards and the prisoners alike. He sat with his staff across his knees, ready to poke or slap the warriors sober, and he kept up a running commentary of mingled disgust and warning, which they mostly ignored. If she'd been able to speak openly, Dalla suspected that she could have talked the old creature round to her side. He had some shreds of honor and decency, at least, some kernel of feeling for other souls that she could use as a counter to his fear of Lord Vulpine. But if she tried, the warband would doubtless take steps to silence her and the herald both.

When she stretched her sore arms above her head, the cage swung, creaking. The herald was on his feet like a shot, waggling the staff at her.

"Now don't you go trying anything," he snapped. "You just stay where you are."

"I might as well. Now that I've disarmed your lord's trap, my lord Evandar will doubtless come rescue me soon enough."

The herald moaned and trembled his wattles so violently that she realized her random arrow had struck a target.

"The army's gone off now, isn't it? Where were they hiding? Somewhere nearby, I imagine, lying in ambuscade among the trees."

The herald merely stared at her with rheumy eyes. Those of the warband still awake had fallen silent to listen. The page as well stood clutching the bars of his cage and looking up at her with hopeful eyes.

"Evandar will come marching in here with his entire host, I should imagine," Dallandra went on. "Hundreds and hundreds of them, armed and mailed, swords gleaming, and spears, too, all sharp and ready to cut you all into mincemeat. Oh, the lad and I will laugh to see it, your blood soaking into the ground, your heads all smashed in and bleeding, your guts hanging out, and all of you screaming for mercy and writhing on the ground."

With sleepy grunts the ursine fellows sat up, scratching themselves and looking round baffled.

"You're going to die," Dallandra called to them. "My lord's on his way, and he's going to kill you all."

They leapt to their feet, grabbing for weapons.

"Hold your tongue!" the herald screeched. "Don't listen to her! Our lord would never let such a thing happen."

"Hah! He's not here to protect you," Dalla said. "He's gone off and left you as sacrifices to his brother's wrath. It might go easier for him that way. Maybe by the time Evandar's done torturing you, he'll have a bit of mercy for your lord, Old Dog Nose himself."

They stared, as ensorcelled by her tale as small children by a bard when he condescends to amuse them for an hour. Dallandra was honestly shocked that her crude and clumsy ruse was working; then she remembered that they had no mind in any real sense of that word, no reason, no logic, no introspection, no ability to analyze a situation or tale. She did her best to leer.

"I'm going to help him torture you. Let's see. I shall heat a bronze knife in that fire and then lay the blade upon your flesh. It'll stink when the metal sears you and scorches all your fur away."

The wolf warrior screeched.

"Hold your tongue!" This time the herald's voice wavered badly. "You lie, elven bitch."

"Don't. You're doomed, too, old man. We'll let the page there amuse himself with you."

The boy laughed and clapped his hands, but whether he was acting a part or honestly anticipating the job she couldn't tell. The herald moaned and began chewing on the end of the staff.

"Oh, Dog Nose is gone to play," Dallandra sang. "Over the hills and far away, and Evandar shall ride where he pleases."

The wolf warrior turned to the old man and snatched his staff out of his hands.

"Go fetch him," he growled. "Go fetch our lord. You know which way he rode. Go get him back here."

With a snarl the pair of fox warriors grabbed the herald, one at each arm, and shook him. The entire warband gathered round, snarling, snapping, cursing, and shouting.

"Get him, get him, fetch him back!"

"Very well!" the herald wailed. "I will, I will. Give me my staff. Give it to me, you ugly maggots!"

When he grabbed, the human-looking fellow grabbed back, hit the wolf warrior by mistake, and got bitten for his clumsiness. Screaming and swinging they scuffled, butting at each other with heads and shoulders, flailing round with fists and paws. The herald wiggled free and rolled clear, clutching his staff, his face bleeding from long scratches.

"Hurry!" the wolf warrior swung his way. "Be gone!"

Shrieking and weeping the herald rushed into the forest, traveling in the exact same direction that the earlier messenger had arrived from, Dallandra realized. She could just see him rush between a pair of strangely identical oak trees and marked them in her mind. Down below the fighting stopped in a wail of curses, a thunder of recriminations. One of the bear warriors picked up a skin of liquor.

"Let us wash this ill feeling away," he announced. "It behooves us to behave like the brothers we are."

Dallandra watched the skin making its round and tried to calculate how far away the herald and his fragment of rational mind might be. She was painfully aware that every beat of her heart meant time passing, an hour perhaps for Jill, or even a day. Besides, what if the old man found Lord Vulpine fast and brought him back? Clutching the bars of his cage, the page stared up at her as if she were a goddess. If only she could get him out of there and away from harm without them seeing, just as Lord Vulpine had winkled the pair of them out from under Evandar's nose!

"Dolt!"

She'd spoken aloud, but fortunately the guards were too busy drinking and bickering to notice. She'd been thinking of the size of her physical-seeming body as immutable, just as it would have been back on the earthly plane, but here in the Lands no such restriction held. She raised one finger, got the page's attention, pointed to herself, then to him, repeated the motion several times since she didn't dare whisper, "Do as I do." He watched with narrowed eyes, as if he tried to understand.

Carefully she built up the linnet image in her mind, then concentrated on size. Immediately she felt her body melting, melding, changing. She clung to the image, made it smaller and smaller in her mind, felt her body shrinking as Lord Vulpine had made it shrink, was aware suddenly of the amethyst figurine as a weight pulling on her neck. She broke the image fast, flapped her wings, and took a few experimental hops forward. The cage towered round her, huge and looming. The little spaces between the wooden bars gaped—doorways. With a cock of her head she looked down and saw a tiny sparrow in the pageboy's cage.

The guards were still talking among themselves, bellowing curses on the herald, shrieking every time a twig snapped in the distant forest. Dallandra hopped to the edge of the cage, chirped to the page, and flew, swooping out over the camp, chirping again as the sparrow flapped up free to join her.

Side by side they darted toward the forest, but just as they reached the trees, Dallandra heard the wolf warrior howl. Shrieking, leaping up, their guards raced after, throwing spears, throwing rocks, cursing and screaming in rage. As the missiles tumbled by it seemed to Dallandra that they flew through falling mountains. Ahead she could see the pair of oaks and between them an unnatural veil of mist hanging like caught moss. With a chirp to the sparrow, she darted straight into it and through.

They were flying across a grassy plain, where tiny streams wound their way between hummocks of yellow flowers. Here and there at deep pools hazels and rowan grew in tangled clumps. Ahead on the horizon she could see a distant roil of smoke, such as marked the battle plain where Evandar and his brother often met. From behind them she heard howls, the baying of a wolf, the sharp yip-yip of foxes. When she risked a glance back, she saw the pack running after them, on all fours and in animal form, the wolf racing ahead, the bears lumbering after, the humanlike thing laboring along in the rear. She felt an exhalation of fear from the sparrow and knew that he'd seen them, too.

With every stroke she flew, the amethyst figurine slapped against her breast. She could feel it pulling her down, slowing her down, aching her already sore body or surrogate of one. Although she considered growing in midair, all her dweomer knowledge warned against any such foolhardy working, no matter where she might be in the vast scheme of interlocking worlds. She forced herself to think only of flying and live each moment as a single wing stroke. Although no natural wolf or fox could have outrun a bird's flight, behind the two birds the pack was gaining. With a shriek the sparrow pulled ahead in a frantic flapping of stubby wings.

Seeing him, Dallandra recovered herself. She'd been thinking like a hunted bird, but with the pageboy free, she could use her dweomer. She deliberately slowed, letting him escape ahead, then wheeled round, letting herself drop low to draw the pack after her and heading for one of the hazel thickets. In bird form she darted among the snarl of shoots and trunks, found a spot of clear ground, and landed, hopping among the twisted roots. She could hear the pack howling and grunting round and smell the bears as they began tearing at the thicket with clawed paws, pulling the withes out, rending the branches. A moment's thought, and she stood in elven form.

The pack yapped and snarled, falling back a few feet. To them she must have suddenly appeared from nowhere, standing among the knotted shafts and foliage. Dallandra threw up one hand and summoned etheric fire. Blue flames blazed round and shot from her fingers and struck the bears full in the face. Screaming, they raised up on their haunches, seemed to shimmer, and re-formed into mostly human creatures, stark naked, batting at their snouts and eyes with human hands, clawing at sparks, and yelping as the flames bit deep into their illusions of flesh. When the wolf warrior leapt for her, she flung a cloak of fire and caught him in midtransformation. Fur scorched but so did skin; a human head screamed on a wolf's body. With both hands she threw blue flames like darts, scattering them across the pack, until the foxes and the wolf creatures turned and fled, howling across the plains. The ursine warriors fought toward her through one last shower of flame, then broke and lumbered after their fellows, dragging the humanish thing with them.

Panting for breath Dallandra pushed free of the thicket and watched them run toward the wisp of dweomer mist, hanging in the far distance. Their tiny figures plunged through; it blew away. She stood alone on the grassy plain, wondering where Evandar might be. Perhaps the page had flown to find him, but most likely the boy had bolted for the only home he knew, the astral river and the gold pavilion beside it. Once again she took on bird form, but full-size, this time, so that she could safely carry her ensorcelled flesh.

In long wing strokes she flew, gliding on the air currents now and again to save her strength, toward the horizon where the yellowish-brown smoke fumed up and swirled. Underneath her flight the grassy plain gave way to rock and a rise of barren hill. With one last swoop she found herself wheeling over the battle plain, where two armies faced one another, the glittering silver swords of the Bright Court, the black enameled mail and spears of the Dark. In the little space between them Lord Vulpine sat on his black stallion, his sword raised high as he taunted his brother.

"I have her, your precious woman!" he was yelling. "Harm me, and she dies!"

His helmet tucked under one arm, his sword still in its sheath, Evandar sat dead-still, like a statue bound to a saddle.

"Heal my lands!" Lord Vulpine bellowed. "And maybe I'll give your elven bitch back to you. You'll never find her now, not where I've kenneled her."

Still his brother said not a word, merely stared, while behind him the Bright Court raged and swore, waving swords and crying vengeance. At last Evandar moved, but it was only to turn in the saddle and shout them into silence.

"Think well upon this demand!" Lord Vulpine snarled. "When the sun rises on the morrow, I'll return to this place to hear your answer."

With a smack of his sword he made his horse rear, then swung round
and led his host away, all of them howling with laughter, screeching
insults, gloating and reveling in their temporary victory. In his flaunt
Lord Vulpine never noticed a plain gray linnet circling the field and
waiting till at last his army rode out of sight, and the dust settled on the
dead brown plain.

Unmoving again, Evandar watched them go, while his court urged
their horses up round him, calling out, begging him to lead them after
into battle. With a little cry Dallandra swooped down. The court burst
out cheering, laughing and waving in their turn, as she circled Evandar's
horse once, landed before him, and transformed herself into elven shape.
He stared at her for a long moment, saying nothing. All at once she
realized that he wept.

"My love," he whispered. "Are you truly free?"

"I am. Did you think they could hold me?"

He tossed back his head in a howl of berserk laughter that reminded
her of Rhodry Maelwaedd, then kicked one foot free of his stirrup and
reached down his hand. When she mounted behind him, he twisted
round in the saddle and gave her one quick kiss.

"Vengeance first!" He turned again, holding out his hand, grasping
from the air his silver horn. "After them!"

The court answered his cascade of silver notes with a war cry. Yelling,
waving swords, they galloped across the battle plain, where far ahead,
warned by the clamor, the Dark Court swung to meet them. Evandar
raised the silver horn and blew the command to hold their ground and
form ranks. In a milling mob his warriors pulled their horses to a halt,
howling their disappointment, while in front of them the army of the
Dark Court did the same.

"Brother!" Evandar called out. "What do you think of this, little
brother? I have my woman back, don't I now?"

Lord Vulpine screamed and turned to flee, but too late. Evandar
flung up one hand and made a circling motion widdershins in the air.
The ground beneath the Dark Court shuddered and began to split open,
with a crack like breaking sticks but so loud it seemed an entire forest
snapped. Round in a circle the widening fissure raced, ringing Lord Vulpine and all his men, penning them inside a vast ditch. Dust plumed,
rocks and clods flew and fell, the Dark Court shrieked and begged for

mercy as the very earth under them pitched and buckled. Horses fell, kicking and neighing; the warriors plunged to the ground and clung to dirt with fingers and claws while the Bright Court laughed and hooted.

Evandar lowered his hand and let it rest on the saddle peak. As the clouds of dust blew away, Dallandra could see the Dark Court, huddled and clutching one another atop an island of solid ground, barely large enough to hold them all. Round this island stretched not a sea, but nothing at all—empty space, a blackness, a depth of naught, falling, reaching, stretching down to a view of distant stars like flecks of ice in a black sky, but stars such as Dallandra had never seen before, because they shone steadily without the slightest twinkling or glint. Evandar urged the horse up to their side of the abyss. After one long exhalation of fear, the Bright Court fell dead-silent behind them. Dallandra had to admit to herself that she felt none too brave, either. She clung tightly to her lover's waist and refused to look down at the distant stars.

"Now," Evandar said mildly. "Let us talk, brother, shall we?"

With a shriek and clatter the Dark Court sprang up and flew. A huge flock of ravens wheeled once, sweeping round its pinnacle of land. For a moment black feathers beat against some invisible wall. As the birds fell back, trapped, taking their usual half-human, half-animal forms, Dallandra realized that there were far fewer of them. Only those with some real consciousness would survive such an ordeal, she supposed.

"Brother! I called you forward, did I not?"

Weeping and trembling, stripped of his fine armor and weapons, Lord Vulpine stepped to the edge of his side of the abyss.

"I will have retribution for this," Evandar called out. "For the pain you've caused my woman and for the mocking of me."

"All my lands are yours, and my vassals as well."

"The lands were mine anyway, and I don't want your stinking pack of monsters. Tell me your name."

Lord Vulpine howled in agony.

"Not that, never that."

Evandar snapped his fingers. A chunk of the Dark Court's island prison broke free and tumbled into the abyss, vanishing as it did so in a scatter of brown dirt that in turn dissolved into naught.

"Your name, brother."

"No!"

Another cliff slid down and crumbled to disappear. The remnant of the Dark Court's army howled and wept, rushing to the center of their island, pushing and jostling one another in their greed to escape the edge.

"Brother, your name. You tricked me out of mine, and now I shall have yours in amends."

The fox warrior sneered and crossed his arms over his chest, glaring at Evandar in silent defiance. The creatures behind him began to beg and weep. Evandar hesitated, then with a flick of his fingers sent a chasm tearing through the prison, separating the warriors from their leader.

"You have one last chance," Evandar said. "Tell me or I'll hurl you back into the chaos you were born from."

His brother spun round, staring at the fissure, staring at his army, as if he'd been counting on Evandar's pity for his men to protect him as well. His own court began to jeer and mock him, taunting him for his weakness, calling out their allegiance to Evandar instead, until the fox warrior howled at them.

"Some dweomer do I have yet, and I'll kill you all myself!"

They fell silent at that and crouched, watching Evandar across the gulf.

"Brother—the name!"

The fox warrior spun back, throwing his head from side to side as slowly, one crumble, one split at a time, the tiny pinnacle of land round him began to fall away, first from behind his feet, then to his left, to his right, then the last little sliver in front of him, till he stood paralyzed with horror on barely enough ground to support both feet.

"Shaetano," he screamed. "And curse you and your elven whore both!"

Evandar laughed aloud and snapped his fingers. With a roar like flooding water the island of land rushed out, spreading to meet the solid ground round it as the fissure healed. Screaming and cursing the Dark Court fled, leaping over the last little crack and racing away in the billowing dust. Only Shaetano remained, sinking to his knees, cringing, weeping, and snarling all at once as he tossed his head this way and that.

"Tell me somewhat," Evandar said. "Who's the elder, you or I?"

He looked up, black eyes glittering, seemed to be about to speak, drew out his silence as long as he dared.

"You," he snarled at last.

"Good. Remember that from now on. Without me, little brother, you'd cease to exist. Defy me again, and I'll ensure that you cease to exist. Now go! I have your name. You'll have to come when I call you now, just as I had to come when you called me, and we shall see, my fine Shaetano, how you like of the feel of it."

He snarled, rose to his feet, the red roach of hair bristling, his clawed russet paws swiping out in a futile gesture. For a moment he tensed on the edge of a spring, then turned and strode off, walking fast, head held high, after his routed court.

"Shaetano?" Dallandra said. "What sort of name is that?"

"I've no idea. A thing he picked up during his wanderings in some other world, I suppose, like the rags and tatters creature he is, rooting through some other world's dung heap for a scrap to eat. What matters is that I know it, you know it, we all know it now." Evandar paused for a laugh. "And we shall continue our hunt beyond his power to stop us."

The Bright Court cheered, but Dallandra caught his shoulder.

"My love, wait! I've got to get to Jill."

He twisted round in the saddle and scowled at her.

"I can't stay," Dallandra snapped. "I absolutely must go to Jill's country. How much time has passed for her?"

"How would I know?"

"Then I'd best find out, hadn't I?"

"I suppose so."

"You *suppose* so? You do know, don't you, that Alshandra's led an army down the mother of all roads?"

"I do. That's why I summoned the court and rode to the border, to look for her, and there I found my wretched brother instead, all puffed up and gloating."

"Well, then! Alshandra must be trying to harm Elessario's mother, back in Cengarn."

"Oh, I'd never argue with you. Why do you think I want to go a-hunting, to flush Alshandra out of my brother's lands? Think about this, my love. She's led one stinking pack through my country to work harm elsewhere, but no one's seen her since. What if she's gone off to gather another?"

"Oh, ye gods! I never thought of that."

"I did," he said with a smug little smile. "I want to keep you with me and safe while I hunt for her."

"Danger or no, I've got to reach Jill. She can't keep a city safe all on her own. She has to sleep, sometime or other, if naught else."

"Well, true, but—"

"Evandar, she needs me."

"Indeed? So do I."

"What is wrong with you? Elessario's in danger. Your daughter! You do remember her, don't you?"

"Indeed I do, and my heart aches from the missing of her, but she's gone from me. No matter whether she lives this life long or dies soon to be reborn again, she rides the wheel now."

"True, but—"

"Hush. Of course I still love her and fear for her, and I'll do all I can for her, too, but I don't want you gone!"

"And I don't want to leave you, but I must."

She twisted round, swung a leg free, and slid inelegantly down over the rump of the horse, which stamped and shied. She nearly fell headlong, in fact, but she caught a stirrup just in time and steadied herself. He leaned over to stare, utterly bewildered. The stallion tossed his head and snorted in a scatter of foam.

"Evandar, please, try to understand. I can't simply do what I'd rather do. If I could, I'd stay with you. I love you."

"If I were in danger, would you put your joy aside and come after me?"

For a moment she thought him jealous; then she realized that he was, indeed, honestly trying to understand.

"I would," she said. "I'd leave the best feast in the world, the happiest day, to come after you."

"Because you love me?"

"Because I love you."

Evandar considered for a long moment. Finally he dismounted, calling to one of his warriors to come tend his horse. A blue-eyed fellow, more human than otherwise, took the reins and led the stallion some paces away. Evandar watched them go, and he seemed to be studying his court, too, as they sat slouched and waiting on their own mounts.

"Answer me one thing," he said without turning round. "When I gave my brother the whistle, he used my mercy against me by capturing you. Now I've spared him again. Will I regret that mercy as well?"

"I have no idea. It was still the right thing to do. What made you forgive him?"

"Forgive him? I've not forgiven him one wretched thing, my love, not one shred of his black deeds, not one jot of the harm he worked you. Someday I'll take my payment for all of it, and he'll not find joy in my doing so, I promise you."

The quiet way he spoke made her shudder.

"Well, then, why didn't you just destroy him when he was groveling in front of you?"

Evandar started to speak, then hesitated, thinking.

"I'll tell you the truth." He turned to face her. "Instead of a riddle, the truth, and then you shall know I love you, because I don't speak cold truth as easily as all that. I need him."

Dallandra goggled, speechless.

"Without me he'd cease to live, just as I told him. But I suspect, my love, deep in my heart I even believe, that without him I'd die myself. Light and shadow, my love, shadow and light. Can there be one without the other? Or hot without the cold, and moist without the dry, fire without water, air without earth? And so I call him brother, because it's true, because we were born a pair, though I'm the elder, because light leaps from the candle flame before the shadow hits the wall."

"I see. And who then lit the candle?"

"That, my love, is a riddle I can't answer. I wouldn't even presume to try. Perhaps those beings your people call gods? Ah, I see from your face that you can't answer it, either. Well, mayhap one day I'll know, but until then it matters little to me." All at once he smiled and turned away, calling to his court. "Wait for me! I'll return in but a little space of time, before you truly know I've gone."

To Dallandra he held out his hand.

"Let us go to Jill, then, since you want to and for no reason more."

She took his hand and allowed him to lead as they walked slowly, deliberately, across the dusty ground. Round them the mist gathered, an opalescent, shimmering mist all light-shot and silvery.

"Mind your step," Evandar said, and rather slyly.

When she glanced down she found a flight of broad stairs, a flow of white marble between walls of gray mist. She looked up and found him grinning like a pleased child.

"I thought I'd make the way easier than usual."

"My thanks, my lord." She made a little curtsy. "There's something about these stairs that makes me feel like a great lady."

"I modeled them upon those in the king's summer palace in Rinbaladelan."

She laughed, glad of a moment's wit and grace before they braved the next battle in their peculiar war. As hand in hand they walked down the staircase, she thought for a moment that she heard music and laughter, the lilt of many harps in some vast room and many voices raised in song, a reminder of better times and peaceful days. The mist whirled, lightened, blew away. Dallandra took one last step down into Jill's tiny chamber, where the dweomermaster sat at her table, fallen asleep over one of her books, her head pillowed on her arms.

"There she is." Evandar's voice was already fading. "When I have news of Alshandra, I'll return."

And then he was gone, relinquishing her to the world of men and elves, caught in the grip of Time and Time's daughter, Death.

6

CAPUT DRACONIS

Some loremasters say that this figure signifies great blessings no matter into which house it falls—save the House of Salt. I myself have grave doubts, for all know that he who would ride a dragon must risk a great burning.

The Omenbook of Gwarn, Loremaster

"I WAS WONDERING ABOUT SOMEWHAT," Rhodry said. "What makes you so eager to see this dragon? Just the glamour of the beast?"

"A fair question," Enj said. "But it be more than that."

In striped shadow they were perched side by side on an outcrop of black basalt like an overturned boat. Behind them rose forest; before, nothing, just a long fall of cliff down, down, down to a tiny riband of water among minuscule trees in a valley below. Far across that rift and to the west another cliff climbed, leveling off to forest. Mountain flanks rose, green-gray waves of a sea, fogged with resinous mist.

"It be due to my father," Enj said abruptly. "He taught me all I know, you see, about the great wyrms, and truly, he did know a great deal, because he found them beautiful. Once when he were very young, he saw a black one flying over Haen Marn, or so he told me, and never could he forget the sight. So down in Lin Serr he studied lore, finding much in books as well as in various tales from bards and priests."

"I didn't realize that the dwarves had lore books. Well, I couldn't have read them anyway, I suppose, when I was there."

"Oh, there's a book hold in Lin Serr, Rori, that's as big as the manse back home in Haen Marn. From what my father did tell me, he spent a long time there, studying dragon lore. But then he came to regret it, not that he should have. You see, when my sister was born, and it came clear that she were, well, so strange, he felt it was his fault."

"What?"

"Oh, it's a daft idea, his blaming of himself, and it did distress my mother sorely, as well you can imagine. Because he'd spent all that time brooding about dragons and talking about dragons and suchlike, he was convinced that he'd somehow summoned a dragon soul to be born into his daughter's body."

Rhodry could only gape at him. Enj looked away, his voice turning unsteady.

"He drowned soon after, of course. I was about a score of summers old, so I remember him well. I loved him well, too. Often we'd take a boat over to shore and go off for days together, hunting. We'd take dogs and bows, you see, and hunt the deer and wild sheep to feed the island. And while we made our nights' camps, he'd tell me tales about dragons, and how his heart ached, just from longing to see another one fly."

"And so you want to fulfill his quest?"

"Just that."

"Well, you know, if you could pass that lore on to me, I'd be truly grateful. It would be a shame to have him gone, and only one person knowing his lore."

"True." Enj's voice choked. "And I will."

They sat together in silence for a few minutes more, until Enj wiped his eyes on his sleeve and stood, stepping back cautiously from the edge.

"And now it be best we get on our way. If we follow the rim of this valley, it should lead us to the waterfall that Avain saw in her basin, and then we'll know we're heading the right way."

Rhodry and Enj had left Haen Marn when the moon was just waxing full. By the time that they were speaking of Enj's father (and this was also about the time that Dallandra reached Jill's chamber), the moon was past her third quarter. Some days earlier, they'd left the hill country behind for the flanks of the mountains. Although Rhodry had been dreading the climb, paradoxically enough it was in one way easier going than the hills. Though the slopes rose so steeply that at times they walked bent double, leaning upon sticks, once they crossed in to high timber the underbrush thinned out. Huge firs of the kind the dwarves call "mountain grays," taller than any pillar in a High King's hall, rose straight and dark, dropping a blanket of dead needles the color of dried blood, thick and spongy underfoot. Although bringing a pack animal through would have been close to impossible, especially since there was no green fodder to speak of, two men could pick their way at a reasonable pace.

"There be little that can grow here, such be this ground," Enj remarked. "I don't know why, but it's as if the firs claim these mountains for themselves alone and choke out any usurpers."

Along the streams, of course, a tangle of shrubs and seedlings fought for water and sun both. In and among them Enj found edible herbs of various sorts as well as fish. Whenever they camped, they set wire snares for rabbits and rodents to supplement what flatbread and cheese they were carrying on their backs. They needed every extra bite they could forage. The forest stretched on and on, a sea indeed, rolling over the high mountains and plunging down into the rare valley. Rhodry felt like a swimmer, making his way underwater to bob up now and then for a view. Whenever they came to the rim of a valley or scrambled over an outcrop of rock, he would always look north, where the white peaks floated far above, still as unreachable as ever, even though he walked among them.

As they worked their way higher, the nights started turning cold, even though their short length told them it was summer still. On dry days they would scrounge dead wood for a fire. Enj was always on the lookout as well for rotting leaves and desiccated needles to augment the meager supply of tow and rotted rags in their tinderboxes. Since Rhodry's entire life had been spent either in towns or along the roads leading between them, how well Enj lived in the woods filled him with admiration.

"This be my home," Enj said simply. "Never have I felt Haen Marn as home since the night my father did drown."

"Well, you still have my thanks from the bottom of my heart. Without you I'd never be able to do this, Wyrd or no Wyrd. Never have I known a woodsman like you, never."

Enj looked away fast, blushing round the ears, then glanced at him smiling.

As they traveled Enj scouted for the landmarks his sister had seen in her silver basin. One after another they found them, the rock face eroded in a pattern like an ear of ripe wheat, the hundred-foot-tall fir, dead some twenty years at least, that still stood stark and black on a hilltop, an enormous boulder split by ancient ice with a young tree growing 'twixt the two halves. Other subtler markers came and went, an oddly shaped hill, a pattern of trees, a waterfall that seemed to break in two round rock. Yet the day came when they reached the last of them, if indeed the outcrop they found really did look like a hound's head. Avain might have seen a resemblance; they were both unsure.

"Hound or no, it does provide shelter from the wind," Enj said. "So let's make camp here."

They set out snares, then scavenged for firewood. While Enj split their haul with their hand ax, Rhodry scrambled to the top of the putative hound's head and stood looking round. They were on a slope downhill to their line of march, and to the west he could see a fair ways into the bluish haze of a summer forest.

"Enj! Here's an odd thing! I see hills, flanks of the big peak due north, but then I think there's a plain of some sort. It's too cursed big to be a mountain meadow or suchlike, way at the horizon."

The ringing of the ax stopped.

"You be the one with elven eyes, not me," Enj called up. "Do the peaks rise again on the far side, like?"

"It's too far to tell." Rhodry shaded his eyes with his hand. "Looks flat, and oddly barren. You don't know what it might be?"

"I've never traveled this far in my life. Truly, I'd wager that no man nor dwarf neither has ever walked this far north."

All at once Rhodry felt dizzy. He slid down from his lookout and sat down in the shade of the outcrop, and as he did so, he patted the firm ground just to make sure it was still there. Enj sank the ax into a log.

"If it be round, that valley might be the 'Gods' Soup Bowl' that Avain kept mentioning."

"It looked long and narrow, actually."

"Well, then, I don't know." He grinned, suddenly as sunny as his sister. "Let's go see, shall we, and be the first men in the world to walk there."

"That would mean somewhat to you, wouldn't it?"

"Oh, as much as jewels and gold, truly. I do see that you don't care in the least."

Rhodry shrugged.

"If I weren't heartsick with worry over this siege, it would mean more. For all I know, Cengarn's fallen to her enemies by now, and me stuck here without one thing to do to save her."

"My apologies. I keep shoving that horror out of my mind, like. Well, then, Rori, on the morrow, let's keep moving in the direction of this mysterious plain, but if you can't see any peaks by the time we camp, then we'll have to turn back. We won't be finding our dragon anywhere but near a fire mountain."

"Truly? Why?"

"That be where they lair in the winter. They be cold-blooded, the great wyrms, and in the winter they'd die without some source of heat."

"I see. I wish we had some scouts to send ahead of us. You know, here's an odd thing! In all of our traveling, I've not seen Wildfolk, not a single gnome or sprite or suchlike at all. Usually they come round me, and every now and then one will run me an errand, too."

"Well, they shun me." Enj smiled, but ruefully. "We Mountain People can see them, but they dislike us, and so I suppose they're avoiding you because I be here."

"Then that's why I never saw them swarming round Avain. Usually they like a person who shows dweomer talent."

"Do they? I didn't know that. You know, when Avain scried, she kept holding the ring, and without the ring she saw little enough. You've elven blood in your veins, and you wear the dragon's name. Can't you scry for it?"

"Not in the least, or I would have."

"Well, true, and my apologies. I just feel that somehow we're missing some thing or other that would help us."

And they needed every scrap of help they could get, Rhodry realized. After they'd eaten, while the late sun still shone golden over the plain far to the west, he climbed the outcrop again and stood staring into the view. The longer shadows of sunset did seem to pick out mountain peaks on the other side of the mysterious plain, though far away, as sharp as cat's teeth, these, if indeed mountains they were. He was painfully aware that he and Enj could wander in this unknown range for months, circling round their dragon, even, or missing the beast by a scant mile or two. When he lowered his hand, the ring glinted a reminder.

"Here, Enj, don't think I've lost my wits, but I think me I'll try calling our wyrm."

It took him a moment to remember what Jill had taught him, and he slipped the ring off, too, to make sure he had each elven letter right in his mind. First he mouthed the words to get the feel of it again, Arzosah Sothy Lorezohaz; then he gathered himself, took a deep breath, and intoned the name.

"Ar Zo Sah Soth Ee Lor Ez O Haz."

In the silent mountains, hushed with sunset, the name boomed out like a gong. Like a gong the sound lingered, quivering to a long stop. For a moment he felt nothing but foolish. Down below Enj was staring gape-mouthed.

"Do it again, Rori," he whispered. "I've never heard anyone but a priest do that."

Rhodry gathered himself again, and this time he imagined himself on the brink of some crucial battle.

"Ar Zo Sah Soth Ee Lor Ez O Haz."

A blare of sound, this time, like the brass horns in the Dawntime style that Deverry priests blow at Samaen, humming and vibrating as much as it trumpeted over the valley, echoing round, racing, it seemed, to the horizon itself. The answer came, a touch, an awareness, a feel of a mind, an alien mind upon his. The dragon lived, and not far, not far measured by the distance they'd already come. He could feel its disquiet— not a fear, certainly, nothing so strong as that—but an ill ease, a wondering that some thought it couldn't understand had touched its mind.

As he shaded his eyes and stared toward the sunset plain, he knew that the wyrm laired to the west. He tossed back his head and laughed his berserker's howl, the mad chortle echoing round the hills, but yet it sounded almost normal after the intoning of that name. Still grinning, he slid down again and clapped his hand on Enj's shoulder.

"We go west. You'll walk upon that plain, lad, just like you wanted."

In but two days more they had solid evidence to match his dweomer knowledge, when they reached the high plain, a sliver of land caught between two ranges. As they hiked down the last slope leading to it, the first thing they noticed was the change in the trees—still the gray mountain fir, but stunted, with scant branches that drooped more and more the nearer they went to the peak. Rhodry found himself sniffing the air like a dog, finally realized what he'd been scenting.

"Ye gods," he said. "The air stinks of brimstone."

"It does, at that." Enj paused to sniff as well. "Just now and again, like, when the wind comes from the due west."

They exchanged a grin and trudged on.

Toward evening they came down at last onto the plain. Rhodry had been prepared for something grim and blasted, but instead it looked ordinary enough at any distance away. As they hiked through, however, they saw that the long stretch of grass grew scant and pale round black rocks, sticking up through thin soil. What few trees there were stood twisted and sickly. Enj hunkered down and dug his fingers deep into the soil, then held up a black and oddly glossy handful, as if it had started life as cinders.

"My father often told me that in the end, the grass and trees take back the land from a fire mountain. It must be happening here."

"Truly, and look, there it is."

At the north end of the valley soared a mountain the like of which Rhodry had never seen. Just like the multiple brochs of a great lord's dun, it seemed formed of three peaks fused together—the highest, a truncated cone, rising snowcapped between a much lower, shambling pair, which looked as if their tops had been bitten off by some unimaginably huge beast. The slopes rose dark, striped here and there with trees, here and there creviced with shadow. A thin mist hung at the apex.

"Smoke?" Rhodry said.

Enj merely shrugged, staring fascinated at the volcano.

"I think your dweomer did lead us here," he whispered at last. "Even if I should die tonight, seeing this mountain would have made the journey worthwhile."

It was, Rhodry supposed, very beautiful, but still, he couldn't understand Enj's fascination. He himself would have preferred a view of the High King's palace or suchlike any day.

"I see water over there," Rhodry said. "Let's hope it doesn't reek of brimstone, too."

They camped that night between the mountain's feet. For the first time since Othara had given him the talisman, Rhodry dreamt, these long and vivid dreams of flying far above the earth, of seeing trees and mountains swoop by underneath as his vision wheeled and soared. Yet along with the delight worry touched the dreams, a faint dread, a wondering if danger lay nearby. He woke suddenly at dawn and lay in his blankets, hands tucked underneath his head, while he stared at the peaks rising above. As the light brightened, deepening the shadows, he could pick out fissures and strange long formations of rock, twining down the mountainside like rivulets of black water between green-gray banks of trees. Here and there the rock pooled as well or made boulders shaped like drops, the record of ancient splashes from a time when the mountain had spilled liquid rock like metal from a blacksmith's spoon. As he studied the slopes, he felt the earth tremble under him, just for a few beats of a heart before it stilled.

"The land of blood and fire," he whispered.

Rhodry sat up and began to study the two side cones. Not only were they lower, the left somewhat more than the right, but they were far more deeply eroded, with the leftward the most heavily forested of the three. The left, then, would probably offer the easiest way up. Given how tired they were, and how little food they had left, it would be best if their first choice were the correct one. He considered calling the dragon to see if he could form some impression of its direction, then realized that to do so would warn it.

Enj woke soon after, and he'd also been worrying about their route. After a scant breakfast of squirrel caught and roasted the day before, they discussed which of the two lower peaks to climb.

"Or should we climb either, for that matter," Rhodry said. "I feel in my very soul that the dragon's up there somewhere, but that's not a rational thought or suchlike. I'd hate to have you depend upon it."

"What else do we have to depend on? I think, Rori, that if you're meant to have this wyrm, then we'll find it easily, and if you're not, well, then, we'll die no matter which way we go."

"Imph. An unlovely thought, that, but I think me you speak true. What we need is an omen. Too bad Otho's not along to cast us a geomancy."

Enj laughed, then went back to studying the mountain. Even though the day was growing sunny and hot, the gray mist still hung at the highest peak. Rhodry rose to his feet and walked a few steps away.

"Well, if there's truly dweomer at work here, then we can invent our own way to take omens, and it'll be good enough. If there isn't dweomer at work, well, then, we're doomed." Laughing, he drew his silver dagger and held it up. "May the gods look down and decide!"

Remembering a chance remark of Jill's, he made sure that he was moving deosil, then spun round and round like a child playing a game. When, after a few dizzy-making turns, he saw out of the corner of his eye the high peak flashing toward him, he let the dagger fly. It arched up, winking in the sun, and fell pointing straight at the leftward of the two low and broken peaks.

"Done, then!" Enj called out. "We'll see what the gods have in store for us."

It took them all day to work their way up the leftward slope. The morning, or so Enj said, they spent learning how to climb, inching from crack to crack, from patch of scrub wood to fissure. Much to Enj's relief they did find decent water, tinged with sulfur and warm, but drinkable, in the occasional pool or cranny. On the lower slope they could make steady if slow progress; by noon they could look back at the plain below and see the trees as tiny marks on barren ground. They rested crammed into a more or less horizontal fissure where trees as gnarled as gnomes were breaking black rock apart, and moss and lichen lay thick, a green if slimy carpet.

After a scant meal they started again. The upper slope rose so smoothly that it seemed they climbed for hours yet traveled not a mile. Up and ever up they went, bent double against the angle, eyes fixed on the next barren streak of black rock, the next patch or pocket of thin soil, slippery with dead grass. All round them the wind gusted this way or that, tainted with brimstone and ancient ash. At last, just when Rhodry's legs seemed to be melting into water, he glanced up to see a horizon of sorts hanging above him—the blackish line of the rock face against blue sky where it lipped over to flatten. When Rhodry hauled himself over, he found another slope ahead, but this one slanted down, broken here and there with flattish spots where a scrawny tree or two lifted its bare branches.

"Almost there," Enj panted. "Hang on."

They rested for a few moments, blowing for breath, pushing back sweaty hair from their foreheads, then settled their packs and moved on. As the slope became a proper cliff top, Rhodry got a glimpse of what lay ahead, a huge rise of distant cliffs, as flat and circling as Lin Serr's wall, with the snowy peak beyond catching full sun, but it wasn't till they reached the edge that he could see the entire view.

"Ye gods," he whispered. "Ye gods."

In front of him the ridge they'd been following dropped away for hundreds of yards to a vast valley floor, unrolling on and on to the distant rise of precipice that had once been the inside of a mountain. These cliffs formed a semicircle, just as if they were the rim of an enormous drinking bowl made of clay, but one ruined on the wheel by a slip of the potter's thumb, that is, the depression where they'd crawled over. Rhodry shook his head, trying to imagine what had made this crater. Over the lip of cold rock on which he now stood fire and liquid rock had once run like wine spilling from the deformed bowl, and the rock had bubbled, too, just like boiling water. He found it hard to believe, yet he knew that Enj's father had taught the truth of the matter. The bottom of the bowl now formed the living valley, covered with grass in places and dotted with trees that flamed red and gold, as if in homage to their home's fiery birth. Autumn came early, he supposed, at this height.

"The God's Soup Bowl," Enj said, grinning.

"It is! Avain was right, after all."

"Good name for it, truly. Lacks a certain poetry, mayhap."

"Whatever we call it, it's huge."

"A fair two mile across at least, I'd say." Enj held up a thumb at arm's length to help himself gauge. "Hard to tell. And those cliffs there at the other lip must stand a good mile above the floor. That be a wretched piece of luck."

"Why?"

"We've got to get over them, that's why. Look, you can just see the apex, rising behind the far cliff. The fire must have burst out partway up the mountain's side first, and as for how long ago, I don't know if we have a word big enough. Then it would have burst out on that other cone, a little closer to our own day."

"And now we've got the peak itself to worry about."

"Worry? I—er, truly. If that thing should blow while we're here . . ."

They stood for a moment, staring at the peak with its scarf of gray mist, whether smoke or cloud, they couldn't tell.

"If we need to be round, hadn't we best just go round?" Rhodry said. "Not go down to the valley at all, I mean."

"Use the cliff tops as kind of a road? You be probably right enough, but I don't fancy camping out here tonight, clinging to this slope like a fly on a tankard."

"Why not? We've slept on worse."

Enj hesitated, staring up at the clear sky while he chewed on his lower lip.

"We're dead tired already," Rhodry said. "If we start down now, and slip or suchlike—"

Enj went on staring at the sky and said nothing. Rhodry waited in silence.

"I was just thinking," Enj said at last. "Suppose the creature be out hunting, and here we be, out walking, where there be neither tree nor overhang for a good mile."

Rhodry started to speak, then merely laughed. Enj winced.

"Ye gods, Rori, when you laugh like that it does creep my flesh. Now, if we head round to the west here for a ways, we might be able to take that slope down. See over there? There's a fissure, like."

In the direction of the fissure, the cliff top seemed to be sloping down somewhat, shortening the distance they'd have to climb, or so Rhodry hoped. Although he'd rested enough to keep going, he could feel his legs and feet aching in stripes of pain along every long muscle. Up in the lead, Enj suddenly cried out and threw up an arm for the halt.

"Now that do be what I call a dropoff! Come up and have a look."

Down at the bottom of an enormous shaft lay a lake, at least a hundred yards across. The pit looked like a giant finger hole, poked by a god, perhaps, into wet earth that had then turned to rock round the poke and caught the rain. From the rim where they stood, cliffs of the usual dark gray stone fell straight as a plumb line down to the water, some hundred feet below. Wisps of steam rose and floated on the surface.

"Somewhat nasty lives in that, I'll wager," Rhodry remarked. "A demon, most like. A pack of evil spirits at the least."

"We're not going to hang about long enough to find out. Quick march."

Once they reached the crack in the cliff face, the eroded slope within its walls did seem more forgiving, a possible though not gentle angle down. Enj studied it for a long moment, then turned to Rhodry.

"What do you think?"

"You're the leader here."

"I think we can manage if we start right now. It's needful that we reach the valley floor before it turns dark."

They did, but only just. They climbed roped, with Rhodry in the lead and the experienced Enj at the rear to anchor the team should he fall. Every yard gained was a matter of careful thought, of a long look down to gauge not only the possible hand- and footholds at the particular spot but whether or not other holds existed farther along the proposed route. They only had to retrace their route once, and even then, if Rhodry hadn't been along, the dwarf might have managed to inch himself past the bad spot. As it was, with a cheerful "better delayed than dead," Enj ordered them back and round to a safer, if slower, route. About halfway down they passed from sun into shade. By the time they stood safely on the flat, the valley floor lay in night, though the very tops of the caldera walls jutted into the gilding sun. Beyond them the volcano's peak, just visible from this angle, shone gold tinged with pink.

"I see a stream over yonder," Rhodry said. "Judging by all those trees. What are they, anyway?"

"I call them mountain larch, but I know not what a loremaster would say to that. I be ready to camp, I tell you. We might be able to scrounge enough dead wood for a fire."

"I wonder if we dare light one."

"True spoken. Well, a summer night without a fire never killed a man."

As they walked on, heading straight toward the center of the bowl, they both kept a good watch, turning their heads constantly, glancing up at the sky often, but the valley lay in the deep silence of coming night.

"I don't suppose the dragon would lair right out here, anyway," Rhodry said at last. "All the tales I ever heard said caves."

"In where it be warm, near the fire in what's left of this mountain, I'd wager. Deep in its belly, most like."

"Not what you'd call a safe place to make your home, then."

"Not for us. Safe enough for a dragon. These ancient fire mountains be full of flues and passages, all smooth and round, where the molten rock poured out fast and left its skin behind like a shedding snake. That outer bit, the skin if you would, hardens to leave a proper tunnel. And heat rises into caverns. They were big bubbles in the melt once, most of them. The wyrm will have found one of those cozy spots to lair in."

"Maybe so, but the mountain could blow again, if it's not dead." Rhodry glanced round, with a cold shudder as he tried to imagine what sort of eruption it would take to gut half a mountain this way. "The dragon couldn't trust it."

"The great wyrms do share a soul with the fire mountains, or so the tales say. Deep, deep in their hearts a fire of their own does burn, just as fire burns deep in the mountains, and there in their hearts they understand each other. The wyrms know when the mountain sleeps and when it's about to rouse. The mountain itself will warn them, like, because at root they're brothers." Then he laughed. "But my father, he did say that the beasts have splendid hearing, that's all, and sensitive bellies. When they plop themselves smack down on the bedrock, they can hear the melted rocks gurgling and scraping below and feel the mountain trembling under them. They learn to judge the noises, he always said, like a midwife with her ear on a pregnant woman's paunch."

"I prefer your way of speaking, but no doubt he was right."

Enj grinned and started to speak, then fell silent, raising a warning hand. By then they'd reached the shelter of the first ratty-looking trees, stunted and half-bald as well, but some sort of cover. They froze, straining to hear, as the sound that had caught their attention came again, distant and more the impact of a sound than a noise. To Rhodry it seemed like the slap of hand on a drumhead when the goatskin cover's got loose with age—a distant thwack, all spongy, but throbbing again and again, and closer and louder until it resolved itself into the beat of enormous wings against still air. Automatically they both looked up, peering through the branches.

Black against the sky, its legs curled under but its tail flung out for a rudder, the dragon flew over the valley. For a dozen strokes its huge naked wings beat the air; then they held steady, and it glided, dipping down straight for the cliffs on the far side, turning a little toward a vast rock formation shaped like a pillar stuck to the cliff by its length. With a smack and rustle of folding wings, it settled. For a moment they could see it clinging to the flume like a woodpecker clinging to a tree trunk. In the darkening light, judging accurately was near impossible, but Rhodry guessed it thirty feet long, not counting its tail. With a little shake it squirmed; the tail whipped; the dragon disappeared inside some crack or cave that not even his half-elven eyes could find. Enj let out his breath in a long sigh. He looked like a man who's just seen his beloved appear briefly at a window, then pull the shutters closed.

"Lucky, aren't we?" Rhodry whispered. "They must hunt by sight, not smell."

"So my father always said." Enj was whispering as well. "So it be not lairing in the high peak, then."

"Let's hope not, but it may have found some passageway through and up. Think we could climb to that hole?"

"Mayhap, but I'll tell you this, Rori. I don't much like the idea of crawling right in after it."

"I've never agreed with a man more. What about a back door, like? The base of those cliffs look as full of holes as a wormy cheese."

"In the morning it'll be worth a look. If we work our way from tree to tree, we'll be safe enough. Maybe."

It was late that night before either of them could sleep. Even though it was quite likely that the dragon had just fed, since it had flown home to lair, this was not a probability either wanted to put to the test. For some time they sat under the trees and talked in low voices about the problem of getting near enough to the beast for Rhodry to enchant it.

"You'll need a few ticks of a heart at least," Enj said. "To call its name in the right way and all."

"Just so, and a place to sit or stand where I can get a good lungful of air, too."

Enj considered for a moment.

"Since they hunt by sight, we should make a run for the base of the cliff now."

"Good thinking," Rhodry said. "Here, we're going about this the wrong way. We keep thinking we're hunting a *dragon,* when we should be saying we're *hunting* a dragon. I'm not the woodsman you are, but I've brought down my share of game in my day."

In the starlit dark he could just see Enj grin.

"So have I," Enj said. "A beast like that will be leaving tracks and signs of its passing you'd have to be blind to miss."

Carrying their packs they dashed across the caldera floor to the rise of cliff, which turned out to offer a wealth of hiding places for two men. They found a shallow cave whose entrance was just big enough for them to squeeze through one at a time. While a dragon might have managed to pry one paw in, they were safe enough from the rest of it. Still, they spent a less than settled night, dozing in turns rather than sleeping straight through. As he sat up with his back to the cavern wall, Rhodry thought he might feel, just every now and then, a trembling as if the rock behind him breathed. When he did doze off, he dreamt of fire that oozed like water through the dark places of the world.

Before the sun truly rose the sky turned light enough for the pair of them to see. Hugging the cliff, staying as much as possible under the overhanging lip, they searched for other caves and fissures, found many, but none that seemed to lead in deep. They went back to their night's refuge and sat discussing plans while they ate the last of the flatbread they'd brought from Haen Marn. They had plenty of smoked meat left from a deer killed early on, but smoked meat alone grows wearisome after a while.

"Well," Enj said. "If this beast doesn't eat us, and if you don't tame it, then it's a slow and hungry walk we're going to have back to Haen Marn."

"Truly. Ye gods, I hope your mother fares well. I know you've both told me about Haen Marn's dweomer and suchlike, but this Alshandra creature can pop out of nowhere like one of the Wildfolk. What if Angmar doesn't have time to work whatever spell this is?"

"Not a spell. Haen Marn goes where the danger be not, that's all."

Enj spoke so calmly, so sincerely, that Rhodry felt his worry ease. Soon, perhaps, he would see Haen Marn safe for himself, anyway, if he could tame this dragon.

"Let's be out and searching, shall we?" Rhodry said. "The more we linger, the better chance it has to realize we're here."

But though they went back and forth along the cliff for hours, they never found a crack or cave more than twenty feet or so deep. They risked walking back a ways, into the open caldera, to study the rock face. Quite clearly in the bright sun they could see the dragon's entrance, a squat half round of cave running back from a tiny slant of ledge. Leading up to it, in fact, ran a number of fissures and breaks.

"Practically a ladder," Enj said. "I wonder if the beast did scrape all that out, with its claws, like, searching for a way in?"

"That would explain our luck, right enough."

"Luck? *Our* luck? Rori, what are you suggesting?"

"Look, we could scrabble round here like moles for days, then find some tunnel and crawl for days more only to fetch up at some dead end. We don't have one of Lin Serr's miners with us, do we?"

"Well, true spoken." Enj looked doubtfully up at the cave for a long time. "Ah, ye gods, naught ventured, naught gained! Let's go get candles and suchlike from our packs, and the ropes, and then up we go."

"I'll go first. If it's waiting inside, it can have a quick bite on me and give you time to get away."

"Get away? From a dragon so close at hand? A fine man with a jest, bain't you?"

They both laughed, but quietly, lest they warn their prey.

Although the first thirty feet or so were slick and thus delicate climbing, once they got well above the caldera floor they found plenty of holds. Every now and then they found a long scratch graved right into the rock, as if an enormous cat had run its claws down leather. Apparently the dragon had searched for a while before clearing its entrance. Where the fissure narrowed, they could brace themselves and rest, but neither ever spoke except for the occasional whispered warning about some loose rock or suchlike. Even with the warnings, occasionally scree fell in a shower of dust and noise. Rhodry found himself wincing every time, but they never heard an answering clatter from within.

Finally, just when the sun had climbed to noon up the greater cliff of the sky, they reached the ledge, which overhung the face itself. By inching sideways and risking a fall, Rhodry managed to flop himself onto it belly first and scrabble forward to security, but the noise was horrendous, at least to his ears. He got to his knees and glanced into the cave. Mercifully it stretched a long way back into darkness, an entrance only, not a home. With a gasp of relief rather than a sigh, he helped Enj gain the ledge as well.

"Not eaten yet," Enj said, a little too cheerfully. "I say we save the candles for a bit."

"Good idea. Both of us can see in the dark."

They stepped into the cave, letting their eyes adjust. From the entrance light filtered in, revealing two tunnels that led deeper, but only one was wide enough for a dragon to pass through. It was possible, of course, that the narrow tunnel wound round to join the wider at some safer place, but Rhodry and Enj looked at each other, shrugged, and took the broad. Its floor was swept clean of loose rock and debris, practically polished, in fact, by the dragon's belly and tail. As they crept along, putting one quiet foot in front of the other, pausing often to listen, the light from behind them dimmed, and the smell rose in a chemical melange—the gagging reek of brimstone, certainly, but mixed with it was another scent, as acrid as sweat.

"The stink of wyrm," Rhodry whispered.

Enj grinned and nodded.

As it sloped down the tunnel twisted, leaving the sunlight behind, yet it never grew completely dark to Rhodry's half-elven sight. Here and there he saw streaks of some pale blue glow, veining in the rock walls. The usual dwarven fungus, he thought at first, then realized that since it had never been exposed to sunlight, it couldn't be phosphorescent— dweomer, perhaps, placed by the dragon to light its way. He'd never heard of their being able to see in the dark, after all. If the beast would mark the way to its lair for all to see, then it must have been supremely confident of its safety. He began to hope that they might come upon it asleep, especially if it had indeed fed the day before.

The tunnel twisted down and in, farther and farther, for what Rhodry estimated as half a mile. The air grew hotter and hotter, stinking of brimstone. Rhodry felt as if the back of his throat were crusted with the stuff, making him want to retch. Far ahead he could just see a different sort of light, pale red like the glow from hot iron on a blacksmith's anvil. He signaled for a rest, and they passed the waterskin back and forth. Though he said nothing, Enj was grinning like a berserker.

As it sloped toward the reddish glow the tunnel narrowed, until its sides and roof turned polished, too, as if the dragon forced a tight way through every time it laired. They walked slower and slower, placing each foot carefully on this slick surface. The glow brightened to a hundred lanterns. Rhodry could smell hot water, the steamy reek of mineral springs and simmering brimstone. Ahead the tunnel mouth gaped. He glanced back at Enj, grinned, and led the way out onto a ledge, perched on the wall of an enormous cavern, formed aeons past, curved like the inside of a bubble, strangely smooth and dead-black, though fissured here and there by huge cracks.

Rhodry realized that they stood halfway up the southern wall and looked across some hundred yards and down some fifty feet. The whole cavern stank of wyrm, and of steam and minerals—the walls dripped and oozed with condensation. Looking down to the misty floor he wondered if this fire mountain was as dead as the dragon seemed to think, because it lay pitted and pooled with springs of sulfurous smelling water, oozing out of rust and yellowish mud, sending out long tendrils of steam to the irregular roof, where in places light shone through in slits. Down to his left, the cavern continued into shadows so dark that he couldn't estimate how far it stretched, although he could see how the floor fell sharply away. Down its slope stood dim shapes of what might be spires of rock and other tunnel mouths.

To his right, half-shrouded by steaming mists the great wyrm lay coiled upon a wide ledge that overhung the hot springs themselves. In the faint light from the cracks in the cavern ceiling, it glittered all black and greeny-black, the great head, resting on one clawed paw, more of a copper verdure, the long body and folded wings tending toward jet.

"Warm in here," Enj whispered. "It'll be awake."

The head snapped up, the eyes opened wide, the color of polished copper and gleaming as they searched out the source of the voice. One wing unfurled with a dry rustle and swept out—and out and out, a vast expanse of green-black skin and delicate bone that roofed half the cavern beneath. Rhodry could only wonder at himself, that he felt no fear, only an awe at how beautiful she was. He was certain—he'd never been so certain of anything in his life—that the dragon was female.

"Get back," Rhodry said. "Leave her to me."

As Enj scrambled into the tunnel, the massive head swung Rhodry's way, and slowly, with a sound like wind in a thousand trees, the wing furled again.

"Leave *her*, you say? You have sharp eyes, elf."

The voice was more a hiss than a roar, but it boomed and echoed through the cavern in a winter flood of Elvish words. Rhodry stepped forward onto the ledge. As he faced her, not twenty feet away, he felt himself laughing, his low berserker's chortle half under his breath. The huge mouth opened to reveal a hedge of crooked fangs like swords.

"You laugh at your dying?" She yawned, extending a long, long pink tongue, then curling it back like a cat. "Very good. I like courage in a male."

"Do you, my lady? Because noble you are, truly, as noble and grand as a thousand queens." He made her a low bow, as courtly as he could manage. "And *my* lady as well, because I'm sure as I can be that my death's riding on your wings, and always have I served the lady called Death."

"Is that why you're here, elf? To die? If the woman you loved left you disconsolate or some such thing, it would have been easier to fall on your sword." She paused, the eyes flashing copper sparks. "Look round you! There's no treasure hoard here. I've nothing to steal, no gold, no jewels, none of those things your stupid stories tell about."

"Why do you think me one of the People?"

"Who else would you be? You smell elven, you're too large for a dwarf, and not hairy enough for a man of the Meradan."

"Half an elf I am, my lady, but only half. My mother was of the race of men. Do you know us?"

With a snarl that stabbed his ears she raised herself up on her forelegs, and at that moment Rhodry saw his death in her eyes. If the fate of literally thousands of souls hadn't rested upon him, he would have welcomed it from such a terrible beauty, but as it was, with a sigh of sincere regret, he flung up his hand and let the silver ring catch the light and flash.

"Arzosah Sothy Lorezohaz!" He intoned her name in a wave of sound that pierced her rage like a spear, that resounded over her like a net. "Arzosah! I call you and command you!"

It seemed that he had cried a dweomer spell that melded her with the rock and turned her to a vein of copper—so still did she become. For a long, long moment she crouched unmoving, unbreathing like a dead thing; then with a rushy moan she slumped, her head flopping onto her paws, the enormous eyes rolling under drooped lids.

"I have hated your race for thousands of years, *Man*!" She spat the name out like an insult. "When you conquered wyrmkind, we fled you, we flew from you, we left our forests and our crags to you, and now you've followed us here. What will you take from me this time, *Man*? My very life?"

Rhodry was too stunned to answer. She lay deathly still, her eyes fixed on his face like a dog watching a cruel master uncurl a whip, and he hated himself for bringing her so low.

"Without your help those I've sworn to serve will die, or I'd turn and walk out of here right now."

"I can tell when someone lies to me, and you speak the truth." Yet still she did not move. "What do you want from me, Man?"

"When have my people harmed you? I've never met anyone who so much as knew that you existed."

She raised her head and tilted it a little to one side to study him. He felt like laughing aloud just to see the life come back into her eyes.

"You're speaking the truth again. This is very odd, Man. Or no, I won't call you by that hateful name. Shall I call you Elf, or will you give me some harmless word to use?"

"My name is Rhodry."

Her eyes seemed to bore into his and through his very soul.

"So it is," she whispered. "So it is. Why would you tell me such a thing?"

"The names of elves have no power to bind them."

For a moment he thought she was growling in a deep rumble under her breath; then he realized that she was laughing.

"Well, so they don't. Very well, Rhodry. If I am to be enslaved, best it be by an elf like you. What do you want from me, Rhodry Dragonmaster?"

"Far to the south of here the Horsekin, the Meradan as you call them, are besieging a city, and they want to kill every soul in it. I intend to stop them."

The rumble of her laughter shook the ledge.

"If I am to be enslaved, best it be for a task like that." She swung her head to stare over his shoulder with one gleaming eye. "That creature behind you? Is it your servant, or may I eat it?"

He glanced round to see Enj standing just at the tunnel's mouth with his arms clasped round his chest, staring at the dragon as wide-eyed as any worshiper seeing the statue of his god.

"Leave him be. He's my friend."

"Stranger yet. Half an elf, half a man, and friend to dwarves. At least you seem to be an interesting sort."

"My lady, I can promise you this: Many a woman has loved me, a few have hated me, but none have ever called me dull."

Again she laughed, the boom rolling and echoing round the cavern till Rhodry felt a lash of fear, running ice-cold down his spine. He knew that he needed to reassert his control of her.

"Tell me one thing," he said. "And then we'll return to the sunlight. Why do you hate the Meradan?"

She curled a vast paw and studied her talons, each as long as a broadsword.

"Now this telling is an order I'll take gladly. Many, many years ago now, it was, but still it burns in my heart, I had a mate who pleased me. The hairy ones hunted him down like a beast and slew him, all to swell their king's vanity. King! If you can call an animal on horseback a king! I slew many of them as they gloated over my mate's dead body, I slew the king himself, chasing him away from the corpse through the grass. Oh, how he squealed and whined and pissed himself when I had him in my claws! King! I pierced him through his stomach and ripped out his guts, then let him die slowly, whining and screeching to the end. But naught would bring back my dead mate. Always have I longed for further revenge, and if you offer it to me, Dragonmaster, then I will serve you well. Why, I'll serve you freely. You don't even need that ring, truly you don't."

Rhodry smiled.

"I think I'll wear it a little longer, though, just for the habit of the thing."

She glared and growled, but just softly under her breath.

"My friend and I are going out now. By your name, Arzosah, I command you to follow where I lead."

"Ych, you're a clever one! Follow I shall."

As they walked back up through the tunnel, Rhodry could hear her, scrabbling and scraping behind, shoving her way through to the wider reaches, where she could pad along after, her feet slapping the rock. Enj seemed to have recovered himself, but even though he and Rhodry would look each other's way every now and then, neither of them could speak in the dark and dreamlike tunnel. Once they reached the open air and stepped out onto the ledge, Enj turned to him and grinned.

"We did it. Against all odds and hope, we did it."

Rhodry laughed just as the dragon stuck her enormous head out in the sun, blinking furiously at the glare. In the sun she shone black, as smooth and fine as a piece of obsidian.

"Do you mock me?" she snarled.

"I don't, no, but my own fears, that never would I find you and fulfill the geas laid upon me."

"A geas?"

"Just so, laid upon me to find you by the greatest master of dweomer in the kingdom of Deverry."

"Ah." She considered this. "Well, then, that pleases me. If there's dweomer at work, no doubt there was naught I could do to turn aside my Wyrd. Shall I carry you down to the valley floor?"

"You shall carry us safely to the valley floor."

"Clever and twice clever. So be it."

Never had Rhodry felt as solemn as he did then, not even when he'd been invested as gwerbret of Aberwyn up in the king's palace of Dun Deverry, not even when the High King himself had taken his hand to bid him rise. He set one foot on her bowed neck and sat between her wings, clutching the rigid scale of a raised crest. With tears in his eyes Enj found a spot behind him.

"If only my father could see this," Enj whispered. "If only he were here."

Arzosah inched forward onto the ledge, then leapt, spreading her wings with a clack like an enormous fan. Wind rushed round them like a slap. Down they glided, circling the caldera once, then landing near the trees and the stream. Rhodry slid down and helped a white-faced Enj to solid ground. He was willing to guess that he looked more than a little pale himself.

"That wasn't the most sanguine ride I've ever taken," Rhodry said in Deverrian, then switched to Elvish. "Arzosah, we'll have to rig up some sort of riding harness with ropes."

"A rope? A rope round my belly as if I were some smelly mule? No! I shan't allow it!"

Rhodry held up his hand and made the ring glitter. Her head drooped, and she rolled her eyes, hissing under her breath.

"Rhodry, please, spare me that, oh, please, Dragonmaster?"

"I can't or I would. I can see what an indignity it is, and I might risk my own death, but I won't have Enj falling to his."

"Oh, very well then. You're a harsh man, though."

"So I've always been told, and so I've always needed to be."

By piecing together the rope they'd brought with them, they managed to make a primitive harness, one loop round her belly, just behind the wings, stabilized with another round her chest, rather like a crude martingale. Rhodry used the ring to reinforce his command that she fly as smoothly as possible.

"And where, pray tell, O master of mine, are we going? I can't fly night and day, you know. I shall have to hunt for a deer now and then as well."

"Fair enough, as long as you promise upon your name to come back when you've made your first kill. You can finish it where we camp."

"So harsh!" She stamped a clawed foot. "Oh, very well then."

"Good. We fly east first, to a place called Haen Marn. Do you know it?"

"No."

"Then I'll guide you there. It's a long journey, so fear not. We'll all rest often, and you shall hunt. And then, after Enj is back home again in Haen Marn, you and I shall fly south, and this time we'll be hunting Meradan."

She gaped her mouth and hissed in murderous joy.

With the rope to cling to, Rhodry and Enj learned, after an uncomfortable while, to adapt to the dragon's flight. Each wing beat thrust her forward in a rolling sort of motion, at times close to a jump, especially when she was gaining height. Sitting on her neck or shoulder felt like standing on the prow of a small boat heading out from shore against the waves. After some hours, though, Rhodry at least found a new balance. He'd been trying to straddle her like a horse, he realized, while he needed to sit forward, steadied by his knees, resting as much on his own heels as her flesh so that he could roll with her wing beats. Bracing himself against them was futile.

When he tried to explain this to Enj, the young dwarf merely rolled his eyes and went on clinging for dear life to rope and crest alike. In the rush of wind and the thwack of the dragon's wings against air, it was impossible to hold any sort of conversation, anyway. At the most Rhodry could bellow orders to the dragon or yell back a few words to Enj during those intervals when she glided rather than beat the air. For both their sakes he ordered her to fly low. Seeing the ground rush by fast scared them less than seeing it unroll slowly from some great height. He supposed that she must be bitterly amused at their clumsiness and weak stomachs, these pitiful creatures who had nonetheless tracked her down.

By late light they left the fire mountain and the Gods' Soup Bowl far behind. With each beat of her wings or long glide Arzosah covered as much ground as they could have by running till they were winded. She also soared over those petty obstacles, valleys and crests, rivers and broken ground, that had claimed hours of Rhodry's and Enj's effort and sweat. After only an afternoon's travel, they'd gone long past the outcrop that may or may not have been shaped like a hound's head. When they camped that first night, Arzosah found them a shallow valley with a stream and set down gently. As soon as they slid off, Enj took a few steps, knelt, and kissed the ground, making Arzosah roll a scornful eye.

"Master?" she said. "May I hunt?"

"You may, as long as you make a fast kill and bring it back here."

"Will you take these wretched ropes off?"

He could, he supposed, with little effort, but always he was aware of the danger they rode by riding a dragon, this creature of air and darkness, so reluctantly tamed.

"No. You need to get used to them."

She snarled and thrashed her head, but when he held up the ring, she quieted immediately. Whatever dweomer Evandar had put upon that ring, Rhodry realized, it must have radiated true power to those sensitive to such things.

"Go hunt," Rhodry said. "But return with your supper."

With a rustle of wing she flapped and flew, circling off to the north. Enj shook himself all over like a wet dog.

"Ye gods, Rori! Never did I think I would see a dragon and finish my father's dream for him, much less ride upon one's back." Enj grinned broadly. "I think me, though, that Da would have had a better stomach for it than his son."

"Well, you know what they always say. Be careful what you wish for."

"Or you may get it. Truly."

It was just growing dark when Arzosah returned, carrying a dead doe in her front claws as easily as a falcon carries a dove. She flew low, dropped it, then circled to settle next to it.

"Do you wish some of this venison, Rhodry Dragonmaster?"

"We have our own kill, my thanks. Enjoy yours, my lady."

"Ah, I do like a courtly man."

Although Rhodry and Enj both had been rather dreading watching her eat, she was a courtly feeder herself, ripping off small pieces of flesh with a delicate fang and turning her head away when she needed to gulp. The bones she cracked, laying one paw upon them and pressing till they snapped, then sucking the marrow with the corner of her mouth. Once done, she buried the hide and other remains with a few scrapes of a paw, then went to the stream and bathed her head and chest.

"Right you were to order me back with that," she remarked. "I'm so sleepy now. A good night to you both."

Without further ado she curled in a grassy hollow like a cat and fell sound asleep.

"Ye gods," Enj whispered. "Ye gods! I wish I spoke the elven tongue, to know what she does say."

"Well, to tell you the truth, my friend, it's all rather ordinary. I doubt me if she's got a large wit, when you come right down to it, or maybe it's just that her concerns are on the simple side."

Enj laughed.

"Very well, then, I won't bother regretting it. I wonder if my sister's scried us out? A fine sight we must be, riding on a dragon."

"You're forgetting about the talisman." Rhodry laid his hand on his shirt over the stone. "And I don't dare take it off to allow her a look at us."

"That's true. Ye gods, Rori. I keep forgetting the grim truths, don't I? About your enemies, and the siege down in Cengarn."

"Well, war or no war, I think me we've a right to gloat."

Although both men woke as stiff and sore as if they'd been in battle, on that second day they learned even more about the proper way to fly. By the end of the day's travel, Rhodry felt nearly as comfortable as he did on a horse—not that he would have wanted to try fighting on drag-onback, mind, with all the swoops and tight turns such would have called for. Enj seemed more relaxed as well, sitting upon rather than clinging to Arzosah's back. When they camped that evening, Arzosah flew out and caught herself another doe, then fell straight asleep again. They were probably tiring her, Rhodry decided, with all this long travel, but soon they would be back at Haen Marn, the place he'd come to think of as home, and the dragon would be able to rest.

"I wonder what she'll think of the beasts in the lake?" Rhodry said.

"Oh, they're not half-elegant enough for her, I'm sure."

They shared a laugh at their own jest. Later, of course, they would wonder how they could have been so at ease, so ignorant, when the dweomer that lay all round them should have at least given them some small hint of danger.

On the third day they left the white peaks behind, swooping lower to fly over the hills that had cost Rhodry and Enj so much time to cross. By Enj's reckoning they would reach Haen Marn before sunset, but long before then they saw their first evil omen. Arzosah was flying along a grassy valley when Rhodry glanced down and saw a peculiar mark, a gash in the grass that stretched east like a road. Without waiting for a command Arzosah dropped some twenty feet to skim the earth. From this height Rhodry could see clearly enough to call her to land. She circled back and settled gracefully to earth at the spot where the trampling began.

Whatever had passed by had cut a wide swath indeed, some hundred feet of grass become mud, hoofprints and horse droppings, wagon ruts and the abrasions of booted feet. Rhodry slid down from her shoulder and ran, dropping to one knee at the edge of the damage where some of the prints separated themselves out. Enj came trotting after.

"What be this?" Enj said, utterly puzzled. "Never have I seen such a thing in my life."

"In your lucky and sheltered life, lad. An army's passed this way, and not long ago at all. Yesterday, I'd say."

"But where did they come from? The tracks just start out of nowhere."

"Dweomer," Arzosah cried in Elvish. "I can smell it!"

Rhodry got up, turning to look at the dragon. She was crouched tense, breathing hard, her great head flung up, her coppery eyes rolling. Her wings trembled as if only sheer will kept her from flying.

"You're right, no doubt," he said. "And from the size of these hoof-prints, the horses were as big as plow stock. That means the riders had to be Meradan."

Her claws shot out to dig the earth in hatred.

"Let's go," Rhodry said to Enj. "And pray that Haen Marn's dweomer held."

Once they were settled on her back, with a flap of wings she leapt up to fly the faster, following the track like a road. Rhodry felt as if the season had changed to winter, and he'd swallowed rocks of ice. Toward midafternoon, when by Enj's reckoning they were close to Haen Marn, the tracks turned south.

"Shall we follow and kill?" Arzosah bellowed.

"Not yet! Keep heading east."

"I want to kill some."

"Arzosah, by your name—"

"Oh, I know! East it is!"

A few moments more brought them their second omen of evil. Off to the south a thin plume of smoke rose at the horizon, as if some large thing burned. Rhodry would have thought that someone had fired a dun, if there'd been a dun there to fire. As it was, the smoke lay dead south, the wrong direction for Haen Marn. Since calculating distances from the air lay beyond him, he could only guess that the source of the smoke was a burning farm, down near Lin Serr's plateau, perhaps. Enj yelled out something incomprehensible, but the fear in his voice spoke as clearly as words. Arzosah put on a burst of speed; she'd seen the smoke as well.

Under them the hills sped by, a dusty green carpet of forest where here and there a stream winked silver. The dragon began to labor, slowing now and then or catching a current in the air to glide and rest. Finally they flew over the last hill to the valley that should have held Haen Marn. Rhodry saw nothing but more hills, stretching green and placid, on either side of the river, the recognizable river that once had sprung from Haen Marn's lake. Now it ran through a narrow valley, not a broad one, and the land was dotted with pines, not oaks.

Behind him Enj howled in grief and rage both.

"Land!" Rhodry called out. "Down by the water, so you can drink."

With a long glide and flap the panting dragon settled to earth. Rhodry slid off, then helped Enj down. For a moment neither of them could speak.

"Are you sure I didn't guide Arzosah wrong?" Rhodry said at last.

Enj merely shook his head no and strode off, heading for a familiar-looking pile of boulders by the riverbank. Rhodry followed and helped him lift the rocks, shoving them out of the way, rummaging round in a kind of desperate hope that they'd find nothing. He was aware of the dragon crouching behind him on the riverbank, her sides heaving in the hot sun. All at once Enj keened, just one wail, bitten off fast. He held up a black and twisted thing, all flattened, tarnished, and torn as if by the passage of a thousand years—the remains of the silver horn that once had summoned the dwarven longboat.

"It's been withdrawn," Enj choked out. "Haen Marn."

"Withdrawn? What do you mean?"

"To its own world. It doesn't truly belong in ours. In times of trouble, it can withdraw. That's the dweomer I was speaking of, when you'd worry and such."

"Speaking of? A bare hint, lad, a bare hint." Rhodry wondered what was wrong with him, that he'd feel so calm, feel nothing, truly, but a strange and distant curiosity.

"You don't dare speak plainly! What if it heard? Or they heard? The spirits, I mean. Whatever guards the place. You could find yourself gone in an eye blink."

"And when, then, will it return? When the danger's past?"

Enj shook his head. His eyes glistened tears.

"I don't know. Maybe never," he whispered. "My grandmother, my father's mother, the Lady of Haen Marn, the true lady, the one Avain should have replaced if she'd not been born a mooncalf—she told me always, when I was a lad, that we ran that risk, living in Haen Marn, that someday it would withdraw, and there we'd be in its true world, whether we wanted to bide there or no."

It be a baleful thing, the hefting of this shield. Pray, Rori, pray that never it be needful.

The thought sounded so loud in his mind that Rhodry turned, thinking Angmar stood behind him, started to ask her a question, in fact, and found he couldn't speak. No one stood there. Only wind sighed in grass. He took a few steps north, toward the spot where the river had once poured from a crack in the cliffs. He was thinking that he really should say something comforting to Enj, seeing as the lad had just lost his mother, when suddenly the view blurred and began to dance in front of him. He dropped to his knees, but he never quite wept, fought himself cold, rather, beside the fast-flowing river, while Arzosah turned her enormous head his way and watched unblinking.

"They slew my mate," she said at last. "And now they've driven yours away. We shall kill many Meradan together, Rhodry Dragonmaster."

"So we will." He smiled, felt that smile burn itself into his face. "Together, so we will."

APPENDICES

HISTORICAL NOTES

Many readers and reviewers have assumed that the Deverry books take place in some sort of alternate Britain or that the people of Deverry came originally from Britain. In fact, they emigrated from northern Gaul, as a couple of obscure clues in the text tell the compulsively careful reader who also knows an awful lot about Celtic history. Since only a few people fall into that rather strange category, myself being one of them, allow me to explain further. For one thing, the great heroes mentioned throughout the series, Vercingetorix and Vindex, are real, historical Gauls. For another, the various gods, such as Bel (Belinus) and particularly Epona are primarily Gaulish gods, though their worship was known throughout the Celtic realms. More to the point, those "vergobretes" who became in Deverry "gwerbrets" are mentioned in Julius Caesar's *Gallic Wars* as magistrates among the Gauls, though, he says, the Britons have no such kind of leader, relying instead upon "kings." The Gaulish king, it seems, was more what we'd term a "warleader," the "cadvridoc" of Deverry, than the ruler of an organized state. Even in Britain, however, the Celts elected their kings more often than they accepted them by inheritance, a pan-Celtic political tradition that lies behind the instability of the Deverry kingship.

The language of Deverry also derives from that of Gaul, but Gaulish was not, as far as scholars can tell, very much different from the Old British that evolved into the language we know today as Cymraeg or Welsh. Thus the Deverrian language, which we might well call Neo-Gaulish, looks and sounds much like Welsh, but anyone who knows this modern language will see immediately that it differs in a great many respects, as it does from Cornish and Breton, the other members of the sub-family of languages known as P-Celtic.

PRONUNCIATION NOTES

Vowels are divided by Deverry scribes into two classes: noble and common. Nobles have two pronunciations; commons, one.

A as in *father* when long; a shorter version of the same sound, as in *far*, when short.

O as in *bone* when long; as in *pot* when short.

W as the *oo* in *spook* when long; as in *roof* when short.

Y as the *i* in *machine* when long; as the *e* in *butter* when short.

E as in *pen*.

I as in *pin*.

U as in *pun*.

Vowels are generally long in stressed syllables; short in unstressed. Y is the primary exception to this rule. When it appears as the last letter of a word, it is always long whether that syllable is stressed or not.

Diphthongs generally have one consistent pronunciation.

AE as the *a* in *mane*.

AI as in *aisle*.

AU as the *ow* in *how*.

EO as a combination of *eh* and *oh*.

EW as in Welsh, a combination of *eh* and *oo*.

IE as in *pier*.

OE as the *oy* in *boy*.

UI as the North Welsh *wy*, a combination of *oo* and *ee*.

Note that OI is never a diphthong, but is two distinct sounds, as in *carnoic* (KAR-noh-ik).

Consonants are mostly the same as in English, with these exceptions:

C is always hard as in *cat*.

G is always hard as in *get*.

DD is the voiced *th* as in *thin* or *breathe*, but the voicing is more pronounced than in English. It is opposed to TH, the unvoiced sound as in *th* or *breath*. (This is the sound that the Greeks called the Celtic tau.)

R is heavily rolled.

RH is a voiceless R, approximately pronounced as if it were spelled *hr* in Deverry proper. In Eldidd, the sound is fast becoming indistinguishable from R.

DW, GW, and TW are single sounds, as in *Gwendolen* or *twit*.

Y is never a consonant.

I before a vowel at the beginning of a word is consonantal, as it is in the plural ending *-ion*, pronounced *yawn*.

Doubled consonants are both sounded clearly, unlike in English. Note, however, that DD is a *single letter*, not a doubled consonant.

Accent is generally on the penultimate syllable, but compound words and place names are often an exception to this rule.

I have used this system of transcription for the Bardekian and Elvish alphabets as well as the Deverrian, which is, of course, based on the Greek rather than the Roman model. On the whole, it works quite well for the Bardekian, at least. As for Elvish, in a work of this sort it would be ridiculous to resort to the elaborate apparatus by which scholars attempt to transcribe that most subtle and nuanced of tongues.

As those who have been following the earlier works in this series know, a certain Elvish professor of Elvish has chosen to waste his supposedly valuable time by disputing this obvious point. Since the man refuses to see reason and stop his scurrilous attacks upon us, my publishers and I have been forced to sue for redress in the malover of the gwerbrets of Aberwyn, much as it distresses us to waste the clearly valuable time of this court. Although the case has yet to be accepted for deliberation, readers will be kept apprised of future developments, never fear.

GLOSSARY

ABER (Deverrian) A river mouth, an estuary.

ALAR (Elvish) A group of elves, who may or may not be blood kin, who choose to travel together for some indefinite period of time.

ALARDAN (Elv.) The meeting of several alarli, usually the occasion for a drunken party.

ANGWIDD (Dev.) Unexplored, unknown.

ASTRAL The plane of existence directly "above" or "within" the etheric (q.v.). In other systems of magic, often referred to as the Akashic Record or the Treasure House of Images.

AURA The field of electromagnetic energy that permeates and emanates from every living being.

AVER (Dev.) A river.

BARA (Elv.) An enclitic that indicates that the preceding adjective in an Elvish agglutinated word is the name of the element following the enclitic, as can + bara + melim = Rough River. (rough + name marker + river.)

BEL (Dev.) The chief god of the Deverry pantheon.

BEL (Elv.) An enclitic, similar in function to bara, except that it indicates that a preceding verb is the name of the following element in the agglutinated term, as in Darabeldal, Flowing Lake.

BLUE LIGHT Another name for the etheric plane (q.v.).

BODY OF LIGHT An artificial thought-form (q.v.) constructed by a dweomermaster to allow him or her to travel through the inner planes of existence.

BRIGGA (Dev.) Loose wool trousers worn by men and boys.

BRIGHT COURT, DARK COURT I've chosen these terms for the traditional divide between the groups of Fair Folk rather than using Seelie and Unseelie Court, names that are localized in our own world to Scotland.

BROCH (Dev.) A squat tower in which people live. Originally, in the homeland, these towers had one big fireplace in the center of the ground floor and a number of booths or tiny roomlets up the sides, but by the time of our narrative, this ancient style has given way to regular floor with hearths and chimneys on either side of the structure.

CADVRIDOC (Dev.) A warleader. Not a general in the modern sense, the cadvridoc is supposed to take the advice and counsel of the noble-born lords under him, but his is the right of final decision.

CAPTAIN (trans. of the Dev. *pendaely*) The second in command, after the lord himself, of a noble's warband. An interesting point is that the word *taely* (the root or unmutated form of *-daely,*) can mean either a warband or a family depending on context.

CWM (Dev.) A valley.

DAL (Elv.) A lake.

DUN (Dev.) A fort.

DWEOMER (trans. of Dev. *dwunddaevad*) In its strict sense, a system of magic aimed at personal enlightenment through harmony with the natural universe in all its planes and manifestations; in the popular sense, magic, sorcery.

ELVES I have chosen this common name for the people the Deverrians call Elcyion Lacar (literally, the "bright spirits," or "Bright Fey"). They are also known as the Westfolk among men and dwarves, though the Dwarvish name for the race is Carx Taen. To the Gel da'Thae they are the Children of the Gods, Graekaebi Zo Uhmveo, while they call themselves, quite simply, Impar, the People.

ENSORCEL To produce an effect similar to hypnosis by direct manipulation of a person's aura. (True hypnosis manipulates the victim's consciousness only and thus is more easily resisted.)

ETHERIC The plane of existence directly "above" the physical. With its magnetic substance and currents, it holds physical matter in an invisible matrix and is the true source of what we call "life."

ETHERIC DOUBLE The true being of a person, the electromagnetic structure that holds the body together and that is the actual seat of consciousness.

GEIS, GEAS A taboo, usually a prohibition against doing something. Break-

ing geis results in ritual pollution and the disfavor if not active emnity
of the gods. In societies that truly believe in geis, a person who breaks
it usually dies fairly quickly, either of morbid depression or some unconsciously self-inflicted "accident," unless he or she makes ritual amends.

GEL DA'THAE Also known as the Horsekin, they are a humanoid, naturally
psychic race that lives to the north and west of Deverry proper. Their
psychic talents manifest mostly as an enormous empathy with animals.
To the elves they are the Meradan (lit. demons) or Hordes, because they
destroyed the elven civilization of the far western mountains in ages past.

GEOMANCY A system of divination, codified during the late Middle Ages,
involving the element of earth. The names of the figures used in this
book having the following meanings: Rubeus, the Red One; Puer, the
Boy; Amissio, Loss; Puella, the Girl; Via, the Road; Carcer, the Prison;
Caput Draconis, the Dragon's Head.

GREAT ONES Spirits, once human but now disincarnate, who exist on an
unknowably high plane of existence and who have dedicated themselves
to the eventual enlightenment of all sentient beings. They are also known
to the Buddhists, as Bodhisattvas.

GWERBRET (Dev. The name derives from the Gaulish *vergobretes*.) The
highest rank of nobility below the royal family itself. Gwerbrets (Dev.
gwerbretion) function as the chief magistrates of their regions, and even
kings hesitate to override their decisions because of their many ancient
prerogatives.

HOB A male ferret. The females are called "jills," though for obvious
reasons I've chosen not to use the term.

LWDD (Dev.) A blood-price; differs from wergild in that the amount of
lwdd is negotiable in some circumstances rather than being irrevocably
set by law.

MALOVER (Dev.) A full, formal court of law with both a priest of Bel and
either a gwerbret or a tieryn in attendance.

MAZRAK (Gel.) A shape-changer. A magician who can turn him or herself
into animal form and back again at will.

MELIM (Elv.) A river.

MOR (Dev.) A sea, ocean.

PECL (Dev.) Far, distant.

RHAN (Dev.) A political unit of land; thus, gwerbretrhyn, tierynrhyn, the area under the control of a given gwerbret or tieryn. The size of the various rhans (Dev. rhannau) varies widely, depending on the vagaries of inheritance and the fortunes of war rather than some legal definition.

SCRYING The art of seeing distant people and places by magic.

SIGIL An abstract magical figure, usually representing either a particular spirit or a particular kind of energy or power. These figures, which look a lot like geometrical scribbles, are derived by various rules from secret magical diagrams.

TAER (Dev.) Land, country.

THOUGHT-FORM An image or three-dimensional form that has been fashioned out of either etheric or astral substance, usually by the action of a trained mind. If enough trained minds work together to build the same thought-form, it will exist independently for a period of time based on the amount of energy put into it. (Putting energy into such a form is known as *ensouling* the thought-form.) Manifestations of gods or saints are usually thought-forms picked up by the highly intuitive, such as children, or those with a touch of second sight. It is also possible for many untrained minds acting together to make fuzzy, ill-defined thought-forms that can be picked up the same way, such as UFOs and sightings of the Devil.

TIERYN (Dev.) An intermediate rank of the noble-born, below a gwerbret but above an ordinary lord (Dev. *arcloedd*).

WYRD (trans. of Dev. *tingedd*) Fate, destiny; the inescapable problems carried over from a sentient being's last incarnation.

YNIS (Dev.) An island.

ABOUT THE AUTHOR

KATHERINE KERR spent her childhood in a Great Lakes industrial city and her adolescence in a stereotypical corner of southern California, from whence she fled to the Bay Area just in time to join a number of the various Revolutions then in progress. Upon dropping out of dropping out, she got married and devoted herself to reading as many off-the-wall, obscure, and just plain peculiar books as she could get her hands on. As the logical result of such a life, she has now become a professional story-teller and an amateur skeptic, who regards all True Believers with a jaundiced eye, even those who true-believe in Science.

Kerr is the author of the Deverry series of historical fantasies: *Polar City Blues*; *Resurrection*; and the new trilogy, *A Time of War*, of which this is the first volume.